Proposals *in* Regency Society

ANNE
HERRIES

MILLS
BOON

Published in Great Britain 2014
by Mills & Boon, an imprint of Harlequin (UK) Limited,
Eton House, 18-24 Paradise Road, Richmond, Surrey, TW9 1SR

PROPOSALS IN REGENCY SOCIETY
© 2014 Harlequin Books S.A.

Make-Believe Wife © 2011 Anne Herries
The Homeless Heiress © 2008 Anne Herries

ISBN: 978-0-263-24632-2

052-1014

Harlequin (UK) policy is to use papers that are natural, renewable and recyclable products and made from wood grown in sustainable forests. The logging and manufacturing processes conform to the legal environmental regulations of the country of origin.

Printed and bound
by CPI Group (UK) Ltd, Croydon, CR0 4YY

Anne Herries lives in Cambridgeshire, England, where she is fond of watching wildlife and spoils the birds and squirrels that are frequent visitors to her garden. Anne loves to write about the beauty of nature and sometimes puts a little into her books, although they are mostly about love and romance. She writes for her own enjoyment and to give pleasure to her readers. She is a winner of the Romantic Novelists' Association® Romance Prize.

Make-Believe Wife

ANNE HERRIES

Prologue

'**D**amn you, sir. I have had enough of your wild behaviour,' the Earl of Hartingdon thundered at his grandson. 'I shall not tolerate the disgrace you have brought upon us.'

'Forgive me,' Luke, Viscount Clarendon, said and looked contrite. 'This should never have come to your ears. Rollinson was a fool and a knave to come prattling to you, sir.'

Tall and almost painfully thin, yet with a commanding presence, the earl's bushy white eyebrows met in a frown of disapproval.

'Do you deny that you seduced the man's wife?'

Luke hesitated. The truth of the matter was that he had no idea whether or not he had seduced Adrina Rollinson. The evening in question was hazy to say the least. He had been three sheets to the wind and, when he'd woken to find himself lying next to the naked and undoubtedly voluptuous beauty, he had hardly been given time to wonder before her husband came storming into the summerhouse to demand satisfaction.

'I can only tell you that I have no memory of it happening, sir.'

'What sort of an answer is that, pray?' the earl demanded. 'You puzzle me, Luke. You have had every advantage and yet you insist on carrying your wildness to excess. If you cannot recall making love to a woman like Lady Rollinson, you must have been drunk.'

'Indeed, that I shall own,' Luke said instantly. 'I would not call the lady a liar, but I doubt I was capable of making love that night.'

'I suppose your taste is for whores?'

'I do not know what you may have been told of me, sir, but I assure you I have done nothing of which I am ashamed.'

'Indeed? I know that you have bought a house and intend to set up your mistress in Hampstead.' The earl's top lip curled in scorn. 'You are a disgrace to your family. Thank God your parents did not live to see what you have become.'

'Perhaps had they lived I might have been otherwise.'

'Are you blaming me? Impudent pup!' The earl's eyes darkened with temper. 'Well, sir, I have done with you. It was in my mind to make you my sole heir, for although the estate is entailed, the patent allows the title to pass through the female line and my fortune is my own to dispose of as I wish. However, I have a cousin who would restore both honour and fortune to the family name.'

'Horatio Harte, I presume? I wish you joy of him, sir.' Luke's temper was barely in check. 'Good afternoon. I shall not trouble you with my presence again.'

'I did not give you leave to go.'

'Yet I believe I shall. You have never liked me, sir. I have done things of which I am not particularly proud, but I am not the rogue you think me.'

'Come back here!' The earl's voice rose petulantly. 'You will hear me out. I shall give you one more chance, but you must marry a decent girl—one with perfect manners who knows how to behave in good society. I need an heir I can be proud of before I die.'

Luke turned at the door, denial on his lips. He would marry when and whom he wished and meant to say so, but even as he began the earl made a choking sound and sank slowly to his knees before collapsing in a heap on the floor.

'Grandfather! Someone, give me some help in here.'

Luke rushed to his grandfather's side. Rolling him on his back, he saw that his colour was slightly blue and acted swiftly in untying the tight starched cravat at his neck. He felt for a pulse and discovered a faint beat and yet his grandfather did not appear to be breathing. He was for a moment unsure of what to do for the best; then, recalling something he had once witnessed a vet do for the foal of an important mare, he opened his grandfather's mouth and made sure there was no obstruction in the throat. Then he pinched the earl's nostrils and breathed into his mouth. Luke repeated the action three times and noticed that a more natural colour had returned, though he had no idea if his actions had helped.

A voice spoke from behind him. 'He has had one of his attacks, my lord. He will recover in a moment.'

'He just keeled over. I thought he was dead or dying.'

'Milord has had one or two close calls, sir. Nasty little attacks that the doctor can't quite make out.'

'Why was I not told?' Luke rose to his feet. The colour was back in the earl's cheeks now.

'He did not wish to bother you, sir.'

'The stubborn fool—' Luke began and stopped as he heard a sound. The earl had his eyes open. He was staring up at them.

'Don't just stand there, fool. Help me up, Marshall.'

'You should have told me you were ill, Grandfather.'

'Stuff and nonsense! It is nothing. As you see, I am perfectly fine now.'

Luke and the butler helped him to his feet and assisted him to a sturdy mahogany elbow chair. Luke felt his body trembling and realised how thin and frail his grandfather had become. When had this happened? Why had he not noticed?

'Forgive me, sir. Had I known you were ill…'

'What? Would you have mended your ways?' The elderly man's eyes gleamed. 'Want to make amends, eh? You know my terms. Get yourself wed and give me an heir.'

'I am sorry you are ill, but I shall not make a promise I cannot keep. However, I will promise not to become so drunk that I do not recall with whom or where I go to bed.'

'Not enough,' the earl growled. 'Leave me to Marshall and come back when you have a wife.'

'Grandfather, that is unfair,' Luke protested, for he was genuinely upset by the news of the earl's ill health.

'Unless you oblige me I shall not leave you a penny—and, what's more, I'll tell the lawyers to cut the allowance you receive from your paternal grandfather's fortune.'

'You cannot do that, sir. I have commitments...'

'To your mistress, I suppose? Well, the choice is yours, Luke. The terms of the Marquis's will state that I can limit your income until you are thirty if I so choose. I have never done so, but now I shall make a change. I need an heir soon, Luke—and I want you to give me a grandson. Marry well and everything will be as it was. Turn your back on me now and you'll find yourself short in the pocket. Show me that you intend to settle down and make me proud of you.'

Luke hesitated, a grim set to his mouth. Had he not just witnessed his grandfather's collapse he would have told him to go to the devil and bought himself a pair of colours while he still had the money. Yet despite his harsh words, there was something vulnerable about the earl, something that made Luke realise that deep within him he cared what happened to the old devil.

'I must have time to think this over, sir.'

'Yes, of course, and to find a suitable girl—but do not take too long, Luke. I may not have more than a year or so left to me.'

Luke inclined his head and left, feeling his temper surge as he curled his nails into the palms of his hand.

He ought to walk out and never return. The lawyers would probably tell him that the earl was lying through his teeth—yet if it were the truth Luke would be in trouble.

He had made a promise to his best friend and nothing would make him break it.

Chapter One

Roxanne glanced back over her shoulder, listening for the sounds of pursuit, but all she could hear were birds calling one to the other as they flitted between the trees and the occasional snuffle of a small animal in the undergrowth. The woods themselves held no fear for her, but she was afraid of being made to return to the camp.

She had been walking for hours without stopping, but now she was hungry. She was fairly certain that no one had followed her. It must be safe now to stop and eat some of the food she had packed. Placing her larger bundle on the ground, Roxanne spread her shawl on the dry earth and sat down, opening the cloth that carried her bread, cheese and the preserved fruit she had brought with her. Sofia had always kept a jar of dried fruits on her shelf, because she said figs, dates and apricots were good to eat in the winter when they could not pick fruit from the hedgerows.

She missed Sofia so much! Her friend's sad death had left her alone and in fear of the future. She had no one who cared for her and no one to care for. She was not sure which felt the worst, because she had enjoyed caring for her friend in her last months when she became too feeble to care for herself.

Blinking away her tears, Roxanne rose to her feet and gathered her bundles. Sofia had been one of a band of travelling players, almost a mother to her, and she had given Roxanne so much, even her name.

'If anything happens to me you should go to London,' Sofia had told her only a few days before she died. 'You are a fine actress, my love. You could find fame and fortune—and perhaps marry a man of substance and be the lady I believe you truly are.'

Roxanne had begged her not to talk of dying, tears stinging her eyes, but after her death it had become clear that Roxanne could not stay with the band of travelling players with whom she had lived for the past five years. She was in danger and her only choice was to run away before *he* returned to the camp.

She had made up her mind that she would get to London if she could, though it would mean walking for many days, perhaps weeks. Before she reached the great city, she would need to find work for a few days to earn her food.

Lost in thought, she was startled as she heard a loud cry and then a horse came crashing through the trees towards her. It was saddled, but without a rider, its reins hanging loose, and she realised that someone must have fallen.

Instinctively, she ran in the direction from which the cry had seemed to come. She had gone only a few yards when she saw a man lying on the ground. His eyes were closed and his face looked pale. Her heart caught and for a moment she thought he was dead. Dropping her bundles, she knelt by his side and touched his face. He felt warm and she drew a breath of relief. His fingers were moving and he was still breathing, though seemed unaware of her. He must have been knocked unconscious by the fall from his horse.

She hesitated, then unwound his white stock from his neck; taking out her precious store of water, she poured some of it onto the fine linen and began to bathe his face. His lips moved, a groan issuing from him, then his eyes flickered open and he looked up at her.

'What happened?' he muttered. 'Who are you?'

'My name is Roxanne. I think you fell from your horse. It came rushing at me through the trees and I heard your cry.'

'It was the fox,' he said and pushed up into a sitting position. His dark grey eyes fixed on her face. 'It started up just in front of us. I tried to stop, but I was riding hard and the stupid horse reared up in a fright.'

'The horse was startled. They are nervous creatures, sir. If you were riding too hard, the fault was yours.'

'The devil it was.' His slate-coloured eyes narrowed, became intent and suspicious. 'What is a lady like you doing alone in these woods—dressed like that?'

Roxanne hesitated, for to tell him her true story was too risky. She did not know him and should use caution.

He was undoubtedly a gentleman and Sofia had warned her to be careful of the gentry, for they were not to be trusted.

'I was with a band of travelling players, but I had to leave. I am trying to get to London to find work as an actress.'

'Are you indeed?' His gaze was unsettling. 'I see you have water, Miss Roxanne. Will you give me some?'

'I used some to bathe your face, but you may have a few sips.' Roxanne handed him the stoneware flask and he lifted it to his mouth, drinking deeply. 'Please leave some. I may not find a stream to refill my flask for hours.'

'I passed a stream not far back,' he replied. 'But if you are making for London you are walking in the wrong direction.'

'Oh…' Roxanne frowned as he handed her back the bottle. 'Perhaps you could—' She broke off as he attempted to stand and shouted with pain. He swayed and would have fallen had she not caught hold of his body and supported him. 'Where does it hurt?'

'My right ankle,' he groaned. 'I think it must be broken. If I sit down again, could you take the boot off for me?'

'Do you think that wise, sir? The boot will probably have to be cut off if your ankle is broken—and a doctor should do it. Sofia would have known how to treat you, but I do not have her skills.'

'Who the hell is Sofia? Is she with you?'

'She was my dearest friend and she died recently.'

'Sorry,' he muttered, his face white with pain. 'I

have a knife. Cut the damned thing off and bind the ankle with the stock. It will have to do until we can find an inn and a doctor.'

'We—are you expecting me to go with you?'

'How do you imagine I can get anywhere alone? Or were you planning to go on and leave me here?'

'Your temper does not help your cause, sir. If you will sit, I shall attempt to do as you ask—and, no, now you mention it, I was not planning to abandon you.'

His eyes narrowed in annoyance, his mouth set hard. 'You speak in the tones and manner of a lady, yet you say you are an actress. You must be a clever one.'

'Sofia said I could play royalty to the manner born,' Roxanne said, helping him to lower himself to the ground so that she could attend to his ankle. 'She was once a courtesan and had both royal and aristocratic lovers in her youth so I imagine she would know how they behave.'

'She sounds quite a remarkable lady?'

'She was wonderful.' Roxanne hesitated, then ran her hands down the length of the boot. Not yet! She would not tell him too much too soon. 'It is difficult to tell while this is on, but I think you may have a break just above your ankle. It will hurt too much if I try to pull the boot off—have I your permission to cut the leather? I dare say it may have cost a great deal of money.'

'I have other pairs; just do it.' He thrust a hand into his pocket and brought out a silver penknife.

'I think I have something better.' Roxanne opened her large bundle and took out a long thin dagger. 'The blade is very sharp. It will slit the leather easier than your knife.'

'Good grief, what are you carrying a dangerous thing like that for?'

'I am a woman travelling alone. I needed to be sure I could protect myself.'

'Remind me never to try to seduce you when I'm drunk.'

'Are you in the habit of seducing women when drunk?'

Roxanne's eyes held a sparkle of amusement as she glanced at him and then back at the boot. It was long and tight fitting and obviously the best quality. She inserted the knifepoint into the leather and began to slit the length of the boot. Her patient groaned once or twice as she worked, a muffled cry escaping him as she finally drew it from his foot.

'Damn!' he muttered as her fingers began to explore his ankle and the region above. 'It hurts like hell.'

'I think there is a small break just above the ankle,' Roxanne said. 'The flesh is not torn, but there is a bump where there ought to be straight bone—it might have been worse.'

'You cannot feel the pain,' he muttered fiercely.

'I am certain it hurts, but I shall bind it with your stock and use the last of the cold water. That may stop the swelling from becoming too bad, but I am not an expert, sir. If we can make you comfortable enough to ride your horse, it will be much easier for you to continue your journey.'

'Supposing we could find the damned creature.'

'I dare say it will not have gone far. I will look for it after I've bound your ankle.'

'You'll go and leave me here.' He looked angry, as if he believed she would simply walk away.

'I promise I shall not. All I have in the world is in these bundles. If I leave them with you, I must return.' She finished her work and rose to her feet. 'Try to rest until I return with the horse.'

'And if you cannot find it?'

'I shall return and try to help you, though it may be best to fetch help. Wait patiently if you can. I shall not be long.'

'Damn you,' he muttered through clenched teeth. 'You're made of iron. You should have been born a lady, you belong with the starched-petticoat brigade.'

'Sofia always said I was from good family.' Roxanne smiled. 'Lady or not, I shall not desert you, sir.'

She walked back the way she had come. The horse had been in a blind panic, but once it stopped its mad flight it would stand and wait to be reclaimed by its owner. She must just hope that it had not injured itself because she needed it to be strong enough to carry them both and her bundles.

Luke cursed as he reached into his coat pocket and took out his pocket flask, which was still half-filled with brandy. His ankle was hurting like the devil and the girl had been gone too long. If she did not come within a few minutes, he would have to try to find help himself. If he ignored the pain, he might hobble far enough to find a farm or a woodcutter's hut. He was attempting to rise when he heard a rustling sound and, a moment later, the girl appeared through the trees leading his horse.

'I thought you had decided to leave me after all,' he said a trifle sulkily. 'You were gone a long time.'

'Your horse was not sure he wanted to come to a stranger. He was a little shy at first, but we have become friends now.'

She led the horse to Luke. 'I think he will carry us both and my bundles, sir. If not, then I can walk beside you. I do not think you capable of riding hard this time.'

'Impertinent wench.' Luke scowled at her and then laughed. 'You remind me of my Great-Aunt Dorethea when she was young.'

'Indeed? I'm not sure whether I should be flattered or insulted.' Roxanne's brows arched. 'Do you think you can mount if I hold the horse?'

'Flattered. I admired her. Give me your arm, Miss Roxanne. I need you as a crutch.' Holding on to her arm, Luke levered himself on to his left foot. He hobbled towards the horse, then, as she held its head steady, took hold of the saddle and belly-flopped over it, using the strength of his arms and body to pull himself into a sitting position. Beads of sweat had gathered on his brow by this time, but he controlled his desire to yell out with pain. Roxanne had fitted her bundles round the pommel of the saddle; then, with an agility that surprised him, she took his outstretched hand and swung herself up behind him. 'You've done that before?'

'I've been riding horses barebacked since I was thirteen or so. We did an act that involved my having to jump up on to a moving horse.'

'You are full of surprises, Miss Roxanne. I thought you a lady at first, but no lady of my acquaintance could do what you just did.'

'A lady might not have been near when you fell,' she reminded him. 'I may not be a gentlewoman in the sense you mean, sir—but I will thank you to show me the proper respect. I am not a lightskirt and shall not be treated as one.'

Luke glanced over his shoulder. 'How do you imagine I would treat you if you were a whore?'

'I have no idea how a gentleman behaves with a lady of easy virtue, though Sofia told me that gentlemen are invariably the worst. I only know that I did not like the way Black Bob looked at me.'

Luke was intrigued. 'Who is he and how did he look at you?'

'He is the leader of the troupe and looked at me as though he could see through my clothes. He told me that now Sofia was dead, he would claim me as his woman—so I ran away.'

'You have run away from your people?'

'Yes. He had to go somewhere on business and so I took my chance while he was gone.'

A rueful laugh escaped Luke. 'And you ran into me. Well, Miss Roxanne, I must thank my lucky stars that you did. If you help me as far as the next inn, I shall return the favour by hiring a coach to take us both to London.'

Roxanne stiffened. 'I told you, I am not a whore—and I shall not be your mistress.'

'Have I said that I wish you to be? I am merely repaying a favour, miss—and if you have any sense you will accept my offer. A girl who looks like you will have offers enough, I dare say, but most of them will not be to your liking. If you are to become an actress you will need patronage, and you may as well accept mine as another's.'

Roxanne's breath caught. She almost wished she had walked away from him in the woods. He could surely manage now he had his horse.

'Put your arms about my waist,' he instructed. 'Hold on tight, Miss Roxanne. My ankle is painful and we had best find an inn before I pass out and you have to cart me there in an unconscious state.'

Roxanne did not reply. She put her arms about his waist, holding him tightly. She did not fear him, as she did Black Bob, but if he were to fall unconscious she might have difficulty in getting him safe to an inn. Perhaps the feel of her at his back would keep him awake long enough to reach the nearest inn. She hoped that he would not fall senseless, because she had no idea of where she was headed and the sooner he reached a doctor the better.

Roxanne could have no idea how very aware Luke was of his passenger, her full breasts pressed against his back. He had noticed her perfume as soon as he became conscious and found her bending over him. It was light and yet sensual, unlike any he had smelled on the ladies he met either in society or in the world of the *demi-monde* he sometimes frequented. She was different, unusual, and he'd felt intrigued from the first.

Roxanne was a woman most men would notice, her figure not willowy slender, but athletic—statuesque, might be a good word. She reminded him of the marble figure of Diana the Huntress he had commissioned for his country house, which stood in a fragrant corner of his garden, but warm with life and passion instead of white and cold. He could imagine what the leader of the travelling players had planned for her and the thought brought a frown of anger to his brow.

Damn the man for his impudence!

Clearly, her friend Sofia had been a person of influence, protecting the girl as she grew to womanhood, but once she was dead, Roxanne was at the mercy of any rogue who saw her. Luke did not know why that thought made him angry, but his protective instincts had been roused and, in thinking of her and ways to make certain she was protected, he was able to fight off his pain.

He cursed himself for riding carelessly as a wave of faintness washed over him and it took all his willpower to stay in the saddle and hold on to the reins.

'I could take control of the horse if you wish, sir. He would respond to me, as he did earlier.'

Roxanne's words jerked him back to reality and her arms about him helped fight off the faintness. He must stay awake, because he needed to be in command. She must not be allowed to slip away when they reached the inn. He could not lose her yet; he needed her help.

'I can manage,' he growled. 'It cannot be much further.'

'I pray you are right,' she said and her arms tightened about him, as if she would save him from falling.

A sharp wave of desire shot through Luke, bringing him to his senses more surely than any words. He laughed deep in his throat—it was like him to want the unobtainable. Luke had met with little resistance in his adult life; the ladies were usually more than willing to share his bed—or even entice him into the summerhouse. It was ironic that the first one to evoke such a strong response in him for an age had placed herself out of reach.

Roxanne had made it clear she would not be his mistress and in all honour he could not use his charm to persuade her after all she had done. However, it would not suit him if she were to run away. He might never see her again, and that thought was sufficient to stave off both the pain and the faintness. An ironic smile settled over his lips. She had already shown herself compassionate; perhaps the best way to keep her with him was to plead his need of a nurse or helper to see him home.

'Hold me tighter,' he said. 'The pain makes me faint. I beg you, do not desert me, Miss Roxanne. In this state I am helpless and at the mercy of unscrupulous rogues—men who would see me dead as soon as look at me.'

'You have enemies?'

'An enemy,' Luke improvised. 'You accused me of

riding too hard, but I was trying to escape from him when the fox startled my horse.'

He justified his lie to himself. His enemy was the bitter anger that had been festering inside him since the interview with his grandfather. The Earl of Hartingdon's unfair accusations and his outrageous demands had smouldered in his brain, making him careless.

'Will you be safe when you reach London?'

'Yes.' Luke waited, holding his breath. 'Once I am home I shall be perfectly safe, but I need help lest I lose consciousness and lie ill by the wayside.'

'It is true that not everyone would help if you became ill of a fever. I know that men like Black Bob might take advantage and rob you.' Roxanne seemed to hesitate, then, 'Very well, I shall not abandon you. I will see that a doctor is fetched, and, if you are ill, stay with you until you are home. I will nurse you and care for you should you need it. However, you must give me your word not to take advantage, sir.'

'You have my word as a gentleman,' Luke said. 'I am Luke Clarendon, a man of independent means and of good family. You may trust me, Miss Roxanne. Watch over me until I am fit again. I shall reward you by taking you to London—and I will introduce you to the manager of a theatre.'

'Very well, it is a bargain,' Roxanne said and her arms clung comfortingly to him once more.

Luke smiled. He did not think she would break her word for she might have done so in the woods. If he could delay their journey for a few days, she might come to like him—and once they were in London, he would find a way of keeping her with him.

Chapter Two

The inn they came to a little later was a small posting inn, not one of those Luke had frequented in the past, but decent in appearance; its yard was swept clean and the groom who came running to help respectful and eager to serve.

'Mr Clarendon has had a fall from his horse,' Roxanne said and slid down from the saddle unaided. 'He cannot walk without assistance. We need a room for him and one for me—and a doctor must be called at once, for his ankle is hurt and he is in great pain.'

Luke moaned as he slid down from the horse and his injured leg jarred. The action had caused the pain to intensify and he swayed as the faintness swirled in his head. Roxanne and the groom rushed to his aid, managing to save him from a further fall. The groom shouted for help and another two came running.

'Ned, take the gentleman's horse—Jeremiah, help

me and then fetch the doctor. Mr Clarendon is in pain with his ankle.'

The two grooms supported Luke towards the inn, which was a modest building, with whitewashed walls, a thatched roof and small leaded windows. Luke glanced over his shoulder and drew a sigh of relief as he saw Roxanne was following with her bundles. His whole leg was throbbing now and he felt very faint. Indeed, he might have fallen had the grooms supporting him not been strong men.

He was supported into the inn. A large portly man came to greet them, his knowing eyes going over both Luke and then Roxanne.

'Would you be needing a room for you and the— lady, sir?'

'We need two rooms,' Roxanne said. 'Mr Clarendon has hurt his ankle. I think there may be a small break. One of your grooms has gone for the doctor. However, I shall be nursing Mr Clarendon until we leave.'

'And who might you be, miss?' The landlord's brows met in a frown.

'I am Mr Clarendon's new governess,' Roxanne said in a clear firm tone. 'He has employed me to teach his nephew. My horse was lost in the woods; it ran off and we could not waste time looking for her. My name is Miss Roxanne Peters.'

Luke glanced at her, resisting a grin. It appeared that she could spin a tale as easily as he. The landlord looked uncertain whether to believe her, but was galvanised into action by a moan of pain from Luke.

'Take the gentleman up to the best chamber,' he

commanded his minions. 'The governess can have the smaller room two doors down.'

'Thank you, landlord,' Luke said and glanced back at Roxanne. 'Follow us up, Miss Peters. I shall want you in attendance when the doctor arrives.'

'I shall be with you in a moment, sir.'

The landlord had gone before them. He gestured at the room that was to be Roxanne's, leaving her to make her own way while continuing further down the passage.

Roxanne went inside the small room. There was a narrow iron bedstead with a white counterpane, blue curtains at the window and a small chest of drawers. To a girl who had been used to living in a caravan it was perfectly adequate. Roxanne dumped her bundles on the floor, took the key from the inside of the door and locked it as she went out, pocketing it safely. Her possessions were not valuable, but they were all she had and she could not afford to lose them—nor did she wish the landlord to go poking his nose into her things.

Walking quickly to the room where she had seen them take her employer—she had decided that the best way to go on was to act the part of an upper-class servant—Roxanne entered and saw that the landlord was standing by the bed. Both the grooms had gone.

'Thank you,' she said. 'I can manage him now.'

The landlord turned, his eyes narrowed and not exactly friendly. Roxanne felt a prickling at her nape. Mr Clarendon seemed barely conscious. She had a feeling that had she not been here to protect him, he might well have been robbed of his possessions. Perhaps she was wronging the landlord, but she was not sure he was honest.

'Right. I'll send the doctor up when he gets here.' He looked at her hard. 'I'll be wanting five shillings a night for this room, two for yours—food and the doctor extra.'

'Yes, of course. You will be paid. Mr Clarendon is a respectable man and we should not dream of running off without paying you.'

'You better hadn't. Jake Hardcastle never forgets a face—and I reckon I've seen yours before, but I can't recall where. You weren't a governess then.' He leered at her. 'If I don't get paid one way, I can take my dues another.'

'Will you please leave us.' Roxanne's manner was haughty, more the great lady than a governess. 'After the doctor has been we shall want food—perhaps some good chicken broth and fresh bread.'

He inclined his head, but made no other answer. Leaving the room, he paused to look back as Roxanne bent over the bed.

'Mr Clarendon,' she said, placing a hand to Luke's forehead. He was feeling warm and a little damp. She thought perhaps he had started a fever. 'Do not worry. I am here. I shall not leave you.'

The sound of the door shutting soundly made Roxanne look round. The landlord had gone and when she turned back, her patient's eyelids fluttered and then opened.

'Has he gone?' he muttered. 'The place looks decent

enough, but that fellow is a rascal. I don't trust him. You won't leave me, Roxanne?'

'Miss Peters. I am your employee, remember?'

A wry laugh was wrung from his lips. 'You will make a damned fine actress, Roxanne. You reminded me of a strict governess I once had—she frightened the life out of us all, except the earl.'

'The earl? Who is he?'

'Oh, just someone we lived with when I was young. He isn't important.' Luke moaned and beads of sweat appeared on his brow. 'I am sorry to make so much fuss. I wouldn't have thought a broken bone could be so painful. I do not recall it hurting this much when I broke my arm as a youngster.'

'You had to ride here and be manhandled up the stairs. I have not been trained to set broken bones and the bandage I applied may have made the pain worse. When the doctor comes he will rebind it and give you something to help you sleep.'

'Will you sit with me while I sleep? Or perhaps you should keep the money with you? I do not trust him.'

'Nor I,' she admitted. 'Do you trust me with your gold?'

'What choice have I?' Luke reached out to touch her hand as she frowned. 'No, that was badly put. Yes, I trust you, Roxanne. It is odd, but I feel I have known you for ever. I know you will not desert me, for you have given your word.'

'Then I shall put the money somewhere safe.'

'It is in my coat pocket, in a leather purse. I do not

know exactly what is there but it should be enough to see us safely back to London.'

Roxanne examined his coat and found the purse. She opened the strings and counted the gold, holding it out on her hand so that he could see.

'You have ten gold sovereigns, sir. I think it should be adequate for the journey, don't you?'

'You did not need to show me. I told you, I trust you. Now put them somewhere safe.'

'Yes, I shall.'

Roxanne turned her back on him. Lifting her skirts, she located the secret pocket sewn into her petticoats and added the gold to her secret treasure. It felt heavy, making her very conscious of its presence, but she would become accustomed to the extra weight.

She turned back and saw Luke staring at her.

'It is the safest place I know. My bundles could be searched or snatched.'

Luke nodded, his eyes narrowed and thoughtful. 'You are a resourceful woman, Roxanne. I wonder what your secret is—what you are not telling me?'

'Why should you think I have a secret?'

How could he know? No, he could not. He was just testing her.

'I shall not pry,' Luke said and yawned, closing his eyes. 'You keep your secrets, Roxanne—and I shall keep mine.'

Roxanne turned her head. How had he sensed that she was hiding her secret? She had not told him about the day Sofia found her wandering, all memory of her previous life gone. Nor had she told him about the jewel she carried in her secret pocket. Sofia had told her she had been clutching it tightly in her right hand when she was found and refused to let go for days. She also carried a lace kerchief with the initials R. P. embroidered into the corner in red. Sofia had said the name Roxanne suited her. They had never bothered with a second name and she had used Peters when the innkeeper asked, because it was the first to come to her mind. She had once done some sewing for a Lady Peters and been given a gold sovereign for her trouble.

Sofia had hidden the ruby safely and Roxanne had forgotten its existence until her friend reminded her as she lay dying. Sofia had said she should sell the jewel, but Roxanne was not certain she had the right to do so, for she did not know whether it belonged to her or someone else. Had she stolen the jewel and run away from her home—or her employer?

Why had she refused to let it go for days?

She hesitated, considering whether she ought to tell Luke Clarendon the rest of her story, but the moment had passed; she heard the sound of voices outside the door and then it opened and a man entered. He was dressed in a shabby black coat and knee breeches, the battered hat he deposited on the chest having seen better days. However, his linen looked clean and he nodded his head respectfully as he approached the bed.

'The gentleman took a fall from his horse, you say?'

'Yes,' Roxanne replied. 'He has been in considerable pain since.'

'I shall examine him,' the doctor said and bent over Luke, pulling back the covers. He unwound the stock

Roxanne had used and ran his fingers over the swollen ankle, frowning and nodding to himself. 'I think this may be a case of dislocation rather than a break. Your employer has been lucky, miss.' Hearing a moan from the patient, the physician turned his gaze on him. 'This may hurt a bit, sir. I am going to…' He pulled Luke's leg out straight, making him yell out with pain as something clicked. 'Yes, I thought so. It will be painful for a while, but I shall put a tight bandage on and visit again tomorrow. You will need to rest for a time, but in a few days it should start to mend. You had dislocated the bones just above your ankle and the ligaments will be inflamed, but I am sure the bones themselves are not broken.'

'I pray you are right,' Luke muttered between gritted teeth. 'It hurts like hell now.'

'Yes, I dare say it may.' The doctor dipped into his bag, brought out linen bandages and rebound Luke's ankle and above to his calf. 'That should help the damage to settle and it will heal naturally. I'll give you something for the pain.' He delved into his bag again and took out a small brown bottle. 'This will help you sleep, but it is dangerous if you take too many doses. You will have to measure it—just four drops into a cup of water every six hours. Miss Peters, is it?'

'Yes, that is my name,' Roxanne lied and took the bottle. 'Is this laudanum?'

'Yes—have you used it before?'

'A friend of mine used it sometimes. I know that it must be handled carefully, sir.'

'Then I can trust you to look after our patient.' He

glanced down at Luke. 'You will sleep soon, Mr Clarendon—and there should not be a fever, but if it happens you may send for me again.'

The physician took his leave. Roxanne carefully measured the drops into a glass of water. She helped Luke to sit up and he took the cup, gulping it down and draining the lot. Then he lay back against the pillows with a sigh.

'I was selfish to ask you to sit with me. You should go to bed and rest.'

'I shall sit here by the fire for a while. The doctor says there will be no fever, but I want to be sure you are peaceful. You were warm and sweaty earlier. I thought you might take a fever, but perhaps now you can rest you will soon feel better.'

Roxanne sat down by the fireplace. Someone had lit the fire when they brought Luke Clarendon up and it was just beginning to draw well. Her room had no fire and she might as well sit here in comfort—but she would lock the door first, just in case she dozed off.

Roxanne woke with a start. The fire was still burning so she could not have been asleep long. She got up quickly and went to the bed, bending over Luke. He appeared to be sleeping peacefully and when she placed a hand to his forehead, he was only slightly warm.

If he had not made a sound, what had woken her? She went to the door and stood with her ear against it, listening.

'Is anyone there?' she asked softly, but received no answer. 'What do you want?'

Another sound alerted her and she turned swiftly towards the window, just in time to see a man's face looking in. Someone must have fetched a ladder to try to gain entrance that way after realising the door was bolted on the inside. Instinctively, Roxanne bent down and retrieved the iron poker from the fireplace. She approached the window, raising her arm high, making it clear that she was ready to repel any intruder. For a moment she stared at the face looking in. The features were coarse and common, unknown to her. Aware that he had been spotted, the man hesitated and then disappeared. Roxanne looked out and saw the top of his head hurriedly descending the ladder, which he then picked up and ran off with towards the stables.

Roxanne's legs felt slightly shaky as she sat down by the fire once more. She had not known the man attempting to enter by way of the window, but she was certain the landlord would. Her instincts had been right. Their host was a rascal and it would not be safe for her to leave Luke Clarendon alone while he was in a drugged sleep.

For a moment she wondered if the doctor had been in with them, but Luke seemed to be easier now and she thought the physician had known his job well enough. She shivered and bent down to place another log on the fire. If Luke were well enough to hire a carriage of some sort, they would do better to move on as soon as they could.

'Have you been to bed at all?' Luke asked as he opened his eyes and looked up at her. She had been applying a cool cloth to his brow. 'That feels good, but I do not have a fever. My mind is quite clear now. I think I slept for a long time?'

'Yes, you did. I stayed with you all night. There was an attempt to gain access through the window, but it woke me and I faced the intruder down with the poker. He ran away, back to the stable.'

Luke's mouth thinned. 'In league with the innkeeper I imagine? Some of these fellows are rogues. Not content with their pay, they will rob the unwary.'

'He must have thought you were alone. I am afraid I have wasted two shillings of your money. I did not use the room I asked for at all.'

'Well, you should go there now and rest. But first, give me my pistol—it's in my coat, the inside pocket— and then ask the landlord to bring food and drink, Roxanne. I doubt he will try anything in broad daylight, but if he does I shall show him I'm no fool. I shall enquire what kind of transport is for hire—but if there is none available here we shall go on together on my horse.'

Roxanne fetched the pistol from amongst his things and handed it to him. Had she known it was there, she might have used it to protect them instead of the poker the previous night.

'Are you sure you can manage to move on so soon? The doctor said you should rest and he would come again today.'

'My ankle feels sore at the moment and there is some pain in my calf, but the excruciating pain of yesterday has gone. I would rather leave if I can manage it.'

'If we can hire a chaise of some sort, will you leave your horse here?'

'I doubt I should see it again. I shall pay the man for the hire of his vehicle and change at the next posting house, but take my horse with us.'

'I confess I cannot wait to see the back of this place. Had I not been with you, you would certainly have been robbed as you slept.'

'I should not be the first vulnerable traveller to die in his bed at the hands of rogues calling themselves landlords.' Luke frowned. 'I have much to thank you for, Roxanne. It seems as if you have saved me from my own folly more than once.'

'I have done nothing any decent person would not,' she said, a faint flush in her cheeks. 'Travelling with you will save my small store of money and I shall reach London sooner.'

'I might not have reached it at all without you.'

Luke's gaze was so warm and so intent that her cheeks flamed and he laughed as he saw her discomfort. 'Now I have embarrassed you. Forgive me, Miss Roxanne. I have not forgotten my promise. I shall not try to seduce you—at least until our bargain is at an end.'

'You should not try it at all, sir. You will be disappointed. I have no intention of becoming your mistress—or any other man's.'

'So you say.' Luke smiled lazily. 'You are far too beautiful to remain untouched for the rest of your life, Roxanne. Someone will persuade you to part with your innocence—I should prefer that it was me.'

'I think you must have a fever, sir. You hardly know me—and you should know better than to mock me.'

'I was not mocking you, Roxanne. Believe me, there are not many women who make me feel the way you do—but I shall not tease you, because I might frighten you away. I may be able to leave this place soon, but that doesn't mean I am safe until I get to London.'

'Are you thinking of your enemy?' Roxanne looked concerned. He might be arrogant and too sure of his power to charm, but she did not fear him, as she had Black Bob. 'I thought it was one of the landlord's rogues trying to rob you last night, but your enemy may have followed you here to try to kill you.'

'No, I do not think so.' Luke frowned and wished he had not spun her such a tale. 'He might want to punish me, but he would not kill me.'

'Oh—then I dare say it was not he.' Roxanne looked thoughtful and he wondered what was in her mind. 'If you truly know a theatre manager who might give me a trial, I should be grateful.'

'I shall help you, as you have helped me,' Luke promised. 'Whatever else I may be, Miss Roxanne, I am not ungrateful. One day I may try to make you my mistress, a position you might find to your liking if you gave it a chance, but it shall not be while we journey together.'

Within two hours, they had left the inn. The groom who had first aided them the previous day was driving a chaise, which was in reasonable order, with Luke's horse tied and trotting behind. Roxanne sat beside Luke on the seat facing forwards so that they could see the groom's back. He had told them his name was Harold and seemed likeable. Hopefully, he was honest, but they would only need his services until they reached a well-known posting inn a few miles further on the London road. Roxanne was not sure what Luke Clarendon had said to the innkeeper, but though he had looked at her in a surly way when they left, he had not spoken to her disrespectfully. She had previously returned Luke's gold to him and he had paid for their lodging and the doctor's fees.

Roxanne was certain their host had added extra to the bill for himself, because his charge of two guineas for the doctor's visit seemed extortionate to her, but Luke had paid it cheerfully.

'It was worth treble for the relief he has afforded me,' Luke said. 'I am still in pain, but it is bearable now.'

'I am glad to hear it.' Roxanne was thoughtful. If Luke Clarendon was capable of travelling alone now, she ought to leave him and make her own way. He had offered her help, but she was uncertain of the price she might be asked to pay.

Sofia had so often warned her to be careful of gentlemen, especially those who smiled and promised her help or a fortune. This man was charming and handsome, but she did not quite trust him.

Well, he might attempt seduction, but she did not believe he would force her—the way Black Bob would have had she stayed with the travelling players. Luke Clarendon was a gentleman, after all.

Roxanne knew that his warnings were valid. If she

became an actress, she would be offered protection by various men—perhaps the manager of the theatre himself or gentlemen who came to watch her perform. If she gained admirers, she might follow in Sofia's footsteps and become the mistress of an aristocrat or even royalty. It was not what Sofia had wanted for her or what she planned for herself, but it might be impossible to avoid some such relationship.

Why not a man she had already begun to like?

The thought had wormed its way into her mind against her will. Roxanne did not wish to become any man's mistress, but if it was inevitable— Her thoughts were interrupted as Luke glanced at her.

'You look pensive, tired. Why do you not lean your head back against the squabs and sleep for a while? I think we may trust Harold. Relax your guard and rest.'

'Yes, perhaps I shall.'

Roxanne leaned her head back against the squabs, closing her eyes. When Luke Clarendon looked and spoke to her in that way her defences crumbled. He was such an attractive man and she was beginning to like him all too well.

When she woke an hour or so later, the chaise was drawing into the yard of what was clearly a prestigious inn. She discovered that she had been leaning against Luke's shoulder and apologised, her cheeks warm.

'Forgive me, sir. I hope I have not made you uncomfortable. Does your leg pain you very much?'

'It is sore and, yes, a little painful,' he said. 'I shall

live, Miss Roxanne—and you did not make me uncomfortable at all.'

The groom had brought the chaise to a halt. One of the inn's employees had come to open the chaise door and let down the step. Seeing that Luke was carrying an injury, his breeches split and opened to allow for the bandages, the man offered his hand, helping him to descend. Luke did so slowly and carefully, his flinch of pain not going unnoticed by either the ostler or Roxanne.

'I have suffered an accident, as you see, Johnston,' Luke said with a friendly smile at the man who clearly knew him. 'If you would have someone care for my horse and ask someone to give this kind fellow something to eat before he goes on his way again. Please help me inside yourself.'

'Yes, sir, of course,' Johnston replied and signalled to his minions, who came running and were given curt instructions to see to the horses.

Roxanne frowned as she thanked Harold for bringing them here safely and gave him a shilling of her own money for himself.

'I'm sorry if you weren't treated right at the last place,' he said and pulled his cap. 'I heard what happened, but I didn't know until I was told what you did, miss. You were right brave.'

'I do not think you belong at a place like that, Harold.'

'No, miss, nor don't I,' he agreed. 'I stayed because it were better than being on the road, but when I take this rig back I shall give me notice and look for work elsewhere.'

'I am sure you will find it,' Roxanne said and inclined her head before following Luke into the inn.

When she entered she saw him in close conversation with a man who looked to be the landlord. He was a very different man from the last one they had met; portly and pleasant-faced, he smiled and nodded at her in a friendly way.

'This gentleman has told me he owes his life to you, miss. I know there's more than one who should be grateful to you. My wife will take you up to a nice comfortable room and look after you. I dare say you are very tired.'

'I slept a part of the way here,' Roxanne replied. She looked at Luke, her fine brows raised. 'Have you asked our host to fetch a doctor, sir? I think your leg may need further attention—just to make certain it has been properly treated.'

'Don't you worry, miss. His lor...his honour is in good hands now.'

Roxanne heard the change in the landlord's tone and his hasty correction. What had he been going to say? It was clear that Luke Clarendon was well known and respected here—but how was he normally addressed?

She frowned as the landlord's wife came to greet her, curtsying respectfully. 'Come this way, miss. We are always glad to have his lordship come to stay—' She clapped her hand to her forehead. 'There, if Sid didn't tell me I was to call Lord Clarendon his honour. My tongue runs away with me, so it does—but everyone knows who he is so why not say it openly?'

'Why not indeed?'

Roxanne felt her cheeks getting warmer. What a fool she was not to have made sure of her facts for a start. He had told her his name was Luke Clarendon and she had assumed his title was plain Mister. He must have been laughing at her behind his hand.

Luke Clarendon was an aristocrat and therefore not to be trusted. Sofia had told her that they were the worst of all and warned her never to lose her heart to a member of the upper classes.

'If you do, he will use you and then abandon you. Take notice, child, for I know of what I speak.'

Roxanne felt her stomach knot with a mixture of anger and disappointment. For a short time she had begun to think that perhaps Luke really liked her—so why had he not told her he had a title from the start?

He had pretended to trust her, but he hadn't trusted her enough to tell her who he really was. She felt the sting of tears, but blocked them out. There was no sense in crying. She didn't know Lord Clarendon at all and, after listening to Sofia's opinion of the aristocracy for years, she was sure she did not wish to. Her friend had warned her that they were all the same: proud, arrogant and ruthless.

'They know how to be charming and they will smile and tell you they adore you, but underneath they are cold and heartless. They will not marry out of their class—and they toss you to one side when they are fin-ished with you. The English aristocracy are the worst.

Some foreign royalty are kinder and more generous. Never trust an English gentleman, Roxanne—particularly if he tells you he will always love you. Just take what you can from him and move on before he does.'

Roxanne kept her anger in check as she followed the innkeeper's wife along a hall and into a room. It was large and comfortable, well furnished and, with a fire burning in the grate, warm.

'This is next to his lordship's chamber,' she said. 'He always has the same one when he visits on his way to stay with the earl.'

'Who is the earl?'

'Why, his grandfather, of course.' The woman gave her an odd look. 'I thought you would know that, miss, being a cousin of his lordship.'

'Yes, of course. There is more than one earl in the family.'

Her quick answer banished the other woman's frown. 'So there will be,' she replied and laughed, her large bosom shaking. 'Silly me. Now, is there anything more you need, miss?'

'May I have my supper here, please? Just something light—and I would love a cup of tea.'

'Yes, of course you would. You ladies love your pot of tea and bread and butter—but I've a nice pie cooking and some chops for his lordship. His lordship is partial to a nice chop or two.'

Roxanne inclined her head. She was so angry that she barely knew how to answer. One part of her mind was telling her to walk out now and make her own way to London. If Harold had not left, he might have taken her a bit further before returning the rig to its owner. Yet if she did that she would not have the chance to tell Lord Clarendon exactly what she thought of him and his lies.

The warmth of the fire was enticing and Roxanne's feeling of annoyance faded as she moved closer, holding her hands to the flames. There was nothing to stop her moving on alone, because *Lord* Clarendon was amongst friends and would be properly cared for. Her instincts told her that she might be laying up trouble for herself if she stayed here and yet she was seduced by the thought of a warm bed, the fire and some hot food.

What harm could it do to travel on with him, even if he had not been entirely honest with her?

It was good to be in a house again instead of the cramped conditions in the caravan… Now *where* had that thought come from?

Try as she might, Roxanne had never been able to remember anything about her previous life. Sofia was convinced she had run away from her home, that she was the child of gentry, but had been in some terrible danger.

'Something happened to you, my love,' Sofia had told her. *'You were frightened and ill. In your fever you spoke of many things, of places you'd seen and people you knew. For weeks you woke crying and screaming, frightened of a dream, but you could never recall it. It is the reason I did not try hard to find your family. If you ran away in such distress there must have been a*

reason—and I would not give you back to people who might ill treat you.'

Had Roxanne's family mistreated her? Sofia had burned her clothes, because she said they were not fit for use and could tell them nothing about her past, except that they were of good cloth.

Roxanne shook her head. If her family had wanted her, she would not have been wandering the roads alone and in such a state. It hardly mattered where she had come from. Sofia had been like a mother to her, giving her all the love she instinctively knew had been missing from her previous life. A wave of grief swept over her, bringing tears to her eyes. She dashed them away with her hand, determined not to give into foolishness. Sofia was gone and she must manage alone.

Faced with walking the rest of the way to London alone or travelling in a chaise with a gentleman, who was truly in no condition to ravage her, she thought she must be sensible and choose the latter. If Lord Clarendon tried to seduce her as he recovered his strength, she could leave him and go on alone.

Removing the black-velvet cloak that had been Sofia's, a relic of the days when she had moved amongst gentlemen of fortune and their mistresses, Roxanne sat on the edge of the bed. Her dress had also belonged to Sofia when she was a young woman; though old-fashioned, it was of good cloth with a low, dipped neckline, in which Roxanne had sewn a frill of soft cream lace for modesty's sake. Amongst her things was a silver hand mirror that she had inherited from her friend, an ivory comb and a bristle brush. She took them out and then tidied her dark red curls, glancing at herself once before replacing them securely in her bundle.

When she heard the knock at the door, she gave permission to enter, but was surprised when Lord Clarendon walked in.

'I thought it was the innkeeper's wife, my lord,' she said and raised her head defiantly. 'Why did you not tell me you were the grandson of an earl? I should not have called you Mr Clarendon had I known your title, sir.'

'It hardly matters. Hartingdon is about to disown me anyway.'

'Why?' Roxanne asked. 'Is he not your grandfather?'

'He brought me up after my parents died, but I was a nuisance. He did not truly wish for the trouble of a young boy and I was left to the care of servants. When he was forced to discipline me, he was harsh. As soon as I inherited my father's estate I left Hartingdon and have visited very seldom since—and yet…'

Roxanne sensed his hesitation. 'You are troubled over something?'

'Hartingdon is an old man. He fell down in some kind of faint while I was visiting there recently and—to be honest, it distressed me. Had you asked me a week ago if I cared a damn what happened to him, I should have said no but now…' Luke shook his head and laughed ruefully. 'I am a fool. His health changes nothing. And if he makes that popinjay Harte his heir… it is not my affair.'

'Why would he disown you?' Her clear eyes disconcerted him and he dropped his gaze.

'He wishes me to marry a suitable young lady, someone with good manners who will not disgrace the family.'

'Why should he imagine you would marry anyone other than a respectable girl?'

'Because he has been told that I have a string of mistresses and it is true that I have found pleasure in the arms of whores. I have found them kinder and more generous than young ladies of my acquaintance.' He frowned. 'I dare say it was my fault that he was ill.'

'You are blaming yourself, are you not?'

'Yes. I thought he was going to die. It shocked me and I realised I did not wish for it.'

'You care for him,' Roxanne said and nodded, looking at him curiously. 'Why do you not do as he asks and marry a suitable girl?'

'Because the only ones I know bore me to tears. I would make him happy if I could, for I believe he may not have long to live—but to marry a woman I could not love is a life sentence. Even for his sake I could not do such a thing.'

'No? I thought men of your class often married for land or money?'

'If one is in difficulty...' Luke glared at her. 'My father was forever having affairs. He broke my mother's heart. As a consequence they quarrelled and...the chaise he was driving went off the road into a ditch filled with water and they were both killed. I was thrown clear and survived. The last thing I remember of that day was my mother screaming at him, crying because he had broken yet another promise. I would not wish to make any woman that miserable.'

'How terrible for you. I think I understand why you feel as you do.' Roxanne frowned. 'If the earl does not have long, could you not let him believe you mean to marry and then…?'

'Break it off?' Luke raised his brows. 'I should be a fine rogue to dash a young lady's hopes, should I not? Society would throw me out and I should deserve it.'

'Yes, it was a foolish idea, though if she knew and it was a business arrangement it might be possible,' Roxanne said and then changed the subject hurriedly because she had been outspoken. 'I have asked for my supper to be brought here. Did you want something, sir?'

Luke was staring at her. He looked as if he had been struck by lightning. 'What did you say—a business arrangement? What exactly did you mean?'

'It was mere foolishness.' Roxanne's cheeks burned. 'I meant nothing—did you want something of me, sir?'

'I'm not sure,' he said and looked thoughtful. 'I came to ask if you would dine with me down in the parlour, but perhaps I shall have my meal brought up to my room, too. You have given me food of another kind, Miss Roxanne—something to chew on for a day or two until I am certain of my own mind.'

Now what did he mean by that? Roxanne would have asked, but her supper arrived and Luke walked away with a nod of the head.

Chapter Three

The sun shone through the small leaded window the next morning, bringing Roxanne from her bed with new energy. She had been up for some minutes when the innkeeper's wife entered bearing a can of hot water and was grateful for her thoughtfulness.

'Thank you. I was about to use the water left from last night and this is a kind thought.'

'His lordship would expect it, miss. Would you like to eat your breakfast here? His lordship is having his in the private parlour. You could join him, if you wish? He has bacon, devilled eggs, kedgeree and also cold roast ham, besides the toast, of course. You could have the same unless there is something else you would like?'

'If I could have some bread or rolls with honey, that would do very well. I shall come down as soon as I have washed and tidied myself.'

'Of course, miss. Whatever suits you.'

Roxanne thanked her and she went away. Despite

some fears about the future and her present situation, Roxanne had slept well and was feeling refreshed. She was ready and downstairs in a very short time. In the private parlour, Lord Clarendon, as she was trying to think of him, was drinking coffee and reading a news-sheet. He looked up as she entered and smiled. She realised not for the first time that he was very attractive and her heart did a funny little skip.

'Ah, Roxanne, did you sleep well? I trust there were no untoward incidents to disturb you last night?'

'None at all, sir. I slept perfectly and feel much refreshed this morning.'

'That is excellent news. I, too, am feeling less strained. I have been thinking about our situation and would like you to consider a suggestion that I believe might suit us both. Am I right in believing that you need to find work almost immediately?'

'Yes, that is so,' Roxanne replied and sat down just as the innkeeper brought in some warm soft rolls in a covered dish, also butter and a pot of dark honey. 'Thank you so much.'

She took a fresh baked roll and spread it with honey. Their host poured her a bowl of fragrant coffee, adding a drop of cream, and then left them alone together. Raising her clear eyes to Luke's, Roxanne questioned, 'I am not certain of your meaning?'

'It is a little difficult to explain. Have you been honest with me, Roxanne? From your story I think you honest and of good character—is there something I should know that you have not told me?'

'I do not see why you should need to know anything

about me, sir.' She hesitated, then, 'I will tell you that I have no memory of my life before Sofia found me more than five summers ago. I was in great distress, near to starving and out of my mind with a fever. I had a kerchief with the initials R. P.—and that is why Sofia called me Roxanne—and Peters was the name of a lady I once did some sewing for. It fits and might be my name, but I do not know the truth.'

'Good grief! So you have no idea who you are?' He frowned. 'That could complicate things…'

'What do you mean? What can my past life mean to you?

'Perhaps nothing, perhaps much.' He glared at her. 'What else have you kept from me?'

Roxanne thought of the ruby but decided she would not tell him everything just yet. 'I do not see what difference it can make to you.'

'It is in my mind to do as you suggested last night—but I should not wish for an unpleasant surprise. I do not want an irate brother or employer turning up on my doorstep causing trouble.'

'I fear you have lost me.' But she was beginning to feel an odd churning in her stomach and her suspicions were aroused. He could not be suggesting what she thought?

'You want work as an actress and you assured me that you can play royalty or the aristocracy to perfection. What I need is a make-believe wife, Roxanne, a woman who can play the part of my fiancée, and, if necessary, marry me. The marriage would be annulled later—and you would receive a generous settlement.

You could then live your own life, abroad should you wish it—or perhaps a nice house in the country, where you could entertain your friends.'

Roxanne was stunned, speechless at first, and then firm in denial. 'That is ridiculous, sir. I do not know how you could suggest such a thing. You do not know me—and I do not know you. Even if I agreed, it would be wrong to deceive your grandfather so cruelly.'

Luke frowned. 'Last night you said it could be a business arrangement. What is different about my proposal?'

'I meant a young woman of good family who would marry without love for the sake of a home and children—a lady who would be content to remain at home in the country while you lived as you pleased in town. Is that not the way many marriages are arranged?'

'Yes, of course, but I explained how I felt about that, the distress and misery it can cause. A proper business arrangement, where the lady in question is paid a sum of money and understands her position from the start—that should not cause unhappiness at all, should it?'

'No, not if the lady was content with the arrangement.' Roxanne saw the slightly excited, expectant look on his face. 'I am not a lady, sir. I told you, I do not know who I am—and I have lived with travelling players for some years. I have appeared on various stages about the country and might be recognised.'

'That might be a drawback, if you had played in London—but I think you have not?'

'No, I have never played at a large theatre. Sometimes we were employed by a provincial theatre, but often we set up on village greens or in the yard of an inn, as travelling players have for centuries.'

'Black Bob is not your relation—or your lover?'

'Certainly not!' she cried indignantly.

'Then I see no reason why you should not oblige me.'

'Do you not?' Roxanne pressed a spotless white napkin to her mouth, then laid it by her plate. 'I am grateful for the bed and my food, but I think we should part company now. I will find some way of reaching London alone.'

'You promised you would not abandon me. We still have one more day on the road.'

'You are perfectly safe now. These people are honest and they know you. Besides, I do not think you are in pain now.'

'I am not in as much pain as I was, but if I wanted to get down from the chaise on the road I could not do so without assistance. If my idea upsets you, I withdraw it. Last night I thought you willing. I misjudged the matter. Forgive me, but allow me to take you on to London and find you a place to stay and at least an interview with the manager of a theatre.'

'I see no reason why you should do anything for me. I have done very little to deserve it, sir.'

'Apart from saving my life twice?' Luke grinned at her. 'Say you are not offended, Roxanne. I assure you that my motives are not those of greed or wishing to deceive—except in a kind way.'

'A kind way?'

'I should like my grandfather to die with an easy mind. Is that so very terrible?'

'No, and if the young lady were willing I should not entirely condemn the idea—but I am not a lady. You would be lying to him if you presented me as a lady of good birth.'

'Supposing I merely said you were a young lady of good character—would that be a lie?'

'No.' Roxanne met his searching gaze. 'I am untouched—if that is what you mean. Sofia kept me safe. She believed I was of a good family and she wanted me to become a lady. She did not wish me to follow in her footsteps—but a lady is born, not made. I could live quietly, perhaps in Bath, as you suggested, but without patronage I should not be accepted.'

'Supposing I could find a lady who would sponsor you? Supposing you found yourself able to mix in company—would you then consider becoming my fiancée or, if necessary, wife for a short time?'

Roxanne hesitated. She hardly knew why she was resisting. Sofia had kept her jewel safe, telling her that she need not work on the stage. The chance to be accepted into society, to live as a respectable young lady, was something that might never come again. If she refused and insisted on finding work as an actress, her future was inevitable. In the end she would be trapped or persuaded into taking a protector.

'I might consent to a long engagement,' she said and then wondered if she had run mad. 'I think marriage might be a step too far, but if you were to introduce me as your fiancée and explain that we could not marry until…my father returns from India, it might serve.'

'Is your father in India?'

'I have no idea who my father is or even if he is alive. It was a game Sofia invented. She said I was the daughter of an English lady and an Indian prince. She was once the mistress of a maharajah and liked to tell me tales of India. I think her stories were so vivid that sometimes I saw the prince in my dreams. She said it would take away the bad dreams and she was right.'

'Your friend was a remarkable lady.'

'She taught me so much and I loved her. Sometimes her stories seem real to me, but I remember nothing beyond waking and seeing Sofia smiling at me.'

'It must have been terrifying for you.'

'Yes, at first, but Sofia helped me through the dark times when the nightmares came.'

'You were lucky to have her.'

'I think had she not found me I should have died— but you do not need to tell your grandfather lies. Surely there must be a young woman of good family who would oblige you?'

'I do not wish to make a marriage of convenience.' A tiny nerve flicked at his temple. 'My mother made such a marriage and was desperately unhappy. I would not inflict that pain on anyone. I truly do not wish to harm anyone.'

'Then…' Roxanne sighed '…perhaps we might have a business arrangement if you wished for it.'

'I begin to see how the story might work,' Luke said, his gaze narrowed. 'I could say that you were the daughter of an employee of the East India Company. You have not heard from your father for some time and, while consenting to an engagement, could not marry until he replies to your letter. If necessary, we could always kill him off at some future date.'

'Do not joke about such things.' Roxanne twisted her napkin in her fingers. 'I feel that we are discussing a wicked trick and I am not sure that I could carry it through. If the earl were to discover the deceit he would be devastated—it might lead to his death.'

'Why should it be discovered?' Luke's cool gaze intensified. 'You are an attractive young woman, Roxanne—but your clothes do not do you justice. Dressed as a young woman of good family you will look very different. No one is going to recognise you as an actress—none of my friends or family will have seen you on the stage. An engagement may be broken. If something goes wrong, we can end it and my grandfather will understand that these things happen. However, he may not live for many months. After his death, you will be free to go wherever you please. Is it too much to ask—to make an old man happy?'

Roxanne considered, then, 'No, that part at least is commendable. Yet I still feel it wrong to deceive him. Could you not bring yourself to make a marriage of convenience to a young lady of your own class, my lord?'

'I fear it is out of the question. If you will not accept, I must forget the idea. Grandfather has given me an ultimatum and if I do not abide by it… He has threatened to disown me and—make life extremely difficult for me and the people I support. Besides, his cousin Harte is a pompous fool and not fit to stand in Grandfather's shoes.'

'What happens to you if the earl disinherits you?'

'I lose the earl's title, his estate and fortune—but do not imagine I care for his money. I have sufficient of my own...or I had. He has told me that he can withhold the inheritance I had from my paternal grandfather until I am thirty if he chooses. I do not know if it is an empty threat. I must speak with my lawyers in town. It would be deuced awkward. I have commitments to some people that I would be loath to break.'

'What kind of commitments?' She saw his quick frown. 'That is not my business. Forgive me. It is just that I would be certain what is in your mind concerning this arrangement.'

'My suggestion stemmed from your own, Roxanne. Forgive me, I should not have mentioned it. After all, you hardly know me. I might be a ruthless rogue out to rob the old man of his money.'

'No, I do not believe that,' Roxanne replied. 'You must allow me a little time, sir. I shall complete the journey to London with you—and then we shall discuss this again, perhaps in a few days.'

His gaze fastened on her face. 'Yes, of course. We have another day on the road and then I shall take you to a place where you can stay until a decision is made.'

The journey was completed without incident. They were obliged to get down from the chaise once so that Luke could relieve himself. He had not lied when he told her he would need assistance to hobble into the bushes at the side of the road and leaned heavily on her arm. From the grimace on his face, she thought that he was still in some pain. She turned her head modestly and ignored the sounds from behind her, waiting patiently to help him back into the carriage when he was ready.

Luke shot her an amused glance. 'You play the part of a long-suffering wife to perfection, Roxanne. If you chose, you could easily fool Grandfather or anyone else into thinking we had been married for an age.'

Roxanne looked at him disapprovingly. 'I know you are jesting, but I do not find the suggestion funny. Marriage would not be an option. Even an engagement seems so deceitful when there is no intention on either side—but I do understand why you wish to please him.'

'He gets so distressed over the smallest thing,' Luke told her. 'I fear a fit of temper may carry him off. Once, that would not have concerned me, but now—I find I should not like to be the cause of his death.'

'You really believe that your refusal to marry may cause the earl to die in distress?'

'Yes.' Luke's expression was serious. 'You are right to accuse me of levity. It has always been my way to make light of things—but it shocked me when he had that turn. I thought he was going to die, and, had he done so, it would have been my fault.'

Roxanne nodded, but made no further comment. Luke sat back with his eyes closed and the remainder of the journey was accomplished in silence. However, he stirred himself as they approached the heath and told her that they had reached Hampstead.

'There has been a highwayman waylaying travellers hereabouts for some months, but last month they caught him and I dare say he will hang. The house I told you of is nearby. It is being prepared for someone—a lady and child. At the moment she is staying with friends in the south of England, but in another week or two she will take up residence. She will not mind if we use it for a few days.'

'You intend to stay there with me?'

'Not to sleep, but I must visit often. You have my word that I shall not take advantage. If you are to play the part of my fiancée, you will need to know certain things and we must dress you accordingly.' He smiled at her. 'Can you trust me, Roxanne? You must know that I would not harm you after all you have done for me?'

'I hardly know you—and I have been taught not to trust gentlemen of your class.' Roxanne was thoughtful. If the house had been prepared for a lady and child, she was probably his mistress and perhaps the child was his. He would surely not attempt to seduce her in the house he had bought for his mistress? 'Yet I believe you to be a man of your word.'

'That is something.' Luke was unsmiling as the chaise came to a halt. 'You may help me down if you will, Miss Roxanne—it is best I address you formally now. Mrs Mills is the caretaker here for the moment and will respect you more if she thinks you a respectable young lady fallen on hard times.'

'What do you mean to tell her?'

'Just what I intend to tell everyone.' His grey eyes were intent on her. 'You do not know who you are. Yet I am certain you came from gentry—and you suggested India, which may be the truth for all we know.'

Roxanne climbed down from the chaise and gave Luke her hand to steady him. He winced as his injured leg touched the ground, but immediately recovered and took the arm she offered. As they approached the front door of the modest red-bricked villa, it opened and a woman of some forty-odd years stood in the doorway, looking at him expectantly.

'Mrs Mills, I am pleased to see you again,' Luke said with the easy charm that had drawn Roxanne to him. 'This is not Mrs Fox, who is to live here, but a lady who has done me the honour of accepting my help.'

'Lord Clarendon, how good to see you,' she said and dipped a curtsy, her curious eyes on Roxanne.

'This is Miss Roxanne Peters,' Luke said without batting an eyelid. 'I have brought her here for a few days, because she had nowhere else to go. Her best friend has recently died and she is alone. Roxanne's father is in India and she is having difficulty in managing. She needs somewhere to stay for a little while—until we can settle things with the earl. In confidence, this lady is to be my fiancée.'

'Then you *are* planning to marry.' Mrs Mills looked surprised and pleased. 'Well, sir, I am sure the earl will be glad to hear your news.'

'We must hope so, Mrs Mills—but you know my grandfather.'

'Indeed, I do, sir, and if you will forgive me, I thought him a harsh guardian after your dear parents died so tragically.'

'I dare say he did his best,' Luke replied, a little nerve flicking at his temple. 'If you will be so good as to look after Miss Roxanne for me, I have business to attend. I shall return later to dine with you, Roxanne.'

Oddly, now that he was leaving, she wished he would stay. She offered her hand and he took it, bending his head to kiss it briefly.

'Until later, dearest,' he said and her heart jolted. He was playing a part, but for a moment she felt something so sweet and delicious that she wished their game was not merely make believe.

Roxanne nodded, turning to watch as he left before following the housekeeper up the stairs to her room.

'Such a kind man,' Mrs Mills was saying and she realised that she had not been listening. 'Always thinking of others. People try to paint his lordship black, but take no notice, Miss Peters, he has a good heart.'

'Yes, I am sure you are right,' Roxanne said as she was shown into a bedchamber. 'What a lovely room.'

'And this is the guest room. It's as I was saying, no expense spared for the widow and her child. Mrs Fox is a fortunate young woman if you ask me.'

'Mrs Fox is the lady who is to live here?'

'She and her son, the poor lady. Such a sad tale—but my tongue runs away with me and his lordship would be cross with me for tattling. I shall leave you to rest, Miss Roxanne—please ring for tea in the parlour when you come down.'

Roxanne looked about her at the pretty satinwood furniture, the silken hangings of green and white and the crystal trinkets with silver tops on the dressing table. If this was the guest room, Mrs Fox's room must be something special. Clearly Luke had deep feelings for the widow.

Was Mrs Fox his mistress? The thought troubled Roxanne. If he had feelings for the lady—and he must, for he would not otherwise have provided her with a house and Mrs Mills to care for her and her son—why had he brought Roxanne here?

If he already had a son, why did he not produce him as his heir and marry the boy's mother? It would surely solve all his problems.

Luke had told her he did not wish for a marriage of convenience. Was that because his heart belonged to a woman he could not marry?

Perhaps the earl thought Mrs Fox unworthy. What would he think of a young woman who knew nothing of her background and might even be a thief?

No, Roxanne was certain she was not a thief. She did not know why she had the ruby in her possession when she was found, but she would not have stolen it—would she?

Sighing, she gave up the attempt to remember. She remembered nothing but her life with the travelling players and Sofia. The vivid pictures that flitted through her mind at times were merely Sofia's stories— put there to fill the blankness that had been there when she woke from her illness and cried for days.

'Oh, Sofia,' she whispered as she sat down on the

bed and ran her hand over the silken covers. 'What am I to do? I like him so much—but I fear that I am headed for trouble. I should run away now, go to London and forget him…but I feel as if something binds me to him.'

'He will break your heart.'

The words were only in her head. Sofia was no longer there to guide and comfort her. She was alone and must use her wits to keep herself safe. Luke Clarendon was offering an arrangement that would make her independent for the rest of her life. All she had to do was to play a part—and keep a little distance between them.

A tiny voice in her head told her it was already too late, but she was no longer listening.

Roxanne smiled and lifted her face to the sun. She had been staying here for almost a week now. Life was comfortable and pleasant; Roxanne was beginning to feel at home, but she did not dare to let herself feel too settled. She was here under false pretences and that made her feel a little guilty. Once or twice she had considered hiring a cab to take her into the centre of London in search of work at a theatre.

'Roxanne…' Mrs Mill's voice calling to her made her glance over her shoulder. She looked at her basket. She had enough flowers for now. 'His lordship has arrived.'

'Thank you.' She saw that Luke had come out into the garden in search of her and her heart quickened as she went to meet him. 'I thought you would not be here until this evening.'

'I was able to get away sooner.' He looked at her approvingly. 'That gown suits you well, Roxanne.'

'I am glad you approve. You chose it.'

'So I did,' he said. 'Fetch your bonnet and a shawl if you wish for one. As I rode here I saw a fair on the Heath. It is an age since I visited a fair. Shall we go, Roxanne? I'll buy you a toffee apple.'

She laughed and shook her head. 'I do not think I should care for it, but there will be other treats I dare say. Yes, if you wish, we may as well spend a little time there for it is a lovely afternoon.'

'Then we shall go and if you do not wish for a toffee apple I will win you a fairing at the shooting range.'

Roxanne agreed and ran inside to fetch her bonnet. She did not know why, but the prospect of spending the afternoon at the fair with him was delightful. She had come to know him a little these past days and to like what she learned of him very much.

The fair had spread out over much of the Heath. There were stalls of all kinds and the smells of hot pies and toffee apples were mouth watering. A man on stilts was walking through the crowds, telling people to visit the bearded lady and the dog with two heads, as well as to watch the wrestling match and the bowling for a pig. Luke paid to try his hand at the shooting range, but his shots went astray and he made a sound of annoyance.

'I am sure the barrel is not straight. I will have one more attempt. Walk a little further and I shall catch you up in a moment.'

Roxanne smiled and left him, feeling amused that

he was so determined to win her a fairing. She would not go too far, but wander around the stalls, which sold all manner of pretty trifles. She would have liked to buy a small gift for Luke, but her few pennies would not stretch far and she was afraid to spend them in case she needed them.

She stood for a moment watching a man swallowing a sword and juggling with fire. Then, feeling a tingling at the nape of her neck, she glanced to her left where a group of men were standing haggling over horses and a shiver went down her spine. A man with black hair and a swarthy complexion was looking at her. She knew him at once and felt the fear sweep through her. How unfortunate that he should be at the fair! If he came to her and demanded she return with him, he might force her to go.

She had to return to Luke! Yet if she did so, she might bring trouble on him; his leg was better than when he fell, but she knew it still pained him. Perhaps she could lose Black Bob in the crowd. Turning away, she began to walk hastily back the way she had come, but almost immediately collided with a man. He put out his hands to steady her.

'Whoa,' he said and laughed as she gave a cry of alarm. 'Where are you going in such a hurry, Roxanne? Were you running away from me?'

'Not from you.' Roxanne breathed a sigh of relief as she looked up at Luke's teasing smile. 'I saw someone I did not wish to meet.'

'The man you ran away from after Sofia died?'

'Yes.' Roxanne drew a deep breath. She glanced

back and saw that Black Bob had followed her but now he was hesitating, looking uncertain. 'Please give me your arm. He is watching us. I was afraid he might try to grab me; but he did not expect to see you. If you seem to be a friend, he may think he was mistaken.'

Luke offered his arm and she took it, her hand trembling slightly. He glanced down, a frown on his face. 'You are afraid of him, aren't you?' She nodded. 'Damn the fellow. Shall I thrash him for you?'

'No, please do not try. He was stronger than all the other men—and you are injured.' She glanced down at his tight-fitting breeches and long, highly polished boots. 'Is your leg better?'

'Much. My doctor bound it and instructed me to rest, which I have as much as I could bear. I have an ache now, but the sharp pain has gone. It was a dislocation after all and not the break I feared—so it seems our rustic physician knew his trade. My own doctor had nothing but praise for his work.'

'I did not doubt it, but you were in such pain afterwards that I feared he might have done some damage.'

'My physician told me I was lucky. Had the fellow not acted as he did, I might have had an infection in the leg and been far worse. I might even have lost the use of it. However, I fear I made too much fuss of a slight thing.'

'I am sure you did not. Do you think Black Bob is following us?'

Luke glanced back. 'I believe he has gone. He will have realised he was mistaken or given up, I dare say.'

'Yes, perhaps.' Roxanne caught her bottom lip

between her teeth. Luke's timely appearance might have put him off for the moment, but it would not stop him if their paths crossed again. 'I do not think I can continue to stay here. If that man discovered where I was living, he might make trouble for you—and for Mrs Fox when she takes up residence.'

'Surely he would not?' He arched his fine brows as if to dismiss her fears.

'You do not know what he is like. He is a violent, brutal man who never considers the wishes of others.'

'I believe you, but surely it is not necessary to hide from him?'

'If he found me, he would try to force me to go with him.'

'Then what would you like to do?'

Roxanne looked at him hesitantly. 'To be honest I do not know. Now that he has seen me here, London may not be the best place for me to find work.'

'Then let me take you to stay with my grandfather. We can announce our engagement—and you can help me do something kind. Had my grandfather not set his mind on this I should simply have ignored his demands. My lawyer tells me that he could in law withhold the income from my trust, though he is not the only trustee and my godmother might take my side. Yet because of his illness I would make his last months happy if I can. To engage in bitter arguments and legal battles could only shorten his life.'

'Are you sure he would accept me?' Roxanne glanced down at herself. Inside she was trembling. The life he offered was a golden prize. Yet she was wary too, conscious that she might be laying up trouble for herself. 'I know the clothes you have given me have made me look the part—but are you sure he will not see through my disguise at once?'

'I do not think it. You are everything Grandfather asked me to provide in the woman that I intend to marry, Roxanne. Charming, good mannered and conscientious—what more could he want in a wife for me? Besides, if he does not approve that will end it. I shall bow to his judgement, take you to Bath and make sure you have all you need to live in comfort for the rest of your life.'

Roxanne gazed at him in silence for a moment. Sofia's voice was in her head, warning her to be careful. Was he merely trying to deceive her into an illicit entanglement? No, no, she believed he had a true concern for his grandfather.

'You are quite sure you wish to do this?'

'I have given the idea more thought since I left you with Mrs Mills. She has served my family all her life and her opinion of you has confirmed mine. You may have lived in the company of travelling players for a few years, but before that you were strictly reared. I had wondered if I should need to teach you how to behave in society, but you know instinctively. Do this for me, Roxanne. Please, help me to make Grandfather's last days more content. Afterwards, you will be free to live your own life.'

'Supposing he lives much longer than you expect?'

Luke gave her a thoughtful look. 'You may have to marry me. I know it isn't what you want—but it would be temporary, and in time you could live your own life. We could have the marriage annulled and you would still be young enough to marry again.'

It would be like an acting contract with a theatre manager. She would play a part for some months, perhaps longer, and then move on. Easy enough, perhaps, yet supposing her emotions became involved?

'An engagement is easily broken but…' Roxanne hesitated, then, 'Marriage is a last resort and only if it becomes impossible to prolong the engagement. It cannot be what you wish for?'

'I have no wish to marry, but it would be a business arrangement, nothing more. I enjoy my life the way it is—but for Grandfather's sake I am prepared to play a game of make believe.'

'It is really just a part I must play, but on a smaller stage and in private rather than public,' Roxanne said thoughtfully.

'Yes, mostly in private—though I dare say Grandfather will give an occasional dinner for us.'

'I can manage that,' Roxanne replied confidently. 'Besides, your grandfather may think me unsuitable and then I can simply go away and disappear.'

'Yes, exactly.' Luke stopped walking and looked into her eyes. 'Will you do me the honour of wearing my ring for a time, Miss Roxanne?'

For a moment it felt as if he were truly proposing and her heart jerked, but then she saw the mischief in his eyes and smiled.

'Yes, I shall do as you ask, sir. Just until you decide that you are ready to abandon the masquerade.'

'Do not think of it as a masquerade. It is a gentleman's agreement between friends—a small deception for the best of reasons, do you not agree?'

'I cannot disagree when you wish only to give an old man peace of mind—and to honour your commitments,' Roxanne said. For a moment she wondered where Mrs Fox came into his plans, but dismissed her doubts. 'You will be my employer and may dismiss me when it pleases you.'

'Please.' Luke made a rueful face. 'You must not think of me in that way or it will show. I am Luke—the man you intend to marry.'

'Yes, of course you are, dearest.' Her manner was light and teasing, exactly right for a woman who had just become engaged to the man she loves. Roxanne placed her hand playfully on his arm. 'Do not be anxious, Luke. I shall not forget my part and let you down. The earl will have nothing to complain of in my manner or deportment.'

'We must order you some more clothes and then we shall leave.' Luke smiled, his eyes thoughtful. 'I am certain Grandfather will like you, but you must look the part. Tomorrow I shall take you shopping. I intend to write to my grandfather and tell him that I shall be bringing a young lady to meet him in one week from now.'

Chapter Four

'Your belongings are strapped to the back of the carriage. Is there anything more you require before we leave, Roxanne?'

She thought of the two trunks packed with pretty gowns for all occasions, silk undergarments, stockings, shoes, slippers and gloves, besides several pretty bonnets. She had taken her pick of the wardrobe when acting in plays on their travels, but never had she seen so many beautiful clothes as Luke had so recklessly purchased for her. Too many by half and expensive, far more stylish than anything she'd ever worn before.

'You have been most generous and I have all I need, thank you.'

'Then we should go.' Luke offered his arm and they strolled towards the carriage. 'I intend to ride most of the way, Roxanne. We shall stop one night on the road—and your new maid will meet us at the inn, where we stopped before.'

'My maid?'

'Yes, of course. A respectable young lady cannot travel without a maid. I sent word ahead and I am sure a maid will have been provided by the time we arrive. Grandfather would be shocked if we visited without one.'

'What would he think if he should learn how we met?'

'It will not happen. I met you at the house of a friend and we liked each other very well. You have consented to an engagement, but we are waiting for your father's permission to wed.'

Roxanne stifled her feelings of unease. 'I pray you will not invent too many lies, sir, for I may forget them.'

'We shall keep your story as simple as possible,' he promised. 'You must expect some questions, Roxanne. Grandfather is bound to wonder why I have given into his request so tamely.'

'You must endeavour to look as if you are in love, Luke,' she said and gave him a smile of positive wickedness. 'Liking will not serve or he will sense a mystery. If you have resisted his plea thus far, he must be convinced of your sincerity or you may do more harm than good.'

'You are very right,' Luke agreed and looked thoughtful. 'Let us hope that I can play my part as well as I expect of you.'

'Watch me often and look pleased or brooding,' she suggested and her mouth pouted at him. 'It should not be beyond you, Luke. I dare say you have wooed enough ladies to know how to court the love of your life.'

'You have a wicked tongue,' Luke remarked and grinned. 'Do not be afraid of Grandfather, Roxanne. I think his bark worse than his bite—besides, he should be happy to meet you. You are exactly what he has looked for.'

'Let us hope that is the case. If not, you can apologise to him and take me away.'

'He wants me married and an heir,' Luke said. 'Play your part well and he will soon be eating from your hand, my love.'

'Yes, that is better,' Roxanne approved. 'You had the tone just right then. I was almost convinced myself.' She took off her smart leather glove, looking at the huge square emerald-and-diamond ring on her left hand. It was proof that she was truly caught up in this masquerade, pretending to be Luke's betrothed. 'This is magnificent enough to convince anyone.'

'I could not do less. Had I given you something paltry Grandfather would not have been fooled for an instant.'

'Any jewels you lend me will of course be returned when we part,' Roxanne replied. 'All I shall ask is a small income so that I can live quietly but respectably.'

'Yes, well, as to that we shall see. That ring belongs to you, Roxanne, whatever may happen when we get to Hartingdon.' Luke helped her into the carriage and stepped back. 'I shall be close by. Should you need to stop, you may tap the roof and the driver will oblige you.'

Roxanne sat back against the squabs and looked

out of the window. She had butterflies in her stomach, for the role she was about to play was important, far more demanding than anything she had accomplished before. If she failed, she would be letting Luke down and perhaps hurting a vulnerable old man.

She would not fail. Roxanne did not think she had come from Luke's class, but she was certain that she had been reared as a gentlewoman. Why had she run away from her home—and what had frightened her so much that she'd lost her memory?

It could not matter. Her engagement was merely make believe and intended to be a temporary arrangement.

Would the earl be fooled by their little charade? Luke wondered as he rode just behind the carriage. It was perfectly possible that he would throw them both out and disown his grandson, as he had threatened. That would be a deuced nuisance and the ensuing row would be messy and unpleasant. He could not let Beth Fox and her son Harry down. He had promised to support her for the rest of her life in comfort and would keep his promise, which meant he must fight for his income if forced. He would also need to keep his promise to Roxanne if things went wrong.

Luke wanted to avoid a quarrel if at all possible. He had no desire to be the cause of the earl's death—nor did he particularly wish to inherit a large and cumbersome estate that would require a much larger commitment than his own did at present. It would suit him if the earl lived for some years longer, yet he needed his own income intact.

It was such a coil and so unnecessary. Why must the earl be such a pompous fool, making unreasonable demands on his grandson? Anger mixed with regret as he considered his childhood. Alone and grieving for his parents, he had looked for a sign of love or softness in the earl and found none. Because he was hurt, he had drawn into himself and rejected his grandfather. The estrangement between them had begun years ago and they had drifted apart. For a long time Luke had believed there was nothing between them, but now he was not so sure.

Had he been as indifferent to his grandfather as he had pretended to be since reaching his maturity, he would simply have walked away and left him to make Harte his heir. However, that particular rogue would rejoice at the earl's early demise and make short work of his fortune. He might behave as if butter would not melt in his mouth when in the earl's presence, but Luke knew him for what he was—and that was something that left an unpleasant taste in the mouth. Naturally, he would never mention Harte's true nature to his grandfather.

On the other hand, Hartingdon might embrace Roxanne with open arms and demand a marriage sooner rather than later. At the moment she was resisting the idea stoutly, but once she had become accustomed to her surroundings she might change her mind. Luke had dismissed the idea of a convenient marriage for years, but since coming up with the idea of this make-believe engagement, he had found that he did not dislike it as much as before—providing the young woman in question was Roxanne.

The calm and enterprising manner in which she had embarked on this whole adventure had made Luke admire her more than any other young woman of his acquaintance. Her circumstances would have broken a lesser spirit, but she seemed resilient and eager for life. She was courageous, honest, and, of late, he had found her both charming and amusing as a companion. It might be perfectly possible to have the kind of businesslike marriage they had spoken of with Roxanne—if she could be brought to agree.

Love was something he still felt belonged to the realms of myths and fairy tales. However, he did like the young woman riding in the carriage ahead of him, and if she were to agree, he would not entirely dislike the idea of marriage and children.

Yet there might come a time when he found someone he truly wished to wed. Luke shook his head. His father had strayed from the marriage bed, not just into the arms of a mistress, but with a woman he professed to want too much to give up. That day in the carriage when his parents had argued so disastrously, Luke's father had been talking of a separation or a divorce. When Luke's mother became hysterical he had begged her pardon, but she would not listen—and then it was too late for all of them.

Thrown clear of the wreckage that had taken their lives and changed his own so dramatically, he had vowed that he would never hurt anyone as his father had hurt his mother. A sham marriage built on lies was bound to end in bitterness and tears—but a business arrangement was another matter and perhaps a sensible young woman like Roxanne would be able to see its advantages.

As yet they hardly knew one another. Some time spent visiting the earl would rectify that and, if they continued to get along, Luke could suggest that they turn this make-believe engagement into a real marriage.

Naturally, she would still be free to lead her own life much of the time, as would he. Their children would be in the nursery, cared for by a nurse and— No! Suddenly, Luke recalled his own childhood after he was left to the mercy of his grandfather. He would wish to spend time with his own children and to help teach them what life was about. They should not be left to the sole care of servants.

Luke frowned, for the thought brought complications. It might not be as easy to partition his life into different compartments as he had imagined.

Perhaps for the time being it would be best to stay with his original idea and separate once his grandfather was dead. He was amazed at how disappointed that thought made him feel.

Roxanne's heart thudded as she glanced out of the window and saw the huge sprawl of Hartingdon. She had known it must be a large house, but this was so big, way beyond her expectation, some parts much older than others and an ancient tower at one corner. How did one ever find one's way about in such a place? She had thought she would find it easy to play the part of a respectable young lady, but suddenly the task seemed far more daunting than she had imagined. She would be unmasked immediately and the earl would have her thrown out on her ear.

Risking a glance at the girl sitting opposite her, she saw that Tilly was looking terrified. The girl had no previous experience of working in a house such as this, though she had sometimes helped ladies who stayed at her aunt and uncle's inn without their own maids.

'Do not be too anxious, Tilly.'

'It is a big house, miss.'

'Yes, it is. I dare say you will soon get used to it.'

Roxanne smiled reassuringly, though her stomach was tying itself in knots as the carriage slowed to a halt and then stopped. A groom opened the carriage door and immediately stood back, allowing a man in a black-and-gold uniform to assist her. She took the footman's hand and was helped down just as Luke gave the reins of his horse to a groom and came to her.

'Have courage,' he whispered. 'It looks daunting, I know, but it is just a house.'

Roxanne lifted her head proudly, but she could not quite control the trembling of her hand as she placed it on his arm. Briefly, Luke covered it with his own and smiled at her. They walked towards the door, where a small group of servants wearing the earl's colours of black and gold had assembled.

'This is Marshall, my grandfather's valet, and Mrs Arlet, the housekeeper.'

A tall thin woman dressed completely in black

dipped a curtsy. 'Welcome, Miss Peters. Please allow me to present the staff.'

Roxanne was led down a line of maids and footmen, ending with the scullery maid and the boot boy. She kept her head high and a smile on her lips, giving just the faintest nod to them all. It was the way a properly brought up young woman would act, she was sure, and brought her a look of respect from the housekeeper. However, she noticed that Luke chatted to one or two of the footmen and smiled at the pretty parlour maid. Such behaviour was acceptable from him, for he had known the staff all his life. She was a newcomer and should keep her distance, at least for the moment.

'Perhaps you would take my fiancée up to her chamber, Mrs Arlet?'

'Yes, my lord, of course. This way, Miss Peters.'

Roxanne glanced at Luke, but he was talking to the earl's valet. She steadied her nerves and followed the housekeeper up the wide magnificent staircase, her gaze moving to the high-vaulted ceiling of the entrance hall. The banisters were heavily carved mahogany, which had darkened with age and polish, the stone steps covered over with a rich blue Persian-style carpet. The entrance hall floor was tiled in black-and-white marble, but the hall upstairs was covered in the same carpet and looked a recent addition to the elsewhere-faded grandeur of the house.

'The earl ordered that you be given the best suite of guestrooms, miss,' Mrs Arlet said as she led the way along the hall and into the east wing. 'They have recently been refurbished. This is a large house and in constant need of repair or refurbishment. Some of the family rooms have not been used in an age, so nothing has been done to them. No doubt that will change when his lordship marries.'

'Yes, I would imagine so,' Roxanne said, her heart racing. Naturally everyone would expect a marriage to be forthcoming. A tiny pang of guilt pierced her, because the housekeeper looked pleased at the idea of change. 'I think—perhaps you would give me a little tour of the house one day, Mrs Arlet? Not just the main reception rooms—but the kitchen and anywhere else I ought to see.'

'Yes, miss. I should be pleased to, though Lord Clarendon will show you his own rooms, I dare say. The west wing is not often used, because the tower is in need of repair. Lord Clarendon's parents once occupied that wing but after the accident the earl closed the whole wing off, and no one bothers to go there.'

'The accident…'

'When the late Lord and Lady Clarendon were killed, miss.'

'Ah, yes,' Roxanne nodded. 'I was not sure of your meaning.'

'No, miss. I suppose there have been a few accidents in the family, what with the earl's only son dying of a fever when he was in his teen years—and then the earl's wife taking a chill after being caught in a rainstorm. I think it broke the master's heart when his daughter was killed so cruelly. He never quite got over it, for she was his favourite.' Mrs Arlet shook her head. 'They have not been a lucky family, but I am certain that is all about to change now, miss.'

'Yes, we must hope so,' Roxanne replied. It was amazing how much she had learned from the housekeeper in just a few minutes. Luke had told her his parents' story, but not the rest of it. She understood now why he was prepared to go through with this sham engagement in order to please his grandfather in his last months. She must not let him down, however hard it might be to carry off the part of a loving fiancée. 'That is up to me in part, is it not?'

'There's been a different atmosphere here since the letter came,' Mrs Arlet said. She unlocked a door and stood back for Roxanne to enter. 'The earl gave orders for most of the rooms to be opened up immediately. We'll be giving a ball to celebrate his lordship's engagement, miss. Everyone will want to meet you.'

'Oh…yes, of course,' Roxanne said and took a deep breath as she looked about her. 'This is beautiful, thank you. When will the ball be held? I am not sure I brought a gown suitable for a grand ball.'

'No doubt that can be rectified, miss. There are bales of silk in the sewing room waiting for just such a purpose. We'll fetch the seamstress from town and she will be pleased to serve you. You'll be the countess one day, after all.'

'Yes.' Roxanne looked round. 'I think perhaps I should tidy myself.'

'Yes, miss. The earl will be waiting for you in the main parlour downstairs. If you could be ready, I shall serve tea in twenty minutes.'

'I can be ready, but I'm not certain I know where to go.'

'Lord bless you, miss. Just go down the stairs to the main hall and someone will direct you. The footmen are here for that very purpose and we are all eager to make your stay at Hartingdon as pleasant as possible.'

Roxanne thanked her and she went away. She was left standing in a small but pretty sitting room and beyond that was a bedroom. The main colours were green, gold, cream and yellow, which gave the rooms a light bright appearance. Roxanne ran her fingers reverently over the surface of a delicate and very pretty desk suitable for a lady. An elbow chair was set ready for use; the sofa was covered in green-striped silk and there was a rolled cushion at each end. Small occasional tables were dotted about the room and a bookcase with leather-bound volumes and porcelain figures behind the glass doors occupied the length of one wall.

Going into the bedroom, which was equally well furnished with a dressing table, matching chests and a padded stool at the end of the bed, Roxanne took off her pelisse and let it fall on one of the pretty chairs. She sat down in front of the dressing table and studied her reflection in the shield-shaped mirror. The frame was fashioned of smooth mahogany and inlaid with satinwood, set on a stand so that it could be moved to give a better view. The table was set out with silver items, including brushes and combs and perfume pots. How much luxury there was in a house like this!

She had removed her bonnet earlier and now took the brush to smooth over her hair, pulling at the tendrils that framed her face. She was wearing a silver brooch in her lace, but otherwise had no jewellery other than her ring. Touching the brooch, she smiled because it reminded her of Sofia and she could almost hear her friend applauding.

'Now we shall see if I really am fit to be a lady,' she said softly. 'Wish me luck, dearest Sofia.'

'You were born to the part, dearest.'

For a moment it was as if her friend were with her and she felt her courage return. Her part here was not to deceive for advantage, but to bring comfort and joy to an old man's last days.

Roxanne's things had not yet been brought up so she did not have the opportunity to change her gown; deciding that she looked the best she could after her journey, she left the bedroom and retraced her steps to the landing.

At the bottom of the stairs two footmen were discussing something and she caught the words *'beauty and better than expected'*, before they became aware of her standing there.

'You were quick, miss,' one of them said, a faint colour in his cheeks. 'Mrs Arlet said to take you to the back parlour when you came down. It is the master's favourite room these days. He mostly uses it when he is alone, though we'll be using the drawing room for tea in future.'

'Shall you?' Roxanne said, controlling the urge to smile. Clearly the servants here considered themselves part of the family and that was somehow fitting. 'There is no need to stand on ceremony for my sake. Please take me to the earl—I believe Mrs Arlet said your name was Jarvis?'

'Yes, Miss Peters,' he replied, seeming surprised that she should remember. 'If you would like to come this way.'

'Thank you,' she said and inclined her head in her most regal manner.

Roxanne's heart was hammering against her ribs as she followed the footman through to the back of the house. He paused before a pair of impressive double doors and then threw them open with a little flourish.

'Miss Peters, my lord.'

Jarvis stood to one side so that Roxanne could enter; when she did so, he closed the doors behind her with a snap. Immediately, she saw the elderly man rise to his feet. He was tall, though a little stooped about his shoulders, thinner than she thought healthy, his hair dark pewter and his white brows bushy and slightly raised, intimidating. His eyes, though, were of a similar colour to Luke's and for some reason that made her smile. She was, she imagined, looking at Lord Clarendon as he would be one day in the distant future. The two gentlemen were very alike despite the years between them.

'Miss Peters? You are down sooner than that graceless scamp my grandson.'

'Since I could not change my gown to greet you, I thought it better to come sooner rather than later,' she replied and moved towards him, her hand outstretched. 'Luke has told me a little about you, sir—and you are very like him.'

'You are the first to say so in an age, though his mother often told me that he would be my image one day. Unfortunately, she did not live to see it. I have thought that a good thing, for she would have been disappointed in the young rogue—but now I am not so sure.'

'I know that Luke has not always behaved in a way that pleased you,' Roxanne said. 'But you must not disparage him to me, you know.'

'You are prepared to defend him if I do?'

'I should be a poor fiancée if I did not—do you not think so, sir?'

The earl glared at her for a few seconds, then gave a harsh laugh. 'I think he has done better than I imagined. I was prepared for you to be one of his doxies—but you ain't, are you?'

'Certainly not. I have been no man's plaything and have no intention of it.' Her eyes flashed a challenge at him. 'Do you really think so poorly of him, sir? It would be unkind to bring a lady of that nature into your home. From what I know of Luke, he would not be so discourteous to you.'

'You're an outspoken miss. I can see why he picked you, Miss Peters.'

'I fear I was taught to speak my mind and to be independent as much as possible. I should be happier if you were to call me Miss Roxanne—or simply by my given name.'

'You have an older sister?'

'No—but everyone always calls me Miss Roxanne. I prefer it.'

'Do you, now? I wonder why?' He stared at her a moment longer, then took her hand and bent over it, lifting it to his papery-dry lips to salute her with a kiss. 'Come and sit down and tell me something about yourself.'

'I am quite unremarkable, sir,' Roxanne replied. She sat in the chair at the opposite end of the imposing fireplace so that he too might sit. 'I have little family and, until she died, lived with the lady who cared for me after…I lost my home.'

'Clarendon's letter said that your father is in India and you do not wish to marry until he gives his permission?'

'Do you not think that the proper thing to do, sir?'

His bushy brows met in a frown. 'Humph. Clever with words, ain't you? No fortune, I suppose—are you after his money, girl?'

'I did not agree to this engagement for money.'

'It was a bit sudden. He told me nothing of you the last time he was down here, then announces he's engaged. Why would he do that—and why should you agree?'

'I should be a liar if I said that Luke's proposal was not appealing. I was in some difficulty and I am almost alone in the world, for I have not heard from my father in years. However, I have respect and liking for Luke and I believe he feels the same. I consented to the engagement—with the understanding that it would not continue if you should dislike it.'

Hartingdon's gaze narrowed. 'Willing to give him up for a consideration?'

'I said no such thing,' Roxanne replied, refusing to be ruffled by his pricking at her. 'I should not wish to cause trouble between you, for I know that he holds you in affection. You do not need to pay me to make me go away, sir. I shall leave at once if my presence here offends you.'

'Do not talk rubbish, girl. You look and behave like a lady. Might not be out of the top drawer, but I ain't fool enough to send you packing—at least until I discover the truth of the matter. If he really means to settle down and provide me with an heir, you will do well enough, I dare say.'

Roxanne was not called upon to reply for the doors opened and a footman announced Lord Clarendon. Luke advanced into the room, looking strangely apprehensive.

'Roxanne, I intended to be with you when you met Grandfather,' he said, his gaze going from one to the other. 'Everything all right, sir? How are you today? Better, I trust?'

'Well enough. Don't fuss, boy. I cannot abide people fussing over me. That fool of a doctor is bad enough without you.'

'I see your mood has not much improved, sir.' Luke's mouth firmed. 'I hope he has not bitten your head off, Roxanne? I assure you he is not always this ill tempered.'

Roxanne looked from one to the other and then laughed. 'Oh dear, you both look so cross—like two bulldogs who have been quarrelling over a bone, which has been suddenly snatched from under your noses by a mongrel pup.'

For a moment there was silence and then Luke grinned. 'You are perfectly right, dearest. It is ridiculous to argue over trivial things. Forgive me, Grandfather. I did not come down here to quarrel with you.'

'Why did you come?' The earl looked at him suspiciously. 'Am I supposed to believe that you truly intend to settle down and do your duty?'

'What is my duty, sir? I hope that you will continue to live for some years yet in the full enjoyment of your estate. If you need help or advice with business matters I should be pleased to give it—though whether you would wish to receive it is another matter.'

'I have agents and fellows enough to run the place,' the earl grunted, 'though you might take the trouble to ride the estate with Tonkins while you are here. Some of the cottages may need renovation. It was in my mind to do it some years back, but I let things slip, though I've no cause for complaint in Tonkins's management as far as I know.'

'I shall be pleased to do so, both with him and on my own, while we stay with you,' Luke told him. 'May I take it that Roxanne and I have your blessing?'

'You puzzle me, Clarendon. You have flouted my wishes since you reached your majority and became independent. Now, it seems you wish to please me— why? Afraid of losing your inheritance?'

'I find that it does not suit me to be at odds with you, sir. Is that so very strange?'

'I suppose it threw you into a blue fit because of

that little incident.' The old man glared at him. 'Well, I mustn't nag on at you or your fiancée will scold me. I am pleasantly surprised, Luke. When your letter came I scented a rat, thought you would try to play one of your tricks on me, but Miss Roxanne seems a decent gel. For the moment I shall reserve judgement.'

'I hope I shall not let you down,' Roxanne said. 'The marriage cannot happen until I have my father's permission, so there is plenty of time.'

'Indeed, I might argue with that,' the earl said. 'What makes you think your father will write if he has not done so for years?'

'I can only hope that he will do so, sir.'

'And if he does not?' Hartingdon's eyes gleamed suddenly. 'I shall give you three months to seek his permission. If after that there is no word, I shall insist on the banns being called.'

Roxanne looked at him and saw the challenge in his eyes. She sensed that he was testing her and smiled, but before she could answer Luke spoke.

'I am certain we could agree to that,' he said. 'After all, your father could not blame you for going ahead if he makes no attempt to contact you, Roxanne.'

'It is so long since I heard anything, he may be dead,' Roxanne said carefully. 'If in three months' time nothing has changed—and we are all content with the situation—I shall agree to the banns being called.'

'Then you have my blessing,' the earl said and looked smug, as if he had gained what he sought. 'However, there is one caveat—and that is that Miss Roxanne remains here with me so that I may get to know her. If you have business elsewhere, Luke, you may leave us for as long as it takes. Your fiancée will reside here.'

'I'm not sure…' Luke looked stunned. Clearly he had not expected anything of the kind. 'Roxanne—how do you feel about living here with Grandfather?'

Roxanne hesitated. She had expected a visit of two to three weeks at the longest. To live in this house for three months under the eye of the earl would be a huge challenge.

'I…' she began and then encountered a strange expression in the old man's eyes. The challenge was there, as she had expected, but there was something more—a vulnerability and frailty that seemed to be pleading with her rather than demanding. 'I think that would be an excellent idea. I have a great deal to learn if I am to be the mistress here, Luke. I hope you will stay with us as much as you can, dearest, but I shall be perfectly content to help Mrs Arlet. I believe she is quite keen to open up some of the family rooms that have been under covers for years.'

'Told you that, did she?' For the first time there was a glimmer of true respect in the earl's eyes. 'Jane Arlet knows quality when she sees it. If she approves of you, miss, I expect you will do. Don't worry that I mean to keep you a prisoner. We shall have guests to entertain and you can visit our neighbours, though I do not go out at night these days. Barely go further than the garden even in summer, but I'm not too decrepit to entertain the family and our neighbours. We shall have a ball in a couple of weeks. Mrs Arlet will give you a list and you can write the invitations, girl. You can write, I suppose?'

Roxanne laughed softly. 'Sofia said I had the most beautiful copperplate hand she had seen, sir.'

His brows met in a frown. 'And who, pray, is Sofia?'

'She was my dearest friend, almost a mother to me. Unfortunately, she died recently. I miss her very much.'

'Humph…' His gaze narrowed thoughtfully. 'Name seems familiar, though I can't think why. Well, why are you both still here? It is a beautiful morning. Get off out and leave me in peace. You should show Roxanne the gardens, Luke.'

'Yes, sir, delighted.' Luke held out his hand as Roxanne rose to her feet. She took it, smiling up at him when his fingers closed about hers. 'Would you like that, my love?'

'Yes, I should,' she agreed and bobbed respectfully to the earl. 'Thank you for receiving me, sir.'

'Come and see me again tomorrow in the morning and we'll talk. I may dine with you this evening, but we have no guests until the following day. I wasn't sure whether you would really come.'

'Or whether I should be presentable,' Roxanne said and gave him a look that was deceptively demure. He glared at her, but she thought there was a glimmer of appreciation in his eyes. 'Please dine with us if you feel able, sir.'

She took Luke's arm and they left the earl's room, going downstairs, through the hall and out of a side door into a small walled garden. It was square with rose beds on all sides and a sundial in the middle. Most of the roses were still in tight buds, though some had begun to show signs of opening.

'Was it too much of an ordeal?' Luke asked and looked down at her, a flicker of doubt in his face. 'He seemed to like you, though you might not have thought it—but believe me, he can be much worse.'

'Yes, I dare say he could. You told me not to be afraid of him and I thought it best to speak out from the start. I believe he prefers plain speaking.'

'He cannot abide mealy-mouthed women. I have a godmother, who was also a great friend of my mother's. Hartingdon was abominably rude to Lady Paula the last time she was here. She left in tears, vowing she would never visit again.'

'I dare say he can be intimidating if he chooses,' Roxanne said. 'Yet I think underneath the growling and the harshness, he is lonely and vulnerable.'

'Good grief.' Luke stared at her in astonishment. 'You saw that too? I thought I might have imagined it—he does his best to drive everyone away, you know. All the time I was growing up, he never showed me any sign of affection. He shut himself away from everyone after my mother died and often went for days without speaking to me. He was a harsh disciplinarian, though, when I look back, I believe he was fair. I dare say I was a rebellious lad and even more so as a youth.'

Roxanne laughed and hugged his arm. 'I can understand why you rebelled when you reached your majority. Sofia always said that if you tied a dog to a short lead it made him wild when let free—and I think it is much the same with us. The best discipline is that which we apply to ourselves, do you not agree?'

'You are amazing,' Luke said. 'You seem to have wisdom beyond your years, Roxanne. How old are you actually, do you know?'

She shook her head. 'I think I may be nineteen or perhaps twenty. Sofia was never certain, but I was with her for more than five years and must have been thirteen or fourteen when she took me in. If I seem wise, it is because I spent all my time listening to her. She was an intelligent woman with great experience of the world and its foibles.'

Luke nodded, his eyes intent on her face. 'You still recall nothing of your past?'

'Nothing.'

'Then what are you hiding from me? I have sensed something, but did not wish to pry lest it was painful for you.'

Roxanne hesitated, then made her decision. She must trust him with her secret. 'I have in my possession a ruby of great value. Sofia says I was clutching it in my hand when she found me. I held on to it fiercely and would not be parted from it for some days. When I finally did release it, she hid it and kept it for me. I had forgotten about the jewel until she reminded me just before she died. She says that when I was found, I was dressed in good plain clothes, but not silk, and I had no other ornament.'

'Are you thinking that you may have stolen it?'

'I do not know. Sofia told me that I should sell it and set myself up as a lady, but I should be reluctant to do so. It is the only clue I have to what happened before Sofia found me. Besides, it may not be mine to sell.'

'You think you took the ruby and ran away? Are you certain it is a real jewel and not simply glass?'

'Sofia thought it valuable. I will show it to you later. I do not know if there is any way to trace the rightful owner…'

'How do you know that you are not the rightful owner?'

Roxanne looked at him, wrinkling her brow in thought. 'Sofia told me that I kept saying it was mine, but after I relinquished it to her, I seemed to forget about it and did not ask for it again.'

'It must have held great importance to you at the time.' Luke looked thoughtful. 'You told me that India came to mind when you thought of your father. It is quite possible that a man who either served with the British army or for the trading company might acquire such a jewel. Perhaps it belonged to your father.'

'Why would I steal a jewel from my own father?'

'He might have given it to you.'

'The memory of India was just Sofia's game.' Roxanne sighed. 'I have tried so hard to remember, but I cannot.'

'Did you keep the jewel hidden in the secret pocket beneath your gown when you travelled?'

'Yes, in the place where I put your gold to keep it safe. It is not there now. I will show you this evening and then you can tell me your opinion of its worth.'

Chapter Five

Roxanne took the jewel from the dressing case Luke had bought for her. She had placed it in the secret compartment for safekeeping. It was as large as a pheasant's egg, a strange oval shape with slightly pointed ends and a deep dark red in colour. When it caught the light from the candles on her dressing table it sparkled and glowed with fire. Something about it at that moment sent a shiver down her spine. She had not noticed before, but there seemed something mysterious, even sinister, about the jewel.

She tucked it into the bodice of her gown and went out of her room, her heart beating faster. It was a relief to share her secret with Luke, because it had lain heavy on her conscience ever since she'd rediscovered the ruby in Sofia's things. Making her way down to the smaller of the two dining parlours, Roxanne wondered if it would be possible to trace the origin of the jewel. She thought Luke was right. It had most likely been brought from India—but was it a gift to her from someone or stolen from its rightful owner?

The earl had decided that he would dine with them that evening. Dressed immaculately in evening clothes that belonged to an earlier age, he seemed more formidable than previously, a proud autocratic man with a strict manner. However, he was the soul of courtesy to Roxanne and did not once give her reason to blush or feel uncomfortable. With Luke he was sharper on one or two occasions, but, receiving only polite answers, he lapsed into silence and then glanced at Roxanne.

'Do you play chess, Miss Roxanne?'

'Yes, sir. Sofia taught me. We played in the evenings for there was little else to do…except sew, of course.'

'You did not have an instrument?'

'No, not for some years.'

'We have some excellent instruments here. You are welcome to use them whenever you wish. I enjoy music. I could employ a music master for you if you wish to be taught.'

'I shall attempt the pianoforte tomorrow,' she promised. 'If I have the aptitude, a music master might be useful to improve my skill. I am good with the needle.'

'Do you like to sketch or paint?'

'I think I have not had the opportunity.'

'Your guardian was remiss in your education. You may need some social skills, Miss Roxanne. Perhaps we should send for your godmother, Luke. She is a foolish woman, but might be of some use in giving our gel a little nudge. What do you think?'

'I believe I shall leave the decision to Roxanne, sir. I am not certain Lady Paula would come.'

'Nonsense. Write to her and ask her to come down for the ball. She will be here before you have time to turn round. Her curiosity will bring her, if nothing more.'

The earl waved the footman away as he offered more wine. 'Nothing more for me. I think I shall leave the pair of you to amuse yourselves. If I stay up this evening, I shall not be fit for guests tomorrow. No, no, do not get up. Finish your meal. Jarvis, give me your arm. Goodnight, Miss Roxanne. My suggestion was for your benefit, not an order.'

'I thank you for the thought, sir.'

'Well, he is certainly taking an interest,' Luke remarked as the door closed behind his grandfather. 'Shall we go through to the parlour, Roxanne? I thought we might use the front parlour when we are alone. It was my mother's favourite and the drawing room is far too large. Shall I ask Mrs Arlet for some tea and coffee?'

'Would you not rather have port or brandy? Tea will do very well for me.'

'If you do not mind, I shall have brandy.' He nodded to the remaining footman. 'In twenty minutes or so, Smith.'

Roxanne proceeded him into the front parlour. It was of a similar size to the one the earl preferred, but its décor was a little in need of refreshment, though comfortable and with a pleasant aspect out over steps leading down to a wide expanse of lawn in the sunken garden. At that moment the light was fading and she could not see beyond the windows, for the candles had been lit.

'Did you bring it?' Luke asked, having made certain the door was closed behind them. 'I must admit I am curious to see this jewel.'

Roxanne reached inside her bodice and took out the ruby. It was warm where it had lain nestled against her breasts. She held it out on the palm of her hand and it glowed in the candlelight.

'Good grief,' Luke exclaimed as he saw it. 'I have never seen its like. This must be worth a king's ransom, Roxanne. It looks as if it came from an Indian maharajah's crown.'

'Then it is valuable,' Roxanne said as he held it to the light between his thumb and forefinger. 'Sofia said as much, but I was not certain. How could I have come by it, do you imagine?'

'I believe it must have come from India. The secret of its origin must lie locked in your subconscious, Roxanne. Could your father have brought it home? Did something happen that made you take it and run away?'

'I truly wish I could answer that question.' She looked thoughtful. 'I have wondered if Black Bob guessed I had something valuable. He was determined I would be his woman—did he know that Sofia had hidden this for me? He would not have dared to steal it from her. The other players respected and revered her. Had he stolen from her or harmed her, I think they might have turned on him.'

'So he waited until she was dead.' Luke inclined

his head. 'It is possible that he might have suspected something. One of the others might have seen it in your hand when you refused to be parted from it.'

'Yes, perhaps. What do you think I should do about this? Would it be possible to trace the rightful owner?'

'I dare say a good few would claim it as theirs if they could whether or not they had the right,' Luke said. 'I suppose I might place a vague advert in *The Times* newspaper and see what happens. I should ask any respondent to contact a solicitor by letter and see what replies we get, but I think we must take great care of the jewel, Roxanne. If Sofia told you that you claimed it was yours, it may be—and this ruby is extremely valuable. If no one likely comes forward in response to the advert, I think you should accept that you own the jewel.'

'Would you have it placed somewhere safe for me? I was nervous enough of carrying it before, but now—I should hate to be accused of being careless if it was lost.'

'I shall have it stored in my grandfather's strong room until I return to London,' Luke said. 'We keep all the more valuable heirlooms there when they are not being worn. Hartingdon thinks them as safe here as in a bank and I think he is right. The strong room was once a dungeon and the locks have been made stronger.'

'Is it in the old wing—where the tower is?'

'Yes. We seldom use that wing, because parts of the tower are unsafe. Grandfather hasn't opened the strong room in years, but I shall ask him for the key. You will not mind if I show him the ruby?'

'Supposing he asks where it came from?'

'I shall tell him it is your inheritance from your friend, which in a way it is. Had Sofia been other than she was, she might have sold it long since.'

'She would rather give me all she had than take something of mine,' Roxanne replied with a smile. 'Yes, it should be safe in the strong room—though if it is claimed we shall need to explain.'

'I doubt it will be,' Luke said. 'The only person who might know of the ruby would be the owner, whoever that might be.'

'My father…' Roxanne sighed. 'I think it must have been his and that it came from India, just as we have surmised, but perhaps I wish to believe it. Perhaps I have invented the fairy tale?'

'Did Sofia never try to find out where you had come from?'

'We were always moving from one place to another. Besides, I think she was afraid someone would take me away from her. She says that I was very quiet and I cried in my sleep for months when she first took me in. It was in her mind that I had been harmed in some way. She would not have given me up to someone who might hurt me.'

'A jewel like that might cause many people to do things they would not otherwise do,' Luke said and frowned. 'I shall seek the advice of my lawyer before placing the advert, Roxanne. It may bring more than we would wish for and I must be certain it cannot be traced back to you.'

'You think I might be in danger?'

'I cannot know for certain—but there must have been something that frightened you or you would not have been in such distress when Sofia found you. If you were so determined not to give the ruby up, you must have had good reason to think it was yours.'

'Sofia has said much the same to me.' Roxanne looked up at him. 'I would willingly return it to its rightful owner if it is not mine.'

'Yes, well, we shall see what happens,' he said and his eyes were thoughtful, as if wondering how much he could believe of what she'd told him. 'Do not worry about it, Roxanne. I think Grandfather seemed pleased with life this evening, do you not agree?'

He had pocketed the ruby and Roxanne was glad to see it in his safekeeping. She did not wish to be responsible for such a jewel and felt she would not mind if she never saw it again—and yet, according to Sofia, as a young girl, she had been determined not to give it up.

'I hope he will be as pleased with me in a few weeks. I am doing my best, Luke, but he is bound to discover gaps in my education. Sofia taught me so much about the world, and I read plays and poetry, but I know little of the things most young ladies learn.'

'And your mind is all the better for it,' Luke said. 'You cannot imagine how boring some of them are, Roxanne. I would swear you could discuss Shakespeare in more depth than most.'

'Yes, at least the roles I have played,' she said and dimpled. 'I shall not mind if the earl employs tutors to rectify my lack. It will pass the time and give me something to strive for.'

'Have you thought about what happens in three months?'

'It is a long time,' Roxanne said. 'I dare say he will have discovered I am a fraud and declare me unsuitable to be the mistress of a house like this long before that, and if he does not...well, that is up to you, I think.'

'Would you go through with the wedding if I asked it?'

'On the terms you offered before?' He inclined his head and Roxanne was silent for a moment. 'If we are both of the same mind in three months, I think I might.'

Why on earth had she agreed to marry him in three months if he should ask her? Roxanne wondered what had got into her head. A sham engagement was as far as she had been prepared to go initially, but, oddly enough, she had begun to find the idea of marriage to Luke Clarendon more and more appealing.

What else could she do with her life that would bring her comfort and safety? A woman alone in her position would be prey to rogues and predators, men who would trick her and seduce her for their pleasure. As Luke's fiancée, and perhaps his make-believe wife, she would have respect and a settled income. Surely that was enough for any woman?

Yet there was something inside her that wanted more. How foolish she was! Luke had never intended more than a temporary arrangement, but now the earl was insisting on a marriage after three months. No doubt he wanted to know a grandchild was on its way before he died.

Luke's child. For a moment the thought sent a warm spiral curling through her and she smiled. How pleasant the picture was, though quite impossible, of course. They must try to please the earl in his last months, but a child would be too much. She frowned as she recalled her first meeting with the earl. He looked frail, but he did not look particularly unwell.

Could Luke have overreacted to the earl's illness? Was he truly as sick as his grandson believed?

What would she feel if Luke expected her to provide the heir?

The questions went round and round in her head as her maid helped her prepare for bed. When she was in her nightgown, Roxanne sent the girl away and curled up on the deep window seat to gaze down at the gardens. She was already beginning to feel more at home here and she could not help but think it might be nice to live in a house such as this, not just for a visit, but as the mistress.

'Foolish,' she murmured aloud as she twirled a strand of red hair over her finger. 'It is not poss…'

The words trailed away as she saw the shadow of a man reflected on the lawn in the moonlight. He appeared to be trying to hide in the shrubbery, but the moon was at his back and cast a shadow for a few seconds before he moved further back into the darkness and was lost to sight.

She did not think it had been Luke and it was certainly not the earl. Perhaps one of the servants? Yet it had seemed to her that there was something furtive about the man, as if he wanted to watch the house without being seen.

Could Black Bob have followed her here? For a brief moment the thought sent cold chills winging down her spine, but then she dismissed them. The leader of the travelling players was an opportunist. Given the chance that day at the fair he might have grabbed her and forced her to go with him, but she did not think he would spend days following her to this house, only to hide in the shrubbery and spy on her.

Now she was being very foolish. Why should the man in the shrubbery be spying on her? Luke had said something about having an enemy when they first met. It might be that someone had followed him, intending some harm.

It was too late to go in search of Luke now. She did not know where his rooms were. Besides, the servants would be shocked if she went looking for him at this hour. She would just have to wait until the morning. Slipping into bed, Roxanne tried to be sensible. The man in the shrubbery was probably only one of the servants.

'Someone hiding in the shrubbery watching the house?' Luke looked incredulous when she told him her fears at breakfast. 'I imagine it must have been one of the keepers. They probably take a walk round the house at night just to make sure everything is secure.'

'Yes, I expect you are right. Though, whoever it was seemed a little furtive, as if he wanted to watch the house without being seen, but perhaps that was my imagination.' She helped herself to a little scrambled egg and ham from the vast array of dishes under silver covers on the sideboard and carried her plate to the table. Luke was finishing his rare beef eaten with sauté potatoes and pickles.

'I dare say he was being discreet rather than furtive. Grandfather would not want the keepers to be patrolling in full view of the house, but I think that is what you saw, Roxanne.' He pushed his plate aside and poured more coffee into a delicate porcelain bowl.

'I am relieved to hear it. I wondered if Black Bob had followed us here, and then I thought that perhaps—you spoke of an enemy when we first met?'

'An enemy?' Luke looked puzzled, then smiled ruefully. 'In truth, I do not have an enemy, Roxanne. Are you anxious about this fellow who threatened you before?'

'No. He would grab me if he saw me by chance, but I do not think he would take the trouble to follow us here. I am sure you are right. The man in the garden was merely a keeper on patrol. I shall not give it another thought.'

'You are safe now, dearest,' Luke said and smiled across the table. 'You have me to look after you—to say nothing of the earl's household.'

'Yes, of course. I am not anxious for myself, but I thought I should tell you what I saw.'

'I am glad you did. What are your plans for this morning, Roxanne?'

'I have been invited to visit the earl at eleven o'clock.

Until then I think I shall try to make myself familiar with the house.'

Luke got to his feet, tossing his napkin on the table. 'I would love to stay and show you round, but I have an appointment with Grandfather's agent and bailiff. Perhaps we can spend the afternoon together? Do not let Grandfather bully you, Roxanne.'

'I have no intention of it. He is a peppery gentleman, but I rather like him.'

'You do?' Luke arched his brow, a smile quirking at the corner of his mouth. 'Well, I wish you luck. He is seldom at his best in the morning. Excuse me, I must go or I shall be late—finish your breakfast at your leisure. Had you wished, I am sure you could have had a tray in your room.'

'I like to rise early. Please do not let me keep you from your appointment.'

After Luke had gone, Roxanne drank her coffee and then pushed back her chair. She examined the contents of the silver dishes and saw that most had not been touched. Leaving the room, she glanced at the maid hovering outside the door.

'You may clear now, Maisie—it is Maisie, isn't it?'

'Yes, Miss Peters.'

'Please call me Miss Roxanne. Everyone does and I prefer it, as I have told Mrs Arlet.'

'Yes, Miss Roxanne. Mrs Arlet said she was at your service if you should care for a tour of the house.'

'I think I should like that very much.'

'I'll tell her you're ready, miss, before I clear.'

'How kind of you, Maisie, but I think I know where

her sitting room is; she told me where to find her yesterday.'

Maisie bobbed a curtsy and went into the breakfast room. Roxanne wandered through the hall to the back stairs and then went down to the area that was used exclusively by the servants. The housekeeper's sitting room was on a small landing just above a short flight of stairs, which led to the servants' hall and the kitchen. Pleased that she had remembered correctly, Roxanne knocked and was invited to enter.

'Miss Roxanne,' the housekeeper said and looked surprised. 'I would have come to you if you'd sent for me.'

'I wanted to see if I could find my way here,' Roxanne said. 'I should like to begin with the kitchen, if you please. I have no intention of interfering with the way you do things, Mrs Arlet, but I think I should know the layout and the way everyone works. It is a long trek for the servants to carry the food to the dining room. I find it hardly surprising that things get a little cool sometimes.'

'Yes, miss, that is a fault. Cook has been asking if we couldn't have a serving hatch somewhere. It would save Mr Marshall going up and down those stairs so much—and the food would keep hotter.'

'Would you like me to speak to the earl for you?'

'If you think he is up to it, miss. When he was down a year or so back, his lordship did mention having a modern range put in and a tap in the scullery to save us fetching water from the well, but nothing happened.'

'I dare say he might have forgotten,' Roxanne said.

'Gentlemen have such a lot to think of, do they not? They tend to leave the house to us.'

'Well, Miss Roxanne, it is a treat to have a sensible young woman in the house. We've servants enough, it's true, but life could be a bit easier for us all and there's no mistake. A house like this needs constant attention to keep it right.'

'I am certain it does,' Roxanne said. 'We shall begin with a tour of the house this morning, then, when I know my way about, we shall discuss menus. Cook is providing a huge choice of food in the morning. That is as it should be when we have guests, but we hardly need so much for the family.'

'The master eats like a bird, miss. I think Cook likes to show what she can do when his lordship is down.'

'Yes, of course. Well, we are to have guests very soon now and she will have plenty of chance to show off her skills.'

Roxanne noticed a glimmer of respect in the house-keeper's face. She suspected that too much waste had gone on for years with no one to keep a check on things and Cook probably sent leftovers to the village or the servants took it home with them. Since there was no need for strict economy, Roxanne would not interfere— providing the neglect was not actually abuse of the earl's laxity. She felt it did no harm to let the servants see she intended to keep an eye on such things.

Where had she learned about these things? Roxanne frowned. She did not know why, but her instincts were guiding her.

'Did you say something, miss?' the housekeeper asked, looking at her curiously.

'No, nothing at all,' Roxanne said and smiled. The memory had been so clear for a moment but she did not wish to think of it now. 'Shall we go down to the kitchen?'

'So, Miss Roxanne, you have been inspecting the kitchens,' the earl said when she bent to kiss his cheek. 'Discovered they are cheating me, have you?'

'I think too much waste has been going on,' Roxanne said. 'I am not sure you have been cheated, sir. Waste food is usually passed on to the poor or beggars, is it not?'

'I can't be bothered with that business,' he said. 'It will be your place to see we are not being abused now—and to sort out any problems. Do not bring them to me. There is an allowance for repairs and maintenance below stairs. Ask Clarendon if you must, but, otherwise, deal with it.'

'In that case, I shall authorise a serving hatch, a new sink in the kitchen and taps, also a larger, more modern cooking range—but I shall not trouble you other than to ask who has charge of the allowance for repairs.'

'Tonkins, of course. Clarendon is with him this morning.'

'Your agent, I imagine. Very well, sir, this is the last you shall hear of it.'

'Good.' He glared at her. 'What do you make of the rest of it—think it an old wreck of a place? Clarendon does. He'll tear it down and build new when I'm gone, I dare say.'

'Oh, I do not think it, sir. I have no idea what it costs to run a house like this, but I imagine it is a great deal. Perhaps if you were to pull down the tower and the wing you never use, you might build a more modern section there—and keep the rest of this lovely house as it is.'

'Humph. Think you're the first to come up with the idea? Clarendon's mother wanted me to do it years ago. She always hated the tower—said it was haunted.'

'Is it?'

'Don't believe in that rubbish, do you? The roof has gone in parts and rooks nest there. The sounds people hear are wind and birds or rats in the eaves.'

'Yes, I expect you are right,' Roxanne said. 'At night it is easy to imagine all kinds of things.'

'You are a woman of sense,' the earl said, his gaze narrowing. 'Is it all an act, Miss Roxanne? The ruby Clarendon showed me—it doesn't fit with the rest. What are you keeping from me, miss—and does Clarendon know it all?'

'The ruby is my inheritance. I wasn't sure it was valuable, but Luke says it is and I believe him.'

'He told me he has to return to London tomorrow. He will be gone for a few days and then he intends to stay until after the ball. What do you think of that, miss?'

'I expect he has some business in town. There is little he can do here, really. I am sure he will have sorted any estate business this morning.'

'Don't mind him running out on you, then? What if

he decides not to bother about coming back until the day before the ball?'

'I should miss him, but I believe he will keep his word.'

'You have a deal more faith than I, Miss Roxanne. He usually stays two days at the most and then I don't see him for months.'

'Things are different now, sir.'

'Are they?' The earl's eyes seemed to pierce her with their intensity. 'I thought this was just a masquerade to keep me sweet—are you telling me that you are really going to marry him?'

Roxanne looked at him in silence for a long moment, then smiled. 'We have to wait for three months—but if you give your blessing and Luke still wants to marry me, yes, I shall.'

'I haven't made up my mind about you yet, miss. There's something you're both hiding—but I'll get it out of you or him. Wait and see if I don't.'

Roxanne hesitated, then, 'Tell me, sir—what is it that you want most in the world?'

'To see my great-grandson and know there will be someone to carry on here when I've gone. Clarendon will never settle here—but you might. Is that the idea? You'll give me what I want and he gets to live in town as he pleases? You won't like that much, girl, and you're a fool if you settle for it.'

'Please, do not think so ill of him, sir,' Roxanne pleaded. 'I know things have not always been right between you—but will you not give Luke a chance to make this work? He is genuine in his desire to mend fences.'

The earl's gaze narrowed, his mouth pursed. 'Hmmm, we shall see.'

'I hope Grandfather did not bully you too much?' Luke said when they met for nuncheon later. Roxanne shook her head and he nodded in satisfaction, looking so much like his grandfather that she had to hide her laughter. 'Well, what would you like to do this afternoon? I know you can manage a horse—have you done much riding? Proper riding, I mean, not as part of a circus show.'

'All kinds,' Roxanne replied. 'Barebacked, astride, but I have not much experience of riding sidesaddle. I can drive a caravan. I dare say I could learn to ride like a lady easily enough.'

'I am sure you could and I will arrange a suitable mount for you when I return from town. For this afternoon I think perhaps we should drive round the estate, just to give you an idea of its size and where it is pleasant to walk when you are alone. When I was out with Tonkins this morning everyone was asking about you. Since it is a pleasant afternoon we can use the curricle and allow the curious to see my fiancée. It is only necessary to wave and smile at this juncture.'

'I think that would be very pleasant. Did you have a good morning with your grandfather's agent?'

'Yes. Why do you ask?'

'I understand the monies for minor repairs to the kitchens are lodged with him. Mrs Arlet has spoken to me about various needs and your grandfather has told me it is up to me to sort out domestic problems in future.'

'Has he, indeed? Clearly he trusts you more than me, Roxanne. I spoke to him about a serving hatch some months back and he sent me about my business, told me he didn't need help with arranging his household.'

'Well, perhaps things have changed. I have been told not to bother him with trivial domestic affairs and I shan't—but the hatch would improve the quality of the food for us and make less work for others. I think it would repay the cost many times over.'

'I can see the future of this place is in safe hands, at least for the moment.' Luke frowned and stood up. 'I shall arrange for the curricle to be brought round. It is warm, but there may be a breeze so you will want your bonnet and a pelisse.'

'I shall fetch them,' Roxanne said.

She was thoughtful as she walked upstairs. Luke had not seemed particularly pleased with the news that the earl had placed domestic affairs in her hands. Perhaps he was beginning to regret bringing her here? His idea of a temporary engagement seemed to be getting out of hand.

Had Roxanne been able to read Luke's mind she would have discovered that he had mixed feelings and was in something of a turmoil regarding the situation between them. It was surely a good thing that the earl should feel able to place his domestic affairs in Roxanne's hands. He was uncertain of her true feelings regarding the situation. She had been quite adamant that there would be no wedding, just a fake engagement for a few months, but she seemed to have changed her mind since their arrival at Hartingdon.

She had been running from a man who was determined to make her his mistress when they met, her future dubious to say the least. It would be tempting for any woman in such difficulty to be seduced by the house and the obvious wealth here. Yet if the ruby truly belonged to Roxanne she had money of her own. Luke did not know exactly how much it would fetch, but he was sure it would be more than a few hundred—perhaps as much as two thousand pounds or more to the right person? With such a sum she could set up her own establishment and live comfortably for the rest of her life or until she found work or married. She did not need to live here at the mercy of a cantankerous old man—or to marry a man she did not love.

So why had she changed her mind? She was unsure if the ruby was legally hers, but she might have sold it and risked the consequences had she been less than the honest woman he believed her.

Having placed the ruby in his safe keeping, she had surrendered her independence and shown great trust in him. Luke could not recall anyone else placing that amount of faith in him and his reactions were a mixture of gratification and panic. At the start he had thought the sham engagement might eventually lead to a physical arrangement between them. Luke would have been very ready to become her protector had she chosen a life in the theatre. He had been aroused by Roxanne's vibrant beauty from the beginning, but did he really wish for marriage? Luke had avoided being caught in what he thought of as a trap for so long, he could not help wondering just what he had got himself into.

It was to be merely a sham marriage, of course. That was the reason Roxanne had agreed to it when the earl insisted on the three-month engagement. She knew that he would keep his word to let her go once the earl had died.

Roxanne would give him his freedom once the earl was in his grave. He was certain that she would keep any bargain he made with her, but by the time he was able to ask for his freedom, would he still wish for it?

Damn the earl for interfering in his life! Hartingdon had no right to dictate terms to him and his threat to restrict his income could be overcome in a court. How could he think of destroying the man who was his only close family? Such a breach would surely kill the old man. Despite the anger and frustration inside him, Luke knew he would never deliberately harm his grandfather. It might be that he would have to make more than a sham marriage and actually give the earl his heir.

Roxanne would never agree to it—would she? He could not expect her to provide an heir and then simply disappear when the marriage ended. Yet need it necessarily end so finally? There was always the alternative of a marriage of convenience.

No, he had vowed he would never go down that road. His parents had been so desperately unhappy. He had witnessed his mother's tears too many times. His father had been a heartless brute who cared only for his own pleasure and Luke suspected he might be the same. To marry under false pretences might cause too much pain in the future.

The Roxanne who had bound his leg and threatened an intruder at the inn was exciting and amazing, but if she settled into a life of domesticity to please the earl Luke might become bored and begin to stray.

He knew his own faults only too well and he liked Roxanne too much to want to hurt her. It might be as well to remind her that this relationship was a temporary affair. It would be best to stick to the business arrangement they had made at the start.

The earl's estate was vast, much larger than Roxanne had imagined. She had no experience of land husbandry, but from what she could see as Luke drove her about the estate it was in good heart. The people looked prosperous and they smiled and waved, the labourers and farmers doffing their hats to her. Some children ran out of one of the farms and stood waving and giggling as Luke brought the curricle to a halt.

'Mam said to wish you happy, sir,' one of the boys said. 'She wants to know if there's to be a bit of a do for the tenants and all.'

'Yes, I am sure we shall arrange something when the wedding happens, but it is not to be just yet.' Luke thrust his hand in his pocket and brought out some silver coins, which he tossed to the children before driving away.

'Your tenants seem pleased to see you, Luke.'

'They will be disappointed if there is no wedding,'

Luke remarked. 'Perhaps we should hold some sort of fête in the park this summer. Grandfather always had a late summer party in the gardens for the tenants and labourers. I suppose an engagement is as good an excuse as any other. I'll speak to him later.'

'Your grandfather suspects you of trying to fool him, did you know that?' Roxanne said, keeping her gaze to the front. 'If we were to break the engagement too soon, he would be certain that he had been right all along.'

'We shall see whether his health improves. We might have to marry to satisfy him, but do not worry, Roxanne. I should give you your freedom afterwards. He can push us into marriage, but even he cannot hurry the arrival of an heir. It should content him to know that I am married—if you are still prepared to go so far?'

'Yes, of course. I know that the last thing you want is a life of domesticity, Luke. You need not fear that I shall cling to you and beg you not to leave me. I will not ask for more than we agreed.'

'No…' A little pulse flicked at his temple. 'Well, we shall see how things go, but you must tell me if the situation becomes too difficult for you here. I know Hartingdon is a past master at inflicting wounds.'

'I think he is a lonely, unhappy man. He shut you out when you were younger, perhaps because he was grieving for your mother—but then, when he might have reached out to you, it was too late. You are very like him, you know.'

'Like Hartingdon?' Luke turned his head to look at her in astonishment. 'What on earth makes you say that? I do not think I have given you cause to fear me?'

'No, you have not—but neither has the earl. He may be grumpy and harsh at times, but I do not fear him. Indeed, I rather like him. I should not wish to be the source of pain to him.'

Luke made a face of disbelief. 'If he appears to reciprocate, beware. He is probably trying to get beneath your guard to discover your secrets.'

'You are unfair,' Roxanne replied and gave him a look of reproach. 'Why does neither of you trust the other? You say you wish to make his last months happy—yet you will not allow him to have a heart or a conscience.'

'If he has a softer side, he has given no sign of it in my presence.'

'You are so used to quarrelling with each other that neither of you can see how foolish it is. If you let down your guard, Luke, you might actually enjoy a pleasant relationship with him—become friends or at least respect one another.'

'If I offered affection, he would throw it in my face. My advice to you is to be careful, Roxanne. Allow him to get inside your head and he will hurt you. Do not imagine that anything he has said of late means he is happy to accept you into the family. I have no doubt that from the moment I told him I was engaged, he instructed agents to discover who you are and where you came from.'

'He is unlikely to do so.' Roxanne kept her face turned from him as she said, 'Since I am well aware that this is all a masquerade I am not likely to be hurt, whatever happens.'

'That is as well,' Luke said. 'Neither of us is to be completely trusted, Roxanne, but you have my word that you will never want for money for the rest of your life. I intend to have the ruby valued when I am in town; I shall try to discover if it has a history—but regardless of what I discover, my promise to you holds true. When this is all over I shall set you up with a house and an income that will be more than adequate.'

Roxanne made no answer. He was merely reminding her of their arrangement. Luke Clarendon had never pretended to care for her. She ought not to feel disappointed or upset. Indeed, she would not allow herself to feel anything. She would simply make the most of her time here—and when it was over she would know what to do.

Chapter Six

After Luke left for London the next day, Roxanne set her mind to the tasks she had taken on in the house. A list of guests for the ball was drawn up and the invitations written carefully in her best copperplate hand. She spent an hour with Tonkins and set the work in hand for the improvements to the kitchen, and, after speaking to the head gardener, arranged for fresh flowers to be brought to the house each day.

When she carried a bowl of yellow roses into the earl's sitting room that evening he stared at her as if she had run mad.

'What is that for, miss?'

'To brighten your room and bring some sunshine indoors to you. The weather is so delightful, sir, and the gardens are glorious. We have so many lovely blooms it would be a shame not to enjoy some of them indoors.'

'Like flowers, do you?' His thick brows knit as he stared at the offering.

'Yes, I love them. I think I should like to improve some parts of the garden—if I stay here for long enough, of course.'

'What would you do?'

'There are some unused areas at the back of the house that are merely grass. I would like to make a wild garden, with your permission, sir. I have spoken to the gardener and he says there were plans to make a garden of box hedges and herbs there once, but it never happened. I thought something similar, but less formal. I should like plants that invite butterflies and birds to visit often, and perhaps some running water—a fountain of some kind.'

'The herb garden was my wife's intention, but she died.' The earl glared at her, seeming angry or at the mercy of some deep emotion. 'I suppose you can do as you please—if you stay long enough.'

'Luke says you will have instructed agents to discover who I am and where I come from, sir.'

'And what if I have? Worried about what they will find, miss?'

'I believe I have done nothing of which I ought to be ashamed, sir.'

'There's something, though. I've sensed it since the beginning. You are a mystery, Miss Roxanne—but I don't dislike having you visit me, and the roses can stay.'

Roxanne smiled. Impulsively she bent and kissed his cheek. 'Perhaps there is a mystery, sir—perhaps even

I do not know its answer, but believe me when I say I would not harm you or Luke. Indeed, I would rather go away, disappear altogether, than bring shame on either of you.'

The earl grunted, making no other reply, but his eyes looked very bright as she glanced back from the doorway. Walking down to the hall, Roxanne felt at a loss. She had become acquainted with all parts of the house, including the disused wing. The tower was out of bounds so she had not attempted it, but, walking up to the stairway to look at the curving stone steps, she'd heard a screech and some fluttering that she took to be the rooks the earl had spoken of once.

The tower had no appeal for her and she decided to walk in the garden for a while. Perhaps she would have a talk to the gardener or the bailiff about the new wilderness. It could not hurt to make plans for her wild-flower plot, even if her stay here was only temporary. Walking round past the tower to the back of the house, something made her glance up. For one moment she saw something at a window about halfway up, but in an instant it had gone. She frowned, because it had looked like a face—a man's face, dark-complexioned and strange—and yet she was sure that the earl had given orders no one was to go up the tower because it was unstable.

It must surely have been a trick of the light? Why would anyone be in the tower? The earl's servants were all aware of his orders—and yet there might be good reason for someone to visit surreptitiously. When he spoke of putting the ruby somewhere safe, Luke had told Roxanne that the earl's strong room was some-where either in the tower or beneath it.

Would a thief try to find the entrance and break in? Roxanne did not know what to think, because it seemed so unlikely. If no one had ever attempted it before, why should it happen now?

Had Luke been at home, she would have told him immediately, but the earl was not to be made anxious or worried about something of this nature. It might be nothing more than imagination, but rather than simply leave it, she decided to speak to someone. Knowing that Tonkins had gone into town that day, she thought of the bailiff. She'd seen Higgins going into his office earlier and turned in the direction he'd been heading, which was towards the stable block.

Higgins was in conversation outside his office with a stout man who looked as if he might be one of the earl's tenant farmers. He lifted his battered brown hat to Roxanne as she approached, nodded to Higgins and went off.

'Forgive me for interrupting you, Mr Higgins,' Roxanne said. 'It is a small matter—but, since Lord Clar-endon is away and Mr Tonkins has gone to the market, one I thought should be brought to your attention, sir.'

'Nothing is too much trouble for you, miss. Was it about the plants for the wild garden?'

'I was hoping to speak to Minty about that later,' Roxanne agreed. 'It may have been a trick of the light, Mr Higgins—but as I passed the tower just now I thought I saw a face at the window—not at the top, but at that little round window halfway up.'

'You didn't investigate yourself, miss?'

'I know it isn't safe, which is why I thought it curious that anyone should be there.'

'Everyone knows it isn't safe, miss. None of our people would dream of going there—unless ordered to by the earl and then we should send a party armed with ropes for safety's sake.'

'No one who knows that it is unsafe would go up the tower—but a stranger might. A stranger intent on robbery or some such thing.'

'Lord Clarendon told you about the strong room,' Higgins said and nodded. 'Only a handful of us know the secret, miss. I've never known anyone to attempt a break in, but I suppose there is always a first time. His lordship may have been seen when he visited it recently—though I cannot think any of our people would consider doing such a thing. The door is solid iron. It would be impossible to break it down—but I'll make sure the lock has not been tampered with. I'll go there myself now, miss.'

'Do you think someone should accompany you?'

'I'll take a pistol with me, but I doubt there's much to worry about, miss. As you said, it will be a trick of the light.'

'May I come with you?'

'Now that I can't allow, miss. I couldn't live with myself if you were to fall and have an accident. You'll find Minty in the hothouses. Go and have a talk with him, discover what he has to say about your wild garden, miss. I'll let you know if I discover anything.'

Roxanne agreed and left him. She was almost sure

that it must have been a trick of the light and half-wished that she had not put Mr Higgins to the trouble of investigating.

Returning to the house after a long and pleasant talk with the head gardener, Roxanne washed her hands and changed into a fresh gown for lunch. She had instructed Mrs Arlet that she would have just a little bread and butter and cold chicken in the small parlour. Her meal was finished and she was about to leave when the housekeeper came in.

'I am sorry to disturb you, Miss Roxanne, but Mr Higgins has asked if you will visit him at home.'

'At home?' Roxanne was puzzled. 'Is he not in his office?'

'It appears he had an accident, miss. Johnson will take you in the governess's cart—if you wouldn't mind travelling in such a way?'

'Of course not. I shall get ready at once. Is it far?'

'Not far, miss, but Johnson says he was instructed you wasn't to walk there alone. He's to take you and wait to bring you back.'

'I shall fetch my pelisse at once.'

'I took the liberty of sending for it. Tilly is waiting in the hall to help you with it, miss.'

Roxanne thanked her. Going into the hall, she put on her pelisse and bonnet and then went out to the courtyard at the back of the house, where the groom was waiting with the governess's cart.

'Is Mr Higgins badly hurt, Johnson?' Roxanne asked as she was helped up into the little seat at the back.

'He's got some nasty cuts and bruises,' the groom replied. 'His wife made him lie on the sofa in the parlour and the doctor told him he should go to bed and rest for a few days, but he won't until he's seen you, miss.'

'Please take me to him at once,' Roxanne said. 'I know this must be important or he would not otherwise have sent for me.'

She twisted her gloves in her hands, feeling a heavy weight of responsibility. Higgins had gone to the tower on her behalf and it was her fault if he had taken a tumble down the stairs. She was distressed because he was hurt and blamed herself.

The bailiff's cottage was through the park, at the edge of the road that led to Harte Village. It would have taken her a good half an hour to walk here, but the drive was accomplished in a fraction of the time. The groom helped her down and, as she walked up the path of the neat garden, the front door opened and a plump, pleasant-looking woman opened the door to her.

'I've been watching out for you, Miss Roxanne,' she cried. 'I am that grateful you've come. Higgins won't go to bed until he has spoken to you—and the foolish man has refused to take his medicine for fear it sends him to sleep.'

'I came as soon as I heard,' Roxanne said. 'I am so sorry, Mrs Higgins. I fear I am to blame for this.'

'You, miss? I should say not—but come through to the parlour and let my man tell you himself.'

Roxanne followed her into a pleasant parlour with

a sunny aspect at the back of the house. Mr Higgins was lying on a large comfortable sofa with his head on a pile of pillows and his eyes shut. He opened them as she approached and sat up, looking anxious.

'Please do not disturb yourself, sir.' Roxanne drew a parlour chair and sat close to him. 'Did one of the steps give way beneath you? I am so sorry for sending you there. I do hope you are not badly hurt?'

'It was not the steps, miss, though one or two are crumbling, but I didn't go up the tower. The place we spoke of is below it. I went to look at the lock and found some signs that someone had tried unsuccessfully to open the door. I was about to leave and report it to Mr Tonkins when something hit me from behind. I went down like a light and it must have been some minutes before I came to myself enough to get up and stagger out. One of the gardeners saw me fall as I left and called for help.'

'You were hit on the back of the head? That is terrible.' Roxanne felt shivery all over. 'So I was right—there was someone in the tower. I am so sorry you were hurt, Mr Higgins.'

'Serves me right for going there alone, miss. I thought you had imagined the face and took a risk. In future I'll be more careful and respectful of what you say. I gave instructions that a search should be made. Six of the men went to take a look in the tower after they brought me home—and I've since heard that someone has been camping out in the tower.'

'Good gracious! How long has this been going on?'

'A day or two at most the men think. It might have

been a tramp, miss—or it might have been a thief, as you suggested. Whoever it was, he didn't want to get caught.'

'No, indeed, but this is serious, Mr Higgins. You must take great care and rest, as your doctor told you.'

'I shall for a day or so, if only to appease Mrs Higgins—but you must promise me you will not attempt to visit that wing or the tower again, miss. His lordship would never forgive me if anything were to happen to you. One of us should have noticed something before you did, and that can't be denied.'

'I shall certainly not attempt to enter the tower,' Roxanne assured him. 'I have been wishing that I had not told you. I am so sorry you were hurt.'

'It was my own fault for not taking anyone to guard my back. I didn't give you credit, miss, and I should have known you're not the sort to imagine things. I've given instructions that the grounds are to be patrolled at all times. If there are dangerous intruders about, we cannot be too careful.'

'I thought I saw a man hiding in the shrubbery outside my room the first night I came here,' Roxanne told him. 'Lord Clarendon thought it must have been one of the keepers, but now… Why would anyone watch the house and then hide in the tower?'

'There's something he's after,' Higgins said and looked grave. 'I don't know what it is, Miss Roxanne. We've never had anything like it before—so why now?'

'I do not know,' she replied. 'I promise I shall take great care when walking in the gardens—and you must rest, sir.'

'I shall for a day or so, miss. It seems I've a tough skull for the blow did no more than knock me unconscious. I may have a headache for a while, but I'll be as right as rain soon.'

'I am relieved to hear it.'

'Shall you tell the earl, miss?'

'No, not unless he has heard something,' Roxanne said. 'As you know, his health is not good. I do not wish him to worry. I dare say the intruder has gone. With the increased security he is unlikely to return.'

'I doubt he will risk it again—unless there is something he desperately wants to get his hands on. You cannot think what that might be, miss?' The bailiff looked at her hard. 'No idea what he's after?'

'No,' Roxanne said. 'I cannot tell you, for I do not know.'

Yet as she was driven back to the house some minutes later, Roxanne was thoughtful. Had the intruder been after her ruby? It would explain why the attempt on the strong room had happened now—but was the jewel valuable enough to bring whoever it was here? It had been in the strong room only one night, because Luke had taken it to London with him to be valued.

Besides, no one knew she had it. How could they? Sofia had kept it hidden for years and no one had tried to take it from them. Roxanne had wondered if Black Bob suspected she had something of value, but would he attempt to break into the earl's strong room? It did not fit with what she knew of him. Petty thieving or cheating a traveller of his purse was the gypsy's style, but not robbery on the scale that had been planned here. To break into an earl's treasury would be a serious matter.

Yet if it was the Hartingdon heirlooms that were wanted, why had it happened now and not at some time in the past?

What was so special about the ruby that it had provoked an attempt to break into the earl's strong room and an attack on his bailiff?

Why had it been in her hand when Sofia found her? She had been so determined to keep it, so adamant that it belonged to her. The earl was right when he said something did not fit with the rest. How could a girl of modest family come to own a jewel like that one?

Roxanne thought about the game they had played when she was recovering from her illness. Sofia was an intelligent lady. Had she suspected that the ruby had come from India? She might have invented the game to try to jog the memories in Roxanne's mind. It was possible that as she lay delirious she had said something that made Sofia believe she had once lived there. Rather than try to force her to remember, Sofia had invented the game.

The face at the tower window had been dark and not English. Roxanne strained for a memory, anything that would make sense of what was happening, but nothing came to her. Yet there was something that warned her she might be in danger, some instinct that told her Mr Higgins had been set upon by someone who wanted that ruby.

The thoughts went round and round in her head

like a trapped animal trying to escape from its cage. If she could remember what had occurred to frighten her when she ran from her home, she might be able to understand what was happening now.

'What is this I hear about Higgins?' the earl asked when Roxanne visited him that evening before going down to supper. 'What on earth was the fool doing in the tower in the first place? He knows it is dangerous.'

She hesitated, then, 'Do you truly wish to know the answer, sir? You might find it concerning.'

'Damn it, I ain't on me last legs yet. Tell me the truth, girl. All of it, for I shall know if you lie.'

'I saw a face at the round window halfway up the tower earlier today. I told Higgins, because I knew the strong room was there somewhere. He went to investigate, found an unsuccessful attempt had been made to open the iron door—and someone knocked him unconscious. The tower has since been searched by some of the men and no one is there now.'

'So the rogue has escaped. Is Higgins badly hurt?'

'No. I think he has a sore head and is shocked—but the doctor said the blow was not severe enough to kill him. Perhaps whoever it was did not wish to murder him, merely to stun him while he made his escape.'

'Humph. Got it all worked out, have you? Answer me this—why now? That strong room has been there for a hundred and fifty years and no one has ever tried to break in before this—couldn't if they tried. It would take a team of men to break that door down—and then they couldn't open it unless they knew the trick. It's a secret puzzle lock known only to me and now Luke.'

'I do not know why now, sir. Why do you think it happened?'

'I knew there was something suspicious about that ruby. Who did you steal it from?'

'I did not steal it.'

'Where did it come from then? It ain't the kind of thing a girl like you ought to have—unless you got it from a lover. Have you been the mistress of a rich man, girl? Did you steal it from him in a fit of pique?'

'No, I have not been a rich man's lover, sir.' Roxanne hesitated, then, 'I am not sure of its history. Luke is trying to find out what he can for me. I had it in my hand when—Sofia found me. I was about fourteen, very ill, alone and frightened—and I had lost my memory. I did not know my own name then and to this day I do not recall it. She says I would not let go of the ruby and claimed it was mine. When at last I did let her take it from me, she hid it and I forgot about it for years, until she reminded me as she was dying.'

The old man's eyes gleamed. 'I knew there was something. You were too good to be true, miss. I suspected something was wrong from the start.'

'Well, now you know it all. Do you wish me to leave?'

The earl was silent for a moment, then, 'You had best tell me all of it, girl. How did you meet my grandson—and why did he bring you here as his fiancée?'

'After Sofia died I was not safe amongst the people we travelled with. One of them wanted me as his mis-

tress so I ran away when he was making arrangements
to give a performance at a theatre in the town nearby.'

'You are an actress?'

'Yes, I have been an actress—but Sofia was certain
I had been properly reared, though I have no memory
of my past.'

'So it was a lie about your father being in India?'

'It was just something that came into my mind. I
believe there may be a connection between the ruby
and India. I do not know who my father was—or if he
is still alive.'

'You think it has a connection with India, but you
do not know?'

'I am not certain, but recently the idea has become
stronger.'

'So how did you meet Clarendon?'

'He had a tumble from his horse. His ankle was
painful and we thought it might be broken, though it
was actually a displaced bone. I helped him and then
recaptured his horse. We went to an inn to stay for
the night and a doctor was called. The landlord sent
someone to break into the chamber and rob Clarendon
when he was sleeping, because he was unwell and vulnerable—but I had stayed to care for him lest he took a
fever. I was awake and I had a poker. When the intruder
saw that I was ready to fight him, the rogue ran off.
The next day, your grandson begged me to stay with
him until he was safe in London—and he took me to
stay with someone called Mrs Mills.'

'Saved his backside for a second time, did you?'

'He insisted I had saved his life, but I dare say it was

no such thing. The lady I visited was very respectable. I might have been in London still, but at a fair on the Heath I saw Black Bob and told Luke I must leave. He asked me to enter into an engagement and—you know the rest.'

'I knew it.' The earl glared at her. 'It was all a masquerade from start to finish.'

'No...not quite. Luke wanted to make you happy. At first I agreed reluctantly, but then I came here—and I wanted to stay. If this had not happened I might have married Luke, if he wished it—and you agreed. I think we might have given you an heir and then, if he wished, parted. Now I think perhaps I should leave before he returns.'

'Leave the sinking ship, eh? Is that all you're good for—running away? I thought you had more spunk than that, girl?'

Roxanne's cheeks flamed. 'No, that is not fair. I would have married Luke if he wished...but you cannot want me to stay now you know the truth. You cannot wish him to marry a girl who does not know her own family.'

'Know my mind better than I do, do you?' The earl stared at her hard. 'You've told me the truth as you know it?'

'Yes, sir.'

'Held nothing back?'

'Nothing, I swear.'

'I ought to send the pair of you packing—but I want that heir. Clarendon isn't going to oblige me in a hurry if I send you away, so you can stay. You will marry him in a month or so. No reason to wait for three months if a letter isn't coming.'

'You want me to marry Luke?'

'Nothing the matter with your hearing, is there? I don't know who your father was or whether he gave you that damned ruby, but I can see quality in you. Tell you the truth, our family goes back to a privateer who came from yeoman stock and rose to be an earl through pleasing Good Queen Bess. Since then we've married into good and bad blood. It may be time we had some fresh blood in the family. If you've lied to me, we may both be sorry, but I'm going to trust you—on one condition.'

'That is?'

'Luke is not informed that I know the truth.'

'You wish me to lie to him?'

'You have been lying to me.'

'No—at least I didn't actually lie. I merely allowed you to think what you would, sir.'

'I said you were clever with words. I suppose that comes from being an actress. Is it all an act or do you actually care for the fellow?'

'I believe you know the answer, sir.'

'Humph. He's bitten off more than he can chew, hasn't he?'

'I shall not demand more than he is willing to give.'

'My grandson chose to play a little trick on me— now I've turned the tables, but it may all be for the best. So—what do you say?'

'I can only say yes—and thank you.'

'Nothing to thank me for, girl. I'll still throw you

both out on your ear if I discover you've spun me a tissue of lies.'

'I promise you I have not—though in truth I do not know who owns the ruby. Perhaps I did steal it. I cannot know for certain.'

'Damn the thing. If the owner wants it back, he can have it. You won't want for jewels as my grandson's wife—there's a strong room full of the damned things if you've a mind to wear them.'

'If there were some pearls I could wear to the ball, I should be glad to borrow them, but I have no great desire either for jewels or huge wealth. However, a beautiful home where I feel safe and might do some good is a precious thing I should value.'

His eyes glittered. 'You are either a treasure or a consummate liar. We shall just have to see whether you fall flat on your face, Miss Roxanne.'

'I still do not know why someone should attempt to break into your strong room. How could anyone know I had the ruby or that I had given it to Luke?'

'Whoever it was may have tried to enter the strong room on the chance it was there. If he followed you here in the first place, the rogue must have discovered you have the ruby. Perhaps he has only just discovered that it is in your possession?'

'Yes, perhaps.'

Roxanne was thoughtful as she left the earl's apartments. It did seem as though the intruder might have been after her ruby—if she was the rightful owner. How could she have come by it unless someone had given it to her?

Why was it so important and why could she not remember her past life? What had happened to make her forget so completely?

She tried to recall more of the game she had played with Sofia. Fragments of Sofia's story came into her mind, but she had forgotten it as the years passed and she had become a woman.

'Who was the prince, Roxanne? What did he look like?'

Had Sofia actually asked her that question or was it merely a part of the game?

Roxanne wished she could lift the curtain that hid her previous life, but it remained as firmly down as ever. Yet she was growing ever more certain that the ruby was part of a mystery that she must solve before she brought danger to the people she had come to care for.

'That is a remarkable jewel, my lord,' Mr Brandon remarked. 'What exactly is that you wish me to do for you?'

'My fiancée believes she was given this by her father as a child,' Luke replied. 'However, she wishes to be certain that she is the rightful owner. She has not heard from her father in years; he may be dead. We were thinking of placing an advert asking for information about the ruby and offering a small reward—say a hundred guineas.'

'You want me to place the advertisement for you so that it cannot be traced to you?'

'If you are willing, I feel that it may be for the best.

We are not sure where the jewel came from and should there be a dispute would wish to hear the claimant's story. However, an advertisement of this kind may bring unscrupulous rogues who would lie to gain something that was not theirs.'

'Your wording is vague.' Mr Brandon read the words Luke had written, *'A ruby of good colour and size. Lost five years ago. Anyone with any information concerning this jewel should apply in writing to Mr Brandon of W. R. Brandon and Associates.'*

'I kept the wording vague on purpose,' Luke agreed. 'Nothing may come of it. If we do not hear within a few weeks, I think we may assume that my fiancée's recollection is correct. We shall at least have tried and may then use or dispose of it with a clear conscience.'

'I dare say most would simply have sold it,' the lawyer said. He frowned as he looked at the jewel. 'If I were you, I should place that in the bank for safekeeping. I do not think I have ever seen such a magnificent ruby—and yet there is something about it that makes me feel it may be dangerous.'

'A ruby is simply a ruby,' Luke said and laughed. 'I shall not ask you to keep it here, sir. If no one comes forward to claim it as theirs, I may have it set as a pendant for my wife.'

'The shape of it is unusual,' Mr Brandon said. 'It could almost be a large eye…'

'It is an unusual shape,' Luke agreed and slipped it back into his breast pocket. 'I think perhaps I shall lodge it at my bank, Brandon. You will let me know if you hear anything of interest?'

'Yes, of course, sir. As for the other little matter, I shall set that in hand at once.'

'If you could bring the papers down, sir? You might like to attend the ball at Hartingdon next week.'

Mr Brandon looked pleased. A short stay at the country house of a wealthy client was a break from the routine of life in London.

'I should enjoy that very much, my lord. I am certain we can have the papers ready for your signature by the fourteenth—and I should be delighted to attend your engagement ball.'

'We shall look forward to seeing you,' Luke said and shook his hand. 'I have ordered a gift for my fiancée. My bank is near the jeweller's, so I may as well kill two birds with one stone.'

Luke left the lawyer's office and crossed the road. He was lost in thought and did not notice the man following a short distance behind as he walked the length of two streets and entered his bank, before making his way, some minutes later, to a large jeweller's establishment at the opposite side of the road.

He did notice the man who entered a few moments after him and asked to look at a tray of diamond rings, because he was young, attractive and spoke in a soft voice that sounded foreign and his skin was deeply tanned. An Indian of a high caste, perhaps, Luke thought as the man took his time examining the expensive rings, perhaps the son of a wealthy maharajah. His English was perfect and he was dressed in Western clothes, but his accent was definitely not English.

'Your pearls, sir,' the jeweller said and opened the

black velvet box to show Luke the single strand of large creamy pearls. 'I hope they are to your liking?'

'Yes, they are perfect. My bank will settle your account as usual.'

'Thank you, sir. Do you wish them wrapped?'

'No, the box will fit into my pocket,' Luke said. He noticed that the shop's other customer had agreed to purchase one of the rings as he slipped the box into his pocket and left the shop.

Outside, he hailed a hackney cab and asked the driver to take him to his club.

A few moments later, the dark-skinned gentleman came out of the shop and stood on the pavement in thought for a few minutes before turning away.

'Luke, you are back!' Roxanne cried as she saw him leave the house by way of the French windows and enter the rose garden. She moved swiftly towards him, her hands outstretched and a smile of welcome on her lips. 'Your grandfather thought you would not arrive until the day before the ball.'

'I told you I should not delay,' he replied and took her hands. 'How are you? I hope the old scoundrel has not been too grouchy?'

'Luke! You really must not.' She laughed and shook her head reproachfully. 'He has been very kind to me. I must tell you that time goes very quickly here. The curate has been giving me piano lessons. He comes twice a week in the morning—and the earl actually left his apartments so that he could listen. They are both of the opinion that I have been taught to play, but need to practise often to become proficient.'

'And do you enjoy your lessons?'

'Yes, I do,' she said. 'No, do not look so dubious. I find playing very worthwhile and relaxing. I may never be as good as your mama was, but if I play well enough for my own amusement and the enjoyment of others it will be sufficient. I tried my hand at sketching, but I do not think it will suit me. I have no talent for it, I fear.'

'You have talents enough, Roxanne. Do not be bullied into doing anything you do not wish to do.'

'No, I shall not. There is more than sufficient to keep me occupied here. I have with the earl's permission begun to plan a wild garden at the back of the house and the kitchen renovations have already started. The invitations for the ball took two days to complete, but since they went out we have been inundated with kind letters—and also some generous gifts. I have written thank-you notes, which the earl was good enough to frank for me.'

'And so he should since he insisted that we hold a ball.'

Roxanne looked up at him, caught by an inflection in his tone. He sounded annoyed, almost bitter. 'Did you not wish for a ball?'

'It makes no difference to me one way or the other—I thought it might be difficult for you, since you do not know any of our friends and relatives.'

'We have had several morning visits since the news got out,' Roxanne said. 'Just a few of the earl's neighbours. They were all very pleasant and friendly. I do not think the ball will make me uncomfortable.'

'I am relieved to hear it.'

The look on his face struck her as brooding and she felt her stomach twist with nerves. He was regretting the ball—and perhaps his impulsive suggestion that they should become engaged. Had he visited Mrs Fox in London? Was that why he seemed moody and disgruntled? If she was the woman he truly loved and could not wed, this arrangement must irk him. A sharp pain struck her to the heart, but she ignored her doubts and lifted her head to meet his gaze.

'Yet the sooner it is all over the better.'

'Is something wrong, Luke? It is not too late. If you wish to change your mind, I can leave. You could cancel the ball and tell everyone I jilted you—or was not suitable.'

'Do not be foolish. Nothing has changed. Why should it? Grandfather seems to have accepted you and I see no reason to disappoint him. If you were agreeable, I might persuade him to have the wedding sooner than later—what do you say?'

'If we are to be married, I see no reason to wait,' Roxanne replied, though she could not meet his eyes. 'I made a bargain with you, Luke—and I shall keep it to the last letter, if you wish.'

'You mean you are willing to give Grandfather an heir?' His gaze narrowed, intent and seeming to penetrate her mind, his look almost an accusation, though of what she did not know.

Roxanne's cheeks were burning, but she did not look

at him as she replied, 'Yes, I think we should not disappoint him if it is possible to oblige.'

'Supposing an heir comes along—and then the old devil dies on us? What terms will you demand of me then?'

'I have never demanded anything of you,' Roxanne replied a trifle haughtily. Her head went up, her manner proud. 'I should want to be a mother to my son, either here or somewhere else. Naturally, you would visit him, or, as he grew older, have him to stay with you wherever you wish.'

'I do not much care for this place, but my son will inherit it one day. You could continue as its mistress, Roxanne. Unless you wish for your freedom, divorce is hardly necessary. I do not believe I should wish to remarry. I think I am not the domestic type.'

'No, perhaps not,' Roxanne admitted, her throat tight. Each word he spoke was like a blow to her pride and her heart, but she managed to conceal her feelings. She held herself stiffly, speaking carefully. 'I believe you are telling me not to expect love or attention. You will continue to live in London and visit us occasionally—is that your wish?'

'Yes. I have come round to the idea you suggested, Roxanne. I do prefer you to almost any other lady I have met. You do not bore or irritate me and I think we should suit—but I want your promise that you will not weep and reproach me if I take a mistress or stay in London for months on end. I cannot give you love and you must not expect it.'

Roxanne hesitated. Could she keep such a promise? Her feelings for him had gradually become deeper since they had first met and she was very much afraid that her heart was already engaged. She ought never to have agreed to accompany him to London in the first place, or to entertain what was meant to have been a sham engagement. Somehow they had been drawn into something far deeper and for her more meaningful. It hurt to realise that for him nothing had changed. Yet Roxanne knew that she could not bear to walk away from him now. She must just bring all her arts as an actress into play and allow him to believe her feelings were not affected.

'You know my situation, Luke. Here at Hartingdon I am safe from Black Bob—and I enjoy living here. I believe I should be happy as its mistress and as the mother of your children. If you truly feel there is no need for a divorce, then we may continue the marriage after the earl dies. However, I must tell you that he seems much stronger of late. He has come downstairs for the last three evenings and says he means to walk in the gardens with me tomorrow if it is fine.'

Luke inclined his head, the tiny flicker of a pulse at his temple. 'I am glad to hear it. However, I have it from his own doctor that he could have a fatal attack at any time, so we must take care not to upset him over small things.' He hesitated for a moment, then, 'We are of one mind that there is no point in delaying the wedding—if Grandfather agrees?'

'None whatsoever,' Roxanne said, though her heart raced and for one second her knees felt weak.

'Then it is settled.' He smiled and her breath fled. 'I

see no reason why it should not be a pleasant arrangement for us both, Roxanne. I may not believe in the fairy tale of romantic love, but I know how to please in bed, and I believe we should suit well enough. Now tell me—has anything much happened since I left?'

Roxanne flinched, but managed to show no emotion. 'Yes. I shall tell you in a moment—but first, pray tell me what happened in London. Is your lawyer to place the advert?'

'We have worded something vague, but enough to arouse curiosity if someone feels they lost a similar jewel.' Luke frowned. 'You have remembered nothing?'

'I remembered that Sofia once asked me what the prince looked like. At the time it was a part of the game we played, but I have wondered if Sofia had reason to connect the ruby with India and if her game was meant to jog my memory.'

'How could she?'

'When I was ill I may have rambled in my mind, said something that made her wonder.'

'Would she not have asked you outright?'

'Sofia cared for me as if I were her own. She would have done nothing that might hurt me—and perhaps she feared what might happen if my memory did return.'

'Yes, perhaps. It seems odd she made no effort to find your family.'

'She had no money to hire agents. Besides, I had bruises on my arms and legs, and she wanted to protect me. I think if anyone had asked after me, she would have lied to keep me safe.'

'My lawyer was of the opinion that the ruby came from India. He thought it sinister and found the shape odd, which I suppose it is in a way. Had you noticed that if you turn it on its side it has the shape of an eye?'

'I cannot say I had thought of it that way, but I suppose it does—an elongated eye with pointed ends, but, yes, I can see what he means. Did you have it valued?'

'No. I placed it in the bank in London. I hope you do not mind?'

'It may be as well,' Roxanne said. She took a deep breath, 'There was an attempt to break into your grandfather's strong room when you were in London and Mr Higgins was struck over the head when he went to investigate a face at the window of the tower room.'

'Good grief!' Luke looked at her in horror. 'Was he badly hurt?'

'Fortunately not. I visited him at home afterwards and he said it was his own fault. I told him that I had seen someone at the window about halfway up the tower. Mr Higgins was not impolite enough to say so, but he thought it my imagination. The tower has since been searched and there were signs that someone had been there, but has now gone.'

'Frightened by what he had done, I dare say.' Luke frowned. 'Did the rogue manage to get inside the strong room?'

'No, I believe not,' Roxanne said. 'Do you think it was because of the ruby? It does seem a little odd that it should happen now, do you not think so?'

'The ruby?' Luke considered for a moment. 'How could anyone know you had given it to me for safekeeping? I placed it there for one night, no more. Only the three of us knew. Unless you told someone, it was impossible for them to know. Besides, there are more valuable jewels in the strong room. It is mere coincidence that it has happened now.'

'Of course you are right.' Roxanne drew a breath of relief. 'It was just that the face I saw was not English—the man had dusky skin and I thought he might be Indian, which was why I wondered if he was searching for the ruby.' It had all seemed to fit in her mind, but now she felt a little foolish. Of course her ruby was not that important.

'Did anyone ever come looking for either you or the ruby when you were with the travelling players?'

'Not to my knowledge. However, Sofia was respected and loved. If she asked the others to keep the secret, no one would have given us away while she lived.'

'So the only man who might look for you is the one you ran from that day at the Heath—might it have been he?'

'No, I do not believe it was, though he would have hit poor Mr Higgins and he might have attempted to break into a door that looked intriguing enough to hide valuables. However, I am almost certain that his was not the face at the window.'

'Then it must have been an itinerant, an opportunist who found himself a place to sleep and attempted to break open a locked door. I am sure the incident had nothing to do with you or the ruby.'

'I am glad of your good sense. I had been feeling

guilty,' Roxanne admitted. 'Now I can forget it and concentrate on other things.'

'You should certainly not let it bother you. Shall we go in and have some tea?'

Roxanne took the arm he offered and walked into the house with him. She was glad to have him back, even though there was pain mixed with the pleasure.

Chapter Seven

Luke paused in the act of tying his cravat before dinner that evening. His talk with Higgins had elicited no more information than Roxanne had given him earlier—apart from one thing.

'There was a strong smell,' Higgins said. 'Just before I was hit I smelled perfume—not the kind Miss Roxanne uses, but something heavy and exotic. Nothing I've ever smelled before. I forgot when I was telling her about it, but then it came back to me. One of my men found a length of cloth in the tower and it had the same smell about it.'

'Might the cloth have been used for a turban, do you think?'

'Yes, sir. As you know, my son is an army sergeant and he sent me a tinted drawing of an Indian soldier he served with when he was in India. The cloth that was found could easily be from a turban.' Higgins seemed puzzled. 'What do you think a person like that would be doing in the tower, sir?'

Luke was thoughtful. 'I think it best we keep this to ourselves, Higgins. At the moment we cannot be sure of anything.'

'Yes, sir. I understand. The men will keep a sharp eye out for any strangers. Do you think there is something odd going on, my lord?'

'At the moment I am not certain,' Luke replied. 'It may just have been a vagrant who saw an opportunity and then panicked when you arrived. Or it may be more sinister. We shall employ more men and patrol the grounds day and night.'

'Right you are, sir. May I say how happy everyone is that you are spending more time here, sir. Mr Tonkins is a good man and I've done my best, but there are times the earl just does not want to listen.'

'He has always been stubborn, but he is frailer than I like, Higgins. Any problems regarding this business should come to me, not my grandfather.'

'You'll be staying here now then, sir?'

'At least until after the wedding. What happened may be just an isolated incident. Unfortunate for you, but over. However, if anything else happens I may have to rethink my plans.'

Now, as he tied his snowy white cravat into intricate folds, Luke was remembering the dusky-skinned gentleman who had followed him into the London jeweller's. He had noticed a rather exotic perfume that day, though of course it could all be a coincidence. Yet

Brandon had disliked the ruby, implying that there was something dangerous or sinister about it.

It could be that there was something significant about that ruby, something that made it worth sending people to England to search for it—but why now?

Luke had told Roxanne not to worry, dismissing her fears that her ruby might have brought the intruder here, but he could not help wondering if he had been too hasty. The ruby might have more worth to someone than the amount it would fetch in a jeweller's shop. Luke had not considered it important at first, but now several threads were running through his mind.

Damn the thing! He had more to concern him than the blasted ruby. Having spoken to his grandfather that afternoon about bringing the wedding forwards, Luke knew that he had committed himself to marriage. While doubts remained, he could not deny a feeling of satisfaction. It was as if he had been resisting subconsciously, but now that had fallen away and he found he was looking forward to the wedding—but first there was the engagement ball.

While in town he had given Roxanne's measurements to a French seamstress and she had promised to deliver the gown he had ordered in time. She was coming herself to fit it and make any last-minute adjustments. He knew that Roxanne had some idea of making a gown herself, but the magnificent creation he had bought for her would be a surprise—as would the pearls he had purchased in the London jeweller's.

Once again he considered whether the attack on Higgins and the man he had seen purchasing a ring in

London were connected. Had he been followed to the jeweller's that day? Had the man he'd noticed hoped to discover the ruby's whereabouts?

'Imagination,' he murmured aloud, fastened a magnificent diamond pin in his cravat and went down to dinner.

After Luke's return the days seemed to fly past so quickly that Roxanne hardly had time to think or worry about what she was doing. The incident in the tower had been dismissed from her mind completely and she was thoroughly enjoying each day.

Luke had purchased a beautiful mare for her. Rhoda, as he informed her the horse was named, was a chestnut and a perfect mount for her, being spirited and yet good natured, even playful. The mare had responded to Roxanne's touch and voice immediately and, if Roxanne did not watch her, would give her new mistress a sharp nudge in the back with her nose.

'She is lovely,' Roxanne cried as she thanked him. 'I am so grateful for your kindness.'

'You must have a horse of your own. The saddle belonged to my mother. It takes time to make one to suit an individual and we shall commission a new one once you have got used to this, which has been worn in and should be comfortable both for you and the mare.'

'It is perfect,' Roxanne said and ran her hand over the soft leather, which, though not new, had a pleasant feel. 'I do not think I need another just yet.'

'My mother was an excellent horsewoman, Roxanne.

I am certain you can do as well if you are willing to learn.'

Roxanne assured him that she was and allowed him to help her into the saddle and to explain how she should hold her reins. Although she had been used to riding astride when with the players, she immediately settled to the new position and needed telling only once how to sit and hold her reins.

Luke watched her walk the mare about the paddock, making only an occasional remark about posture or commands to the mare. After some minutes had passed, he nodded his head and walked up to her as she halted the mare.

'Are you sure you have not ridden this way before?'

'I may have done years ago…'

'When you were a child in India?'

'If I was ever there. Sometimes in my mind I seem to see a beautiful pink palace with cool rooms and fountains in the gardens—but it may just be one of Sofia's stories.'

'Are there people in your dream?'

She shook her head. 'No, I have no real memories, Luke. I think the palace was where Sofia lived with her prince.'

'You are sure she never mentioned anything you told her when you were ill?'

'No, I am not sure of anything.'

Luke's eyes were very intent. 'You have not been lying to me, Roxanne? I would rather hear the truth from your lips now than discover it is all lies later.'

'Are you accusing me of trying to deceive you?'

She raised her head proudly. 'Why should I do such a thing? I have no wish to be other than I am.'

'Forgive me, that remark was uncalled for. It is just odd that you should have this feeling about India—and now it seems as if there may be a connection. Does that not sound strange to you? In my place would you not wonder?'

'Yes, perhaps,' she agreed. 'May we speak of something else now? Your grandfather spoke of dancing lessons, but it may have slipped his memory. The curate is coming this afternoon. If he played for us, would you teach me some steps, please?'

'Yes, of course. I should be delighted. I will call the groom. You have done enough riding for today. You should learn at least one or two dances before the ball.'

'Count in your head, Roxanne…one two three, one two three—and follow me. Trust me and you cannot fail.'

'Thank you, I shall try.'

Roxanne stood as he placed his right hand at the small of her back and let herself relax, feeling the warmth that flowed through her. The curate's playing was pleasant and she felt as if she floated on air as they waltzed the length of the gallery, where the ball was to be held.

'Yes, that is exactly right,' Luke told her. 'You were born to dance, Roxanne. It is a natural talent that may be learned, but you feel the music and you are like thistledown in my arms.'

Roxanne closed her eyes. In her head she seemed

to hear strange music and for a moment she felt light-headed, as if she were not quite herself. Luke's voice came from a distance. The dreamlike state still held her and she stumbled, falling into his arms.

Luke caught her and carried her to a sofa, sitting her against the soft cushions as she stirred. She opened her eyes, looking at him in a puzzled way.

'What happened?'

'You were faint for a moment. Are you ill?'

'No, I do not think so. How foolish of me.'

Luke placed a hand to her forehead. 'You do not seem to have a temperature, but you said something just before your faint.'

'Did I?' She looked up, feeling bewildered. 'For a moment I thought I was somewhere else.'

'You said a word I did not recognise. I think it may have been another language—perhaps Hindu or some such thing.'

'How could I know an Indian word?'

'Easily, if you were truly brought up there.' He frowned. 'This business of the ruby has been playing on your mind. It might be that the face you saw at the window was Indian. A turban cloth was found at the tower when the search was made.'

Roxanne shivered. 'That is a little worrying, Luke. What is so important about the ruby that someone would follow us here and attempt to break into your grandfather's strong room?'

'If we knew that, I think the mystery might be solved.' Luke offered her his hand as she attempted to rise, catapulting her into his arms. It surprised them

both and Luke's kiss was completely without intention. He kissed her lightly at first, but it deepened to
intensity before he let her go. 'It was the look in your
eyes,' he excused himself. 'There is no need to fear,
Roxanne. I shall protect you.'

'Yes…' Roxanne spoke in a faint voice unlike herself. 'I am not afraid, just curious as to why the ruby
is so important.'

'Yes, it is curious,' Luke replied. 'I think enough
dancing for today. We shall send for some tea—and I
think our kind pianist should stay and enjoy it with us.'

'Yes, of course, Luke,' Roxanne said and went off
to speak to the curate.

Luke's eyes narrowed as he watched her. She looked
every inch a lady—but supposing she had lied in an
attempt to ensnare him? Supposing she'd stolen the
ruby? She might be Black Bob's accomplice; they could
have stolen it together. Perhaps she'd wanted the jewel
for herself and run off with it. That might be the reason
she was frightened of being found and dragged back to
her former life. He knew a moment of intense pain at
the thought. If she had played him for a fool, he would
feel betrayed.

Luke was aware of a sense of unease. He knew that
he was being drawn into something beyond his control. What exactly did Roxanne want of him? She had
refused to enter a sham marriage at first, but now she
seemed prepared to become his wife and to give him
an heir.

Could he trust her? More importantly, perhaps, could
he trust himself? The feelings he'd had for Roxanne

from the beginning had grown stronger, but surely a night in her bed would satisfy his hunger. It had always been that the chase was more important to him and he soon tired once the game was won. Perhaps he was a shallow fellow, incapable of feeling more than a fleeting affection—if that were so, why was he beginning to feel obsessed by Roxanne and a need to know the truth about her past?

He was a fool to let down his guard. Until he was certain this was not all an elaborate plot to ensnare him he refused to feel more than liking for her. He had met many beautiful women, but none had touched his heart—why should it be different now?

Roxanne glanced at herself in the mirror as she prepared for dinner that evening. Why had Luke kissed her that way earlier? She could not convince herself that he cared for her, so why had he suddenly kissed her with such intensity? Was it merely a passing impulse—or lust?

He'd told her that he did not believe in romantic love, yet he knew how to please a woman in bed. Her mouth felt dry and her stomach cramped with nerves. Luke felt physical desire for her and he would be a passionate lover.

She supposed men often felt desire for a beautiful woman. Roxanne had seen lust in the eyes of men many times, but she had never been kissed like that because she'd always avoided any involvement. Sofia had warned her to be careful, telling her that men were not to be trusted—especially the aristocracy.

Was she a fool to let herself be used both by the earl and his grandson? They both wanted something from her, but were either of them prepared to give her anything of value in return? Luke had offered an income, but money was not important to Roxanne. She wanted to be respected, liked, even loved for what she was—especially by Luke.

How foolish she was to have let down her guard even for an instant. Luke had made it plain from the start that he did not wish for a true marriage. It was a business arrangement and she must accept it—or walk away.

To walk away would cause too much pain. She had become fond of the earl and must do nothing that would bring on his illness. Luke might come to admire her qualities in time and it should be possible to have mutual respect.

Was that enough in a marriage? It had to be, because Roxanne knew that she could not expect more from a man who refused to give his heart.

'Would you like to wear your hair up this evening, miss?'

Roxanne's thoughts were recalled to the present. She looked at the face of her young maid and smiled.

'Yes, thank you, Tilly. I shall have it dressed with a ringlet for the ball, but tonight I would prefer it to be quite plain.'

'Yes, miss.' The girl took up the brush and began to stroke it through her hair, leaving Roxanne free to continue her thoughts.

* * *

That evening they dined with friends of the earl and Roxanne began to understand what her life would be like here. Although curious, the earl's neighbours were friendly and prepared to accept her, because Hartingdon had made his wishes clear.

'This young woman has done wonders for the house already,' he remarked to a gentleman of similar years. 'I never expected to see such a day and I am truly grateful to her. Clarendon is fortunate to have found her.'

'I'm sure he knows it,' General Forster said and nodded approvingly. 'Luke, you must bring Miss Roxanne to dinner soon—and I should be delighted to take you fishing in our lake one day, should you care for it.'

'Very kind of you, sir,' Luke said and sent a brooding glance at Roxanne. She thought that he was learning to play his part very well. 'It is a while since I went fishing.'

'Do you enjoy music, Miss Roxanne?'

She turned to the young man sitting beside her. 'Yes, Sir James, very much. I fear I am an indifferent pianist, though I am attempting to improve.'

'Do you sing at all?'

'Yes, I do,' Roxanne said, recalling some of the performances she'd given when with the players. 'I enjoy listening to others play and sing. I also enjoy the performance of a play.'

'Ah yes, I'm fond of the theatre myself.' He beamed at her. 'You put me in mind of something, Miss Roxanne. I mean no insult when I say that you remind me of an actress I once saw. She was very talented, but just a provincial actress, not famous at all—however, the likeness is superficial.'

'I am glad to hear it,' Roxanne said and laughed, hiding the fact that his remark had made her heart beat fast. 'Tell me, where was she performing?'

'I hardly remember—an open-air performance, as I recall, at an inn or somewhere like. Do not be offended by the comparison, for I meant none.'

'I am not offended.' Roxanne smiled as the moment of panic receded. He did not remember her. 'If the lady was talented there is no reason.'

She had been apprehensive for a moment but she saw there was no need. Even though the young man had undoubtedly seen her performing, he did not dream that Roxanne was the actress he'd watched. He thought the likeness superficial, which indeed it was for she had changed considerably since those days. That girl had been left far behind as she became more confident and sure of her place here.

'Oh, very talented. I thought she belonged on the London stage. I would have spoken to her about it, but I could not stay until the end of the play.'

'Roxanne, may I speak with you?'

She stood up as Luke came up to her, nodding her head to her companion and moving aside to the window.

'You looked slightly disturbed. James was not annoying you?'

'He wished me not to be offended, but saw a vague likeness in me to an actress he'd once watched performing somewhere.'

'Ah, I see…' Luke nodded, his gaze intent on her face. 'You are not distressed?'

'No, certainly not.' Roxanne lifted her head proudly, every inch the great lady. 'You wished to speak with me?'

'I forgot to mention it earlier, but a seamstress is coming down in a couple of days. She has made a gown for the ball for you and will fit it and make any adjustments needed while she is here. I thought you might like her to make a wedding dress for you? We shall buy most of your trousseau in Paris after the wedding—if that suits you?'

'Of course, if you think it necessary.' Roxanne's heart thudded in her breast, her throat tight suddenly and for no good reason. 'Your grandfather looks a little tired. If there is nothing more, I shall see if he wishes to retire.'

'No, nothing more,' Luke replied with a little frown.

'Then please excuse me for the moment.'

Luke watched as she walked to the earl. The old man listened to what she said to him and then inclined his head. Roxanne gave him her arm and they left the room together. For a moment the earl's face was unguarded and his grandson saw real affection in his eyes as he responded to her caring.

It was evident that a bond had formed between them while he was absent. Luke wasn't sure how he felt about the situation. Roxanne seemed fond of the earl and sure of her place here. For a moment he was irked by the affection between them. Roxanne had found a way past the prickly outer skin the earl had used to shut out everyone else, including his grandson. Why was he prepared to accept her when he had shown little but indifference towards his own flesh and blood?

Luke ought to be delighted that his plan to make his grandfather's last days happy was working so well and yet once again he had a sense of unease—almost fear. It was ridiculous to feel trapped. He could walk away, go back to London whenever he chose, and yet something was holding him here. It was as if invisible chains bound his limbs and he did not understand his own feelings.

It was not as if the marriage was to be a true one. He felt passion for Roxanne and knew that he would find great pleasure in teaching her the delights of the bedroom—but he was not sure that she felt anything for him.

She was always welcoming, pleasant and amenable to his wishes, but was that what he wanted from her? Was this show of affection and content merely a consummate actress at work? He had made a bargain with her and Roxanne was playing her part all too well.

Luke wasn't sure what he wanted or expected of her—or what he hoped the future might bring. His uncertainty had not improved his mood and he was on edge, moody, anger simmering beneath the surface—but he did not know why he was angry.

Roxanne was surprised at how many people had come to wish them well. She had written the invitations to whole families and it seemed that uncles, aunts and cousins had turned out in force. They had been arriving for the past two days and the house was already overflowing. The arrival of neighbours and friends later that night would ensure that the ball was a success.

'That's a beautiful gown, Miss Roxanne,' the housekeeper observed when she brought up a posy of fragrant lilies the gardener had sent. 'I think you will be the centre of attention this evening—as you deserve to be, miss.'

'Thank you, Mrs Arlet,' Roxanne said. 'Lord Clarendon ordered the gown in London, as you know. He has excellent taste. Those flowers are lovely—did they come from his lordship?'

'I think it was Minty's idea, miss—though I dare say his lordship asked for flowers suitable for the occasion.'

'Well, they are delightful,' Roxanne said and the housekeeper left. She glanced at her reflection, thinking that the gown called for an ornament of some kind. Her request to the earl for the loan of some pearls had not been met and she regretted her lack. She was just considering whether she could pin a single flower to her gown when someone knocked. Opening the door, she was surprised to see Luke. 'Oh...I am nearly ready.'

'You look beautiful, Roxanne,' he said, staring at her in such a way that her heart fluttered and her mouth was suddenly dry. 'I brought you a little gift to wear this evening—if it pleases you.'

Luke offered her a black velvet box, which Roxanne took and opened. Her breath caught in her throat as she saw the single string of beautiful creamy pearls fastened with a clasp of emeralds and diamonds.

'Oh, these are beautiful. My maid has gone—would you fasten them for me, please?'

'Yes, of course.' Luke followed her into the bedchamber. Roxanne lifted her hair and he placed the pearls around her throat, his fingers lingering against the sensitive skin at her nape. 'The clasp is meant to be at the front.' He turned the necklet, his hand just brushing against her dipping décolletage for an instance.

The dizzying sensation that shot through her at that moment almost took her breath. Roxanne's lips parted on a sigh and she felt a spasm of desire and need so strong that it required all her willpower not to melt into his arms. Just for a moment she wished there was no ball, nothing but Luke and a soft bed where they could lie together.

The sensation was sweet and overpowering, but Roxanne forced herself to remain aloof. To beg for kisses and more would shame her and she had no intention of allowing her feelings to become plain. Luke wanted a business arrangement and that was what she must accept because anything else would end in pain. The last thing Luke wanted or needed was a clinging wife who would love him and make him feel guilty for neglecting her when he returned to the life he enjoyed.

She would be a poor actress if she could not hide her feelings for him, but she must remain outwardly in control. He would hate her to fall in love with him. He had no wish for a clinging wife.

Glancing in the mirror, Roxanne was satisfied that apart from a faint flush in her cheeks she had given no sign of the intensity of her feelings. She touched the emerald clasp and smiled.

'How did you know that I longed for such a necklace?' she asked, for all the world without a care as she met his brooding look. 'The pearls are wonderful, Luke, and the clasp goes so well with my ring.'

'That was my intention,' he said, a faint smile in his eyes. 'Grandfather asked me to find something for you in the strong room, but I told him I had my own gift for you.'

'I see.' Roxanne nodded, because that explained why the earl had not kept his promise. 'I must thank you so much for my gifts, Luke.' She looked up at him, seeing a blaze of passion that made her tremble. 'Luke—what are you thinking?'

'I think we should go down before I am tempted to lock the door and stay here with you instead of entertaining our guests.'

Roxanne's heart pounded. Her stomach clenched with something she instinctively recognised as desire. The look in his eyes was so hot that she could not doubt he felt desire for her, but she was certain that his feelings were no more than that; he wanted her, but love was not something Luke was prepared to give. His touch would make her flesh sing, but love was the forbidden fruit she must not taste.

'Yes, we must not keep our guests waiting or the earl,' Roxanne said, painting a smile in place as she lifted her head. 'Our audience awaits, Luke.'

'A performance? Is that all this is to you, Roxanne?'

'Of course. What else?' she said. 'That is what you required of me, as I recall.'

She moved past him into the hall, then turned and waited expectantly. Her composure was perfect, she was ready for the stage.

'You're a clever actress, Roxanne. I dare say you will have our friends eating out of your hand, just as you have Grandfather. He prides himself on his judgement, but you have him purring like a kitten.'

She felt as if he had pricked at her with long thorns, but kept her smile in place. 'If I have the ability to make people like me, that is a good thing, is it not?'

'I think they will love you. Grandfather certainly does.'

Loved by all, but not by you. The words were in her head, but not spoken aloud.

Lifting her head, she looked into his eyes. 'His happiness is your main concern, is it not? That is the reason you brought me here?'

'Yes…' Luke's gaze narrowed. 'I would not wish to see him hurt, Roxanne.'

'Then we are of one mind,' she said and took his arm. 'Come, Luke, need you look so sober? This is meant to be an evening of pleasure for us as well as our guests. You must try to look as if you are enjoying yourself or your friends will wonder.'

'You are right.' He smiled suddenly and her heart skipped a beat. 'I have no right to expect more than you wish to give. We shall dance and enjoy ourselves this evening. More serious matters can wait for another day.'

Now what did he mean by that? Roxanne wondered,

but she put the little puzzle from her mind. Tonight she was playing the part of a girl very much in love who was announcing her engagement to the man she loved. It was not a difficult part to play, as long as she did not remember that Luke did not love her.

Chapter Eight

As Roxanne had imagined, the evening was a huge success. The ballroom was decorated with banks of fragrant flowers from the hothouses and reels of white-silk tulle hung in drapes above the dais where the musicians were seated. Sparkling chandeliers threw out showers of light, which were picked up by the glittering jewels worn by both ladies and gentlemen. They had come dressed in their best finery, prepared to enjoy the celebrations, and laughter reverberated through the rooms, the sound of chattering voices almost deafening.

Roxanne soon discovered that she was the centre of attention.

'To tell the truth I never expected to see this day,' Luke's Uncle Frederick on his father's side told her as he claimed one of the first dances of the evening. 'I believe Hartingdon had given up all hope of Clarendon ever doing his duty.'

'Surely not?' Roxanne gave him an amused smile. 'Luke is not in his dotage, I think?'

'Good lord, no, he's a young man, but he seemed set in his ways. I always knew it would take an exceptional young woman to catch my nephew and it seems I was right.'

'Thank you for the compliment,' Roxanne replied mischievously. 'I shall do my best to live up to what is expected of me.'

'You'll do very well,' the talkative gentleman said. 'Beauty and brains, to say nothing of charm. Now that is a combination not often found, Miss Roxanne. Luke is a lucky fellow.'

Since that seemed the consensus of the guests, Roxanne did not find herself left without an admirer at her side all evening. She danced every dance, sipped at, but did not finish, several glasses of champagne brought to her by a string of helpful gentlemen and ate sparingly of the delicious supper that had been provided for them.

'Where did you meet Clarendon?'

The question had been asked again and again by curious aunts and cousins throughout the evening. Roxanne gave the same reply to all of them.

'I was staying with a friend and we met by chance when Luke was out riding,' she told them, embroidering the truth only as necessary. 'We were mutually attracted and liked each other immediately.'

Surely that much was true. Roxanne *had* felt an instant liking for the man she'd helped in the woods, despite his hostility. He'd been angry and in pain at first, but later he'd been grateful for her help. That meeting seemed so far away now, her life revolving round the earl and his grandson these days. Sometimes she almost forgot that she had ever known another life.

The Roxanne who had lived with a band of travelling players was someone different. *She* was Miss Peters and her father lived and worked in India… The story she'd invented for herself was now so real that she believed it must be the truth.

As far as she understood, Luke's lawyer had heard nothing from the advertisement. Roxanne might never discover whether the ruby was truly hers or the property of another person. Perhaps it was not important. She had become a part of Luke's family, welcomed and accepted amongst them. It did not matter that she could not remember her own family—at least she must try not to let it matter.

She had danced three times with Luke during the evening. Each time it had been a waltz and Roxanne felt as if she had been floating on air, his nearness giving her such pleasure that she felt she could melt into his body. The feeling was so perfect that she knew she could become his lover easily. There would be no hesitation on her part, because already she felt as if she belonged to him, in his bed, in his arms. He had called her a clever actress, but he gave such a convincing display of affection towards his fiancée that Roxanne might have been deceived herself had she not caught a hint of mockery in his smile once or twice. It was as if he were showing her that he, too, could play his part.

What was in his mind? What did that look mean?

Sometimes she thought he was like a cat playing with a bird it had caught in its claws.

'Have you enjoyed this evening?' Luke whispered as the hour grew late. 'I believe you have charmed all my uncles and my cousins have fallen in love with you. Cousin Horatio is quite eaten up with jealousy, though I am not certain whether he envies me you—or my grandfather's estate, of which he had hopes before you arrived.'

'Luke…' Roxanne tapped his arm with her fan '…that was not well said of you. Mr Harte was charming to me and told me how pleased he was that you'd decided to marry.'

'Horatio is charming when he wishes to be, Roxanne, but do not be fooled by him. I dare say he is spitting venom in private.'

Roxanne shook her head at him. She had noticed a certain underlying tension between the cousins, but there was often rivalry between gentlemen and she took little notice. Cousin Horatio was one of those staying overnight and she noticed that he was absent for a while towards the end of the ball, reappearing just as the guests that lived locally were leaving.

The earl had gone to his apartments soon after supper, and when there were only a handful of gentlemen left, all of them related and preparing for a last nightcap before seeking their rooms, Roxanne said her farewells.

She went upstairs to her own bedchamber and entered. She'd instructed her maid that she was not to wait up, because she could manage to unhook herself and would not need assistance. However, when she opened the door and walked in a feeling of shock ran through her. It was immediately obvious that the room had been searched.

The drawers had been pulled out of the chest and the contents scattered on the floor, her underclothes, scarves and gloves scattered in little heaps. The armoire had been opened and dresses pulled from the shelves, as if whoever had been searching had been in a hurry. Yet there was more, a kind of venom, almost as if the mess had been intended to punish and hurt.

Since the only things she had of personal value were her ring and the pearls Luke had given her, which she was wearing, there was nothing much for a thief to steal. The silver pots on the dressing table, which were the earl's property, were still there, though lids had been removed and the contents examined.

Who had been here and caused such upheaval? It did not seem to Roxanne that anything had been taken, but it was obvious that someone had been searching for something in particular. Who would dare to do such a thing when the house was full of guests?

Roxanne trembled, a slither of ice sliding down her spine. It was a most unpleasant feeling to discover that her room had been ransacked in this way. What had the intruder been looking for—was it the ruby?

She hesitated for a moment, wondering what to do for the best. It was too unsettling to sleep in her room like this, but she was unwilling to rouse the servants at this late hour.

Luke ought to be told. Roxanne knew that she must speak to him at once about what had happened here. There might still be an intruder in the house. He would know what to do, because the house ought to be checked. If an outsider had broken in while they were all at the ball, he might be dangerous. Perhaps other guests had had their rooms searched.

Still fully dressed, Roxanne made her way through the halls and up a short flight of stairs to the wing where Luke had his rooms. Would he have come up yet or was he still downstairs, taking a last drink with his cousins?

She tapped at his door and after a short pause, during which Roxanne wondered what to do if he were not there, Luke opened his door. He was still dressed in his breeches and shirt, but he'd taken off his coat and neckcloth and his feet were bare.

'Roxanne—what are you doing here at this hour?'

'May I speak to you, please?'

'Of course, come in,' Luke said, then took her arm and drew her inside his sitting room. It was furnished with two leather elbow chairs, a bookcase and a writing table and chair; there was also a collection of paintings of horses, also two bronze figures holding torches aloft, which held lighted candles.

'I am sorry to disturb you, but I did not know what else to do—my rooms have been ransacked.'

'What?' Luke looked startled. 'Your rooms—was anything valuable taken?'

'I was wearing the only items of jewellery I possess,

but the silver pots on the dressing table are all there and they have been opened.'

'Someone was searching for something they did not find.' Luke's brow creased. 'Do you suppose it was the ruby?'

'Yes, perhaps it was,' Roxanne said. 'Whoever it was must have taken the opportunity to search while we were all dancing. I suppose there were so many people about that he was able to slip in without being noticed.'

'Yes, I imagine it must have seemed a good opportunity.' His gaze narrowed. 'You saw no one—you are not harmed?'

'I saw no one and I am not harmed—but I felt uneasy and wondered whether to call my maid to tidy the room or sleep elsewhere this evening.'

'You must stay here for now,' Luke said. 'I shall put on my boots and check your rooms and the downstairs rooms also, Roxanne. I want to make sure the windows and doors are locked, though I prefer not to rouse the guests or Grandfather. I do not wish to disturb him.'

'No, of course you must not,' Roxanne agreed. 'I was not certain what to do, but I hope no one else need know about this unfortunate incident.'

'Mrs Arlet must be told and the servants will know, but it is best if the guests do not learn of this—unless any of them have suffered something similar.'

'Had they done so, I'm sure someone would have told you,' Roxanne said. 'I think it was just my room, Luke—and I believe it must be because of that ruby.'

Luke had sat down to pull his boots on. He looked at her thoughtfully for a moment, then inclined his head.

'It seems the most likely explanation. Unless Horatio wanted to see what he could find to discredit you. He knows what he has lost because we are to wed and he was absent for a time this evening.' He saw her look. 'You don't believe it was him. Well, you may be right. Stay here, Roxanne, and lock the door behind me. I shall take a look at your room and make a tour of the house. When I return we'll talk about this again.'

'Yes, of course. Please take care, Luke. I would not have you come to harm for the sake of that wretched jewel.'

'I shall be perfectly safe. Whoever wants that ruby seems not to mean harm to either of us. There has been plenty of time for him to attack me had he wished it. No, it is the jewel he wants for some reason best known to himself.'

Roxanne went to the door with him and he locked it after he went out. She chose one of the elbow chairs and sat down, but could not rest. As she paced about the room, the minutes dragged by and, when Luke did not return after more than half an hour, Roxanne went into his bedchamber. Luke was not particularly tidy and she noticed discarded neckcloths and a dressing gown lying abandoned over a chair. She sat on the edge of the bed, then laid down, resting her head on a pillow that smelled faintly of the cologne he sometimes wore. Lying with her knees pulled up to her chest, she closed her eyes.

* * *

Movement close by woke Roxanne and she opened her eyes and then sat up as she saw Luke standing there looking at her.

'Is all safe?' she asked, her heart pounding.

'I discovered a window catch in the library that was loose and I believe that may have been how our intruder got in. There was a smear of earth on the window-sill and what may have been a footmark. I think our intruder was bare-footed.'

'He wore no shoes?' Roxanne frowned. 'I remember that Sofia told me shoes are not worn in the house in India. The face at the window in the tower might have been Indian—it all seems to point to the ruby, do you not think so?'

'Yes, it would seem the jewel is important to some-one,' Luke agreed. 'I wish whoever it is would just ask for the damned thing. My concern is for your sake, Roxanne. If he becomes frustrated, he may attack you...'

Roxanne got to her feet. She shivered, feeling chilled and uneasy.

'I'm sorry to have caused you so much trouble. I wish I could remember what happened…why I had the ruby…' A tear spilled from the corner of her eye. 'Who am I, Luke? Am I a thief? Why did I have that ruby? I wish I could remember.'

'Don't cry, dearest,' Luke said softly. He reached out and wiped away the tear with his fingertips. 'You mustn't be upset over this. I'm here. I shall protect you, Roxanne.'

'But why is all this hap—' She got no further for Luke's arms were about her. He drew her close to his body, his head bent towards hers, his mouth covering hers in a kiss so hungry and intense that all else fled from her mind. Roxanne's arms folded about his neck, her fingers reaching into his hair at the nape as the kiss deepened between them. Then Luke was lifting her in his arms, carrying her back to the bed. He placed her amongst the covers and lay down beside her, gazing into her eyes.

'I want you so much,' he whispered passionately against her ear. 'I've wanted you from the moment I first saw you, Roxanne. You are so beautiful and you're mine. I swear that no one shall harm you. I will protect you with my life. You must never be afraid while I am with you.'

'Luke…' she whispered hoarsely. 'Luke, hold me, love me. I want you, too. I love you…'

As soon as the words left her lips Roxanne regretted them. She had not meant to say the one thing she knew he would not want to hear, but her feelings had rushed to the forefront because of her distress and the words had slipped out. She thought that for a moment he stilled, as if he would withdraw from her, but then he was kissing her again, hungrily, passionately, as if his need was as great as her own.

Giving herself up to desire, Roxanne responded to Luke's loving with an equal passion of her own. She had never known that such feelings lay within her, waiting to burst forth in a torrent of need and hunger. All the years of not knowing who or what she was, all the pain, uncertainty and fear, the need to be loved came out of her in a frenzy of wanting and loving. His hands were gentle but firm as they explored her body, seeking out the secret places of her femininity, touching her where no one else had touched her, bringing her sweet pleasure. Her hands moved over his arms, his back, following the firmness of his shoulders and the honed muscles, moving over skin that was now naked and slicked with sweat as their bodies came together in sweet ecstasy. His throbbing manhood sought entry and she felt pain, but then the pain was forgotten in the sweet pleasure of his kisses.

'Yes…' Roxanne moaned as he moved within her, deep and firm, bringing her to such exquisite delight that she writhed and arched beneath him. She moaned and clung to him, her breath soft and sweet as she sighed. 'So good…so very good.'

'My sweet, beautiful Roxanne,' Luke murmured against her ear. 'Such passion and heat. No one has ever made me feel as you do, my darling. You are exquisite, perfect. I want to hold you and make love to you always.'

His words were so tender and loving that Roxanne felt tears of joy on her cheeks as they lay together, entwined, satiated and at peace before they slept. During the night, they woke, loved again, as sweetly and as urgently as before. Roxanne slept deeply, curled into his body, her legs captured and held as he clasped her against him. Her long red hair was spread over the pillows and had entangled itself about him as they loved.

* * *

When in the morning Luke moved her hair from his face, carefully disentangling himself from her limbs that curled about him, Roxanne did not wake. She was caught up in a dream so sweet that her lips curved in a smile of content.

'Love you,' she murmured. 'Always love you…'

Luke knew that she was still sleeping and that she did not know she had spoken. He frowned as he moved carefully about the room, collecting the clothes he needed for riding. He watched Roxanne sleep while he dressed, a look of gravity on his face, then went out, leaving her to rest.

He needed to ride and to think about the future. Roxanne's distress the previous evening had led him into something he had not planned and he was not sure what it meant for the future. In her dreaming state she had spoken of love, but was it real or part of the story she'd invented for herself—and did he want his marriage to be more of a real marriage than he'd intended?

He suddenly felt trapped again. He was being drawn into something that threatened to overturn all he had believed and he could not handle the feelings churning inside him.

He must think about what had happened the previous night and what it meant—and he must question the men he'd had patrolling the grounds. Why had they not seen the intruder and who had been so desperate to find Roxanne's ruby that they had risked breaking into her room when there was a house filled with guests?

* * *

Roxanne stirred and stretched, a feeling of well being stealing over her as she opened her eyes. What had happened the previous night to make her feel so good? Letting her gaze move about the room, she realised that she was not in her own bed and then the memories came flooding back. Suffused with warmth, she felt herself blush as she recalled how gladly she had surrendered to Luke's loving the previous night. She had gone to his arms like a wanton instead of the gentlewoman she was supposed to be, giving no thought to propriety or the future.

What did that say about her? What kind of a woman was she truly?

Sitting up in bed, she saw her clothes strewn over the floor and recalled the way they had come off with such abandon. Indeed, she'd behaved like a harlot. No well-bred young woman would behave in such a way—and yet she did not regret it. Roxanne knew that she would do it again, because one night of love like that was something she would never forget. Even if Luke did not love her in his heart, he'd made her feel loved and needed, and something deep inside her had responded, had been waiting for him. She'd felt as if her whole life had been waiting for that moment—the moment she became one with him.

Rising, Roxanne picked up her clothes and dressed. It was time she returned to her own room. She was about to do so when the door of Luke's bedchamber opened and a maid entered. She did not seem surprised to find Roxanne there and bobbed a curtsy.

'Lord Clarendon said to tidy your chamber, Miss Roxanne, and then inform you that you could return. He told us he gave up his room for you last night because of what happened, miss. It must have been such a shock to find it that way.'

'Yes, it was,' Roxanne replied and glanced towards the bed. The sheets were open, as she'd left them, and she could see some small bloodstains. Her cheeks felt warm as she left the room. Luke had told the servants that she'd slept alone, but the maid would see the evidence of what had taken place here and she could hardly be expected to keep such knowledge to herself. The servants would smile to themselves and whisper that Lord Clarendon had anticipated his wedding night.

It was an embarrassing thought, but there was nothing she could do to change things. She could not go back and act differently, nor did she wish to in her heart. The dice was cast now. She had given herself to Luke body and soul. Roxanne had no intention of drawing back. If Luke did not wish for a loving wife, he would make his feelings known. She loved him, but she was strong enough to let him go when he needed to be free. She would not cling and weep as his mother had to her husband. Perhaps next time Luke came to her bed she would be more prepared and be able to control her feelings, giving herself with less abandon.

Making her way back to her own room, Roxanne wondered where Luke was. At what time had he left her and where had he gone?

Her bedchamber had been put to rights, everything back in its place and the scent of fresh lavender polish making it seem welcoming and normal. A frown touched her forehead as she remembered her distress the previous evening; it was that distress that had prompted Luke to kiss her and carried them both on a tide of passion.

What must he be thinking of her now? Roxanne knew that she had been abandoned, almost wanton in her passion, and wondered what Luke thought of the bargain he'd made. Was he regretting it? Was that why he'd left without waking her, because her passion had disgusted him—or did he simply want to ride in the early morning, as she knew he often did?

Roxanne washed in the warm water she found waiting for her and dressed in a fresh morning gown. She had brushed her hair into a knot at the back of her head and was about to leave when the door opened and her maid entered.

'I did not ring, Tilly,' she said. 'I was able to manage for myself—but if you will take away my soiled things and see to them, please.'

'Yes, Miss Roxanne.' The girl bobbed a little curtsy. 'I've washed all the things that were on the floor, miss, because I knew you would wish it. I came to tell you that you're needed in the earl's chambers. Marshall said to tell you that Lord Hartingdon is a little out of sorts this morning. It may have been all the excitement of last night, miss.'

'Yes, perhaps.' Roxanne looked at her in dismay. 'Is he just a little tired or unwell?'

'I'm not sure, miss. Marshall said to ask if you would come at once—and I think the doctor's been sent for.'

'I see…thank you,' Roxanne said and went hurriedly from the room. If the doctor had been sent for, it was more than just a little tiredness.

Her heart was thudding as she walked along the hall to the earl's chambers. She had become more than a little fond of the elderly gentleman and it would distress her if he were seriously ill. Luke had known that his grandfather was frail; it was for this reason that she had been brought here as Luke's fiancée, but somehow she hadn't expected anything to happen. Indeed, she'd hoped, expected that Hartingdon would go on for some years yet. If he died now…Roxanne shut out the unwelcome thought. She did not wish to think about such a prospect.

Reaching the earl's room, she knocked softly and then entered. His manservant was in the small sitting room, but there was no sign of the earl.

'How is he?' she asked, her throat catching with emotion. 'I was told he wished to see me?'

'His lordship had a bit of a do first thing, miss,' Marshall said. 'I've persuaded him he should stay in bed and called the doctor just in case. His lordship wanted to see you, miss. He's very fond of you—if you don't mind my saying it.'

'Not at all.' Roxanne smiled at him. 'The feeling is mutual. I was most concerned to hear he was unwell. May I see him, please?'

'Go right in, miss. He might be dozing, but if you sit in the chair I've put ready he'll see you when he wakes.'

'Yes, of course. Thank you, that was so thoughtful, Marshall.'

'We're all pleased to have you here, miss. The family and servants both. We've taken you to our hearts, Miss Roxanne.'

She thanked him, her cheeks a little warm. Marshall would never show by gesture or innuendo that he knew she'd spent the night with Luke, but she doubted it was a secret. If her first child was not long in coming, the servants would count the months after the wedding back to the previous night.

The earl was resting as she walked softly into his bedchamber. He was lying back against a pile of pillows, his eyes closed, but as she bent over him to kiss his cheek he opened them and looked up at her.

'Ah,' he said in a satisfied tone. 'There you are, girl. You did me proud last night, Roxanne. I was complimented on Luke's happy choice many times. Most of them seem to think I must've arranged the whole business. I didn't contradict 'em. You're either a truly great actress or you were born to be a lady.'

'Does it matter now, sir?' Roxanne asked. She sat down on the edge of the bed and took his hand. 'It was a tiring evening for you. I hope you mean to be sensible and keep to your bed for a few days?'

'You're right, it don't matter where you came from,' he said and sighed. 'You'll make a good mother for my boy's children and that's what counts. I'm not sure he'll make you a good husband, but you took him on and I think you'll see it through. You won't let me down?'

'Do I look like a bolter?'

He gave a harsh laugh. 'It's a while since I heard that expression. Luke's godmother used it when she was younger. She didn't come to the ball. I was disappointed that she stayed away. Her influence on Luke was always for the good—but I suppose I scared her off with my harsh tongue. I must make it up to her before the wedding. I've mellowed a bit. In the old days I was sharper than a razor.'

'I'm glad you've mellowed, sir.'

There was a hint of laughter in her voice and his brow lowered. 'Are you mocking me, miss?'

'Just a very little, sir. Do you not think it is time that someone did? Perhaps you have taken yourself a little too seriously at times—would you not say so?'

He glared at her, then made a sound between a snort and a guffaw. 'You're a minx, Roxanne. Think you've got me eating out of your hand, do you? I'm not to be fooled by a few smiles, miss.'

'Why would I wish to fool you, sir? All I wish for is that we should live together happily as a family. I want to make you happy.'

'Want to make Luke happy too?' He raised his bushy brows at her. 'Planning on getting him to settle down to married life—is that it?'

'I am not sure that would be possible,' Roxanne replied honestly. 'However, it seems to me that you are very alike, sir. If what you both want is an heir for the family, I shall do my best to oblige.'

'And what do you get out of it?' The earl's eyes were very bright. He was intent as he waited for her answer.

'A home and perhaps affection,' Roxanne said. 'I shall make no demands on you or your grandson, sir—but if things go well I shall have children and perhaps they will give the unconditional love both you and Luke seem incapable of giving.'

'Will that satisfy you, girl?'

'I think it may have to,' Roxanne replied. She saw his eyelids flicker and moved to the chair beside the bed. 'You should try to rest for a little before the doctor comes, sir.'

'You're a fine girl, a decent girl,' the earl said. 'I'm not sure we've been fair to you. This is a selfish family, Roxanne. I think you deserve better.'

He closed his eyes and she saw that he was drifting into sleep. It had been a huge effort for him to attend the ball and he was very tired. She hoped that he was not actually any worse than before. Perhaps all he needed was a little rest.

Luke was greeted by the news that the doctor had been called when he returned from riding. He threw his crop and gloves on the sideboard in the hall and took the stairs two at a time. When he entered his grandfather's sitting room, Marshall was just tidying the grate with a small brush. He put a finger to his lips.

'He's sleeping at the moment, sir. Miss Roxanne has been with him for the past two hours. The doctor came and said he was exhausted. He's not to be upset and he must rest for at least a couple of weeks. Miss Roxanne was reading to him just now, but I think he may have gone off again for a while, because she stopped. Now she's started again. She has a fine reading voice, sir. Your grandfather was chuckling away for a while there.

Reading Shakespeare she was, but in a way I've not heard before.'

'Thank you.' Luke said. 'Perhaps you have something you need to do elsewhere? I shall sit with my grandfather for a little now.'

'Yes, sir. I'll fetch up some brandy and warm water. It helps his lodship to sleep sometimes and the doctor said anything that made him rest was good.'

'Yes, you do that,' Luke said. He walked to the door of his grandfather's bedchamber and then listened. Roxanne was reading *The Taming of the Shrew* and acting out the parts. He heard his grandfather chuckle and hesitated, hardly liking to intrude on what was clearly an enjoyable companionship.

'You are a wicked minx, as I said before,' the earl said and laughed. 'I think you have missed your calling, Roxanne. You are wasted here. You should be on the London stage.'

'I would much prefer to be here with you and Luke.'

'I think you mean that,' the earl said. 'It isn't just an act with you, is it, Roxanne?'

'No, sir. I am very fond of you and…'

Luke walked in before she could finish. Roxanne was standing at the foot of the bed, a book of Shakespeare's plays in her hand. She was smiling, but when she saw him, her cheeks turned pink and she glanced away from his searching gaze.

'How are you, sir?' Luke asked and went to his grandfather's side. 'I hear the doctor has been to visit you. I think you found the ball too much, sir. Perhaps we should postpone the wedding for a month or two?'

'You will do no such thing on my account,' the earl said. 'It will take place as planned in three weeks from now or I'll want to know the reason why.'

'Please do not distress yourself, sir,' Luke said quickly. 'I was merely concerned for your health.'

'My health is neither here nor there. I did not summon the family here for you to change your mind the next day, Clarendon.'

'Please do not get upset, sir,' Roxanne said and bent to touch his cheek. 'I shall leave you with your grandson—Luke, you should not tire him. The doctor told me it is important that your grandfather rests as much as possible.'

'Of course.' Luke inclined his head stiffly. 'I shall speak to you later, Roxanne.'

'Of course, Luke. Whenever you wish.'

'You'll come to visit me again later, girl?'

Roxanne looked at the earl and smiled. 'Of course. You must have a sleep when Luke leaves you, but I shall come back before dinner.'

Roxanne was sitting in the back parlour she favoured when Luke entered later that day. He frowned to find her alone and asked why she was not in the drawing room with their guests.

'I wanted a period of quiet reflection,' she said and stood up. 'I shall join your Aunt Jane and Uncle Frederick for tea. Most of the others left an hour or so ago. Your Cousin Horatio asked for you, but I was forced to say that I did not know where you were, since I was told you were not with Grandfather.'

'The earl asked to be left alone. He seems weaker than before. I fear that he may not live much longer. The doctor told me that if he takes a turn for the worse it could be his last illness.'

'I know he seems very tired, but the ball took a great deal of his energy. I pray that he will recover. He so longs for an heir. It would be wonderful if he could at least know that a child was on the way.'

'After last night that may already be the case.' Luke frowned, turning to gaze out of the window. 'I should apologise for what happened, Roxanne. I did not behave, as a gentleman ought. If I could change things, I would, but unfortunately we cannot turn back the clock.'

His words stung like the lash of a whip. If the previous night had been as wonderful for Luke as it had for her, he would not need to apologise.

'I think no harm was done since we intended to marry as soon as the banns are called,' she said. 'It need only be a small affair. I see no reason why Grandfather should be forced to attend. He will be satisfied if all is done as it should be.'

'You seem to be on excellent terms. I must bow to your superior judgement in this matter.'

She glanced at him. His lips were white and set in a thin line.

'Are you angry with me for caring about his welfare?' Roxanne asked in a carefully flat tone. His manner was so rigid, his anger barely under control. 'The earl requested that I call him Grandfather. If it annoys you, I can be more formal.'

'Why should you? He clearly likes it and you.' Luke frowned as he turned to look at her. 'Forgive me. I was anxious and when I'm anxious I become angry. I had no right to interfere.'

'You have every right. I have not forgotten the reason you brought me here, Luke—but I find that my affections are engaged. Grandfather has been generous to me with his own affection and I genuinely wish to make him happy. I hope he will rally again, but I know that he could take a turn for the worse.'

'If he should die, you would not need to keep your bargain.'

'Should I not? That would be your decision, naturally.' Roxanne got to her feet. 'Excuse me, I should go and take tea with your family. If you wish to disappoint everyone, you must take the necessary steps, Luke. I gave my word to the earl and I shall not break it. However, I shall not hold you to a bargain you dislike so much. Please inform me of your wishes when you are ready. Now, if you will excuse me.'

She walked out of the room with her head high. Luke cursed himself for a fool. She had been on the verge of tears, but hiding it as best she could. He had hurt her and it was the last thing he wanted to do and yet he was hurting too, so badly that he was striking out blindly. He was so confused at this moment that he did not know what he wanted.

Waking to find Roxanne sleeping so sweetly in his bed had thrown his senses into disorder. She was beautiful, generous and passionate—what more could any man want in a wife? He knew that he had discovered a treasure beyond price and it frightened him. How could he ever deserve such a woman?

One day he would break her heart and she would leave him—she might be killed in an accident because he'd broken her heart. To know that he was guilty of bringing her to such misery would destroy him. If he loved her, he would lose her. Far better not to love than to love too much.

Chapter Nine

Roxanne saw the last of the guests leave and then went upstairs. She knocked at the earl's door and was invited to enter by his manservant.

'How is he now, Marshall?'

'Not so clever, miss. I was just about to send for you to ask what you thought. He doesn't want a fuss, but I wondered if we should have the doctor again?'

'I think he would prefer just to rest. There is very little the doctor can do for his condition, you know. I'll sit with him for a while now. He seems easier when I'm with him, I think.'

'Yes, he does, Miss Roxanne. I've not seen him take to anyone as he has to you, miss, not for years. He's laughed more these past few weeks than he has since his wife died. He became almost a recluse after his daughter died young. If it had not been for Master Luke he might have given up altogether. Yet he found it hard to show his feelings—just as Master Luke does. I know the earl better than most and I can tell you that his heart has been broken more than once.'

'I dare say he missed both his wife and his daughter a great deal.'

'Not that he let on. He just became more buttoned up, if you'll excuse the phrase—but I think you're right, miss. Shut himself off, he did, but he's come back to us since you arrived. I don't know what he'd do without you now, miss.'

'Yes, I think he is happier than when I first came,' Roxanne said and went into the bedchamber. The earl was lying with his eyes shut, but when she sat down close to his side, he opened them and looked at her.

'You've come, then,' he said. 'I hoped you might when they'd all gone. Has that grandson of mine gone too?'

'No, I do not think he plans to leave us just yet,' Roxanne said. 'He cares for you more than you might think, sir.'

'He never showed it before you came. Mind you, I haven't exactly been loving towards him. I was grieving and so was he. We lost touch and when a breach opens up it's hard to cross it. We're both too damned proud for our own good and that's the truth. We can't say sorry—and neither of us knows how to love.'

'I would not say that, sir. Perhaps you find it hard to show your love. I imagine it must be difficult, particularly for two very prickly and stubborn gentlemen.'

'You've worked us out, haven't you?' The earl nodded as she merely smiled. 'I underestimated you when you first came. I wonder if Luke has too. He doesn't wear his heart on his sleeve, girl. I was just the same as a young man. It took my Emily to make me realise what love should be and when she died she took my heart with her.'

'Yet you do love Luke and he loves you. Do you not think you should tell him before it is too late?'

'Perhaps you're right,' he agreed. 'I've held back all my life—afraid of making a fool of myself or being hurt again, I suppose.'

'It is hard for everyone to trust once they've been hurt. Now, would you like me to read to you for a while or would you prefer to sleep?'

'I've all night for sleeping. Tell me about yourself, Roxanne. Tell me about Sofia—and the life you led with her and the travelling players. I knew a young woman by that name once. She was very beautiful, but she never looked at me. Who knows, had she given me encouragement everything might have been different.'

'While Sofia lived I was happy with her,' Roxanne said. 'She was like a mother to me and she took away the dark emptiness inside me. I wish I might tell you who I am, sir, but apart from a vague feeling about India, which may be merely a game we once played, I remember nothing.'

'I can tell you that you're a lady born,' Hartingdon said. 'I've watched to see if you would let the act slip and you never have. If it were an act, Roxanne, you would make a mistake. No, you're a lady—and you love my grandson, whether he deserves it or not.'

'Yes,' Roxanne said softly. 'I do, but please do not tell him that for he may not wish to hear it. Sofia was a lady, too, though she did not care for society. She found the social drawing rooms shallow and too insipid. For her drama and life lived to the full was more exciting than a life of domestic cares. She led an exciting life, but in the end I think she regretted that she had not known a true and lasting love.'

'And you—are you like her, Roxanne?'

'No, I do not think so. I believe I should enjoy a life in the country, devoted to family and friends and the service of others. I do not wish to be a courtesan and have princes fight over me, as she did.'

'You're like my Emily,' he said and closed his eyes. 'Tell me some more…about your acting and…' His voice trailed away and she knew he was sleeping.

Roxanne sat quietly by his side. He woke after a little while and smiled at her, then drifted off to sleep again, reassured that she was there. She held his hand for a while and gave him a drink when he asked.

It was almost midnight when the door of his bed-chamber opened and Luke entered, wearing a long silk striped robe, his feet bare.

'Are you still here?' he said softly. 'You should go to bed now, Roxanne. I shall sit with Grandfather for a while.'

'I will return in a few hours,' Roxanne said. 'I do not want him to be left alone, Luke. It is important that he feels loved and wanted, because then he will have the strength to go on.'

'You really do care for him, don't you?'

Roxanne inclined her head. She wanted to tell him

that the earl was not the only one she cared for, but the words remained unspoken. She'd said too much the previous night and Luke's anger had shown that he did not wish for her love. He had offered her a business arrangement, not a loving relationship. Unless she wished to end it, she must let him think that her emotions were not truly involved. Luke had been deeply scarred; he was afraid of loving, afraid of commitment.

'Yes, I have become very fond of him,' she said. 'I shall sleep because I must, but call me if you need me.'

'Yes, of course. If he wakes and asks, I shall send for you, Roxanne. Goodnight, sleep well.'

Roxanne made no reply as she walked from the room. Her thoughts were with the earl, but as she opened the door of her bedchamber, for a moment she was apprehensive as she recalled the events of the previous night. However, her room was just as it ought to be.

She refrained from summoning a maid and managed to unfasten her gown without help. In bed she lay for a moment, her eyes stinging with tears she would not allow herself to shed. It was her fault for allowing herself to fall in love. Luke had never promised her love, only comfort and a home. She told herself it was enough and then at last she slept.

Roxanne was not summoned to the earl's side that night but at half past six the next morning she went to his room and found that Luke was still there, his long legs stretched out before him as he dozed in the armchair. He woke as she entered and looked at her sheepishly.

'I must have dozed off,' he apologised. 'I do not think he called out or I should have heard.'

Roxanne looked down at the earl. His eyes were closed, but as she bent over him, he opened them and then deliberately winked at her.

'Good morning, Grandfather,' she said and bent to kiss his cheek. 'How are you this morning?'

'Better,' he grunted. 'What on earth that grandson of mine wanted to sit there all night for I've no idea.'

Luke had risen to his feet and was stretching his shoulders, clearly feeling the effects of an uncomfortable night. 'Roxanne would have insisted on sitting with you had I not taken a turn,' he said. 'I'm glad to see you better, sir. I will call and see you later. Please excuse me.'

'Much good he would have been,' the earl said as the door closed behind him, but there was no malice in his words, just a hint of amusement. 'His snoring would waken the dead.'

'I'm sorry Luke's snoring disturbed you. How long had you been awake?'

'An hour or so, perhaps. I hadn't the heart to wake him, but I need Marshall's assistance. Fetch him to me, girl, and then take yourself off for a few hours. You must have something you need to do?'

'I believe I shall speak to Minty about flowers for the wedding,' Roxanne said and smiled. 'You're a sly old fox, sir. If I didn't know better, I would think you had a plan to bring us all to heel.'

'Do that graceless scamp good to think of someone else for a change. He's like me, too selfish and careless of others—but you were right, girl, I do care for him and I shall tell him so next time he comes. No good leaving it until it's too late.'

'I shall see you later,' Roxanne said and went off to summon his manservant before going in search of the head gardener.

After an hour spent in delightful discussions about the various flowers needed for the church and the reception, Roxanne returned to the house. Entering the hall, she discovered Luke reading a letter. He turned to look at her with a frown.

'This is from my solicitor. He writes to tell me that he has had no replies to his advertisement as such—but his office was ransacked by persons unknown the night he stayed here for the ball.'

Roxanne went cold all over. 'You think someone was searching for that ruby? What is so important about it? I know it is valuable, but it is not priceless—or is it? Is there something special that draws others to it?'

'I think we can be certain that someone is desperate to recover the ruby. I should be prepared to give it back to whoever is the rightful owner—if that is your wish?'

'Yes, of course.' She shivered. 'It is a dangerous thing, Luke. I wish I'd never seen it.'

'When Grandfather is well again I shall place another advertisement and offer to return the damned thing to the person who has been searching for it. We shall all sleep sounder in our beds once this business is over.'

'Yes, I believe so,' Roxanne agreed. 'I think Grandfather is better this morning. His health is clearly still fragile, but I believe he was just exhausted after the ball. We should keep the wedding list to a minimum so as not to tire him too much.'

'If I know Grandfather, he will insist on having a grand affair, even if he goes to bed for a week afterwards. This wedding means a great deal to him.'

'Yes, but if we told him we wished for a quiet ceremony I believe he would agree.'

'I'll have a word later,' Luke said. 'You look very well, Roxanne. Have you been for a walk?'

'Only to the hothouses. Minty has been showing me his pride and joy, which are some very rare plants. We were discussing flowers for the wedding.' She looked at him uncertainly. 'You do wish to continue with this?'

'Yes, of course. If I have given you reason to think otherwise, I apologise, Roxanne. I will admit to having a temper and I am sometimes rash when anger gets the better of me.'

She swallowed hard, her heart thumping. He was not saying that he loved her, merely that he wished to continue with the make-believe wedding they had planned.

'Then I shall begin to write out the cards. I will send the family invitations first and you must tell me if there are friends you wish to ask, Luke.'

'You have none you would wish to ask yourself?'

'Perhaps Mrs Mills if it would not be too far for her to travel? I have no other friends or family, Luke, or none that I know of—but I shall content myself with yours. Your Uncle Frederick is a very pleasant man and I like his wife. Some of your neighbours are very companionable and I am sure I shall make friends here.'

'You are quite settled here,' Luke said with a rather odd look. 'I think you would be happy to make it your home, even after Grandfather dies?'

'It is such a lovely house and the estate is thriving, the people honest and hard working—and I should enjoy helping to keep it in good heart. To live as the steward of such a house and care for its people is a good life. Do you not think so?'

'I like London,' Luke said. 'When a man is tired of London he is tired of life.'

'A profound sentiment, Luke. Is it your own?'

'No. I believe it was once a favourite saying of Dr Johnson.'

'Ah, yes. Grandfather spoke to me of Dr Johnson's dictionary, something he would like to add to his library, I believe.'

'I must see if a copy can be subscribed,' Luke said. 'I will enquire when I go up to town—which puts me in mind of your wedding gift. Is there any particular jewel you like, Roxanne? I gave you pearls and emeralds, but you might prefer something different.'

'Oh, no, I am very happy with what I have,' she denied, her cheeks warm. 'I do prefer simple things—a gold brooch for wearing in the mornings might be nice, but I have no particular need.'

'People will expect you to have jewels to match your status, Roxanne. If I did not give them to you, they would imagine I neglected you and my duty. I am very sure Grandfather would have given you something for the ball had I not had my own gift to give you that night.'

'We have been given several gifts for our engagement,' Roxanne said. 'Mrs Arlet told me that a silver tea service arrived from your godmother this morning. Your uncles and aunts have also been generous, and Cousin Horatio gave us a particularly beautiful silver inkstand. Shall I write to thank them all or would you prefer to do it yourself?'

'If you have time, I shall leave you to do the honours,' Luke said. 'There are estate matters enough to occupy me while I stay here.'

'Are you thinking of leaving for London soon?'

'I may go up in a day or so. I should probably get this business of the ruby over as soon as possible, Roxanne. I will arrange for an agent in London to handle the affair. We do not need to be involved ourselves.'

'Yes, of course,' she said, conscious of a feeling of disappointment. No longer angry, Luke was being considerate and generous once more, but he had given her no reason to think that the feelings that had boiled over on the night of the ball had been anything more than an impulse he had since regretted. 'It must be just as you wish.'

'Must it?' Luke's gaze narrowed, becoming brooding and thoughtful. 'I wonder what you would say if I told you what I wish for, Roxanne?' She raised her brows and he shook his head, laughing ruefully. 'If only I knew, my dear. I fear I am an impossible fellow and I dare say you are wishing you had never come to my aid that day in the woods.'

'No,' Roxanne said. 'I have never wished that, nor shall I. You may have regrets, Luke, but I regret nothing.'

With that she walked away, leaving him to stare after her and wonder what was in her mind.

'Ah, you look better, sir,' Luke said as he saw his grandfather sitting propped up in bed reading the latest newssheet from London. 'I wanted to see how you were. I have some business to attend in London, but did not wish to leave until you were over the worst.'

'Running off before the wedding?' The earl looked at him over the small round glasses that he wore perched on the end of his nose for reading. 'Do you think that entirely fair on Roxanne?'

'Roxanne will not mind. She does not expect me to dance attendance on her all the time, sir.'

'No, of course not. She made a bargain with you and she'll stick to it, because she is honest and decent—but there's no cause for you to treat her as if she were a doormat.'

'I cannot think I have done so,' Luke replied, stung by the accusation. 'Roxanne has not complained to me—has she said something to you?'

'She would not complain, but I've had the truth out of her. She told me after that fellow attacked Mr Higgins. The gel doesn't know who she is or where she came from before Sofia found her. She's afraid she stole that wretched ruby, but I don't believe she's a thief.'

'Roxanne told you all this?' Luke frowned, his mouth thinning. 'Did she tell you everything?'

'About the bargain you made to give me something to please me in my last days?' The earl's gaze narrowed. 'I'd guessed some of it and I made her tell me the rest. Did you imagine I should be fooled, Luke? You haven't been behaving like a man who has fallen head over heels. She's a better actress than you—though I'm not so sure she's acting now. She's a tender-hearted woman, Luke—and I don't want to see her hurt.'

'What do you mean?'

'If you're doing this for my sake, perhaps you shouldn't,' the earl said. 'I know I've pushed you towards marriage, but that girl means something to me. If you don't love her, let her go and stop this masquerade before it's too late. I'll do something for her myself. Indeed, she is welcome to stay with me for the rest of my days if she chooses. You can go back to the life you enjoy. I know now that I was wrong to demand so much of you, Luke. It isn't right to force you into marriage for my sake. I don't want either of you to ruin your life for me. That gel cares about us both and I won't see her hurt. If you marry her, make it a proper marriage and forget this foolish bargain.'

'I think marriage to Roxanne would suit me well enough. It is no different to many marriages made for position or money. I doubt I shall ever fall in love or want to settle for domesticity. I'm a loner like my father. It wouldn't be fair to make any woman love me, because I should hurt her.'

'Your father may not have been what you think him,'

the earl said and sighed heavily. 'This marriage and an heir before I die would make me happy, Luke—but I've been selfish too often in the past. I want both of you to be happy and I'm releasing you from your promise. If you marry her, let it be because it's what you want.'

'Thank you, sir.' Luke inclined his head stiffly. 'I shall leave you to rest. You may be certain that I shall give this some thought.'

Luke left his grandfather's bedchamber, striding along the hall and down the stairs. He could feel the anger building inside him. Why hadn't Roxanne told him that the earl knew everything? Why had she allowed him to think that she was still going through the motions of a make-believe marriage?

She was in a plot with his grandfather to trap him into making this a proper marriage. Once his ring was on her finger there would be no going back. Luke could divorce her, but the scandal would be horrendous and he would never be able to face it. Hurting Roxanne would be like inflicting pain on himself. He'd meant it to be a simple arrangement with no ties on either side, but Roxanne had broken the terms of their agreement.

He felt resentful and bitter, because she had taken his grandfather's side against him. He could imagine them smiling over their plot, reeling him in like a fish on a line. How dare she talk about him behind his back?

Luke knew that he was the one who had swept her off on a tide of passion on the night of the ball, but he was struggling to keep his head above water and only by transferring the blame could he justify his own reactions. He'd meant it to be the way it was when he took a mistress, passion and pleasure but no emotional entanglement. Roxanne had declared her love in the heat of desire and it had sent him running in a panic.

He couldn't handle love. Luke's mouth was dry and his stomach was tying itself in knots. Love hurt too much. It was a black choking sensation that made small boys weep in the darkness and cry out for the mother they had lost. He wasn't in love with Roxanne. He couldn't love anyone. He was like his father. She had lied to him by keeping it secret that the earl knew of their bargain.

Roxanne was in her favourite parlour. She was matching silks against a piece of embroidery she'd found somewhere, a look of such perfect content on her face that his fury broke loose in a torrent of bitter words.

'How dare you lie to me?' he demanded without preamble, ignoring the look of shock on her face. 'Have you been plotting together—you and Grandfather? Did you laugh at how easy I was to fool?'

'I have no idea what you mean? Why should I wish to lie to you—or to make a fool of you?'

She rose slowly to her feet, looking as if he'd struck her. It was the way his mother had looked at his father so many times and it made Luke feel guilty. He struck out blindly, because he could not stand to feel her pain.

'You did not tell me that you had confessed everything to him.'

Roxanne's cheeks burned. 'Grandfather made me promise I would not tell you he knew. I could not keep it from him because he guessed a part of the whole and was angry. I thought he would send me away and I did not wish to leave.'

'It suits you to live here as a grand lady, I suppose,' Luke thundered, his expression one of fury and disgust. 'You've been fooling us both, haven't you? Laughing at us all the time. Who are you really? An adventuress out for what you can get? I fell right into your little trap, didn't I? You played me so well, pretending to be reluctant and making me persuade you into marriage and giving me an heir. You must have been laughing at my gullibility all the time.'

Roxanne was deadly white. He saw her hands shaking and knew that she was fighting her desire to weep, but his anger was so intense that he could not control it.

'Have you nothing to say to me?'

'I believe you have said it all,' Roxanne murmured between stiff lips. 'Excuse me. I think I must leave.'

'I'll save you the bother. I'm going to London.'

Luke strode from the room. His temper carried him as far as the stables and then he suddenly felt all his energy seep away. Leaning against the wall, he discovered that tears were streaming down his cheeks and he could not stop them. A choking sob broke from him as he mumbled, 'Roxanne, forgive me. Such a fool. I'm so sorry. So very sorry.'

What had he done? He'd said such dreadful things to her. Terrible, cruel, wicked things that she did not deserve. He knew that she was not an adventuress, nor had she planned this for material gain. Yes, she was glad of a settled home, but she was prepared to give so much in return—all the things that he had lost when his mother died. All the things his soul craved and he feared. He was a craven coward and deserved a horsewhipping for the way he'd spoken to her.

Roxanne would hate him. He had destroyed any feeling she had for him.

She'd said she must leave. In his rage he hadn't listened. Did she mean leave the room—or leave him? Go away for ever?

He might never see her again. The thought sent such a wave of agony lashing through him that Luke groaned. He had not realised what he had and he'd cast it away without a second thought.

Perhaps it wasn't too late. If he went back now and begged her pardon on his knees, perhaps she would stay—if not for his sake, for his grandfather's. She loved the earl. Surely she would not desert him?

Luke strode towards the house. Please let him be in time. If she'd already gone, he would find her. He would find her and bring her back for the earl's sake.

Even now he was in denial. Even now he could not quite admit that he needed her, needed her more than he had ever believed possible.

He had no right to care. He was not worthy of her love. He did not know how to love. She had the right to walk away if she chose, now that she knew him for what he was. His damnable temper and the way he hurt people—how could Roxanne ever love him?

Roxanne had left the sealed note on the silver salver in the hall. Mrs Arlet would find it and deliver it to the earl later. It would hurt him, though she'd promised that she would return to see him if she could one day—one day when Luke was back in London and she would not have to see him or the lashing scorn in his eyes.

How could Luke have said such things to her? Roxanne felt her throat tighten with pain. It hurt so much to know what he truly thought of her. How could he believe that she was pretending to care for the earl? He must know that she loved him. He must know that she loved them both so much that this was tearing her into shreds.

She was carrying one small bundle, very similar in content to that she had taken when she left the camp of the travelling players. She'd had no choice but to take the gown she was wearing, some underclothes and a spare skirt and bodice, but the ring and necklace Luke had given her were left on the dressing table in her room.

She had less money than when she'd fled from Black Bob. She'd had no need of money in the earl's house and none had been offered to her. Instead, Luke or the earl had met all the bills for her clothes and anything else she needed was provided.

She would need to find employment quite soon. Roxanne had packed her things, written her note and left in haste. She had not given a thought to what she would do in the future. Now she realised that she must begin working almost immediately. The ruby had gone and she was without friends. Her dream of becoming an actress must be put to one side for the moment. To eat and have a roof over her head, she must take any work that was offered.

She could not look for a position too close to the estate. People might know her and gossip and she did not wish to cause a scandal for Luke and the earl. There would naturally be some scandal when it was discovered that the engagement was over, but Luke could explain to his family that he'd been mistaken in her; they would sympathise with him and it would blow over after a few months.

Roxanne recalled that they had passed a staging inn on the way here. That meant that the mail coach would call there on its way to and from London. She might just have enough coins to travel a part of the way to London. She could find an inn or perhaps a farmhouse where they were looking for a girl to help with the chores. It was not the life she would choose for herself, but she must make the best of it until she could earn enough to set up for herself. Perhaps she could become a seamstress. She had some talent for sewing and she would prefer that kind of work.

She had left by a side door in order to avoid being seen and made her escape through the walled garden and out into a lane that led through the earl's estate to the village. Once there she could find her way to the staging inn and then… Roxanne choked back her tears and looked about her.

The lane had come to an end. She must either cross over a stile and a meadow, which appeared to be filled with cows and what she thought might be a bull, or go through the wood. She'd imagined the way across the field would lead her to the village, but now she knew she was lost. Hesitating, she avoided the meadow and the bull, which was eyeing her in a way that she preferred not to challenge. If she kept walking, the wood must lead somewhere and eventually she would find a main road or a village where she could ask the way.

She had been walking in the cool shadow of the wood for some twenty minutes or so when she heard something rustling in the undergrowth and then a stick snapped. Someone was close by. She turned her head, eager to find whoever it was and enquire the way, and then something struck her on the side of the head and everything went black.

'Fool,' the voice said as a pair of strong arms caught her as she fell. 'His Highness will be angry if you've harmed her. He gave orders that she was to be taken, but not harmed. May the goddess protect her and keep her from harm.'

Roxanne heard nothing of the argument that ensued, nor was she aware of being carried through the wood to where a closed carriage and four horses awaited. Although she was treated with respect after the first crashing blow, she had no knowledge of what was happening to her, her eyes closed and her face pale as the darkness held her mind.

'What does she say?' Luke asked as he watched the earl open his letter and read its contents. Discovering that no one had seen Roxanne, he had found the letter on the salver in the hall and taken it at once to his grandfather. 'Has she gone away? Has she left me? I think she left nothing for me.'

'What on earth did you say to her?' Hartingdon handed him the letter after skimming its contents. 'You have a careless tongue, but this was more than a harsh word, Luke. She begs my pardon for breaking her promise and regrets she must leave—though she promises to let me know how she is and to visit often if I wish it. Damn it, why does she need to ask? I did not wish her to leave me.'

'It is my fault. My fault entirely,' Luke said. 'Forgive me for hurting you like this, sir. I know you care for Roxanne. I was abominably rude to her and I said things I did not mean in temper.'

'She said we were very alike,' the earl grunted. 'I can imagine what you said, what you thought. You're a damned fool, Luke. You've thrown away your chance of happiness, boy. Couldn't you see that she was perfect for you? She loved you.'

'I know, at least I thought…' Luke caught his breath as the pain knifed through him. 'It was fear of her love that made me cruel, sir. I didn't want to do to her what my father did to my mother. I was afraid of hurting her, of breaking her fine spirit—and I've done just that, haven't I?'

'Your mother should never have married,' the earl said. 'I loved her, but she was a foolish silly girl and your father needed a woman with passion in her bones to help him forget. I should never have pushed them into marriage.'

Luke's brows knit in a frown. 'Help him forget—what? I do not understand you, sir.'

'Your father married on the rebound, Luke. As a young man he was very much in love. Your mother liked him when they first met at a society ball, but he didn't look at her that night. He was in love with Helene Digby, the woman he planned to wed, but she died of a sudden and terrible fever. I believe your father was with her, held her in his arms as she died. He never truly recovered from her death. A love like that comes but once in a lifetime.'

'My father was in love like that—really, deeply in love? I thought him a shallow fellow given to affairs and not capable of love.' Luke stared in disbelief, his memories in disarray.

'He loved too deeply, that was his trouble,' the earl said. 'When I coerced him into marrying my daughter he told me that he couldn't love her. I thought it an ideal marriage for my silly girl. She would live here with me, give me an heir for the estate, and her husband would go his own way. My silly Sarah couldn't let him go. She didn't truly enjoy the physical side of marriage, but she wanted a romantic husband to fuss over her and bring her presents. Clarendon wasn't that kind of man. If she'd had passion in her, she might have held him, but she didn't and so he broke her heart with his affairs. She should have let him go, been content with what she had, but she demanded too much of him.'

'Good grief.' Luke sat down heavily, his legs going weak as the shock went through him. 'I had no idea. All these years I've thought…'

'You thought you were shallow and worthless and I let you believe it. Instead of appreciating your qualities, I drove you away, blaming you for what your father did to my silly girl. It wasn't his fault and it certainly wasn't yours, Luke. I don't believe you take after either of them. You're like me—Roxanne knew it instinctively and she loved us both.'

It was like a light breaking over him, the realisation that he loved Roxanne with all his heart. Tortured by his memories that were false and seen through the eyes of a child, who did not understand what was happening between his parents, he had fought against his love for her. When he realised there was no longer a reason to hold her to her promise, he had lashed out in fear and despair, driving her away.

What had he done? All he had ever secretly longed for and needed had been within his grasp and he had thrown it away.

'I am a crass fool and I have to pray that she will forgive me.'

'She might if you can find her,' the earl said and frowned. 'You rode to the village and enquired, but no one had seen her?'

'One of the gardeners thought he saw her in the lane that leads to the meadow where the cows are. If she'd crossed that, she would have come out on the high road and followed the signs to the east, but there is also the wood and if she took that route she might end up on the road north.'

'Where would she go?'

Luke moved his shoulders negatively. 'She was heading for London when I first met her…'

'You must find her,' the earl said urgently. 'Don't blame yourself for the whole, Luke. I made her promise not to tell you that I knew the truth. I am as much to blame as you are in this.'

'No, sir. Roxanne certainly didn't run away from *you*. I'm the one that hurt her. I intend to find her, however long it takes me, and when I do I shall beg her to return, but it may be too late. Some things are unforgivable and, in truth, I do not deserve her forgiveness.'

'I think she may give it,' the earl said and smiled at him. 'You haven't yet realised how lucky you are, Luke. Roxanne is a wonderful and very loving person. You must find her because if you do not you'll regret it for the rest of your life.'

'Yes, I know,' Luke said. 'I think I must travel to London. Will you forgive me for leaving you at such a time?'

'I'm not going to die just yet, boy,' the earl said. 'Find Roxanne and bring her back for all our sakes.'

Luke smiled oddly. 'I promise I shall leave no stone unturned, sir, but for the moment it seems that she has disappeared into thin air.'

'That isn't possible, Luke. Roxanne was on foot. It would have taken her hours to walk anywhere.'

'Unless…' Luke shook his head. He would not distress the earl yet by suggesting that she might have been kidnapped. Somehow Roxanne had avoided detection, but he would find her if it took him the rest of his life.

Chapter Ten

Roxanne stirred and moaned, turning her head on the soft pillow. She was dreaming and tears were on her cheeks as she cried out, 'Mama, please don't leave us. Papa, why must she die? I want Mama, I want my mother…'

'Your mother is dying of a fever. Her heart is not strong enough to fight it. You should blame me, child. I should never have brought you both out here to this dreadful climate. It is my fault, but you shall not fall victim to this accursed place, as she did. I shall take you home to your aunt.'

'Mama…please don't leave us. Mama…'

'Hush, memsahib,' a soft voice said and gentle hands stroked her brow. 'You are ill, but you will be better soon.'

'Mama is dying…' Roxanne's eyes flicked opened and she saw a face, the face of her nurse. The Indian woman was kind and loving and she was comforted. 'Mama is so ill.'

'That was long ago, little one. Rest now and when you wake you will be well again.'

Roxanne closed her eyes as the soft hands stroked her forehead and she smelled the exotic perfume of flowers and spices.

The dream was changing. She was in a different place and someone was saying she must die. Now she was lost...running from something...someone. Her uncle wanted her father's ruby, the precious jewel Papa had asked her to keep for him until he returned from India. Her uncle had demanded that she give it to him, telling her that she could not look after it properly.

'No...' she cried out. 'Please help me. He will kill me...he wants Papa's ruby.'

A cool dark hand touched her brow and a woman's beautiful, dusky-skinned face appeared through the mist for a moment.

'Do not fret, little mistress,' the woman's soft musical voice soothed her. 'You are safe now. My lord is angry they hurt you so. He will not let more harm come to you. Rest now and sleep.'

'My uncle...he wants the ruby,' Roxanne moaned, her eyelids fluttering as the words came tumbling out. She clutched at the bedclothes with restless hands. 'My aunt said she would steal it while I slept, but he said it would be best if I were dead. He says they will tell my father I died of a fever and the ruby was lost. I must get away...I must get away...'

'Hush, little one. You are safe now.'

'No…Luke, I want Luke…' Roxanne's cheeks were wet with tears as the fever raged through her. 'Please, ask him to come to me. I need him so…' She was sobbing, tossing restlessly on the pillow, her long hair damp and clinging to her forehead.

'The memsahib is very ill,' another voice said. 'Those fools hit her too hard. If she dies, the lord will be angry and he will punish them harshly. She must drink this medicine; it may ease her. She must live or all will be lost. Without her to help us, the ruby may never be recovered and our people will continue to suffer.'

'Give me the cup,' the woman's soft voice said. 'I will get her to swallow your potion, honourable doctor, but she is wandering in her mind and she may not remember where the ruby is or even her own name.'

'It is in the hands of the gods,' the doctor said. 'I shall pray for her life, for if she gives back what was stolen our people may prosper again.'

'Help me…' Roxanne cried. 'Sofia…help me. Papa, why do you not come back to me? I need you…I need you so.'

'Drink this and it will ease you.' The woman's soft voice was close to her ear and gentle hands stroked her face.

Roxanne gave a cry of fear. 'They are searching for me. I'm so hungry and thirsty. I want Papa…if they find me they will kill me.'

'No one will kill you. You are going to get well and strong again.'

'Sofia, please don't leave me, don't die. I shall be so

alone…' Roxanne sat up, her eyes wide open. 'Luke! Please don't hate me. I love you. I love you.'

'Hush then, the medicine will work soon.'

The soothing hands were stroking her brow, helping her to relax. Roxanne knew there was something she must do or say, but she was sinking back into the darkness and a strange lassitude was binding her limbs and her mind. She fell back against the pillows, her eyes closed.

'She will sleep now,' the doctor said. 'We must pray that the fever will leave her and when she wakes she will tell us what we need to know.'

Roxanne felt that she was dying and feared she would never see Luke again. The words she wanted to say were in her mind, but would not come. She was slipping away, away into a deep dark place. For a moment everything had been so clear, but the drug claimed her senses and she slept.

'She has not been seen in the village and she did not board the stage for London. The coachman and ostlers were quite adamant that they had not seen her. I do not know where to look next.' Luke ran his fingers through his thick hair in frustration. There was a shadow of beard on his chin and his clothes were less than immaculate. 'Where could she have gone?'

'She must either have been picked up by a carter or she has walked in another direction,' the earl said, looking at Luke in concern. He'd hardly slept for the past week, spending every daylight hour out riding or walking in the hope of discovering Roxanne's whereabouts. 'She cannot have gone very far on foot, Luke. Perhaps she has found work somewhere, in an inn or a farmhouse.'

'She would not?' Luke stared at him in horror. 'I think she had very little money. I gave her jewels, but she left them behind. She is proud and independent and would take nothing we had given her.' He sank down onto a chair, a look of despair on his face. 'What can I do, Grandfather?'

'You cannot give up yet,' his grandfather said. 'She must be somewhere, either hiding or working.'

'Unless…' Luke held back the fears that haunted him night and day.

'What?' The earl's brows met in a frown. 'You are hiding something from me, Luke. Tell me the truth or I shall worry more.'

'Someone has been searching for that damned ruby. I don't know why, but it is important and these people might do anything to recover it.'

'But she no longer has it. You placed it in a bank in London.'

'The men who want it may not know that—they may think Roxanne has it or that, if they hold her captive, we shall give it back to them.'

The earl looked at him in horror. 'You think she might have been kidnapped?'

'I don't know,' Luke said honestly. 'No one has seen her, but one man did tell me that a closed carriage was seen in the lane near the woods on the day Roxanne disappeared. It is possible that she might have been abducted.'

'Surely we should have been sent a ransom note? They must know she does not have the ruby by now.'

'Perhaps.' Luke shook his head. 'I think I shall search again in that direction. I will ask at the inns and farms, too, anywhere that she might have enquired for work. She must be somewhere and I intend to find her.'

'Yes, you must.' The earl looked anxious. 'If she was kidnapped her life may be in danger, Luke. We shall offer a reward for her return.'

'Yes, I'll arrange it before I leave. I may be gone for a while—you will be all right here alone?'

'I have Marshall and a house full of servants,' the earl grunted. 'I'm not about to die on you, Luke. Get out there and find our girl or neither of us will know a moment's peace again.'

Roxanne's eyelids fluttered and her eyes opened. She looked up at the woman bending over her. Her perfume was deep and sensual and it had become familiar as Roxanne lay in her fever, because the woman had tended her day and night, caring for her when she was raving and out of her mind.

She had thought when she was ill that she was her ayah and that she was a child again, growing up in India with her tall strong father and her sickly mother, but now she knew the woman was a stranger.

'Who are you?' she asked, her voice cracked and hoarse. 'Where am I?'

'My name is Shulie,' the woman smiled down at her

as she eased herself up against the pillows. 'You are at the house of my husband, Prince Ranjit.'

'Prince Ranjit…' Roxanne wrinkled her brow in thought, trying to remember. 'I think…I believe I used to know a Prince Ranjit. We played together in the gardens of the palace in India. My father…my father was the prince's tutor.'

Suddenly, it was as if a curtain had been pulled aside and she remembered everything: her life as a child in India and what had happened when her father had taken her to his sister's home and left her in her aunt's charge while he returned to his work.

'My lord has told me that you were his friend,' Shulie said and smiled at her. 'I am my lord's first bride and he trusts me. He gave me the honour of caring for you when you were ill.'

'I was ill? What happened to me?' Roxanne frowned and then gave a little cry. 'I was in the woods and someone hit me on the back of the head.'

'The prince was very angry that you were harmed,' Shulie told her. 'You must not think that he wanted you to be hurt, memsahib. He remembers his playmate Rose Marie very well and he did not believe that you would withhold the ruby if you knew its importance to our people.'

'That will do, Shulie.'

The man's voice made both women glance towards the door. A man of perhaps five and twenty, dressed in rich clothes and wearing a purple-silk turban with a magnificent diamond in its folds, was standing there, watching them. Shulie fell to her knees, bowing her head.

'Forgive me, my lord. I only wished to reassure the memsahib that she was with friends.'

'So, you have returned to us,' the man said and moved towards the bed. His dark eyes went over her. 'You look better, but I see that you are still not truly well. Shulie will continue to care for you and we shall talk when you are better.'

'Is it the ruby you seek?' Roxanne asked, holding the sheets against her defensively as she looked at him. This man was very different to the thin and gangly young prince she'd known and admired as a child. 'How is your family, sir?'

'My father is sick and we fear his death. Before he dies he wishes to see the eye returned to its rightful place.'

'The eye?' Roxanne was puzzled. 'I fear I do not understand, sir.'

'You may think of it as merely a ruby, but to others it is a sacred thing—but I shall tell you the whole story when you are able to leave your bed.' He turned to Shulie. 'Bring Miss Rose Marie clean clothes and food. She is to be told nothing more until she is able to hear the story from me.'

'Yes, my lord.'

Shulie approached the bed as the prince left the room. 'My lord has spoken. Please do not ask questions, for I may not answer them. I shall bring food, water for you to wash and clothes. You will feel much better when you have eaten.'

'Please, one thing,' Roxanne said. 'How long have I been here?'

'You lay in a fever for ten days,' Shulie said. 'We feared you might die, but the honourable doctor has saved you. It was the will of the gods.'

'Yes, perhaps,' Roxanne said. She lay back against the pillows, closing her eyes as the woman left the room. Ten days. She'd been here ten days—but what had happened just before she was brought here? Someone had hit her on the head, knocking her unconscious—but where had she been and where had she been going?

She could recall running away from her aunt and uncle just before her fifteenth birthday. Her father had written to tell her he would be home before Christmas and would be taking her to live with him.

I've made my fortune here, Rose Marie, he'd written. *It is time I came back to England to live and made a home for us both. The ruby will be the icing on the cake, though I have other jewels and money enough. Take good care of it, Rosie my love, for it is special.*

It was two days after her letter arrived that she'd heard her uncle telling her aunt what he planned for her as she went down to have afternoon tea.

'She is old enough. He wants her and when he's done with her he'll put her to work for her living. She'll not last long enough for her father to find her. If she doesn't die of the whore's disease, she'll be beaten to death.'

'Frank, you cannot do it,' her aunt had protested. *'Rose Marie doesn't deserve to be treated that way.'*

'She should have given me the ruby when I asked her. It's either the whorehouse or the river—make up

your mind. My debts must be paid and that ruby will see us in comfort for the rest of our lives.'

The past was so clear now. Her name was Rose Marie Pearson and her father's name was Captain Peter Pearson. He'd been an Indian Army officer and then left the service to work for a rich maharajah, first to train his private army and then to teach his sons how to be gentlemen.

When her gentle mother died of a fever, her father had sent her home to live with her aunt and uncle. He'd sent the ruby to her a year or so later with a special messenger he trusted. She had been so proud of being trusted to care for the jewel, but her aunt had seen her admiring it and demanded to know where it came from.

'Papa sent it to me. He told me to take great care of it, because it is worth a small fortune.'

'It is far too valuable to entrust to a young girl. Your father meant me to look after it for you, Rosie.'

'No, Aunt. Papa told me to wear it inside my gown always and never be parted from it. If he'd wanted you to care for it, he would have sent it to you. He trusted me, not you and my uncle.'

'How dare you speak to me that way?'

'The ruby is mine. I shall not give it to you or anyone.'

Even then, Rose Marie had not trusted her aunt and uncle. They had called her Rosie and she had disliked the name, but they had said her own was too fanciful. She'd known instinctively that if they once had the ruby they would keep it, but she had not dreamed they would kill her to get it. She'd run from them that very moment, clutching the ruby and in fear of her life.

Roxanne's mind was clear now and she recalled that she'd run until she could run no more. After that she'd wandered for days, perhaps weeks, always in fear of being caught, hungry, thirsty and cold. Then one night as it grew dusk a vagrant had attacked her and attempted to rape her. She'd fought him off and run away into the night with no more than a few scratches and bruises, but the smell of him had sickened her and she'd been terrified. She had not dared to approach anyone to ask for food and she had wandered, her stomach aching for want of food. She had fallen and hit the side of her head. After that she had been very ill. As she starved, her mind became hazy and she could recall nothing until Sofia found her and nursed her back to health.

Sofia…Black Bob…Luke.

The memories slotted into place one after the other. Tears trickled down her cheeks as the names came to her mind and everything became crystal clear. Now she remembered both the past and recent events. She recalled meeting Luke and falling in love with him and his grandfather.

She loved Luke so very much, but he did not love her. He did not truly wish to marry her.

What was she going to do? Prince Ranjit wanted his ruby back—but surely it was her father's ruby? Roxanne did not believe that her father would have stolen the jewel from his employer.

There was still a mystery here to be solved.

* * *

Roxanne seemed to have vanished into thin air. No one had seen her. Luke was met with shakes of the head and blank faces wherever he enquired for her. With each day that passed he grew more desperate. If she were lost for ever, he did not know how he would live with himself. He must search and search until he found her.

'No, sir,' one innkeeper told him. 'We did have a coach stop to change its horses on the day you mention. I recall it particularly because of the odd clothes the servant was wearing. They were foreigners, your lordship. The servant who arranged everything was wearing a white turban and inside the carriage I saw two women, but they were wearing odd clothes, too, and had veils over their faces. One was enveloped in a thick dark cloak, though it was a warm day. I did think that odd—also that she never moved or spoke.'

'I see…' Luke frowned as icy chills crawled over his body. 'You did not notice anything else—any sign that one of the women was captive?'

'I wasn't allowed to speak to either of them, sir—but I did think that the one in the cloak seemed to be sleeping heavily; at least, that's what it looked like from a distance.'

'You have no idea of where the carriage was heading?'

'I think one of them spoke of London, but I couldn't say for sure, sir. It's a while ago now. I doubt I'd have remembered anything if it hadn't been for their clothes.'

'Thank you, you may have provided a clue,' Luke said and gave the man a gold sovereign.

He was thoughtful as he left the inn. If the men who were searching for the ruby had captured Roxanne, they would know by now that she did not have it with her. What would they do next? Pray God they would not harm her.

His search had widened the last few days and this was the first clue he'd discovered, but it was of little real worth to him. If Roxanne had been taken to London, it would be like searching for a needle in a haystack. He must certainly make enquiries, but a team of agents would do that far more efficiently than he could, especially in his present state of mind. He could not concentrate long enough, his thoughts wandering to her smile, the touch of her hand and the knowledge that he felt devastated by her loss.

He might do better to return to Hartingdon to discover whether or not a ransom had been demanded for Roxanne's safe return. Luke was praying hard as he made his decision. He would retrace his steps, make certain that he hadn't missed anything, but first he must send word to the agents who had worked for him on various occasions and instruct them to search for the mysterious owner of the carriage. Surely such a man and his servants could not hide themselves completely. If they were in the vicinity of London or its outskirts, his agents would find them.

Luke saw the gypsy camp gathered on the common at the edge of Hartingdon woods. Suddenly, he recalled that Roxanne had been frightened of the man called Black Bob. It was possible that he had taken her. He might have been following the wrong theory all this time.

Dismounting, he tied his horse to a bush and approached a woman who was stirring something in a large black pot on a trivet over a fire. She glanced at him suspiciously and called out to someone. A man came down from one of the caravans and stood looking at Luke as he walked up to her, his arms crossed and a menacing look in his dark eyes.

'Good day, mistress,' Luke said politely and doffed his hat to her. 'I mean you no harm. I am looking for someone and wondered if you might help me?'

'It depends whom 'tis you want, sir.' The woman spoke in a voice that surprised him; looking closely, Luke was certain she was not a gypsy, as he'd first imagined.

'The man I seek is named Black Bob and he leads a troupe of players—actors who perform all over the country.'

'And what would you be wanting of him, sir?'

'You're not Romany,' Luke said. 'Your voice has a good resonance. I believe you are an actress—am I right? Did you know Roxanne? She lived with Sofia until her friend died.' He saw a startled look in the woman's eyes and knew that he'd touched a raw nerve. She did know Roxanne—or she had once. He moved towards her, taking hold of her arm. 'You do know her. Is she here? Has he got her?'

'Leave me be.' The woman cried, a look of fear in

her eyes now. 'I don't know this woman you speak of—leave me be.'

'Leave her be.' The man who had come out of the caravan moved towards Luke threateningly. 'You take your hands off my woman or you'll be sorry. You damned aristocrats think you own the world. If you persist, I'll thrash the life out of you.'

'I mean your lady no harm,' Luke said and let his hand drop from her arm. He was armed with a loaded pistol, but had no wish to use it, for he would lose all chance of discovering Roxanne's whereabouts then. 'I do not fear to fight with you, sir—but I came here in peace. I am searching for Roxanne and I thought you might know of her.'

'Clear off or I'll bash your head in,' the man said fiercely, but another man had come up to them and the first moved back out of respect or fear. 'We've told him nothing, Bob.'

'Quiet, fool,' the tall dark-eyed man grunted. He scowled at Luke. 'Run away from you, too, has she? She's an ungrateful wretch and a thief. Has she taken something of yours?'

'No. Roxanne is not in trouble with me. I am afraid her life may be in danger. Why do you call her a thief?'

'*He* told me she had something that belonged to him.' Black Bob's eyes narrowed. 'I saw it once before Sofia hid it—a huge ruby bigger than a pigeon's egg. Stands to reason a girl like that weren't the rightful owner of a valuable jewel. *He* told me if I knew where she was he would pay me so I gave him the direction of the house she was living in. Followed you, I did, out of curiosity.

When they come looking for her I knew something didn't smell right. There alus was somethin' odd about the girl.'

'Where is she? Have you got her?'

'I ain't got her. She's got the mark on her—I wouldn't have her now if she came crawling on her knees.'

'What are you talking about?'

'She's cursed. *He* told me that whoever has the ruby is cursed. Until it is returned to its rightful place the mark of doom is on anyone that touches it.'

'Whoever this man is, he meant to scare you,' Luke said scornfully. 'Roxanne is not a thief. She was given the jewel to keep for someone. Tell me, was the man who offered you money for information an Indian?'

'I reckon he might be. He were dressed much like you, a wealthy man—but his servants were dressed strange and their faces were darker than his. Some of them wore turbans on their heads and one had a curved sword hanging from his belt. They looked a strange lot and I didn't trust them, though he paid me my money.'

Luke inclined his head. He believed Black Bob was telling the truth. It tied in with what the innkeeper had said and pointed towards the ruby. Roxanne had been kidnapped because of that damned jewel.

'If this man speaks to you again, tell him to come to me at Hartingdon. I shall give him what he wants, but first he must release Roxanne. If anything has happened to her I shall punish him—and you.'

'All I done was tell him where he could find her.'

'Roxanne was once one of your people. If you cared for her at all, you would have come to us and told us about this man instead of betraying her.' Luke's eyes flashed scorn. 'You are a greedy rogue and deserved to be punished. I cannot prevent you from camping here, but I would not advise you to return once you leave.'

He was furious as he mounted his horse and rode off. It had taken all his strength of will not to go for the man and give him a good hiding. Only the knowledge that there were more than a dozen men watching him prevented him from seeking physical revenge. The whole tribe would no doubt have set him on and it was more important to keep searching for Roxanne than to make a fool of himself by indulging in a fight merely for his own satisfaction.

Feeling frustrated by his inability to discover Roxanne's whereabouts and afraid of what might be happening to her, Luke rode towards his grandfather's house. It was six days since he'd last visited. Perhaps there might be some news. The earl might have received a ransom note. He must speak to his grandfather before going out to search again, though he did not truly know where to look next. He'd tried every posting house, every inn and every village within a thirty-mile radius of the estate. He was beginning to think she must be in London—or, worse still, on a ship bound for India. Her beauty would be appreciated by certain men who thought nothing of holding women captive in their households.

No! It must not be. The thought was so terrible that it tore him apart, a groan leaving his lips. Rumours and tales of the white-slave trade passed through his mind. Roxanne was so beautiful. Once this man had her, he might think she was of more value than that damned ruby.

* * *

Roxanne looked at the clothes Shulie had brought her and smiled. She had wondered if she would be given something similar to the clothes her nurse wore, but instead she was being offered a beautiful silk gown of French design and make. As she slipped it on, her heart raced wildly. She had remembered more about Prince Ranjit and she seemed to recall that he was charming, but a little selfish, inclined to lose his temper if he did not get his own way. Yet as a child she had admired him, following him about and hanging on his every word. He had grown up to be a handsome man with an exotic and slightly dangerous air.

What did he want to tell her himself? Why had he not allowed Shulie to tell her about the ruby?

She decided to fasten her hair back in a severe knot at the nape of her neck, but, glancing at her reflection, Roxanne knew that it did not make her look any less attractive. The gown was so very elegant and flattering that she needed no jewels to appear to advantage.

'The memsahib is beautiful,' Shulie said and looked at her oddly. 'My lord has always admired you—and I think he looks for another wife. I have been his wife for nine months and I have given him no sons.'

'Nine months is not long,' Roxanne said and smiled. 'You do not need to fear me, Shulie. I would not seek to take your place. I am grateful for all you have done.'

'My lord does not acknowledge the word no,' Shulie replied and looked doubtful. 'If he wants you, he will take you for his wife.'

'At home Prince Ranjit may soon rule in his father's

place,' Roxanne said. 'This is England and he cannot take me as his wife against my will. Besides, I am already promised to another man. I am betrothed. I do not think Prince Ranjit would take the wife of another man.'

'No, perhaps not, if you belong to another.' Shulie's face cleared and she handed Roxanne a spangled drape to wear over her head and shoulders. 'If my lord wished you for his wife, I think I should not mind too much. You are lovely of nature as well as face; there are some who look for the honour who do not deserve it.'

'Perhaps the prince will be satisfied to have just one wife.'

Shulie shook her head sadly. 'It is the custom for a man to take several wives. If I had given him a son, my place as his chief wife would be assured, but now he may put another in my place.'

'You must make him understand it would hurt you. If he loves you, you will remain the first in his heart even if he takes other wives.'

'Perhaps.' Shulie beckoned her. 'We should not keep my lord waiting, memsahib. I know he will want you, but if you belong to another perhaps he will not insist that you become his wife.'

Roxanne's heart raced as she followed Shulie out of the room and along the hall. There was no point in thinking of trying to escape. She had no idea of where she was being held and the prince's men would be watchful. They had not gone to the trouble of kidnapping and then nursing her when she was in a fever simply to allow her to escape. The prince wanted something. Roxanne must pray that it was only the ruby he required from her. She knew that Shulie believed he wanted her for his second wife, but Roxanne had no intention of being taken off to India to live in a harem as one of the prince's wives.

'Nothing,' the earl said and shook his head. 'I cannot understand it, Luke. How could she have disappeared so completely? Had she been seen walking the roads we should have heard. She has not visited an inn or attempted to buy food at the markets or someone would have reported it to us for the reward money. I fear that she is either dead or kidnapped.'

'From what I now know, I think she was taken by the servants of a wealthy Indian man,' Luke said, his mouth pulled into a grim line. 'I believe they want the ruby. It may have some religious significance, but that is merely a guess. Why they did not simply come and ask for the damned thing I do not know. I would willingly have given it.'

'That gypsy fellow told you it is cursed,' the earl said and his hand trembled. His eyes held an urgent appeal as he said, 'You don't think…she's not dead, is she? Our girl's not gone?'

'No, Grandfather. I'm sure she is still alive. I would know if she were dead.' Luke ran tormented fingers through his thick hair. He had dark shadows beneath his eyes and his face looked haggard from lack of sleep. 'She can't be dead. She must be a prisoner somewhere. I'm certain she would have written to you otherwise. It is too cruel to just disappear like this. I do not believe

Roxanne is that careless of another's feelings, especially someone she cares for. If she could have got word to us, she would by now.'

'We must pray for her safe return,' the earl said. 'Have your agents heard nothing?'

'I shall ride to the village and ask if there is a communication for me,' Luke said. 'Do not look so distressed, Grandfather. I shall find her. I swear to you that I will never rest. She shall be brought home...' The words he added in his own mind were not meant for his grandfather's ears.

Even if she is dead I shall find her body and bring her home to us. His throat closed and the agony in his mind was fearful. *Roxanne, my love, please be alive. Your death will kill him...and me.*

'Come, sit here near me,' Prince Ranjit said and captured her hand, leading her to an elegant little sofa. He took the gilded chair just opposite and waited for her to sit before sitting himself. She recalled that his father the Maharajah Jankara had had impeccable manners and he, too, behaved as a gentleman should. 'Please tell me what happened to you, Miss Pearson. My father has been trying to find you for many months. Your family had no knowledge of your whereabouts and believed you dead.'

'Some years ago I found myself in danger and I ran away from my aunt's home. I became very ill and was rescued by a wonderful lady; she cared for me and became like a mother to me. Her name was Sofia and she lived with a band of travelling players. She had been a lady and the mistress of aristocrats and princes and we travelled together until she died.'

The prince nodded and Roxanne realised he already knew this part of her history. Somehow he or his agents had managed to trace her, not only to the camp, but also to the Hartingdon estate. He wanted to know the things his men had not already discovered about her life.

'My father gave me a ruby to keep for him, your Highness,' she said. 'He said I must keep it with me always because it would make our fortune. He was returning to England to set up a home for us. However, my uncle and aunt coveted the jewel and they planned to sell me to a revolting man—a man who meant to use me in a way I cannot bring myself to mention. This was the reason I ran away.' She paused, then, 'Can you tell me where my father is living, please? Has he been looking for me?'

'Forgive me, Rose Marie,' the prince said and leaned forwards to touch her hand. 'Your father believed you dead—a letter came from your uncle saying that you had run away and were believed to have died of a fever in the poorhouse. They said you had the ruby with you when you left—did you?'

'Yes, I took the ruby when I fled—but my father?' Roxanne's throat tightened. 'Please tell me, sir.'

'Your father *had* planned to return to England and make a home for you. However, when he believed you dead, he decided to remain in India. He left my father's employ and lived in solitude doing good works amongst the poor and sick. He died of a fever about eighteen months ago.'

'My father is dead?' A single tear trickled down Roxanne's cheek. For years she had forgotten the tall handsome man she'd adored as a child, but the last few days had brought him back to her. It hurt to know that he had died not knowing that she was alive and well. 'Then I shall never see him again.'

'I am so sorry to be the bearer of this sad news,' the prince said and touched her hand again. 'When he knew he was ill, Sahib Pearson left you a letter and also a small inheritance, which I have placed in a bank in London for you. You see, in the last months before he died, he had begun to believe you were not dead, though his reasons for this belief are not clear. He sent the letter with another of explanation to my father and asked that you might be searched for. It was then that he told my father of the ruby he'd given you. It was only at that time that my father learned yours had possessed the eye for a time. My father sent his men to England to search for you, but it was many months before we traced you to the camp of the travelling players and by then you had disappeared once more.'

'You did not begin your search until eighteen months ago?'

The prince shook his head. 'Until we had your father's letter, the eye was thought lost and you were believed to have died.'

'The eye? Was it stolen? Surely my father would not have stolen from yours?'

'No, the ruby did not belong to us—it is the eye of the goddess Bersheira and it was stolen by thieves who raided the temple. My father believes that your father

bought the eye in good faith. He did not know that it
was stolen from the goddess, for he would never have
bought it and given it to you. Until the eye is returned
to its rightful place, all those who touch it are cursed.
Since it was stolen the people of our province have
suffered in many ways: sickness, fires in the villages,
mysterious deaths and other evils. They believe that
they will be cursed until the eye is returned and it was
for this reason that my father decided to send me to
discover you and the eye. I arrived in England only a
few weeks ago. Our men had failed and it was I who
finally discovered the man who revealed your whereabouts to me.'

'Black Bob—was it he who told you?'

'The leader of the travelling players, yes. I had
advertised with posters for a missing girl who disappeared five years ago and offered gold for information
of her whereabouts. We had heard vague whispers of a
girl travelling with the players, a girl who had lost her
memory, and I wondered if it might be you. But until he
came to me I had no idea of where you might be. Then
I saw the advertisement for a lost jewel and I began to
link the pieces together. When that rogue told me you
had a fabulous jewel I was sure it must be you.'

'Why did you not simply come to me and ask for its
return? Was it necessary to kidnap me?'

'You must forgive me, Rose Marie. It was not my
men who attacked you—though we took you from the
aggressors and brought you here.'

'Not your men? I do not understand.'

'My father has a brother—my Uncle Sangyo,' the

prince said and looked angry. 'He is a ruthless man and covets my father's throne. Sangyo believes that, if he finds the eye and returns it to the goddess, the people will place him on the throne when my father dies instead of me.'

'So it was your uncle I saw in the tower—it was he who tried to break into the earl's strong room and he that hit the bailiff?'

'I fear this may be so,' Prince Ranjit said. 'I was in London for a time on other matters and, when I was informed of your whereabouts, did not immediately send men to the earl's estate to watch for you. When I did, they reported to me that Sangyo was lurking, intent on mischief. I decided to let him make his move and then punish him. Until he tried to abduct you I could not prove he was guilty of anything. He has been made a prisoner and sent home, to be punished by my father. It was necessary to do this or he would have remained a threat to us all.'

'Yes, I understand,' Roxanne said. 'Though I cannot help wishing that you'd acted sooner for you might have spared me an unpleasant illness, sir. Had you asked for the ruby it would have been given to you.'

'I have suffered for your suffering,' the prince told her. 'I must beg your forgiveness and shall do what I can to make reparation for your pain. I am sincere in my regret, Rose Marie.' He hesitated, then, 'Do you still have the ruby?'

'No, I gave it to my fiancé. Lord Clarendon has placed it somewhere for safekeeping. He will, of course, give it to you if you take me to him and offer him proof of your identity. I remember my friend Prince Ranjit, but the years have changed us both, sir. I think Lord Clarendon would require proof that you are the prince before giving you the ruby.'

The prince frowned. 'It is easy enough for me to supply proof of my identity, but this man—Lord Clarendon—he is truly your husband?'

'Yes—at least, we are legally betrothed and intend to be married soon, sir.'

'I see…then it is my duty to take you to him,' the prince said. He gave her a brooding look that told of his displeasure in the discovery that she was betrothed to another. It seemed that Shulie was right to suspect the prince had entertained ideas of making her his second wife. 'I am disappointed. I had hoped we might renew our friendship—the warm affection we had as children, Rose Marie.'

'I am called Roxanne these days,' she said and smiled at him. 'You are right to think I remember you with affection, sir. You were as a brother to me when I lived at the palace and we played as children. I have to thank you and Shulie for your care of me, Highness. I believe that your wife saved my life. She is both beautiful and wise. I think she will give you handsome and clever sons.'

'We have no sons yet,' the prince said and frowned.

'You will have sons, I am certain of it,' Roxanne said. She hesitated, then, 'Perhaps it is the curse of the eye that has prevented you from having a son thus far, sir. When you return it to the goddess, she will favour you and your wife will give you healthy sons.'

The prince looked struck by her words. He took her hand, bringing her to her feet, then bowing to her before placing a kiss on the back of her hand.

'The Lord Clarendon is a fortunate man,' he said. 'I envy him his wife, Rose Marie. Your words are wise and I am sure that you speak truly. It was my destiny to find the eye and restore it to the goddess. When this is done, Shulie will give me sons.'

'Yes, I am certain this is your destiny, sir.' Roxanne smiled at him. 'If you would please take me to Hartingdon, I shall arrange for the eye to be returned to you.'

'I shall escort you myself,' the prince said. 'It has been a privilege to speak with you, Rose Marie. If things had been otherwise...but a betrothal is sacred and I must follow my destiny.'

Chapter Eleven

Luke sighed as he dismounted and gave the reins of his horse into the hands of a waiting groom. He was tired and hungry and, as he noticed the carriage and horses waiting in the courtyard, resentful of whoever had come calling at such a time. He was in no mood for visitors. What he needed was a hot bath, food and some sleep. His search had once more been in vain and he was beginning to think he would never see Roxanne again. The thought was like a heavy weight, dragging him down.

'My lord…' the groom began, but Luke waved him away in frustration. 'But, my lord…'

Ignoring the man's attempt to attract his attention, Luke walked into the house. He was heading for the stairs and his own room when Mrs Arlet came rushing into the hall.

'Thank goodness you're back, sir,' she cried. 'She's

home, my lord. Miss Roxanne is in the back parlour with the earl this very minute.'

'Home? Roxanne is here?' Luke stared at her in disbelief. A great wave of euphoria and relief rushed over him, making him weak. He had been at the end of his tether, afraid that she must be dead, and now he could hardly believe she was here. He must go to her at once, tell her how sorry he was for the things he had said to her. If need be he would beg for her forgiveness.

Flinging open the parlour door, Luke stopped abruptly on the threshold as he saw that his grandfather and another gentleman were in conversation but there was no sign of Roxanne. Luke instantly recalled the stranger as being the rich Indian he'd seen in the jeweller's shop in London. Where was Roxanne? Had she run off again?

'Where is Roxanne?' he burst out as his heart suddenly plummeted in fear. 'I was told she was here.'

'Luke,' the earl said and both he and the stranger stood up. 'This gentleman is Prince Ranjit and the son of the ruler of a great province in India. He saved Roxanne from rogues who might have taken her life. His wife has nursed our girl through a severe illness and now he has brought her back to us.'

'Then where is she?' The question came out of Luke in a rush of agony.

'I am here, my lord.' Roxanne's soft tones made him swing round to discover that she was standing a little way behind him in the hall. 'I went up to change my gown, for I wish to return this to the prince.' Luke saw she was carrying a rich silk gown that looked as if it had come from Paris. She was now wearing a simple grey gown that he'd purchased for her in London. His eyes ran over her, seeing her as pale and tired, a shadow of the girl he adored, and his heart caught with pain. 'I am sorry to have caused you so much trouble. Grandfather says that you have been searching for me. Had I been able I would have let you know where I was. It was not possible.' Her eyes conveyed a message that silenced him.

Luke inclined his head, standing back to allow her to enter the parlour before him. He followed and took up a position between the prince and the door, standing rather than sitting, his manner one of belligerence that seemed to say he was prepared to throw the intruder out if he attempted to take Roxanne with him.

'Perhaps someone would explain,' he said in a carefully controlled tone, his hands clenched at his sides. 'You seemed to have disappeared from the face of the earth, Roxanne.'

'Yes, I think the prince wanted to keep our whereabouts a secret until he was certain that his uncle's men were all taken and rendered harmless. It was Prince Sangyo that attacked our bailiff and his men that tried to abduct me. I was fortunate that Prince Ranjit was able to rescue me, otherwise I fear I might have died.'

Luke's brow lowered. He glared at the prince, but resisted the impulse to throw himself on the man and strangle him. How dare he sit there looking so pleased with himself—and why did Luke get the feeling that the prince wanted more than the ruby?

'May I ask why that ruby is so important that your life was at risk in the first place?'

'It is a sacred thing—the eye of a goddess—and Prince Ranjit's people have been cursed since it was stolen. My father bought it from the thief. He did not know that it was stolen and I have agreed that we should return the ruby to Prince Ranjit so that he can take it back where it belongs.'

'What proof do you have that he will return the ruby and not sell it?'

At a movement of anger from the prince, Roxanne held out her hand. 'I know you are angry, Luke. Please save your anger for later. Prince Ranjit is my friend. I knew him as a child and he has letters for me from my father and others from his own father. He is the man he claims to be and I trust his word. He is an honourable man, as is his father. I know that the ruby must be returned to the goddess and I beg you to arrange it with your bank, Luke. Please do this for me as soon as it may be arranged. We shall speak of other things later.'

Luke clenched his teeth. She claimed the man was her friend and the accord between them was obvious. From the way the prince looked at her, he admired her, wanted her—and she seemed dazzled by him.

After the way he had treated her it would not be surprising if she preferred the exotic prince to a man who had bullied and insulted her.

Prince Ranjit rose to his feet. His manner was haughty as he approached Luke.

'May I assure you that my father was willing to pay

the price asked so that the ruby could be returned. He would have paid twice its worth to a jeweller—but Rose Marie has given it of her own free will.'

'Rose Marie…?' Luke's gaze went over her, his heart catching. She was so beautiful and she deserved so much more than he could give her. He loved her, but he had discovered his love too late and she must hate him. 'Is this what you truly want, Roxanne?'

'Yes, of course it is. You know that we always meant to give it back if we could discover the rightful owner. My father has left me an inheritance and the prince placed it in a bank in London for me. I have ten thousand pounds, which is more than sufficient for my needs.'

Now that he had had time to look at her, he saw that Roxanne looked different. Despite her pallor she was confident and sure of herself, with a glow in her eyes that he had not seen before. She no longer needed his help. She had a fortune of her own—and an ardent admirer in the prince. Luke had no claim on her. If she wished to be free, he must let her go.

He inclined his head to the prince. 'Very well. If you will come to the library with me, sir. I shall write a letter to my bank and they will release the ruby into your care.'

'As you wish, sir.' The prince bowed to the earl. 'I thank you for your hospitality, sir.' He took Roxanne's hand and kissed it. 'Should you wish it, my father would welcome you to our palace, Rose Marie. I myself have a deep admiration and warmth for you; it would be my pleasure to serve you if you came to me. May the gods watch over you and keep you from harm.' He shot a look of dislike at Luke and then followed him from the room.

Roxanne stood undecided for a moment, but the earl shook his head at her. 'Let them settle it between them, girl. Sit down and tell me again what happened. Is that rogue truly what he says—and do you believe that it was his uncle's men that attacked you?'

Roxanne smiled, drew her chair close to him and reached for his hand. 'Yes, Grandfather, I do,' she said. 'Prince Ranjit is a terrible liar. When we were children he often lied to us to get his own way, because he was spoiled and a little selfish. We always knew when he was lying and I'm certain I would have known this time. His uncle wants to rule in Prince Ranjit's stead after the present ruler dies. If he could have found the ruby and taken it back to the temple, the people might have rejected the prince and placed him on the throne.'

'Yes, I understand that part of it,' the earl said. 'But why could he not have told us that he had you? You said you were ill?'

'I lay in a fever for some days and then I was weak and unable to rise from my bed. Shulie nursed me and the doctor helped me to recover. When I was well enough to leave my bed, Prince Ranjit told me the truth. I think…' She hesitated, then, 'I believe he may have hoped to make me his second wife. Shulie seemed to fear it, but when I told him I was Luke's betrothed wife he brought me back to you.'

'Where you should always have been,' the earl grunted. 'It was foolish running off the way you did, girl. I shan't demand that you marry Luke if you'd rather not—but your home is here with me. I need to see your pretty face, Roxanne. If you're not here, what is there to look forward to in the mornings?'

'Forgive me,' she said and reached for his hand once more. 'I regretted running off as I did and I think I might have returned sooner had the kidnap not happened. I was distressed, but it was foolish of me. I know that Luke does not love me, as I love him—but I did give my word that I would marry him and I should like to live in this house with you, sir.'

'What about my foolish grandson?'

'Luke must tell me what he wants,' Roxanne said and her eyes shone with the tears she was too proud to shed. 'If he still wants me, I shall marry him.'

'My grandson is a very mixed-up young man and a part of that is my fault,' the earl said. 'I resented him because of his father and I blamed John Clarendon for not loving my daughter.' He sighed deeply. 'I pushed them into the marriage and I almost did the same to you and Luke. Please forgive me and stay with me, Roxanne. You are as a granddaughter to me and I hope you will make this your home—whatever you and Luke decide.'

'I shall be glad…' Roxanne's words trailed away as the door opened and Luke entered. The look on his face was so harsh that she caught her breath. 'Has the prince gone?'

'That damned fellow,' Luke said in a haughty tone. 'He had the effrontery to tell me that he would be happy to wed you if I no longer wished for the connection.'

'I'm sorry he made you angry,' Roxanne replied. 'I believe he had some idea that because we had been childhood friends he would like to make me his second wife.'

'Insufferable.' Luke fumed, his eyes glinting with temper. 'You may think yourself fortunate that you did not have the ruby with you, Roxanne. You might otherwise have been left in a ditch to die.'

'Luke, that is despicable. You should not talk about him in such a disrespectful manner. I believe the prince honourable in his own way,' she replied stiffly. 'I know his father sent him to recover the ruby, but they gave me my father's fortune even though they might have withheld it had they wished.'

'Your father bought the ruby in good faith. It was yours by right, Roxanne, and worth twelve thousand pounds if a penny.'

'I did not want it. Such a jewel could only bring ill fortune to anyone who kept it, knowing its history. The prince will return it to the goddess and perhaps his people will prosper again. They are a superstitious people and the curse may only be in their minds, but with the ruby back in place they may be happier.'

Luke threw her a smouldering look. 'I was merely thinking of your rights. Since you do not choose to take anything I gave you…' He glanced at her left hand and saw that she was wearing her emerald ring. 'You are wearing your ring, yet you left it behind—why the change?'

'I did not wish the prince to think I had lied to him concerning my situation. I believe that he wished to marry me and I wanted to make it clear that I was not free without hurting his feelings.'

Luke frowned. 'I shall not keep you to your promise, Roxanne. I can see that you no longer need me. Marry your prince if that is your wish. I have no right to hold you here.'

'Luke, how could you? You are too cruel.'

'Luke, do not be a fool,' the earl said. 'Roxanne has just come back to us. You should not quarrel with her. Besides, she has decided to stay with me—whatever the pair of you decide between you, Roxanne's home will be here with me.'

'How very convenient for you both,' Luke snapped and turned on his heel, striding from the room without another word.'

Roxanne's eyes filled with tears. 'He is angry again. I did not mean to make him angry. What did I say?'

'He is a pig-headed fool,' the earl said, making a sound of exasperation. 'I fear we are too much alike. It is his pride talking, Roxanne. He will apologise to you when he has cooled down and beg you to marry him.'

Roxanne felt the prick of tears and blinked hard. 'I fear Luke no longer wishes me to be his wife, Grandfather. He never did truly. The engagement was make believe—I would have been his wife only for as long as you lived. Then he would have asked for a separation.'

'Stuff and nonsense. Luke is in love with you, girl. When you were lost he searched for you constantly. He was like a man possessed. He neither slept nor ate and I think, had you not returned, he would have gone

mad with grief. Why should he react so strongly to a
rival if he is not in love with you?'

'You cannot mean it?' Roxanne stared at him in disbelief. 'He is so angry. Surely…was he really in distress
because I was lost?'

'I would never lie to you,' the earl told her and
smiled. 'Go after him, girl. Sort it out between yourselves—but please do not run off again. My heart won't
stand it.'

'I promise I shan't leave you again, sir—though I
think you a fraud. I am certain you will live many years
yet.'

The earl laughed. 'You may be right, especially if I
have good news.'

Roxanne bent and kissed him and then went hurriedly from the room. Where would Luke be? She prayed
that he had not gone off to London in a temper.

His grandfather was right to call him a fool. Luke
left the house with his pride in tatters and his temper
still raging, but he had not gone farther than the rose
garden when he realised that he was in the wrong. Why
must he always quarrel with the woman he loved? The
desolation that had come over him when his search for
her had proved in vain was surely enough to tell him
that his life would be empty without her. He should
have taken her into his arms rather than raging at her,
but the interview with Prince Ranjit had not improved
his temper, and Roxanne's defence of her old friends
had made him snap at her once more.

Yet his honour would not allow him to force her into

a marriage that she might regret. The prince had made it clear that she would be honoured in his country and she had changed since meeting him. Had she rediscovered a lost love? Why did she have that new glow about her? She had always been vibrant and beautiful, but now there was something more—a certainty that had not been there before.

He was a fool and he did not deserve her. No wonder she'd decided that she did not wish to marry him. Why should she? He'd asked her to enter a make-believe engagement, spoken of a convenient arrangement, seduced her and then lost his temper with her. No woman with any pride could accept such treatment. It was not surprising that she'd walked out on him. Now she was back and he had insulted her again. He was a damned fool and he was very much afraid that he'd lost her for ever.

'Luke, please wait for me.'

Turning, he saw Roxanne walking towards him and his heart took a flying leap. The gown she wore was simply cut, but she looked like a queen, regal and proud. In the sunshine her thick luxuriant hair was touched by fire and she was so beautiful that he felt weak with longing. If he lost her, he would have no reason to live.

'Roxanne,' he began hurriedly. 'I know what I said was unforgivable. I had no right or justification for speaking to you so harshly. You have every right to do exactly as you wish.'

'Yes, Luke, I do.' Roxanne raised her head and met his eyes with a cool frank look. 'I am very fond of

Grandfather and I shall not leave him here alone again, though I believe his health is more stable than you may imagine. It is true that he has bouts of illness that could be his last, but he has a very strong will. For as long as he has something to live for he will fight to live.'

'What are you saying?' Luke's gaze narrowed as he tried to gauge what was in her mind. 'Are you suggesting that we should go ahead with our marriage to please him?'

'Perhaps.' She took a deep breath. 'When I left this house that day I felt that your harsh behaviour towards me made a marriage between us untenable. However, after my distress eased, I came to realise that I did not wish to leave Grandfather—or you. I believe I should have returned to discuss the matter with you in a sensible manner had I not been kidnapped.'

She seemed so calm, so in control that Luke hesitated, not knowing what to believe. 'I am not certain what you mean,' he said. 'Are you intending to go on as before—or is this to be a genuine marriage?'

'That is up to you,' she replied. 'My own preference is for a true marriage. I wish for children and—I am very fond of you, Luke. I like you when you are not in a temper and I believe we could go on very comfortably together.'

'You like me when I am not in a temper?' His hands curled into balls at his sides, tension creeping into his voice. 'The evening of the ball you said…I thought there might be more to your feelings than mere liking.' His gaze was intent on her face and he was pleased to see a slight unease dawn in her eyes. She was not truly as calm as she pretended. Roxanne might be a superb actress, but she could not quite shut her feelings out. Making a giant stride towards her, Luke took hold of her, one hand on each of her upper arms, staring down at her fiercely. 'Supposing I want more than mere liking? Supposing I want passion and love—the kind of love that blazes out of control and takes over your life?'

He felt her tremble and she caught her bottom lip between white teeth. Luke smiled, the despair inside him beginning to give way before a new certainty and hope.

'Is that what you want from me?' Roxanne asked, a tremor in her voice now. 'I thought you did not wish to commit to such feelings? You said you did not believe in romantic love, only passion.'

'It was my belief that I could never truly love,' Luke said and smiled. 'Grandfather speaks the truth when he calls me a fool, Roxanne. Everything I ever wanted was there—mine for the taking—but I did not have the sense to see it. Only when I thought you lost, perhaps dead, did I begin to understand how deep my feelings for you actually were. I love you, Roxanne. Not mildly or with fond affection, but with a passion I hardly know how to control. I find the idea of life without you appalling. I want to see you every day, to wake up and find you beside me in my bed—to know that you are mine and always will be.'

Roxanne held back a sob, her face pale and tense. 'Luke, I do love you. You must know it. Surely you must have known that night?'

'I discovered something so sweet in your arms that night,' he murmured huskily, his arms going about her waist as he pulled her close. 'Yet I feared it. I fled from you before you woke because I was terrified of letting you discover my vulnerability. I was uncertain whether you truly loved me.'

'You must have known when I clung to you and held nothing back? Surely you knew then?'

'Yet you so rarely let your feelings show. You are a clever actress, Roxanne. It might have been an act—and it was not all fear that you did not feel as I did; I was afraid that I would hurt you, destroy you, if I allowed myself to offer you a true marriage. I believed my father shallow and thought I might be as he was, but I misjudged him. He lost the woman he truly loved and married my mother just to have an heir for the earldom. He could never love his wife because his heart was in the grave with his one true love. When I thought you might be dead, I knew just what my father felt, Roxanne. Even had I married for an heir in years to come, I should never have loved another woman. You mean everything to me; if you leave me, I shall have nothing left to give anyone.'

'Oh, Luke…' Roxanne's voice caught and a tear escaped, sliding down her cheek. He wiped it away with his fingertips and then bent to kiss her lips. She gave a little moan and pressed herself against him, melting into him so that he felt as if they were one person, one being. 'Luke, my dearest. When I recovered my senses I knew all that I had lost and I feared I might never see you again. Shulie believed the prince meant to make

Make-Believe Wife

me his wife and for a short time I feared he might take me with him whether I wished it or not.'

'But you admired him. I saw it in your eyes—and there is something different about you…'

'I know who I am now, Luke. Before I wondered if I might be a thief or worse. I was not sure that I was good enough to be your wife and the mistress of this house.'

'Grandfather knew you were a lady born. He saw quality—as I did had I the sense to realise it.'

'Yes, but I did not know. I wanted to be worthy of you, Luke. Now the shadows of the past have gone and I know who and what I am.'

'The notion of India was more true than you knew?'

'My father was the prince's tutor. When my mother died of a fever my father brought me home to live with my aunt and uncle—but her husband was a greedy rogue. When Papa sent me the ruby to keep for him, my aunt saw it and her husband was ready to give me to a man who would have used me for his pleasure and made me work as a whore until I died of some disease. I heard him telling her it was either that or he would kill me himself.'

'Damn him! If I'd known, I would have killed him myself!'

'My aunt pleaded with him, but she was frightened of him. I ran away that night. I was afraid he would catch me and I ran and ran for a long time…then I was attacked by a vagrant and after that I became ill and I must have wandered in a daze. I remember now that I told Sofia some of the story when I was ill, just little things about India. I cried for my mother and my ayah.'

'Why did she not tell you later?'

'Perhaps because she knew it distressed me to try to remember. She invented the game to try to jog my memory, but it did not work and so she decided that it was best to forget the past. She loved me and wanted to keep me safe. Because she feared for me she tried to keep my past a secret, and that is why no one found me for a long time, even when the prince's men began to search. When she was ill she told me she was sure I was a lady and that I should sell the ruby and set up with a companion. She hoped I would marry well.'

'She thought you enamoured of the prince,' Luke said, a hint of jealousy in his voice.

'I was but a child when we were friends,' Roxanne said and smiled at him. 'Sofia asked me about the prince once, but I could not recall him, though I must have said something to her when I was rambling. When she spoke of him I thought she meant one of her lovers, because when I recovered from the fever I had no memory of anything.'

'He remembered you. He wanted you.'

'Then why did he not simply take me? I should have found it difficult to escape had he decided to keep me.'

'He wanted the ruby more,' Luke said. 'He knew that I would never give it up while he had you and that's why he brought you back to me.'

'Yes, perhaps, though I believe he understood that I belonged to you. I know he made you angry, but his father was always an honourable man and the prince did what was right in the end.'

'You may think so, but I cannot excuse the fellow. He had the effrontery to offer to buy you from me,' Luke said, a grim look on his face. 'He said that he would pay my price whatever that might be. I told him that you were a pearl beyond price and not for sale.'

'He tried to buy me from you?' Roxanne was stunned, incredulous. 'Is that what made you so angry?'

'What would you expect? He said that if I was making a marriage of convenience, he would make it worth my while to give you up.'

'How could he?' Roxanne felt a surge of anger. 'He had no right. I am not your property. I am not anyone's property.'

'That is the gist of what I told him, though perhaps not quite in those words,' Luke said. He hesitated, studying her face and trying to read her mind. 'Can you forgive me, Roxanne? Will you give me another chance?'

'Are you asking me to marry you?'

'Yes, of course.' Luke suddenly dropped on one knee before her, gazing up at her in earnest. 'Roxanne, will you do me the honour of becoming my wife? I love you and your agreement will make me the happiest man alive.'

She seemed to hesitate for one instant and Luke's heart sank; then she smiled and inclined her head.

'Yes, of course I shall, Luke. Please get up. There was no need to kneel to me. All I want is to know that I am truly wanted and loved. I do not require homage, nor shall I tie you to me. You may live as you wish, visit London as often as you choose. I ask only that you love me and return to me when you are ready.'

'Unless forced by business, I shall never want to leave you for more than a few hours, my darling.'

Luke was on his feet, drawing her into his arms. He crushed her against him, knowing that she must feel the heat and force of his arousal and he held her pressed into his body. He wanted her to know how fierce was his need and his desire.

'I wanted you from the first moment we met,' he said hoarsely. 'At first I thought to make you my mistress, but…' His hold tightened as he felt her stiffen, pressing her even closer. 'For a long time now I've known that making you my mistress would not serve. I suspect that even when I first asked you to enter a make-believe marriage, I knew somewhere deep inside me that once I had you I should never wish to let you go.'

'Luke…I hoped, but was never certain…'

'You do care for me a little? I know I am far from perfect—but you do truly love me?'

Roxanne smiled tenderly. 'I think I fell in love with you the moment you opened your eyes and looked at me, but I did not admit it until much later. I was afraid that you would never love me—afraid that if you sensed my feelings you would feel trapped.'

'I did for a short time,' Luke admitted honestly. 'I did not want to feel love, because I know that it can bring so much pain. I saw my mother's misery and my father's chafing at the bonds that tied him to a woman he did not love. I was a coward to run from love, Roxanne—but I swear I shall never give you cause to doubt me again.'

'Then we shall be married as soon as it can be arranged,' Roxanne told him. She offered her hand, her eyes bright with love. 'I believe we should tell Grandfather. He cares for us both so much, Luke. Before we came here he was lonely and unhappy. The breach between you was too wide for either of you to cross. Now I think you have reached an understanding?'

'Because of you the breach has closed and we are a family once more.' Luke reached out to touch her cheek. 'While you were missing, our mutual despair drew us together and we realised that we loved each other. Grandfather told me I was a fool and he was right. I had no idea how fortunate I was that day my horse took a tumble in the woods.'

'If I had not run away from Black Bob that day, we might never have met.' Roxanne shuddered and moved closer to him. 'How much we might both have lost, Luke.'

'I think it was our destiny.' He leaned down to kiss her once more. 'Come, we should put Grandfather's mind at rest, though I am certain he already knows.'

'I think the old rascal is truly content now,' Luke said as he took Roxanne's hand. The earl had retired to bed after eating supper with them in the parlour and they were strolling in the moonlight, enjoying the warmth of a summer night. 'He seems much better now, though at times I see that he is still frail.'

'We must make his life as full as possible,' Roxanne

said. 'We shall live here for most of the time, Luke, though I know you have other estates and a house in London.'

'Once I thought the country boring, but it cannot be so when you are here, my love. It may be that I shall have to tend to business at my own estate from time to time and if you cannot accompany me I must leave you here—but I shall return as soon as I can.'

'Perhaps one day we shall spend more time in London or at your own estate, but for Grandfather's sake we must be here as often as we can, dearest.'

'You are as caring as you are beautiful,' Luke said and drew her near, bending his head to kiss her mouth. 'I want you so much. I can hardly bear to wait for our wedding night, Roxanne.'

'And why should you wait?' she whispered against his mouth. 'I do not think you need to consider my modesty or my reputation since the servants all knew what happened on the night of the ball.' She gurgled with delicious laughter and pressed herself against him. 'Take me to bed, Luke. I am as impatient as you—and it is only another ten days to our wedding.'

'Wicked seductress,' he murmured and touched her cheek. 'Since it is too late to save either your reputation or mine, I believe I shall take you at your word.'

'You look beautiful, Miss Roxanne,' the housekeeper said when she brought up the posy of white roses and lilies tied with red ribbons. 'It's a shame that you've no family to share your special day.'

'My family is here,' Roxanne said and impulsively

kissed her cheek. 'You are as a friend to me, Mrs Arlet. Everyone has made me welcome, right from the first moment I came here. If I have no mother, I have my memories and I have my friends. Grandfather is to give me away. Why should I need anyone else?'

'You're a proper lady, miss, and no mistake,' Mrs Arlet said. 'We're all so happy that you and his lordship intend to make this your main home.'

'We shall honeymoon in Paris and we shall spend a few weeks in London sometimes, but I love this house. Lord Clarendon knows that and it is the reason that he has agreed to live here.'

'We are all so excited, Miss Roxanne. His lordship was telling us about the plans he has for bringing the house and estate up to modern standards.'

'Yes, I know. Grandfather had allowed things to stagnate a little, but Clarendon will change all that— and that is as it should be. I know the earl is delighted with the way things have turned out.'

'Is there anything I can do for you, miss?'

'No, thank you. I am almost ready. I shall come down in a few moments.'

'I'll leave you with Tilly then.' Mrs Arlet nodded as the maid entered bearing some floral tributes, gifts and cards. 'We all wish you happiness, Miss Roxanne.'

'Thank you,' Roxanne replied and nodded as she went out, closing the door behind her. 'So many people have sent gifts,' she said as her maid laid the packages on the dressing table. 'Where have all these things come from?'

'Some were delivered by hand, miss. I think his lordship sent this one.'

Roxanne took the small package she offered and opened it, smiling as she saw the diamond-and-pearl earrings, which would go with the pearls he had given her and the bracelet of pearls and diamonds that the earl had sent her earlier that morning. She read the card, smiled and then slipped them into her ears. Looking at her reflection, she nodded in a pleased way. She picked up a posy, held it to her nose and smiled, then indicated another small parcel.

'What is the other package?'

'That came from London this morning, miss.' She picked it up and handed it to her.

Roxanne opened it and gasped as she saw the huge pearl. It was pink, flawless and shaped like a teardrop. Set in gold at the pointed end, it could be worn as a pendant. She picked it up, looking at it as it lay in her palm and thinking that it must be very valuable, then saw the card that had lain beneath it.

For a pearl beyond price, she read and frowned as she saw the signature. *This comes from Prince Ranjit on behalf of his family.*

Replacing the pearl in its nest of black velvet, Roxanne fastened the pearls Luke had given her about her throat.

'I shall go down now, Tilly,' she said. 'Please finish packing my things for me. There are only a few trinkets for my dressing case. Everything else we have not already decided on can remain here. Clarendon says that we should not take too much, because he intends to buy clothes in Paris.'

'Very well, miss.' Tilly couldn't keep the note of excitement from her voice. 'I've never been to France, miss.'

'I visited with friends when we travelled as a group,' Roxanne said with a smile. 'I liked it well enough then, but I think it will be wonderful this time.'

Picking up her posy, she walked from the room and negotiated the stairs with care, her train flowing behind her. The earl and most of the servants had gathered below to greet her. She kissed the earl and then turned to a young woman whom she had met for the first time and immediately liked the previous evening.

'Mrs Fox, I am so glad you could come to us—and I hope you like the gown we chose for you. Luke has told me so much about you. Your husband was his dearest friend and I am so pleased that we are to be friends.'

'It is a lovely gown and it was kind of you to invite me to be one of your attendants,' Beth Fox said. 'Please, you must call me Beth. I owe so much to Luke, as you know. After my darling Harry died and I was left alone with a child and no money, Lord Clarendon found me and provided me with a house of my own. I believe you stayed there for a short time before I moved in?'

'The charming house in Hampstead? Yes, I stayed in your guestroom for a short time. Luke told me your story recently,' Roxanne said with a smile. 'Your father and your husband's family rejected you because they did not approve of the marriage. It was unkind of them to leave you to fend for yourself with a young child to bring up alone. I am glad Luke helped you and I want you to visit with us whenever you choose.'

'Luke is fortunate in his choice of a bride,' Beth said and kissed her. 'Many would have believed the whispers and thought me his mistress—though it has never been so, nor could it be. We both loved Harry and felt only friendship for each other.'

'Luke is an honourable man and those who think otherwise malign him,' Roxanne said. 'Now that you are here for our wedding people will see that they were mistaken. Luke ought to have told Grandfather the truth before, but his stubborn pride would not let him defend his honour. It made him angry because the earl believed the tittle-tattle that you were his mistress.'

'You are all so kind. I was not sure I should be welcomed by the earl, who was a close friend of my father-in-law, but I have been invited to bring my son and stay whenever I wish. The earl is so generous, Roxanne. I am not surprised you are so fond of him.'

'Grandfather has made me welcome here from the beginning,' Roxanne said and went to his side, taking his hand. 'Shall we leave? I should not wish to keep Luke waiting.'

Luke turned his head as the organ began to play. Roxanne had just entered the church, standing at the far end of the nave with his grandfather, Beth and some young girls as her bridesmaids. She was so beautiful. His heart caught with pride as she walked towards him. As she reached his side, he offered his hand and she took it. He smiled and whispered, 'You look lovely, my dearest one.'

'Thank you.'

Her hand trembled slightly and he pressed it as the ceremony began.

'Dearly beloved. We are gathered together to see this man and this woman joined in Holy matrimony...'

The words droned on and Luke gave his responses in a firm strong tone. Roxanne's voice was clear and light, carrying to the rear of the church. Luke reached out to lift the white veiling that fell from her satin bonnet and leaned forwards to kiss her softly on the lips.

They advanced towards the high altar to be blessed and then to the vestry where they both signed their names. Then the bells rang out joyously and they were walking into the sunshine. A small crowd awaited their coming and rushed forwards to shower them with flower petals and rice.

After receiving good wishes and small tributes from the villagers, Luke took his bride's hand and hurried her to the carriage drawn up in the lane. He helped her inside, waiting until the door was closed fast before drawing her into his arms to kiss her.

'My sweet love,' he murmured huskily. 'I was afraid this day might never happen, but it has and I am the happiest of men.'

'Thank you for my surprise gifts,' Roxanne said and touched the magnificent earrings she wore. 'You have given me so much...'

Luke smiled, touching her cheek with his fingertips. 'The earrings are just one of many gifts I intend to make you, my darling. I have others for this evening when we are alone—and in Paris I shall buy you all the clothes and trinkets you could desire.'

'You are intent on spoiling me,' Roxanne said and leaned closer to kiss him. 'I love the gifts you've given me, Luke—but it is your love I prize more than any jewel.'

'My love is yours for ever,' he murmured huskily. 'I shall show you later how prized you are, Roxanne.'

'This is the happiest day of my life.'

She reached up and kissed him.

'My beloved.' Luke drew her close as passion surged between them. 'How fortunate I feel.'

The large reception hall was overflowing with guests. They spilled over into the parlours and out on to the terraces in the sunshine, the sound of laughter and chattering voices resounding throughout the house.

The bride and groom stood together to welcome all their guests. It was a glittering occasion, for friends and relatives had come from all parts of the country to stay and witness the wedding.

'I never thought I should see this day,' the earl said to Roxanne when she brought him a slice of rich fruity wedding cake with thick white icing. 'I don't know when I've ever seen Luke look this happy, girl. I never expected to see him head over heels in love, but there's no doubt of it. It's a transformation and one that gives me a deal of pleasure.'

'We are both very fortunate,' Roxanne said and took his hand, holding it to her cheek. 'I owe this to you,

Grandfather. Luke told me what you said to him—the way you made him realise that he was in danger of losing everything he truly wanted.'

'I told him the truth about things he should have known long ago,' the earl said, shaking his head. 'If it made the difference, I'm glad.'

Music had begun to play. Luke came to Roxanne and took her hand, leading her out to the middle of the floor. They danced together, a slow stately performance, then suddenly the music changed and he swept her into his arms as they waltzed.

'I want to take you somewhere quiet and make love to you,' he whispered against her ear. 'How much longer must I wait?'

'Luke…' Roxanne drew back, her mouth soft and seductive as she smiled. 'Be patient, beloved. We shall be together very soon now—and we have the rest of our lives to make love.'

'Hardly enough,' he murmured throatily. 'I want you for ever. Eternity is not long enough for all the things I want to tell you.'

It was as if Luke had suddenly discovered a well of emotions and feelings that he'd never known existed and they spilled over, engulfing her in a tide of love and desire.

'Well, I shall go up and change very soon,' Roxanne told him. 'You could follow me if you wish and…' She left the words unsaid, but her eyes told him all he wished to know.

Roxanne slipped out of her wedding gown and put on a soft silk wrap. She took the brush in her right hand

and began to stroke it over her hair, letting the dark red tresses fall over her shoulders and down her back.

'Come back when I send for you, Tilly,' she said. 'I want to rest for a little while before I change for this evening.'

'Yes, miss—I mean, my lady.' The girl blushed and bobbed a curtsy. 'Ring when you need me.'

Roxanne nodded and smiled. She was dabbing a little light perfume at her wrists when the door opened and Luke entered. She stood up and moved towards him, a smile of invitation on her lips.

'I told Tilly I wished to rest before I change for the evening,' she said huskily. 'I am not tired, but the sheets have been turned back. Shall we rest for a while together?'

Luke moved in closer and reached for her, his arms sliding about her waist. 'Those of the guests who are staying have gone up to change for the evening and the others are departing. I do not think we shall be missed for an hour or so, dearest.'

'Luke…' Roxanne lifted her face for his kiss, melting against him as his lips took possession of hers. 'I love you so very much.'

Then she was in his arms, responding to his kiss, and the next instant he was carrying her to the bed, placing her carefully amongst scented sheets.

Going to him without reserve, Roxanne shuddered with delight as his hands stroked up the arch of her back. Luke reached for her wrap, slipping it back off her shoulders to kiss her soft skin. The touch of his warm mouth on her breasts and then the inside of her thighs made her whimper with pleasure and she trembled, arching to meet him, lips parting as his kiss swept her away on clouds of exquisite pleasure.

Luke removed his own clothes and she saw the urgency of his need as he lay down beside her and drew her into his body. She felt the burn of his desire next to her thigh and then her legs were parting and he was between them, thrusting up into her. She gave a cry of pleasure, opening to him, wanting him deeper and deeper inside her. Her back arched and her hips thrust forwards to meet him as the desire pooled and grew into a raging need.

Together they reached for and found that wonderful place that is known only to true lovers. Luke gave a great shout of joy and triumph as he came inside her and she found her climax rolling through her as it came and came again in waves.

Afterwards, he lay with his head against her breast, their sweat mingling as they held on to each other, replete and content.

It was some time later that they left the bed. Roxanne sat at her dressing table and began to brush her hair.

'I must go and change,' Luke said and lifted her hair to kiss the back of her neck. He moved round to look at her and watch as she brushed her hair, perching on the edge of the dressing table, reluctant to leave despite his avowal that he ought to go. He picked up a small box casually and opened it, then stiffened as he saw what lay inside. 'Where did this come from?'

Roxanne looked and saw the magnificent pearl.

'Oh—that arrived just before the wedding. Tilly brought it up with some other things. Prince Ranjit sent it on behalf of his family.'

'It must be almost priceless,' Luke said and frowned, taking it out so that it lay on the palm of his hand. 'You did not choose to wear it today?'

'Of course not. I wore the gifts you gave me—and Grandfather's bracelet. Why should I wear that pearl, Luke? It is lovely, but I think we should send it back. I have no need of such gifts from the prince.'

Luke's expression eased, anger and tension gone. 'I would return it except that to do so would cause offence. I shall acknowledge the gift, Roxanne. There is no need for you to do anything.'

'I shall not wear the pendant, but if you think it rude to return it…'

'It can stay in the strong room. Perhaps one of our children or their wives will take a fancy to it in the future.' Luke smiled and leaned forwards to kiss her lips. 'He said you were a jewel of rare value. I replied that I did not need to be told. I was well aware of your value to me. I was so angry that I wanted to kill him for daring to think you could be his for a sum of money.'

'You have no need to be angry, my love.' Roxanne stood up and put her arms about him. 'No jewels could buy what we have, Luke. Love such as we feel for each other is a gift from God. It is all that either of us need now or in the future.

'I am so happy,' Roxanne said. 'Paris will be wonderful, but all I truly need is to be at home with you and Grandfather.'

* * *

'So you're home again,' the earl said and nodded with satisfaction as Roxanne came to kiss him on the cheek. 'You look happy, girl. Paris was a success, then?'

'Paris was exciting and I enjoyed the experience,' she said and pulled her elegant satinwood chair closer to his. It had a shield-shaped back, spindly legs and was one of a set of fourteen from Mr Adams's workrooms scattered throughout the house. 'However, I am glad to be home again, sir. Luke will be down shortly. He thinks he must go to London for a few days soon on business, but he will not be away for long.'

'You must neither of you feel tied to my coattails, girl. As long as you visit often I shall be content.'

'Well, I dare say I shall go to London or Bath for a visit sometimes, but not just yet.' Roxanne smiled, hardly able to contain the delight she felt inside. 'Now, I hope you will not think this too soon, Grandfather— but Luke and I...' She paused to watch his face, saw his frown and then a look of enquiry in his eyes. 'Yes, I am to have a child. I know it may seem too soon to be sure, but I think...it may have happened before the wedding. We did anticipate our wedding a little. I hope I have not shocked you?'

'A child...' The earl looked at her eagerly, a hint of tears in his eyes. 'You're certain, girl?'

'I saw a doctor just before we left Paris and he was sure that I was with child, perhaps two months or a little less. If I take good care and do not rush about all over the place, I believe you may have your first grandchild sooner than you had anticipated.'

'An heir…' The earl grinned at her. 'I thought I might have to wait months, years even. You're a clever girl, Roxanne. I knew you were just what this place needed when Luke first brought you here.'

'I may have a daughter,' she cautioned. 'But if I do we shall have to try again. I must confess that I shall not mind if we have a brood of children, both sons and daughters, to fill this big house with laughter.'

'You've already done that,' he said. 'The house has not been empty since you left for France. Your friend Beth Fox brought her son to stay for a few days and I gave him a pony of his own to keep in our stables—so I think we can be sure they will visit regularly. They might find a home here on the estate if you wished it, somewhere close enough for you to visit each other often. Besides, I've had a stream of visitors, neighbours and friends I hadn't bothered with for years—even Luke's godmother stayed on after the wedding—and guests are what this place has needed since Luke's parents died.'

'The tragedy was a terrible thing and it blighted all your lives, but the past has gone and we have a future filled with love and happiness to look forward to.'

'Luke knows of the child?'

'He is delighted. He thought I should tell you alone, but he will be down soon and then we can all celebrate together.'

She glanced up as the door opened and Luke walked in. 'Here you are, dearest. Grandfather is pleased with our news.'

'You've done well by me, sir,' the earl said. 'I'm

proud of you—proud of you both. And this is one of the happiest days of my life.'

Luke looked at Roxanne, his eyes warm with love. 'We both hope there will be others as happy, sir.'

'Yes.' Roxanne stood up and went to him. She glanced back at the earl. 'We have decided that you shall name our first child—boy or girl, the choice shall be yours.'

'Emily for a girl or Selwyn if it's a boy,' the earl said. 'To tell the truth, I have a fancy for a little girl first, but we must wait and see what the good lord sends us.'

'Yes, I do not think even Roxanne can arrange that, though she leaves little else to chance,' Luke said and laughed as his wife pulled a face at him. 'For myself I care not whether the child is male or female—as long as Roxanne is well after the birth I shall be quite content.'

'I have decided we should have at least two boys and two girls,' Roxanne said and smiled. 'But as long as we are all well and content together little else matters.'

'We should send for champagne,' the earl said. 'I want to toast my new grandchild—and the staff must share in our good fortune. We shall give a fête for the people, Luke. I'll leave it to you to organise the affair, but I shall attend if the day is fine.'

'I shall set it all in order before I leave for London— and I'll be back within a week so you need not pull caps with me, Grandfather. My home is here with the people I love and I have no wish to stay away an hour longer than I need.'

The door opened to admit Mrs Arlet. A few words from the earl and she left, face wreathed in smiles, to communicate the news to the rest of the household and order their champagne and lemonade for Roxanne.

'You know that they will be counting back the weeks after the birth,' Roxanne said. 'I think we shall shock our neighbours a little, sir.'

'Nonsense,' the earl replied and winked at her. 'Have you never heard of a babe coming early? My Emily had our son a month sooner than expected—big bonnie boy he was, too.'

'Grandfather,' Roxanne said and laughed. 'You are a rascal.'

'I was a bit of a rascal when I was younger,' he agreed and glanced at his grandson. 'It might be that Clarendon is more like me than any of you thought...'

Afterword

'So, Selwyn Luke John Arnold Hartingdon, future Lord Clarendon and one day heir to this old pile,' the earl said, looking down at the child in the cot beside Roxanne's bed. 'How does it feel to be the first-born of a clever girl like your mama? I dare say you are pleased with yourself and will lead us all a merry dance one day.'

'Grandfather,' Roxanne scolded with a smile of affection. 'He is but a day old and interested only in feeding and sleeping.'

'He is my great-grandson and will take after his father and his great-grandfather,' the earl replied with satisfaction. 'He is going to be a fine big chap and will make us all proud of him. I dare say he might be the Prime Minister or a famous general if he chose.'

'I think he may have some of Roxanne's qualities,' Luke said and raised his brows at her. 'I certainly hope he has more sense than either of us ever had.'

'Well, yes, of course—but he's got my nose and his mouth is just like yours, Luke.' The earl chuckled. 'And I am an old fool clucking over him as if I'd never seen a babe before. Roxanne, I am proud of you, girl. I wanted to tell you that I love you and make sure you were well—but there never was such a beautiful child.'

'Thank you, dearest Grandfather. I love you, too.'

'Well, I'll leave you together for a while—but you should let Roxanne rest, Luke. She needs to get her strength back.'

'I shall do so in a moment, sir.'

Luke grinned as the door closed behind him. 'I've never seen him look so happy and proud. Anyone would think the boy was his son.'

'He loves us all,' Roxanne said. 'Are you proud of me, Luke? Are you pleased with your son?'

'You know I am,' he said and perched on the edge of her bed, reaching for her hand. 'I am the happiest man alive—except perhaps for Grandfather. He looks younger and I begin to think he is an old fraud. He will live for years.'

'His health is not good,' Roxanne said and held his hand tighter, 'but he is content and will have some time with us yet.'

'Yes, I know.' Luke bent his head and kissed her. 'Now I must do as Grandfather bid me and leave you to rest. Beth will be here later and I know she will be eager to see you. Rest now and you will feel better when she arrives.'

'I am perfectly well, you know,' Roxanne said. 'I

shall rest, but only for a little time. Come and see me soon, my love.'

'Of course. I have no intention of going anywhere else,' he said, blew her a kiss and went out.

Roxanne lay back against her pillows, a smile on her lips as she closed her eyes and slept.

* * * * *

The Homeless Heiress

ANNE HERRIES

Chapter One

Captain Richard Hernshaw paused, glanced back into the menacing darkness of the narrow alley behind him and frowned. He was being followed. The instinct he had acquired over several years working for the British government as a secret agent was on full alert. He knew that he had taken a risk by agreeing to meet his contact here in the rookery of these terrible slum streets, but the man would not dare to show his face elsewhere, for he was a rogue and perhaps worse. The meeting had gone well and Richard had what he'd come for, but, since leaving his contact, he had picked up a shadow. The question was—who was following him and why?

He needed to know the answer to that question, because of the papers he was carrying, which were important and could hold the answer to a mystery that he and other colleagues had been investigating in recent times. It was feared that an attempt on the lives of several prominent men in the government, even that of the Regent himself, was being prepared, and Richard believed that the names of the ringleaders were in the documents he carried inside his coat pocket. If the person following him knew that he had them, he might be in danger—of losing both the papers and his life.

Better to attack than be attacked! Richard turned the corner, and pressed his back against the wall, waiting for whoever it was to catch up with him. His suspicions were proved correct, for an instant later a small, dark shadow came hurtling round the corner. He stepped out, and grabbed the rascal's arm, gripping it tightly.

'Let me go!' a voice cried in a tone halfway between anger and fear. 'Watcha think yer doin'?'

'That is exactly what I was about to ask you,' Richard said, his gaze narrowing as he looked down at the rather grubby face of a street urchin. He smiled as he saw the indignant look in the youth's eyes. 'You have been following me for a while now, lad. I don't like being followed unless I know why.'

The youth rubbed his hand under his nose and sniffed hard. 'Weren't doin' no 'arm, sir,' he said defiantly. 'Let me go or I'll kick yer!'

'You would be sorry if you did,' Richard replied. He hesitated, his hold slackening a little as he considered. A lad like this might be after his purse, but he was far from the sinister enemy he had imagined. A smile was beginning to tug at the corners of his mouth when the youth lunged at him, kicked him in the shins and wrenched free, setting off at a run back the way he had come. 'Damn you!'

Richard realised instantly that he had been robbed. The boy's hand had gone inside his jacket, removing the package he was carrying seconds before the toe of his boot connected with Richard's leg and caused him to loosen his hold enough for the lad to break free. He felt a surge of annoyance—how could he have fallen for a trick like that?

Richard yelled and set off after the boy at once. He was angry that he had been so careless, but there had been something almost angelic in the boy's face and he had been lulled into a sense of false security. Damned fool! It was the oldest trick in the book, using a boy to take your enemy off guard. He could see the lad ahead of him, running for all he was worth. He moved fast, but Richard was a match for him, his longer legs and superior strength making it inevitable that he would catch the boy. And then fortune stepped in. In his haste, the lad had not seen the rubbish on the pavement. As his foot touched the rotting filth left there by some careless trader, his heel slid and his legs suddenly went from under him, sending him tumbling into the gutter. He was getting to his feet when Richard arrived, clearly none the worse for his tumble.

'Watcha want ter make me do that fer?' he complained bitterly. 'I ain't done nuthin', sir. Honest I ain't.'

'You stole something from me,' Richard said, holding out his hand. 'Give it back and don't try another stunt like that or you will get a good hiding. Do you hear me?' His strong hands hauled the youth to his feet. He gave him a little shake. 'Did you hear what I said, boy?'

'Me name's Georgie,' the lad said and sniffled. 'I ain't 'ad nuthin' ter eat fer days. I only wanted a few coins. If yer hadn't grabbed me, I wouldn't 'ave done it.'

'Indeed?' Richard's eyebrows rose as he looked at the lad. 'Georgie, is it? Well, Georgie, had you asked I might have given you a shilling, but you deserve that I should hand you over to the law…'

The lad produced the package, holding it out to Richard, who took it and replaced it in his coat pocket. The seal was still intact. It would have meant little to anyone who did not have the code and was able to decipher it, but he could not be sure the lad was not working for someone.

'Let me go, sir,' Georgie said, putting on the wheedling tone again. 'I swear I've never done nuthin' like that afore and I'm hungry…' He sniffed and wiped his nose on his sleeve. 'I didn't mean no 'arm…'

'What you meant was to steal from me,' Richard replied with a stern look. 'But I have the packet back and, if you are truly hungry, I shall feed you.'

'Give me a shilling, sir, and I'll trouble you no more.' Georgie's hand shot out.

Richard was on the point of putting his hand into his pocket when something made him hesitate. There was something about the urchin that did not ring true, though for the moment he could not place it.

'I'll not give you money,' he said. 'But I shall feed you. We'll go to an inn I know. Not here. I don't trust the service in these drinking dens. I'll take you somewhere we can both enjoy a meal.'

The lad hesitated and for a moment Richard thought he would try to run away, but then he shrugged his shoulders. 'All right, if that's what yer want, sir.'

'Come with me then,' Richard said, taking hold of his arm. 'And don't try to run away, Georgie—no funny tricks, do you hear? This package is important to me, but it would be of no use to you. Try stealing from me again and I shall not be as forgiving next time.'

'Don't go on about it,' the lad said, glaring at him. 'And you're hurting my arm. I shan't run orf. I give yer my word.'

There was a touch of unconscious pride about the lad then that alerted Richard's suspicions. Somehow he was certain that Georgie—if that was his name—was not an ordinary street urchin. There was more here than met the eye. He slackened his hold of the lad's arm a little, but made sure it was sufficient to bind him to him as they left the last of the mean streets behind. The lighting here was better, and, glancing at the boy's profile, Richard knew that his suspicions were right. Just what had he discovered here? If he knew anything at all, this lad had not been born to these poor streets of the London slum. Was he a runaway from school or a tyrant father? He was almost certain that the accent was a sham, for it had slipped once or twice. Just what was Georgie up to?

'Where do you go to school?' he asked.

'Don't go,' the lad replied. 'Ain't never bin, sir.'

He was not telling the truth; Richard's instinct never lied. His curiosity deepened. The boy was clearly very young, and, despite what he had done, Richard felt it his duty to try to help him if it were possible. He knew only too well to what depths of degradation some unfortunates were forced to sink in these stinking alleys. A grim expression dwelled briefly in his eyes as he remembered. He would not think of that now! It was behind him. He had buried himself deep in his work to forget and he would not allow that past tragedy to haunt him.

The lights of a respectable inn were just ahead of them, a lantern shedding a bright yellow glow over the pavement. More lanterns lit the archway that led behind to the inn yard, but Richard headed for the main door. He felt Georgie's hesitation, the slight resistance, and looked down.

'There's nothing to fear here, Georgie. You may not be used to such places, but we shall be served, never fear.'

'I ain't frightened,' the lad replied. 'You don't need ter hang on to me any longer. I shan't run away. I ain't frightened of yer no more. Besides, I'm starving!'

'Well, they serve decent food here,' Richard replied. He glanced at the lad's face as they went inside. Now he could see the delicate profile and the pale complexion. Georgie was very slight and he found it difficult to assess his age. At first he had thought him a child of perhaps twelve or thirteen. His height was below Richard's shoulder and he had felt the thinness of the lad's body as he held him after he slipped on the rubbish. Looking at his face in the light, he thought now that the lad must be older—fifteen, perhaps.

'Yes, sir?' The host came bustling up to them, a smile on his face that dimmed somewhat as he saw the boy. 'Captain Hernshaw, isn't it? I believe I've had the honour of serving you before, sir?'

'On a couple of occasions,' Richard replied easily, ignoring the host's expression. 'You serve excellent chops, landlord, and a good pie. My young friend here is hungry and so am I. We shall have the best of whatever you have on offer this evening.'

'Yes, sir. Would you be wanting the parlour, sir?'

Richard hesitated. He sensed tension in his companion and wondered what the lad could be thinking. 'Yes, Goodridge. We shall have the parlour, if you will spare it to us.'

'Just as you wish, sir. Will you want wine or ale?'

'You may bring me some wine,' Richard said. 'Do you have any cordial that you might prepare for the boy? He is my groom's lad and he has been helping me with the horses. I am afraid he has got himself into something of a state.'

'Ah.' The innkeeper nodded as he was enlightened, relief in his eyes. 'Boys will be boys, sir.'

Georgie eyed him resentfully as they went into the private parlour, but said nothing until the innkeeper had left, shutting the door behind him.

'Whatcha want ter say that fer?'

'I thought it best to concoct some tale lest our host imagined something for himself. I do not wish to acquire a reputation for molesting young boys.' Richard smiled wryly. 'In case you had some such suspicion yourself, you may rest easy that my tastes do not lie in that direction.'

'Oh…' Georgie's dark eyes studied his face for a moment, searching, all too wise and yet naïve at the same time. 'I didn't think it. I've met that sort afore and you ain't. I'll vouch for it if he turns up rough.'

'Thank you,' Richard said, a note of sarcasm in his voice. 'If I need your help, I shall ask for it.'

'No need to be so superior,' Georgie said. 'I was just offering…'

'Thank you,' Richard replied, a slight smile on his lips. Something in Georgie's manner at that moment had confirmed what he had been thinking for a while now. This was no street urchin! He wasn't sure why Georgie had tried to steal from him or why he was living rough, as he clearly was from his appearance. There was dirt on the delicate features and the lad's clothes were disgusting. He smelled unpleasant! 'I think we should call a truce, don't you—just for long enough to eat our supper.'

Georgie didn't answer but went to the fire, standing in front of it and holding his hands to the flames. He rubbed them together, shivering as if he had just realised how cold it was outside, but he did not speak. He continued to look into the flames when the door opened, admitting the innkeeper's wife and a maid with two large trays filled with plates of food.

'Come and eat, boy,' Richard said. 'This food smells delicious.'

The lad turned, stood looking at the food for a moment and then came to the table. He sat down on the bench, reaching for a plate of lamb chops. He took one and began to eat it with his fingers, tearing at the tender meat with his teeth—very white teeth for a street urchin, Richard noticed! He ate that chop and reached for another, demolishing that in much the same way, and licking the fat from his fingers—slender, delicate fingers.

'That's enough,' Richard said when the second chop had gone down in a hurry. 'Eat properly now and slower. If you haven't eaten for days, it will make you sick if you stuff too much down at once. Try some of the pork pie. It is delicious.' He cut a slice for himself, putting some pickles on to his plate and breaking a bit of the bread.

Georgie watched and then did the same. He began to eat small pieces of pie with a little relish, buttering his bread. He had small, smooth hands, Richard noticed. Now that he was eating properly he appeared to have table manners too. He sipped his lime cordial and appeared to have no fault to find with the taste.

Richard smiled inwardly. The lad had come from a good home. What had caused him to flee that home for a life on the streets he could not tell, but thought it would be worth discovering. When Georgie put down his knife and sat back, clearly having eaten his fill, Richard drank a little of his wine and observed in silence for a moment.

'Better?' he asked at last. His brows arched as the boy nodded. 'Want to tell me about it?'

'Whatcha mean?' A look of uncertainty came into the lad's eyes.

'Your accent is false,' Richard said. 'You don't always use slang and it slips from time to time. I don't think you were reared in the slums, George. So where have you come from and why?'

'You really want to know?' The boy looked at him oddly. 'Why?'

'Because I should like to help you if I can. A life of thieving is not for a lad like you. I think you have run away from your home or your school—why?'

'I ran away from—' Georgie said and caught his breath. 'I can't tell you. You wouldn't believe me.' He got to his feet abruptly. 'Thanks for the food…'

Richard stuck out his leg, preventing the lad from passing. 'Sit down and tell me the truth.'

'No! You can't make me…' Georgie tried to push past. Richard leapt to his feet and grabbed him. As he did so, Georgie's disreputable cap came off and long dark locks came tumbling down, framing a face that now looked decidedly feminine. Richard gave a grim nod of satisfaction. He had thought something was wrong! This was no fragile lad but a girl! 'Oh…' Georgie put up her hand, trying frantically to hide her hair, giving a very unladylike oath. 'Damn it! I thought you promised to let me go…'

'And I may—if you give me a satisfactory answer. Who are you and what were you doing in that slum?'

She hesitated for a moment and then gave a reluctant sigh. 'My name is Georgie Brown and I worked as a lady's maid,' she said, sitting down again. 'I ran away from my place because my lady's son would not stop pestering me. He kept trying to kiss me and…well, I couldn't stay there any longer so I took some old clothes and ran off.'

'Surely you had family who would have taken you in?' Georgie shook her head. He arched his brow. 'Friends? Another employer?'

'I couldn't ask for a reference, because she would have blamed me…she wouldn't have given me one…' Georgie's eyes dropped, her hand clenching nervously in her lap. 'You don't know what it's like to be at the mercy of—' She broke off on a choked sob.

Richard's gaze narrowed. 'Why live on the streets and try to steal from people? Surely you cannot want to live this way?'

Georgie sniffed, a suspicion of tears in her eyes, but she was obviously trying not to cry. 'I had some money, but it was stolen from me the first day I got to London. I thought I could find myself a job and I had enough money to live decently for a while, but…' The tears were trickling down her cheek despite her efforts to stop them. She rubbed the sleeve of her disreputable jacket over her face, streaking the dirt. 'After my purse was stolen, I did not know what to do and no one would give me money or food.'

'So you thought you would turn to pickpocketing for a living?' Richard smiled oddly. 'Unfortunately, you chose me for your first victim—or was I the first?'

'I stole some fruit from a stall and…and a kerchief from an elderly gentleman, which I sold…' Her cheeks were uncomfortably red now. 'Don't look at me like that! I was hungry!'

'Yes, you were,' Richard agreed, watching her face thoughtfully. He wasn't certain that she was telling him the whole truth even now, but he was prepared to go along with it for the moment. 'Are you sure you have no family? If they live in the country, I could help you get there.'

Georgie hesitated for a moment and then shook her head. She had bundled her long hair back under her cap and her tears had dried. 'Let me go now. You gave me supper, but you promised to let me go.'

'I have no hold on you,' Richard said. 'But I know someone who might take you in. She is elderly and needs someone to look after her—and she might take you for my sake.'

'I'll be all right.' Georgie eyed him suspiciously, clearly not quite trusting him. 'I'm not sure.'

'Well, I am leaving,' he replied. Getting up from the table, he threw some coins down for the serving wench. 'You can come with me or find your own way…it's your choice.'

Georgie didn't answer, though he noticed that she followed him from the room, waiting a few feet away as he paid the host for their supper. Richard refrained from looking at her as he went out of the inn, standing for a moment under the street lantern, its smoky light spilling a yellow pool on the pavement. Some gentlemen were approaching the inn as he turned away, feeling the press of Georgie's body suddenly, as she appeared to take shelter from something or someone. He said nothing until they had left the inn behind them, but he noticed that she looked back over her shoulder several times, seeming nervous.

'What is it?' he asked a short time later. 'What frightened you after we left the inn?'

Georgie hesitated. 'Did you mean it when you said you would help me get to the country?'

'I never say what I don't mean.'

'Then will you—please? I have to leave London. I can't stay now…' She took a deep breath, her eyes filled with a silent appeal. 'Please help me. I'm frightened…'

'Yes, I can see that,' Richard replied and frowned. She hadn't been frightened earlier, but she was now. 'Do you want to tell me why?'

Georgie shook her head, saying nothing. Richard sensed that he was being drawn into something that would cause him a great deal of trouble he could do without and yet there was an unconscious appeal in those eyes that tugged at his heartstrings, reminding him of something…someone else. He had failed that person through no real fault of his own, but he would not let that happen again.

'Very well, I'll take you with me,' he said, reaching a decision. 'I'll give you a place to sleep and some decent clothes and then we'll see. If I'm going to help you, you have to trust me. I promise you I shan't harm you, but I can't help you either—unless you tell me the truth.' He sighed as he saw her face close down. She wasn't ready to trust him yet. 'Well, keep your secrets for the moment, child. You will at least sleep in a decent bed this night, and perhaps tomorrow you may feel like telling me the real story.'

Georgie glanced at the stern profile of the man walking beside her. He was tall and strong, his face attractive rather than handsome and just at the moment he looked annoyed. She supposed he was within his rights to be angry with her, because she *had* kicked him in the shins *and* she had stolen that packet from him. Most men would have cuffed her round the ear or sent for the watchman, but he had taken her to a decent inn and fed her. On the face of it he seemed trustworthy, but Georgie had learned in a hard school and she knew that people were often not what they seemed. She wanted to trust him, needed to be able to trust someone, because the last two weeks of living rough had shown her that she wasn't very good at looking after herself.

She hadn't thought much about what she was doing when she ran away. In her innocence she had thought it would be easy to fend for herself for a while—just until she thought about what she ought to do next—but losing her purse the very first day had changed everything. She had been so naïve, taking her money out to pay for food and just holding the purse loosely by the strings rather than tucking it away again. The man who had snatched it had been so quick that she had had no idea of his intention and he was away with it before she could recover from the shock. Since then she had been roaming the streets, wondering how she could earn or steal enough money to survive, and she had been desperate when she saw him...Captain Hernshaw, the innkeeper had called him.

What kind of a man was he? Georgie wondered. He looked like a military man, and, considering his title, he probably was—but he was nothing like the officers she had met in the past. There was something hard and wary about him, an air of being alert at all times...and the look in his eyes could send shivers down her spine.

One part of her was telling her she ought to run now while she had the chance, because he would make a bad enemy and when he discovered she had lied to him he would be angry. But she'd seen *him* when they left the inn and it had sent shock waves through her, because she knew what would happen if *he* found her.

She had shrunk closer to the side of the man she had felt her protector, her fear very real until they were well away from *him*. Should she confess the whole truth to Captain Hernshaw, throw herself on his mercy and trust in him to help her? He was a stranger to her! If he knew the truth, he might try to take advantage. It was difficult to know who she could trust…if indeed she could trust anyone.

Georgie shivered. They were approaching a row of terraced houses in an elegant square. At least it was a respectable address, a place where she might be able to hide for a few days while she recovered her strength and took stock of her situation. She stayed close to her protector as he rapped at the door, which was opened by a gentleman of advanced years dressed in discreet black.

'Ah, there you are, sir.' The faded blue eyes flicked to Georgie's face, but he gave no sign of curiosity. 'You are early this evening, Captain Hernshaw.'

'Yes, Jensen,' Richard replied with a faint smile. 'As you say I am early, though I may go out again later. Has Mrs Jensen retired yet?'

'No, sir. She is in her sitting room. Shall I tell her that you require her services?'

'She may attend me in the front parlour at her convenience. I wish to place this young lad under her care.'

'Young lad in her care?' For a moment Jensen's face froze, but in seconds he had recovered. 'Yes, of course, sir. I shall tell Mrs Jensen immediately. Is there anything else you require, sir?'

'Well done, Jensen,' Richard said and Georgie saw a gleam of appreciation in his eyes. 'Nothing throws you, does it? No, I require nothing further. It is my intention to go out again once I have this small matter in hand.'

'Just as you say, sir.'

The manservant went off. Georgie followed her protector into a parlour of medium proportions. It was furnished with heavy mahogany pieces that gave it a stately air, rather ponderous and definitely the home of a man who lived alone. There were cabinets filled with objects that looked to be of a scientific nature made of brass or steel, and two large globes on stands were placed one at either side of the window. A desk stood beneath the window, so that the light fell on it, and was cluttered with what looked like old pieces of bone to Georgie.

'Are you a scientist?' she asked, looking at her rescuer curiously.

'No, but my uncle was,' Richard replied. 'He left this house to me and I have done nothing with it, as you see. Uncle Frederick never married. He left me his estate because I was his favourite and—' He broke off, a look of pain in his eyes. 'I shared some of his interests at one time, but I have been away for some years.'

'Oh…' Georgie picked up one of the pieces of what she now saw were fossils. 'What is this?'

'A part of the thigh bone of a dinosaur,' Richard replied. 'My uncle studied fossils of all kinds. I have no particular interest in bones myself, but I hardly ever use this house, except when I stay in town. I prefer the

country and of course I have been away.' He frowned
at her. Here in the brighter lights of his house, he saw
that she looked older than he'd first imagined, not truly
a child. 'You can't be interested in any of this. Will you
not tell me who you really are and why you ran away?'

'I...' Georgie began. She was still uncertain whether
to trust him with the whole story and was relieved when
someone knocked at the door. She saw his quick frown,
but he did not hesitate.

'Come in, Mrs Jensen.'

An elderly woman entered. She was plump, white-
haired and looked approachable, though a little surprised and anxious. It was obvious that she did not
know what to make out of the tale her husband had
clearly been telling her.

'There was something I can do for you, sir?'

'Yes, Mrs Jensen,' Richard replied. 'I want you to
help this young lad. He is in some trouble and I have
rescued him and brought him here for his safety. He has
eaten, but needs to bathe and requires more suitable
clothes and a bed of his own to sleep in. Do you think
you can help me out please, Dora?'

'Yes, of course, sir.' Dora Jensen gave him a look of
such adoration that Georgie knew at once that the
woman had known Captain Hernshaw many years and
trusted him completely. 'The poor little mite. I'll take
him away now, shall I, sir?'

'Yes, if you please.' He turned to Georgie. 'Dora
was my uncle's housekeeper for many years, and we
have known each other since I was in short coats. She
will look after you, Georgie. I have to go out again on
business, but I shall see you in the morning. We shall
talk further then.'

'Yes…thank you,' Georgie said, giving him an uncertain smile. 'You have been…kind.'

He nodded to her, but made no further comment. Georgie saw the housekeeper was looking at her expectantly and she went to her dutifully, following her from the room and up the stairs.

'We always keep a couple of rooms ready in case the captain decides to invite a guest to stay, though he doesn't trouble us much,' Mrs Jensen told her as she looked back, making certain Georgie was just behind her. 'I often say to Jensen that things hardly changed when the old gentleman died.'

'Was that Mr Frederick Hernshaw?'

'Sir Frederick,' Mrs Jensen corrected. 'He was a gentleman of learning, quiet and scholarly. He sometimes had a few of the dons to dinner—university men like himself—but never ladies. There has not been a lady in this house for as long as I can remember…' A speculative expression came to her eyes. 'That brings me to you, young sir—if it isn't rude of me to ask. Who are you and how did you come to meet the captain?'

Georgie took a deep breath, then smiled. 'It is a long story, Mrs Jenkins. Captain Hernshaw doesn't know it all yet, but if you promise to keep it to yourself I shall tell you a part of my secret.' She swept off her disreputable cap, letting her long dark hair cascade over her shoulders. Her melting brown eyes met the housekeeper's astonished look bravely. 'I shall not deceive you, Mrs Jensen. I am not as I presently appear,' she said, and then tucked her hair back under her cap.

'Well, bless my soul,' Dora Jensen said. 'You're a lady, miss! I thought there was something odd as soon as I laid eyes on you. You looked like a girl, but in your present dress it seemed unlikely—if you don't mind my being blunt. It isn't quite proper for a young lady to be in an unmarried gentleman's house.'

'No, you are quite right,' Georgie said. 'But when I tell you that I was near to starving when he found me, you may find it in your heart to look kindly on me.'

'Never fear that I shan't,' Mrs Jensen said in a gentle tone. 'I know a lady when I see one and something tells me you are in terrible trouble.'

'Yes, I am,' Georgie replied and her bottom lip trembled. 'I am in such a mess—and I'm frightened, that's why I came here to the house of a stranger. He gave me food and promised to help me, but he doesn't yet know the real story, though he does know I am a girl.'

'You never told him lies, miss!'

'Yes, well, I couldn't tell him the truth, not at first,' Georgie said, warming to her new friend. 'But I am in terrible danger. And I can't tell you any more, because…well, I just can't!'

'Well, I never,' Dora said and shook her head. 'That is a shocking thing, miss—if you are telling me the truth?'

Georgie crossed her fingers behind her back. It was nearer to the truth than she had confessed to Captain Hernshaw, but still not the whole story. But she was afraid that if he knew the real story her protector might refuse to believe her and pack her off back to her family—and that was something she was determined to fight at all costs.

'I wouldn't lie to you, Mrs Jensen. I just can't tell anyone the whole story.'

'I hope you wouldn't,' the housekeeper said, her eyes going over her. 'I am not sure what we ought to do with you, miss, and that is the truth. There are no young girls in this household and my clothes would fall off you.'

'Oh, I don't want to dress like a girl,' Georgie said hastily. 'I couldn't stay here if people knew it was me—and I might be recognised if I went out in a girl's clothing. I have been into fashionable society, you see. I should have no reputation left if people knew I was here in this house. Can't you find me something suitable to wear—a youth's clothes, perhaps?'

'Well, I don't know, miss.' Dora looked doubtful. 'This is a house of menservants for the most part, because it was always a bachelor's home; there are no boys—but the captain might have something.'

'You could always wash my things.' Georgie looked down at herself doubtfully.

'That I will not,' Dora said decisively. 'Those things are for the rag bag if I have my way. You can wear one of the master's bathrobes. I'll ask Henderson to find you something—he's the captain's valet and he served him when they were both in the army.'

'Oh…' Georgie hesitated. 'Yes, I see…well, it will have to do for the moment. But you do see it is better if people think I'm a boy, don't you?'

'Yes, miss,' Dora said, though she was still doubtful. 'Well, here's your room, miss—or perhaps I should call you master?'

'Call me Georgie. It is my name and it could be for a boy or a girl, couldn't it?'

'You're a rare one,' Dora said and shook her head. 'I don't know what to make of you, and that is the truth, but the master put you in my care, and I'll do the best I can by you. Now, this is your room, and I'll send Henderson up with the bathtub. I'll bring the hot water myself. Make yourself comfortable, Master Georgie, and I'll be back soon.'

Georgie thanked her and went inside the room. It was a bedchamber of handsome proportions, though once again it was furnished in heavy dull furniture, the curtains and bedclothes in sombre shades. Very masculine and not at all what she had been used to all her life, but much better than the streets.

She sat down on a stool near the window and looked out as the door closed behind Mrs Jensen. At least she was safe here for the time being. No one would think of looking for her in this house. It had given her a shock to see *him* when she left the inn with Captain Hernshaw and she had been glad of her new friend's protection. She closed her eyes for a moment, because she was feeling sick and frightened. To be so near to that man! It had made her feel very nervous, though it was unlikely he would have recognised her dressed in her filthy clothes. Yet the fear that he would had been very strong, because she would rather die than be taken back to her home and forced into a life that she knew would be unbearable.

She had run from her aunt and uncle, and they were in collusion with another person to rob her of what was rightfully hers. Not by murdering her, but by marrying her to a man she hated.

She would never marry him! Never, never, never! She would much rather be dead than *his* wife. For a moment the tears were very close, but she held them back. The worst of her ordeal was over now. She was no longer hungry or cold and could put the memory of her time on the streets behind her. She must think hard about what she was going to do next, because her situation was still precarious.

Her head came up as she heard a knock on the door and she called out that whoever it was might enter. A man of about three and thirty came in carrying a large metal tub, which he placed down in front of the fireplace. He then knelt down, striking a tinder and putting the flame to the dry kindling, which caught with the help of a little work with the bellows.

Georgie wandered over to watch him. He glanced up at her and she saw the fearful scar on his cheek. Instead of flinching, she felt an immediate sympathy for him and smiled, hoping that he would see his disfigurement did not cause her revulsion.

'Thank you, that is very kind of you, sir.'

'Call me Henderson,' he told her, his dark eyes narrowed. 'I'm the captain's valet now. I served with him in the army. He saved my life when I was wounded, and he gave me a job. Mrs Jensen tells me you're here because he rescued you too.'

'Yes…' Georgie hesitated because she wasn't sure what else the housekeeper had told him. 'I need something to wear, Henderson. Has the captain got anything suitable?'

'His things will be too big for you, but I'll find you something,' he promised. 'The captain's things will do for tonight, young master, though you couldn't go out in them.'

'Thank you, but I do not wish to go out just yet,' Georgie said. She glanced over her shoulder as Mrs Jensen entered, carrying a jug of water. She was followed by a younger footman carrying two cans of water, which he poured into the bath, before throwing her a curious glance on the way out.

'You can leave us now, Henderson,' Mrs Jensen told

the valet, who had the fire going nicely. 'I'll help the lad.'

'I'll find you something to wear,' Henderson promised and went off, leaving Georgie alone with the housekeeper.

'You'd best lock the door until you've done,' Mrs Jensen said with a frown. 'If we're to keep your secret for the time being, you don't want anyone walking in without warning. I'll bring you a robe—there's one in the armoire that belonged to one of the guests and was left behind. Make sure you put it on before you open the door, and keep a towel round your head. You don't want anyone guessing the truth.'

'No, I don't,' Georgie agreed. 'Thank you so much, Mrs Jensen. I wasn't sure what you had said to Mr Henderson.'

'I told him no more than he needed to know,' Dora replied. 'But he's no fool. I doubt it will take him long to work it out for himself.'

Georgie nodded. She locked the door after the housekeeper left and then stripped down to her skin. The sight of steam issuing from the bathtub was enticing, because she hadn't been able to wash since her flight from her uncle's house and the water smelled nice, as if it had been perfumed. She sighed with pleasure as she stepped into it and sank down into its warmth; it was just right, not too hot or too cold. Closing her eyes, she leaned her head back against a towel and relaxed. It felt so good! She had missed being able to indulge in the luxuries she had known all her life and had hated being dirty. How could people live that way? The answer must be that they had no choice, as she'd had none after her money was stolen.

A single tear trickled down her cheek, because until two years previously she had been the cherished only child of indulgent parents. The tragic carriage accident that had robbed her of both mother and father in one go and cast her into the arms of her mother's older brother had changed her life completely. At first her aunt and uncle had seemed kind enough, but as she approached her nineteenth birthday, and the fortune that would soon be hers, she had noticed a change in their manner towards her. It was just a look, a conversation that ended abruptly as she entered the room, and then one morning she had overheard them discussing her.

'He says he will settle the debt if we give him the girl,' her uncle Henry Mowbray had said as Georgie hovered outside the parlour door. 'I am deeply involved with him, Agatha. If I refuse he could ruin me—and he will. Believe me, he will!'

'You should never have been drawn into his schemes,' Aunt Agatha said harshly. 'She is nothing to me, of course, but even so…that man gives me the shivers. I do not like this, Henry. Are you sure there is nothing else you can do?'

'He wants her and the money, but at least he is willing to let the debt go. If I refuse, he might snatch her anyway—and he could ruin me in more ways than one.'

'But that man…he frightens me, Henry. And she is little more than a child. I do not like the sound of this.'

'Well, he says it is her or what I owe him, and you know I cannot pay.'

Georgie had run away swiftly as her uncle walked towards the door. She knew that she must not let him realise she had overheard their conversation, because he might decide to lock her in her room until he could force her to marry *that man*! And she was certain she knew exactly who he meant. She'd seen *him* looking at her when he visited her uncle and he made her feel as if she wanted to scrub herself all over! She would never marry him, whatever they did to her.

Georgie had left her uncle's home that very night, determined that she would find a place to hide until she came into her fortune. Once she had it, she could set up home somewhere and pay a respectable companion to live with her. Her plans had been vague to say the least, and she had been acting on instinct when she took the mail coach for London, with some idea of visiting her father's lawyers at the back of her mind, but when she lost her purse everything had changed. Her priority then had been to stay alive until she could work out what to do for the best, and now she was here in the home of a gentleman she had met for the first time that evening!

She had been fortunate, she knew that instinctively. There were worse perils on the streets of London than she had yet encountered, and, if she played her game skillfully, Captain Hernshaw might help her. She had to decide what to do for the best. There was one person who might help her, though she was reluctant to approach her great-aunt, who had always seemed remote and distant—but it might be the best way in the circumstances. It would perhaps have been best to seek her help in the first instance, but she had acted on impulse, afraid of the consequences if she delayed.

Georgie stayed in the bath until it began to get cold, then got out and dried herself, before putting on the striped soft velvet robe that the housekeeper had put out for her. It was so big that it kept falling off her shoulders and she had to hitch it up with the belt so that she didn't trip over it all the time, but it felt warm. She went over to the dressing chest, looking at herself in the small mirror that hung from a stand above. Her dark hair was hanging about her shoulders, still slightly damp and curling in wisps as it dried, a complete giveaway of her true sex. She bit her lip, because she knew that she wouldn't be able to hide the truth for long with her hair this way. She hadn't wanted to cut it, but now she felt driven to do so.

She opened the top drawer of the military chest that formed part of the furnishings and saw a pair of scissors lying there. Her hand reached for them, hesitated and then grasped them determinedly. If she wanted to escape detection, she would need to be brave. She took a handful of her hair and held it up above her head, positioning the scissors. There was no help for it, her hair must go!

'I wouldn't do that if I were you,' a voice said and Georgie turned to see that Henderson had entered the room via what must be a dressing room. She hadn't realised that there was another door until this minute. 'Proper shame to hack off all that lovely hair, if you ask me.'

Georgie got to her feet, staring at him in dismay. 'I locked the door...'

'I used the adjoining one, though I waited until I heard you moving about, miss. I did knock, but you didn't hear me.'

'I was lost in thought.' Georgie stared at his face. 'You knew I was a girl all the time, didn't you? Did Mrs Jensen tell you?'

'I sort of guessed it,' Henderson agreed. 'I've seen

delicate young boys, and you might pass for one in poor light, but anyone looking at you now would know for sure. I've brought you some clothes—and a cap, so you can hide your hair.'

'I think it should come off,' Georgie said. 'Would you help me, Henderson? I'm not sure I can do the back.'

'I'll cut it if you really mean it,' the valet told her, 'but I think it is a wicked shame, miss.'

'You must call me Georgie,' she said. 'If anyone discovers the truth…I am in such terrible danger, you see. There is…someone who wants to…harm me.' It was all she could tell him, as much as she dared to say for now. Tears stood in her eyes as she looked at him.

'Not if I was near enough to stop him,' Henderson said and scowled. 'You should tell the captain, Georgie. He wouldn't stand for it.'

'But I can't impose on him,' Georgie replied. 'He has already helped me. I have to get to my great-aunt's house. She lives in Yorkshire and is the only person I can trust.'

'You talk to the captain. He will help you get where you need to go,' Henderson said, looking doubtful. He came towards her, looking at her long hair and the scissors. 'Are you sure you want to cut this?'

'Yes—' Georgie began, but her next words were lost as she heard shouting and then someone knocked frantically at her door. She sprang to open it and Mrs Jensen almost fell into the room. 'Is something wrong?'

'It's the master,' the housekeeper cried, clearly in a state of shock. 'He has been badly hurt, miss, and not far from the house. He just staggered in, covered in blood. He's soaked in it! I never saw the like in my life.

He needs you, Henderson!' Her hands were trembling. 'Nothing like this ever happened when the old master was alive. I can't abide the sight of blood. I never could.'

'Where is he?' Henderson barked at her. 'Pull yourself together, woman! I am going to need help.'

Mrs Jensen was shaking and in terrible distress. 'They carried him to his bedchamber. I can't help you. I'm sorry, but I just can't...'

'I will,' Georgie said at once. 'I'm not afraid of a little blood. Go to him, Mr Henderson, and I'll follow as soon as I am dressed.'

'Oh, miss,' the housekeeper said, forgetting discretion in her distress. 'The poor master. We've sent for the doctor, but he looks in a bad way.'

Chapter Two

Henderson went off without another word or a look in her direction. Georgie scooped up the clothes he had left for her and turned her back on the housekeeper as she dressed hastily in breeches and shirt that were far too big for her. She rolled up the sleeves of the shirt and legs of the breeches, tying them round the middle to hold them in with a neckerchief the valet had brought, then scraped her hair up under the cap.

'Show me where,' she said and Mrs Jensen stared at her, clearly still in shock. Her wits had gone begging and she looked dazed. 'Mr Henderson will need help if Captain Hernshaw has been badly hurt.'

'Yes, come this way,' Dora said, coming out of her trance. 'I'll show you, but don't ask me to help, because I shall faint at the sight of it. I never could stand blood, and that's a fact!'

'We can manage,' Georgie said, understanding that she felt bad because of the way she had reacted. 'My aunt was just the same. When my uncle had a shooting accident, I was the one who patched him up until the doctor—' She stopped abruptly, because she had already said too much. She hadn't intended to mention her uncle at all!

'I thought…' Dora shook her head, because the sight of her master stumbling into the house in such a state had shattered her nerves and she did not know where she was. She had assumed Georgie was alone in the world but now it seemed she had an aunt and uncle. However, it wasn't her business, and there was no time to think of anything but Captain Hernshaw for the moment. 'You had better come at once.'

Georgie followed her swiftly along the hall to a set of double doors at the end, which led into the master suite. She went in, leaving Mrs Jensen to hover outside. The first room was a sitting room, which she noticed seemed less dark and dull than the rest of the house, and might have been refurbished recently, but there was no time to stare, for a voice summoned her from what was clearly the bedroom beyond.

'In here!'

Hurrying to answer Henderson's call, Georgie found him bending over the figure of his master. There was blood everywhere and he was frantically trying to press down on an open wound in Captain Hernshaw's shoulder and directing the footman to do the same to another wound in the captain's thigh.

'What can I do?' Georgie asked, going to the bed.

Henderson glanced up. 'Not going to faint on me?'

'No, I shan't do that,' she replied. 'Can I do that while you attend to the wound in his thigh? It looks as if it is the worst. Shall you stitch it or apply a tourniquet until the doctor arrives?'

'We don't have time to wait,' Henderson replied

tersely. 'Unless I can close that wound, he will bleed to death.'

'You'd better do it, then,' Georgie said. 'I'll apply the pad to his shoulder and the footman can hold him down for you. He will likely come to his senses and fight you when you start.'

'You've had some experience of this,' Henderson said, giving her a knowing glance. He moved the footman to one side and looked at the deep wound to his patient's thigh. 'I'll sew it roughly for the moment to stop the blood. It won't be pretty, but it may save him.'

'Get on with it,' Georgie said, pressing down as hard as she could on the secondary wound. 'Otherwise he will certainly die. No one can lose this much blood and live.'

Almost an hour later, Georgie looked down at the man lying amongst the stained sheets. His face was very pale and she thought he was completely out of it now, for he had fought them so hard when the cauterising iron was applied to his thigh that Henderson had had to knock him out with a strong dose of laudanum, forcing it down his throat as he raged at them in his agony.

She shuddered, because she knew that he had come very close to death that night. The experience had been far worse than when her uncle was shot in an accident, and she was feeling weak after their efforts to save his life. Even now there was no guarantee that he would live. It was likely he would take a fever or his wound might turn bad, as wounds so often did, the poison going inward.

'You look terrible,' Henderson said, glancing at her

in concern. 'You should go to bed, Georgie. I can mange him now.'

'He will take a lot of nursing,' Georgie replied, frowning. She did not know why, but she was reluctant to leave the man lying there so still and pale. 'I've seen something like this before. It wasn't as bad as this, but bad enough. Your master could still die of a fever—and he has lost a lot of blood.'

'Yes, I know. I'll have the doctor to him, but I don't see what else we could have done.'

'You did everything any doctor would have,' Georgie said. 'Did you learn that in the army?'

'My father was an army surgeon,' Henderson said. 'It was his wish that I should take it up, but I wanted to be a soldier. I soon learned that my father's skills were necessary out there and I made it my business to learn all I could—from him and from books.'

'You saved Captain Hernshaw's life.'

'If he lives.'

'If he lives,' Georgie agreed, because she knew the outcome was still in doubt. 'I'll go to bed now, but I'll come back later so that you can rest.'

He nodded his head, not bothering to answer. Georgie left him to finish clearing up the mess they had created. She was feeling so very tired. Everything had happened so fast that she hardly knew what had happened. But as they fought for Captain Hernshaw's life she had known very clearly that she did not want him to die!

As she walked back to her room, Georgie was thinking about the man she had helped to tend. Seeing him lying there, his life in danger, had affected her more than she would have expected. She had only known him a few hours, but already she was praying for his recovery. She did not know why, but for some reason it was very important to her that he should live.

Georgie had fallen asleep almost as soon as her head had touched the pillow. When she woke again it was to see the first rays of the morning light creeping in at the window. For a moment she lay, stretching, feeling relaxed, and then suddenly it hit her and she recalled all the events of the previous night. She had slept in her clothes in case she was needed, and sprang out now, hurrying along the hall to Captain Hernshaw's apartments. As she went in she saw that Henderson was applying a cloth to the patient's forehead and went to him.

'How is he?'

'Feverish, I think,' Henderson replied. 'The laudanum kept him quiet most of the night, but he is starting to fight now.'

'You've been up all night,' Georgie said. 'I meant to come, but I slept too soundly. Give me the cloth. I can do that and you should rest.'

'Yes, I need an hour or two,' Henderson agreed. 'The doctor came and gave me some medicine for the fever. I've given him one dose and he shouldn't have more for two hours. If I'm back, I'll give it to him, but the measure is one spoonful, no more.'

'Yes, I see,' Georgie said and glanced at the dressing chest where the dark brown bottle and a spoon had been placed. She took note of the time by the clock on a tall chest. 'He has the next dose at nine forty-five.'

'Yes, good.' Henderson looked approving. 'I shall leave it to you, then—and thank you.'

'He helped me. It is only fair I should help him.'

Henderson studied her in silence for a moment, but said nothing more, just turned and left her to get on with the job of bathing the patient's brow.

'Justin…' Georgie turned her head as she heard the feverish mumbling. 'Forgive me…I should have been there…don't die…I'm sorry…it wasn't your fault…it wasn't your fault…'

Georgie wrung out her cloth in cool water and stroked it over his heated forehead. His dark hair was damp with sweat, hanging in rat-tails about his face. He wore his hair longer than most men did these days and she thought it gave him the look of a rebel, a man who did not conform to the fashion of the day.

'Justin…no…' He gave a tortured cry and sat up in bed staring wildly in front of him. 'You can't die… forgive me…forgive me…'

'He forgives you,' Georgie said as he fell back against the pillows with a sigh. She wasn't sure if he could hear her in his fever, but she stroked her fingers down his cheek, soothing him. Touching him made her feel a little strange, because she felt he needed her and she longed to help him. He was in such torment and his pain tugged at her heartstrings, bringing tears to her eyes. 'He knows you wanted to save him…it isn't your fault if he dies…'

His hand shot out, gripping her wrist, his eyes staring at her, but seeing something beyond her. 'I knew,' he muttered. 'I knew what they did to him! I should have stopped them. It wasn't his fault…he was gentle…so gentle…they killed him…'

'It's all right,' Georgie told him, her fingers caressing his cheek once more. 'Rest now. Justin is safe…'

'No, he died…' Tears were trickling down his cheeks now. 'He died because I wasn't there to help…'

'But you wanted to,' Georgie comforted, her heart wrenched by his obvious distress. 'You would have if you could…'

'Failed him…' His eyes had closed now, but she thought he seemed a little easier. She stroked his hair and his face, using the cool cloth to wipe away the sweat from his forehead and the tears from his cheeks. His outburst had been a revelation, for who would have guessed that he could be so moved? He seemed such a stern man, giving no sign of any deep emotions, but clearly he felt them. He had inadvertently revealed another side of his character, one that she might not have known was there if he hadn't been struck down like this, and it had reached out to something inside her, arousing tender feelings she had not known she had. Georgie wondered who Justin was and what had happened to him—and why did Captain Hernshaw feel so very responsible?

It wasn't her business, she decided as she sat back in the chair Henderson had drawn close to the bed. At least he was resting for the moment. He was still hot, but the mutterings had stopped and he appeared to be more comfortable.

She sat watching him, studying the curves and angles of his features. He wasn't a handsome man by the standards of the day. His features were much too harsh, his nose straight and patrician. His mouth looked softer when he was sleeping, not hard or angry as it did when he was annoyed, and his lashes were thick and dark. She could not see his eyes at that moment, but she knew they were grey—eyes that could be cold or sparkle with amusement. He intrigued her. What kind of a man would bring a thief he had met on the streets to his home? What kind of man was tortured by something in his past? Had he done something dreadful? Was that why he begged forgiveness in his fever?

She would probably never know, Georgie realised. She had hoped to persuade him to help her reach her great-aunt's, but he was unlikely to be able to leave his bed for some weeks. Could she stay here all that time— ought she even if he allowed it?

She was torn by uncertainty as she sat watching him. One part of her told her that she should leave as soon as she could, because it would be foolish to become more involved with him. Perhaps one of his servants would lend her enough money to take the coach to Yorkshire…and yet she could not desert this man while he lay ill. Against her will, she felt drawn to him in a way she could not explain. Besides, Henderson would need help until his master was over the worst. And, Georgie admitted, she wanted to help take care of him, to see him strong and well again, to touch him and… She shut out the foolish thoughts. She wouldn't run away while he needed her, but she wouldn't allow herself to have foolish thoughts either!

Henderson returned exactly two hours after he had left. Georgie wondered if he had slept at all, but when she asked if he had, he merely said he was rested.

'I got used to not having much sleep when we were fighting on the Peninsula,' he told her. 'I don't need a lot. Mrs Jensen said you were to go down when you are ready, Georgie. She will give you breakfast in the small parlour.'

'Oh…thank you,' Georgie said, becoming aware that she was beginning to feel hungry. 'Yes, I shall. Do you want me to help with his medicine first?'

'I can manage him,' Henderson said. 'He is easy enough when he's like this; it's when he begins to feel more like himself that he gets restless. He doesn't make a good patient.'

'You have nursed him before?'

'He wouldn't thank me for telling you, but, yes, he has been wounded badly a couple of times.'

'He was lucky to have you.'

'I'm the lucky one,' Henderson said. 'When I was caught by a blast from a cannon, it cut my face to ribbons, and I had a stomach wound that should have been fatal. They thought I was finished, but he wouldn't leave me. He carried me back to base over his horse and he forced the surgeon to sew me back together, and then he sat with me until he knew I would live. He paid for someone to nurse me until I was on my feet again. A good many would have left me to die—and when they told me I was no more good for the army, he told me I had a place with him for life.'

Georgie looked at him intently. 'You love him, don't you?'

'I'm not sure whether it's brotherly love or gratitude,' Henderson said with a grimace, 'but I know I would die in his place if it came to it.'

'I call that love,' Georgie said and smiled. 'I'll come back later. We'll look after him together.'

'Yes, miss, if that's what you want.'

'It is,' she said, 'and you can call me Georgie.'

Henderson shot her a curious look, but didn't answer. She was discovering that he was a man who spoke only when he thought it necessary, and she felt pleased that he had told her his story. It must mean that he liked her and trusted her. She felt that she had made a friend, someone who might help her if she were in need.

She went downstairs to the small parlour and discovered that Mrs Jensen had set out a table for her. There was a dish of scrambled eggs with ham and some good fresh bread. It smelled wonderful and she ate most of what had been left for her, gathering the dishes afterwards just as Jensen entered.

'There's no need for you to do that,' he said, his expression doubtful and a little sad as he looked at her. Georgie suspected that he thought her no better than she should be. Perhaps he believed she was masquerading as a boy so as to carry on an illicit affair with his master. 'Mrs Jensen and I are used to taking care of things in this house.'

'Have you been here a long time?' Georgie asked.

'Forty-odd years,' he replied. 'I served the old master until he died. I thought I would leave when that happened, but I've stayed on to take care of things for the captain.'

'I am sure he is grateful,' Georgie said. She sensed that he was not as willing to be as friendly as his wife, and that he didn't quite trust her. 'But you should tell him if you wish to leave.'

'Don't you go saying a word to him!'

'No, I shan't, but if you would like to retire you should consider telling him yourself.'

'When he has time to settle down…' Jensen shook his head. 'That's if he recovers from what happened last night…terrible to think such a thing could happen so close to home.'

'It may be as well it did,' Georgie said. 'Had he not been able to get home, he might have bled to death in the street.'

Jensen looked grey in the face. 'Nothing like that ever happened when the old master was alive. I can't think what things are coming to…'

He looked suddenly old and his hand trembled as he gathered the dishes. Georgie felt sorry for him, because he was so obviously upset.

'I am sure Captain Hernshaw will recover now,' she said. 'Mr Henderson was very quick and clever last night. He saved the captain's life.'

'You helped him,' the old man said and shook his head sadly. 'Mrs Jensen told me she couldn't have done it. I'm not sure why he brought you here, but it may be a good thing.' He sounded and looked doubtful even as he said the words.

'I was in trouble,' Georgie said. 'Captain Henderson helped me—but I would have done it for anyone. I am not frightened by a little blood.'

'It was a lot of blood,' the old man said, giving her a reproachful look. 'We've never had young ladies in this house…and certainly not dressed as you are.'

'I am sorry if you disapprove, but I am in hiding, you see. If a certain person discovered where I am, he might…kill me.' She had decided to stick to this part of her story, because she couldn't be sure of the reaction she would get if she told the truth.

'Such goings-on! The old master would turn in his grave if he knew…' Jensen grumbled to himself as he picked the tray up and went out of the room.

Georgie sighed. She would have felt better if she had been allowed to help, but it was obvious that Jensen would not allow that. His wife would probably resent it if Georgie offered to help in the kitchen. There was nothing for it but to find a book to read, though she doubted she would find anything of interest in this room.

She wandered over to the bookshelves, looking at the volumes of history and scientific volumes. They would send her to sleep in five minutes! She looked further along, almost giving up until she saw the book of poetry. It was new, bound in red leather, and very much out of place amongst all the others. Picking it out, she frowned as she opened it and a folded paper fell out. Georgie replaced it without opening it because it wasn't hers to read. She took the book and curled up in a chair by the window, beginning to read, but after a while she saw that it had been marked in ink in the columns and some words had been underlined.

What a terrible way to treat a new book! And it was by Lord Byron, something she had wanted to read for a long time! Who could have done such a thing?

She frowned over it, trying to ignore the ink marks, but they annoyed her and she found herself fixing on them when she ought to have been reading the poetry. She was caught by the regularity of what seemed to be a pattern, and began to wonder if perhaps it was a code of some kind, though she couldn't make much sense of it. She flicked through the book and found the folded paper someone had left inside, hesitating because it wasn't hers and yet intrigued.

Oh, what did it matter? It shouldn't have been left there for anyone to find if it was important. She unfolded it and read through the few lines of explanation, a spiral of excitement curling through her as she realised that she was right. It was a code and with this she could break it easily. By studying the text in the poetry book and then comparing it to the instructions in the letter, Georgie soon realised that if you took out the letters that had been marked you could make new words and sentences.

It was a message of some kind! She looked at what she had thought was just scribbling in the margins and realised that the numbers and letters referred to certain lines. Someone had already done a lot of the work and Georgie found it easy to work from that person's notes. Counting along the lines, she found the words that had been underlined and suddenly the message began to jump out at her.

It concerned a plot to kill members of the government and an important man, who, she thought, was meant to be the Regent! She sat holding the book for some minutes, staring at it in disbelief, thinking she must be mistaken. Surely she was wrong! If she had translated this correctly, the man she had tried to steal from the previous evening might be concerned in a wicked plot to bring down the English government and the throne!

She couldn't be right! She must have made a mistake…and yet the terrible attack on Captain Hernshaw that had happened close to his house might be directly connected with what she had just discovered. No! She would not believe he was capable of such infamy! Georgie got to her feet, placing the letter back where it belonged and closing the book with a snap. She returned it to its place on the shelf. She had made a mistake when deciphering the message…or perhaps Captain Hernshaw was concerned with this plot because he was trying to stop it happening…

It had to be that, she decided, because she could not—would not—believe that the man who had treated her so well when he might have handed her over to the watch was a traitor to his country.

Besides, she had no right to pry into his private affairs. Glancing at the clock, she saw that some hours had passed. It was time that she went up to give Henderson a chance to find himself something to eat.

They took turns to watch him throughout the rest of the day and during the night, but there was little change, though once while Georgie was with him he seemed to be feverish. Once again she heard the name *Justin,* though what he was saying wasn't clear this time. She smoothed his damp hair back from his forehead, talking to him softly, and after a while he quietened. She smiled down at him, thinking how much younger he looked when he was resting. She knew a strong temptation to kiss him and stroke his face, but fought it because it wouldn't be right to take advantage when he was vulnerable. She sat down again to watch over him from a distance. When Henderson came back, he was sleeping peacefully.

'He seems better,' the manservant remarked. 'I think he may be through the dangerous time, Georgie.' He smiled at her. 'Go to bed now. I can manage him from now on.'

'I'll come back so that you can have your breakfast,' Georgie replied. 'You told me that the trouble will start when he comes to his senses, didn't you?'

'Yes, but…' He shook his head at her. 'It isn't fitting for a young lady to be in a gentleman's bedchamber.'

'Who will know?' Georgie asked and grinned. 'I shan't tell if you don't.'

He tipped his head to one side, considering her.

'Who are you, miss? I'd swear you were a lady if I didn't know he found you on the streets.'

'My name is Georgina, but I can't tell you any more than that,' she said. 'I ran away from…where I was, because something terrible would have happened if I hadn't.'

Henderson gave her a look of disbelief. 'Are you sure you're telling me the truth?'

'I wish I could tell you more, but I can't.'

'The captain will want to know when he's himself again.'

Georgie looked at their patient. 'I want to trust him, but I am afraid he might not believe me.'

'If you tell him the truth, he will help you.'

'Will he?'

Henderson looked at her hard. 'You will have to trust someone eventually—and he is the one who can help you.'

'Yes, I know. I will try, honestly, I will—and could you please call me Georgie? I don't want anyone outside this house to know I'm a girl.'

'They've only to see your hair,' Henderson told her. 'I shan't betray you, but you must be very careful.'

Georgie agreed that she would and he went away to have his breakfast. She stood watching over their patient for a while; he seemed to be resting more easily. She bent to stroke his hair from his forehead, smiling at him as he murmured in his sleep, and then she leaned down to kiss him lightly on the cheek. His eyelids flickered, which made her back away hastily. She wandered over to the window, where she discovered a rather battered-looking chess set on a little table near the window. She began to set out the pieces and had just finished placing them when Henderson returned. He smiled as he saw what she had done and came over to the table.

'We played this many an evening during the campaign,' he told her. 'There wasn't much else to do, miss.'

'Shall we play a game?' Georgie suggested. 'I used to play with my father, but I haven't played for ages. I'll take white and you have black.'

'Yes, if you wish,' Henderson agreed and moved a piece for his opening gambit.

Georgie moved a pawn to block him and battle was joined. She gave a chuckle of delight as he removed her first piece, for it was obvious that he was a worthy opponent and she need not fear to play her best game. Neither of them noticed when the man in the bed opened his eyes.

Richard lay with his head resting against the pillows for some seconds before he became aware that he was not alone in the room. He was at first conscious only of the throbbing agony in his thigh. There was some soreness in his left shoulder, but it was his thigh that pained him the worst. He could not for a moment think where he was, his pain swirling him back to the battlefield and the agony he had endured from wounds gained there. The girl's laughter penetrated the fog that held him, making him focus on the two figures near the window.

It was a few moments before he realised that one of the two was Henderson and the other…was a rather odd-looking urchin dressed in clothes that were far too big for him. He inched his way up against the pillows and the sharp stab of pain cleared his thoughts. No street urchin, but the girl he had brought home the night he was attacked.

Richard grimaced as he continued to watch them. Her laughter was infectious as she moved her chess pieces with lightning speed and gave a chortle of glee.

'Check!'

'I didn't see that coming,' Henderson told her ruefully.

'I am sorry to interrupt your game, but could I have some water?'

Richard's words brought their heads round instantly. Somewhere beyond the pain and the need to relieve his thirst, he felt amusement at the guilt reflected in the girl's face. She got up at once and went swiftly to pour water into a glass.

'Come back to us, have you, sir?' Henderson said, unperturbed. 'I thought you were over the worst last night. You gave us all a fright, captain. What happened?'

'I had been somewhere and it was on my way back…' Richard frowned as he recalled the murderous attack. He had delivered his package to the man who waited for it and returned home. He had had no sense of being followed and the attack was silent and deadly, his assailant stabbing him in the leg viciously and then the shoulder. 'Rather like you, Henderson, I didn't see it coming.'

'That's unusual for you, sir. You hadn't been drinking?'

'Not sufficiently to lose my awareness. Whoever it was must have been a professional.'

'And good at his work,' Henderson said. 'If you hadn't been so close to home, that thigh wound would have done for you, captain. You almost bled to death.'

'Who patched me up?'

'Mr Henderson,' Georgie said, bringing him the glass of water. 'He did everything a doctor could, but much more quickly. We couldn't wait because you were losing too much blood.'

Richard's gaze centred on her face. 'You didn't let this rascal help patch me up, Henderson?'

'Georgie was very good. She has helped me look after you, captain. She didn't flinch at the sight of blood. I should have been hard put to it to manage without her.'

'So you know she is a girl?' Richard sipped the water she offered, his hand closing over hers as she held the glass to his lips. He drank a little and then nodded. 'Thank you, that is enough.' He sighed and lay back against the pillows, his eyes closing as he felt a shaft of pain. Georgie started to move away, but his hand came out, gripping her wrist with surprising strength. 'Where did you get those ridiculous clothes?'

'Henderson gave them to me. I think they belong to you.'

'Indeed?' His eyes opened once more. He looked at his manservant, who nodded. 'We must buy her something suitable. Perhaps Mrs Jensen will know.'

'I can't stay here dressed as a girl,' Georgie said. 'I don't mind wearing your things.'

'Get her something that fits her, Henderson,' Richard said. 'If she is determined to keep up the masquerade, make it a youth's clothing.'

'Yes, sir, I'll do that,' Henderson said. 'Frederick has a young brother. I'll ask him to buy a few things.'

'Yes, do that…' Richard sighed and closed his eyes. The girl was a problem he could have done without at this particular time, but she had made herself useful. Besides, he just did not have the energy to deal with her for the moment. 'I need to rest…'

He was vaguely aware of some whispering going on, but the strange tiredness was creeping over his body and he was slipping away, his eyelids too heavy to open.

Georgie left the bedchamber. Henderson had told her that she should find something to eat for herself, and she went down to the parlour. Some cold ham, pickles and fresh bread had been left out for her. There was also a pot of coffee, but it was nearly cold. She drank some because she did not wish to trouble Mrs Jensen for more.

After she had eaten, she gathered the dishes and took them through to the kitchen. Mrs Jensen was there but there was no sign of her husband.

'You shouldn't have bothered with those, miss.'

'I like to help,' Georgie said. 'I don't want to cause more trouble for you than I need, Mrs Jensen.'

'Well, you're not a bother, whatever Jensen says,' Dora told her kindly. 'I rather like having a young person in the house. It makes a change, and I told Jensen so. He was ready to retire years ago, but I'm younger. I still enjoy my work, and that's a fact, miss.'

'I am glad I am not a trouble to you,' Georgie said. 'I know Mr Jensen thinks it is all very shocking, and of course he is right—but I have nowhere else to go. If Captain Hernshaw would hire a post-chaise for me, I could leave, but I couldn't ask him while he was unconscious, could I? As soon as he is well enough, I will ask for a loan of some guineas and then I can leave.'

'Well, as to that, miss, it is up to the captain who he

brings home, and that is what I told Jensen. We're here to look after the house, not to judge. Besides, there's nothing going on—couldn't be with the master so poorly.'

'He has come to his senses this morning,' Georgie said. 'I helped to nurse him when he was in the fever, Mrs Jensen, but he is a strong man and he will soon recover, I think.'

'I am sure you are right, miss,' the housekeeper said and nodded her head as if she had the same thought. 'Mr Henderson told me he had been wounded badly before. It was a good thing you were here to help, that's all I can say, miss.'

It was on the tip of Georgie's tongue to ask her to remember that she was supposed to be a boy, but she decided it didn't matter. As long as she stayed in the house, and out of the way if the captain had visitors, she would be safe enough. She didn't know that the man she disliked so much was in town to look for her. He could be here for a quite different reason. All she had to do was stay here until she could persuade Captain Hernshaw to help her.

She had decided that she must try to get to her great-aunt's home and ask her if she would take her in. It need only be for a short time, after all, because as soon as she was in possession of her fortune she could hire a companion and set up her own establishment.

In the meantime, Georgie needed something to amuse herself. She went to the parlour that she had made her own since coming to the house and began to wander about the room. She took down the book of poems and began to read through it, trying to ignore the scribbling in the margin.

After a while, she laid the book aside. Obviously, Captain Hernshaw was mixed up in something nasty. It had not occurred to her previously to wonder why he should have been in those mean streets where he'd found her, but now she frowned over it. Had he gone there to meet someone? She knew from her own experience that the slums were haunted by rogues, thieves and worse—so what had a man like that been doing there? And what was in the package she had snatched from him?

It must have been important for him to chase after her the way he had. Could he possibly be involved with the kind of people who would work against the government and the Regent? She had begun to like him rather a lot and tried to dismiss the thought.

Getting to her feet, she was about to replace the book, but then changed her mind, taking it with her as she went back upstairs. She paused outside Captain Hernshaw's rooms, then knocked and entered. She saw at once that their patient was awake, sitting up against the pillows. Henderson had clearly been busy, for his master was clean-shaven and looked much better than he had when she'd left earlier.

He gave her an odd look as she entered. 'What are you doing here? I must thank you for helping Henderson, but you should not continue to visit me here now— unless you have no reputation to lose?'

Georgie blushed. 'I came to see if I could do anything for you,' she said. 'If you would like me to read to you…' She hesitated and then approached the bed, showing him the book. 'I found this downstairs.'

'Did you indeed?' Richard glared at her. 'And have you been reading it?'

'Yes…' She looked away from his hard gaze and then back. 'It has writing in the margins and some words are underlined.'

'And what do you make of that?'

Georgie took a deep breath. 'I am not sure. It might be some sort of a code…'

'What makes you think that?'

'Because I tried making sense of it.' She hesitated, then confessed, 'There was a paper inside that gave me instructions for breaking the code.'

'And did you?'

'Yes…at least I was able to form words and sentences.'

'And that has made you wonder if I am a spy or an assassin?'

'No, of course not,' Georgie denied, a flush in her cheeks. 'I mean…it does look bad, but I didn't think you…but you were attacked and I wondered…'

'I should have left you where I found you,' Richard said ruefully. 'I knew you were trouble from the start.'

'You're not involved in a plot to kill the Regent, are you?' Her eyes opened wide.

'If I were, you would have just signed your own death warrant,' Richard said, a gleam of annoyance mixed with laughter in his eyes. 'No, I am not involved in it—but I may be involved in trying to stop someone who is.'

'Yes…' Georgie let out a long sigh of relief. 'I thought it must be that. I am so glad it isn't you.'

'Are you?' He arched his right brow. 'Are you able to keep a secret, Georgie?'

'Yes, of course. I shan't breathe a word.' She hesitated, feeling uncomfortable at what she must do now.

'Could you lend me some money—enough to travel post-chaise to Yorkshire?'

'Lend you—or give you?'

'Oh, I should pay you back soon,' Georgie said. 'If you would do that, I could leave at once and I would not trouble you again.'

Richard's gaze narrowed. He studied her face for a moment or two. 'I could lend it to you,' he said. 'I may do if you tell me the truth. I know you told me some story of having been forced from your post as a lady's maid because of your employer's son, but I think you were lying to me. I don't think you were ever a maid, were you?'

She hesitated, and then met his eyes. 'I didn't know you then,' she said. It was no use, he wouldn't believe her if she told him more lies. She was going to have to tell him the truth! 'You could have been anyone. My real name is Georgina Bridges. My father was Sir John Bridges, my mother the youngest daughter of Lord Nairn. They were both killed in an accident two years ago—and they left a fortune in trust for me. I inherit in a few weeks' time. My uncle, Sir Henry Mowbray, wants me to marry a man he owes money to—but I hate him, so I ran away. They want my money and they think he will give some of it to them if they make me marry him, but I know he would keep it for himself. He is so horrid…the way he looks at me makes me feel…dirty.' She ended on a sob of distress. 'I ran away as soon as I heard them discussing it. I would rather die than marry him.'

'And what is the name of this man?'

'He is a Frenchman. His name is Raoul Thierry. He seems to be a rich gentleman, but there is something sinister about him.' Georgie shuddered. 'I did not know what to do when I heard my aunt and uncle talking so I ran away, but then…I told you what happened. I suppose my lawyer would give me money if I asked, but he might not believe it really was me.'

Richard's eyes went over her. 'In your present attire I am certain you would not get past his clerk. The money isn't a problem, Georgie. But I am not certain you are telling me the truth.'

'I am this time! I promise I am.'

'Even so, you are vulnerable. You obviously aren't capable of looking after yourself.'

'I should have gone to my great-aunt the first time. I was wrong to stop in London.' She bit her bottom lip. 'I know you must be angry. I tied to rob you and now you are ill and you do not want the bother of me.'

'No, I do not want the trouble of a young lady,' Richard admitted and frowned. 'However, Henderson told me how you helped him and I owe you for that, Georgina.'

'Please do not call me that! My Aunt Agatha calls me Georgina and I hate it. I am Georgie—and you don't owe me anything. I did what anyone would have in the circumstances.'

'No, that is not strictly true. Apparently Dora nearly fainted at the sight of the blood. You did far more than I could have expected of a stranger.'

'You gave me supper and somewhere to sleep.'

'And by doing that you became my responsibility,' Richard said. 'I am confined to bed for the next week or so, but once I am on my feet I shall take you to your great-aunt.'

Georgie looked at him doubtfully. 'You cannot want that trouble, sir. Lend me the money and I shall go alone.'

'No, you will not,' Richard said. 'If you have told

me the truth, you may be in some danger. Therefore it is my duty to see you safe.' He closed his eyes. 'Forgive me, but I am weary. Please go away now. You have my promise that I shall take you to your great-aunt when I am able. For the moment you must be patient and wait.'

Georgie stared at him for a few seconds, but he had leaned back against the pillows, his eyes closed. She placed the book of poetry on the bed and then walked softly to the door, glancing back at him as she went out. She felt frustrated, for she knew that without money she could not hope to reach her great-aunt's house. She could go to her lawyer, but it was doubtful if he would see her in her present state of dress—and if he did he would hardly believe that she was Miss Georgina Bridges.

If she ran away again, she might starve or become ill before she could reach safety. It seemed as if she must stay here, and wait for Captain Hernshaw to recover his strength sufficiently to accompany her to Yorkshire.

Richard opened his eyes as the door closed behind her. Her story was believable enough, though she had lied to him previously. If he accepted it this time, it would be wrong to let her go anywhere alone. Besides, she had mentioned a name—a name that he had learned to associate with treason.

It could be coincidence, but it was possible that by delivering Miss Bridges to her great-aunt, he would learn more of the man—or group of men he sought.

For a moment he wondered if she had been sent to rob him that night. She had certainly tried to take the package containing new information about the plotters—perhaps the names and whereabouts of men concerned in the conspiracy to bring down the government and cause chaos in England. He had not yet had the chance to decode it, though he'd delivered it to others who might recently have done so.

They needed the information, because the plot must not succeed. With the Regent dead, as these villains planned, there would be men in England who would not hesitate to settle with the French. Napoleon Bonaparte was barely contained in his island prison of Elba, where rumour had it he reigned like a prince. If he were to break free and march again, the Allies would join together to defeat him—but if England were in chaos…

Richard knew that without the British the Allies would not stand long against Bonaparte. It was imperative that this plot be foiled and quickly before things got out of hand.

If Georgie was involved with these people, he would be best to stay close to her. His instincts told him that she was innocent—and yet she had decoded the message in the poetry book. It was that first clue that had been instrumental in alerting other members of the intelligence service that a plot was afoot. He believed that the near-fatal attack on him had been because of his involvement in the affair, but he had not seen the face of his attacker for it had been covered by a muffler and only a pair of cold eyes had been visible.

Looking into those eyes briefly, Richard had known that his life was in the balance. It was merely the sound of approaching voices that made his attacker run off before his work was done. From somewhere he had found the strength to stumble the few yards to his home, and Henderson had done the rest…with the girl's help.

Richard frowned. If his manservant were to be believed, Georgie had done well. He'd never had cause to doubt Henderson and must therefore be grateful to her for her contribution, and she was certainly entitled to the benefit of the doubt.

Richard knew that he had been feverish, and wondered what he had said in his muddled state. Had he mentioned his work for the government…or had he spoken of more intimate things? He knew that in the fever he had thought of Justin, his cousin. He felt the sharp grief strike at his heart, because the memories were still painful. Justin had been clever, a bright future his for the asking, but he had been led astray, his mind corrupted by opium and wine. He had sunk lower and lower, beyond the reach of his studious father, until at the last they destroyed him…those evil men who had drawn him into a web of bitter despair.

Richard had been away fighting and had known nothing of it until he returned. At his uncle's behest he had gone looking for the cousin he loved as a brother, but when he found him it had been too late. Justin had been living in squalor, lying amongst his own filth in a disgusting house, his mind destroyed, his body wasting with a disease that could not be cured. Richard had taken him to a place of safety, staying by him until the last, holding him as he choked on his own blood. The memory haunted him, would never leave him. It had made him the man he was, harsh, stern, living only for his work.

The girl was an interruption, nothing more. Yet she had touched something that had been dead, something deep inside. For a moment as she stood there smiling down at him, he had wished that he had the strength to take her in his arms and kiss her until those wonderful eyes turned smoky with desire. It was ridiculous, for, even had she not been a lady, he was as weak as a kitten. However, she had stirred his heart in a way that no one had for years—and he found that he could not simply desert her.

He sighed and closed his eyes.

There was nothing much he could do for the moment. It would be a few days at the least before he could think of getting up, let alone taking a long journey.

Chapter Three

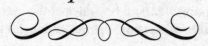

'But that is so silly,' Georgie said, looking mutinously at Mrs Jensen. 'Why will you not allow me to carry that tray up to Captain Hernshaw? I have nothing else to do and I am sure you have other jobs you could be doing.'

'The master says it is not fitting that a young lady should wait on him in his bedchamber, and I agree with him, miss.'

Georgie scowled at her and walked away, finding her way to the front parlour where she usually sat unless she joined Henderson in the servants' hall below stairs. He had taken pity on her a few times these past days, playing cards with her to help pass the time. But he was often busy with his duties, and since Georgie had been banned from her host's bedchamber she was feeling bored and frustrated. More than once she had considered leaving this house and setting out on her own, but the lack of funds meant she would need to walk all the way to Yorkshire, which she knew was impossible, or hitch a ride—and that was too dangerous.

'Oh, damn him,' Georgie muttered. She wandered

round the room at a loss for something to do, and ended up standing in front of the window. As she glanced down into the street, she saw a man crossing the road towards the house and flinched back. Was he coming here? Did he know she was staying here? Surely he couldn't?

She felt a thrill of horror as the knocker sounded. He was coming here! She opened the parlour door and listened, poised for flight and hearing the sound of Jensen's voice as the man inquired for Captain Hernshaw.

'I am sorry, sir,' Jensen said. 'Captain Hernshaw is not available at the moment. If you would like to leave your card, I shall tell him you called.'

'Very well. You may tell your master that I shall hope to hear from him. Good day.'

'Good morning, sir.'

Georgie crept to the top of the stairs as Jensen placed the calling card on a silver salver on the hall table. He went off to the rear of the house and she ran down the stairs, picking up the card. She read the few words printed there: Raoul Thierry of Westbury House, Thraxton Morton, Yorkshire. On the back were scrawled the words: 'We may be of some use to each other if we could meet, Thierry.'

What could he want with Captain Hernshaw? Had he learned that Georgie was staying here? She frowned over the card and then slipped it into the pocket of the jacket she was wearing. She dare not take the risk that he would come here to meet Captain Hernshaw while she was here. She would keep the card for now and give it to Captain Hernshaw when he delivered her to her great-aunt's house.

Georgie went quickly up to her own room. She

glanced at herself in the small mirror on the dressing chest, her melting brown eyes wide and fearful. Henderson had found her some clothing that fitted her much better than Captain Hernshaw's. She looked like a very young boy until she took her cap off, letting her luxuriant hair tumble down over her shoulders. She knew that anyone who saw her dressed this way would think her shameless. She was slender and the short buff-coloured coat covered her breasts, which would otherwise have given the game away, but when she took it off they were noticeable beneath the soft linen. It was after she had wandered into the captain's bedroom looking like this that he had banned her from visiting him.

'Have you lost all sense of modesty, Georgie?' he had asked, sounding annoyed. 'Dressed like that with your hair loose—it is too provocative and not the attire for a gentleman's bedchamber, even if he is still as weak as a kitten.'

The look he had given her then had made Georgie blush. She had replaced her cap, but the ban had not been rescinded. She was barred from visiting him in his bedchamber and as yet he had not attempted to come out, though it was more than a week.

How much longer would he be confined to his bed? Her restlessness had increased since catching sight of the visitor that morning. She thought that Captain Hernshaw did not know him, for he had not reacted to the name when she mentioned it, though it was obvious that Raoul Thierry wanted to meet him. It was imperative that they did not meet until after Georgie had reached her great-aunt's house!

How much longer must she stay here! If only he

would lend her enough money to pay for her fare, but she knew that it was useless to ask. He was determined not to let her go alone and so she had no choice but to wait for him to recover.

Some days later, Georgie was curled in a large wing chair when the door opened and she sensed someone looking at her. She glanced up, her heart jerking as she saw Captain Hernshaw. He looked as powerful as ever, his strong shoulders clothed in a coat that fitted him closely, his breeches pale and elegant with only a slight thickening at the thigh to show that he had recently been wounded and still wore a bandage.

'Oh, are you better?' she said, uncurling and getting to her feet. 'This is the best chair. Perhaps you would like to sit here?'

'So this is where you get to,' Richard said. She wasn't wearing her coat and the shirt clung to her curves, making him realise that she was far from being the child he had thought her that first night. 'Why don't you use the parlour? It is more comfortable than this room.'

'Mrs Jensen always lights a fire here. I didn't like to ask her to light the parlour fire.'

'I shall do so,' Richard said and limped towards her. He grimaced from the pain. If Henderson had had his way, Richard would still be in bed, but he was tired of lying there when there was so much needing his attention. 'What are you doing here? I shouldn't have thought there was much in this room to interest you.'

'There isn't,' Georgie said and pulled a face. 'But Dora would not let me visit you.'

'She was obeying my orders,' Richard said. 'You are

bored. I am sorry. I had no intention of staying more than a few days for I have business elsewhere.'

'It's my fault,' Georgie said, voicing thoughts even she hadn't realised were there until now. 'If you hadn't taken a detour to help me, you would not have had to go out again that night.'

'If it hadn't happened then, it would another day,' he said, voice and face expressionless. 'Besides, I am on the mend now. We shall be ready to leave in a couple of days.'

'Really?' She discovered that she was no longer in a hurry. 'You must take your time, sir. I should not wish your wound to break open again on my account.'

'I heal quickly,' Richard said. His eyes narrowed. 'Be careful no one sees you like that, Georgina. I'm afraid your secret would not remain a secret for long if you were seen without your cap and coat.'

'Perhaps I should cut my hair?'

'No!' he answered swiftly, a note of authority in his voice that made her stare at him. 'No, it would be a shame to cut such glorious tresses. After all, this masquerade will soon be over.' His gaze narrowed. 'I think it best if you retain the boys' clothes as we travel, but I will purchase a gown for you to change into before we arrive at your great-aunt's home. You will not want to shock her by arriving dressed like that, Georgina.'

'No, I think she would be angry.' Georgie looked at his face, noting the tiny nerve that flicked at his temple. 'Please, will you not call me Georgie? My aunt always used Georgina when she wished to punish me for something.'

'Did you often deserve that she should punish you?'

'Perhaps. I dare say I tried her patience, but my

mother…' She blinked as she felt the sharp sting of tears. 'We were a happy family. I was given a great deal of freedom. Mama told me to remember my manners, to be kind to others and to speak my mind if I saw injustice or deceit—but always to be myself.'

Richard saw that she was emotional. 'You must miss your parents terribly?'

'Yes, I do.' Georgie lifted her head. 'Mama would have been so angry if she knew what her brother planned for me. She would never have tried to force me to marry someone I did not like. Indeed, I do not think she would have thought that man a suitable husband for her daughter.'

Richard studied her thoughtfully. 'Just what is it you find so distasteful about Monsieur Thierry?'

Georgie shivered. 'It is the way he looks at me…something secretive in his manner, sly. I trust nothing he says. Besides, a man who truly cared for me would not try to buy me from my uncle. He would have courted me in the proper way and taken his answer in good part.'

'That is certainly the way of a gentleman,' Richard replied, a faint smile on his lips. 'But can you be certain that he used your uncle's debts to secure you in marriage? Are you sure you heard correctly?'

'Yes, quite certain,' Georgie said. 'I heard my uncle talking to my aunt. She was quite shocked and tried to persuade him that it was not right, but he told her that he had no choice. I knew that they would use every method of persuasion to try to force me to take him and so I ran away.'

'And into more trouble!'

Georgie bit her lip. 'You do not have to go on about it! I have learned my lesson.'

'It is to be hoped that you have,' Richard told her severely.

Georgie glared at him. 'If you do not wish the trouble of taking me to my great-aunt, you could send me in a carriage with a servant.'

'Yes, I could,' Richard said, his eyes narrowed in thought. He was not sure why he had not arranged it while he lay confined to bed. Henderson could have secured the services of a lady's maid and they might have travelled by post-chaise. 'But I feel responsible for you. It would not be sensible to send you all that way when we cannot be certain of your reception. Have you thought what you will do if your great-aunt refuses to take you in?' Georgie shook her head. 'She is bound to be elderly and may not wish the trouble of a young woman. What will you do if she sends you back to your mother's brother?'

'I have no idea,' Georgie said honestly. 'However, once I have my money I intend to set up my own establishment.'

'At your age? Impossible!'

'I am nineteen,' Georgie told him. 'At least, I shall be in a few weeks. Besides, I have no choice if my great-aunt does not want me. She and my mother's brother are the only relatives I have.'

Richard nodded, his expression giving nothing away. 'Well, we must see what she has to say when we arrive. And now you may join me in the parlour.' He offered her his arm, which she took shyly, making certain that she put no pressure on him as they walked. 'I saw you playing chess with Henderson. You will oblige me by giving me a game. I have found it extremely tedious being tied to my bed these past days.'

'Well, it is your own fault,' Georgie replied, a sparkle

in her eyes. 'Had you not banned me from your chamber, I should have enjoyed spending some time entertaining you before this, sir.'

'And what would my servants have made of that?' Richard replied a glint in his eyes. 'I am past thirty, miss, and you are eighteen. If it became known that you had come to my bedchamber—made regular visits—your reputation would be gone. Even now, you run the risk that your great-aunt will think you sunk below her notice.'

'Oh…' Georgie flushed. 'I didn't think of it like that, because, after all, you were not likely to get up and ravish me—and I think I could run faster than you at the moment.'

Richard heard the lilt of laughter in her voice. Had she no idea what she looked like in her breeches? She was more enticing than she could imagine! 'You would not think it amusing if it became common knowledge. After all, you will want to go into society one day, perhaps marry? You would not want people to think you shameless?'

'No…' She blushed and hung her head. It hurt to know that he thought her shameless. 'Please do not scold me. I know that my behaviour has been reckless. I have been trying not to think of the consequences, for I cannot change things now—can I?'

'No,' Richard agreed. Glancing at her face, he saw the sparkle of tears. 'Well, do not turn missish on me now, Georgie. No tears! We are in this scrape together and we must brush through it as best we can. No more talk of going off alone. I shall escort you to your great-aunt and see you settled. Besides, I find my business takes me in that direction and it is possible that I may kill two birds with one stone.'

'May I ask the nature of your business in Yorkshire, sir?'

'No, you may not,' Richard said and grinned as he saw a flash of annoyance in her eyes. Better she should be angry than weep! 'It is for your own sake, miss, believe me. I am involved in something dangerous—as what happened the other night proves only too well. I am hoping that my enemy will not follow us from town. Henderson is to follow us on horseback, to keep a watch on my back, though I hope he will not be needed, at least while you are with me.'

Georgie raised her eyes to his. Her heart was racing, because the thought that he might die at the hands of an assassin was more painful than she cared to admit. 'You almost died last time, sir. I hope that whoever it was will not try again. I should not like you to die.'

'Would you not?' Richard laughed softly. It was an attractive sound, his features softening as he shook his head at her. 'Then I shall do my very best to oblige you by staying alive.'

Georgie glanced round the room she had occupied for several days now, feeling pleased that they were leaving at last. The past two days had been pleasant enough, for she had enjoyed Captain Hernshaw's company, playing chess and cards with him in the afternoon and after dinner. She had discovered that he had a good sense of humour and took a wicked pleasure when he could beat her at either game, though she had given a good account of herself and the score was fairly even between them. She was sure that she had won fairly on the occasions when she had beaten him, for he enjoyed winning, as she did, especially when faced with a worthy opponent.

But they were leaving at last, and she knew a sense of relief, not the least of it because she had noticed Captain Hernshaw was not limping as badly as the first day he had come downstairs. She suspected that he might still have some pain, but he had said nothing of it to her and she knew that Henderson still changed his bandages regularly; she had seen the old ones brought down for burning on the kitchen fire.

As she went downstairs she saw that Captain Hernshaw was waiting. His manservant was dressed for riding, and she saw him slip a bulky pistol into the pocket of his greatcoat, which had one simple cape over the shoulders. Captain Hernshaw himself wore a coat with three capes and his waistcoat was a thing of beauty. She had not seen him dressed so finely and blinked— he was a fine figure of a man, though she still did not think him truly handsome. However, he was certainly dressed as befitted a gentleman, and, oddly, she found herself wishing that she was wearing a pretty carriage gown and bonnet rather than her youth's clothing.

Do not be foolish, she told herself silently. He sees you as a duty, not a pleasure.

Her words were spoken only in her mind for Mrs Jensen had come to take her leave of her. 'I wish you a safe journey and good fortune, miss,' she said, giving her a sad, anxious look. 'I've told Captain Hernshaw to look after you. You should be with your great-aunt in a day or two, Miss Georgina.'

'Georgie,' she said and kissed the lady's cheek. 'Thank you so much for looking after me, and I am sorry if I have been a trouble to you. I should like to give you a present, but I have nothing—though I shall send you something as soon as I can.'

'There's no need for that, miss. I don't care what Jensen says, I don't think you're a bad girl and it has been a pleasure to have you.'

'How kind you are,' Georgie said and sniffed. She felt close to tears, but blinked them away as she felt Captain Hernshaw's eyes on her. 'Goodbye and thank you again.' She nodded to Jensen as she passed, for she could see that he felt it was a good thing she was going.

'Are you ready?' Richard asked, giving her an odd look. 'It won't be long now and you'll be with your great-aunt.'

'Yes, thank you,' Georgie said. She shot a shy smile at Henderson, who grinned at her and made her feel much better. 'Are you sure you feel up to the journey, sir?'

'I am perfectly recovered,' Richard lied, for he still felt the pain, as he was bound to for a while yet, but no more than he could cope with at the moment. 'Come along, then. My groom has the horses standing and I know they must be restive, for I have not driven them for a while.'

Georgie followed him out to his curricle. A young groom was holding the heads of a pair of magnificent black horses; they pawed the ground with their hooves, seemingly impatient.

'Do you want me to drive them, sir?' the groom asked, glancing at his master whom he knew to be just up from his sick bed. 'They've got the devil in them at the moment.'

'You can ride behind, Ned,' Richard said, his mouth thinning with determination. 'I'll tell you if I need you to take over.'

'Right you are, Captain. Just asking.'

Richard nodded. He handed Georgie into the curricle

and then got up beside her, the young groom jumping up at the back. Richard's progress was clearly hampered by the wound to his thigh, but he managed it without a wince, though Georgie saw his cheek tighten and guessed it had hurt him to do it. She wondered then if he were quite well, but decided to say nothing. His tone to the groom had been sharp and she did not wish to bring his anger down on her own head.

If he was in pain, it did not affect his handling of the superb matched pair and they were soon bowling along at a fair pace. Once or twice people walking in the street put their hand up to him, and she saw a few curious eyes turned on her, as if they were wondering who she might be. Of course they saw a young lad, not a lady, and must imagine she was Captain Hernshaw's nephew or some such thing. She pulled her cap on tighter, making sure that it could not become dislodged by a gust of wind. She did not want any of these fashionable ladies and gentlemen realising that she was not a boy, but a young woman—especially as she had seen two ladies whom she recalled as being friends of her mother. They would think her behaviour shocking, and, she acknowledged, they would be perfectly right.

She had run away from the protection of her mother's brother, spent two weeks living rough on the streets of London amongst thieves, prostitutes and worse, and then she had gone to the house of a gentleman she did not know, living in his house for more than a week without a proper chaperon. It was a scandalous tale and anyone hearing it without explanation would think her lost to all shame. Indeed, if it became common knowledge she would be ruined.

She would not allow any of it to weigh with her,

Georgie decided. Once this journey was over she would put the memory behind her, forget she had ever met Captain Hernshaw and his servants. Yet even as she thought it she felt a pang of regret. A part of her longed to be back where she belonged, wearing pretty clothes and mixing in society, but another part of her wished that their journey might go on for much longer than two days.

In that, at least, it looked as if she might have her way, Georgie realised when they stopped later that afternoon. The journey had been delayed twice so far for Captain Hernshaw had pulled over into a quiet country lay-by about an hour after leaving the busy streets of London behind. He had given his groom the reins and sat back, allowing the youth to take over. A glance at his white face had been sufficient to tell Georgie that he had found driving more of a strain than he had imagined. After a longish stop for nuncheon at an inn, he had called a halt at just past four in the afternoon, declaring that they would stay the night at a pleasant country inn some ten miles short of the destination he had planned.

'This is very pretty,' she said as he gave her his hand to help her down. 'It will not be as noisy as the posting inn you planned on using.'

'No,' he said, his mouth thinned and pale, as if he were holding himself on a tight rein. 'But I cannot vouch for the beds. They do not always air them as they ought in these places.'

'Oh, I am sure it will be quite comfortable here,' Georgie said. 'We must hope that they have enough rooms for us.'

'Yes, that is a point,' Richard said. 'We need three, but at a pinch I could share with Henderson.'

'Should you not find that uncomfortable?'

'Perhaps.' He smiled oddly. 'But I can hardly share with you, can I? Though I might find it preferable. Ned will sleep with the horses, for he is used to it, and tells me he snores proper dreadful—his words, not mine.'

Georgie blushed and turned away, for there was something in his eyes at that moment she found strangely disturbing. It was one of the few times he had said anything that made her aware of their situation.

'No, of course you cannot sleep in my room,' she replied. 'We must hope they have three rooms to let.'

Fortunately for all of them the landlord did have three rooms to offer and seemed pleased to have company. He said that his wife was preparing supper and that she would cook an extra capon or two to cater for the gentleman's needs.

Richard thanked him for his consideration, telling him that they would be content with whatever was served. He asked Georgie if she could amuse herself for an hour or two and went straight up to his own chamber. Georgie realised that he probably needed to rest his leg and she went to her bedchamber, which was small but suited to the young lad she was supposed to be. She made herself comfortable and returned to the public rooms. She did not stop there, but went out of the back door into a garden.

It was a country inn and the host was a family man. His wife had washing blowing on a rope line in the backyard, and there were three children all under the age of eleven playing games. The eldest, a girl, had a hoop, which she was rolling along the ground by means of a stick, hitting it at just the right moment so that it continued to turn and stay upright. The smallest, a boy, was running behind her, laughing and begging for his turn, and a girl of about six was sitting on an upturned bucket nursing a rag doll.

Georgie went up to her. The child was singing a song, her face intent as she nursed her baby. 'What is her name?' she asked, squatting down on a bale of hay close by. 'She is very pretty.'

'I call her Rosie,' the girl said with a shy smile. 'She is my baby.'

'I can see that she is,' Georgie said. 'Do you like nursing her?'

'My name is Rose,' the girl told her in a confiding manner. 'Ma had a baby, but she died. I don't want my baby to die.'

'Oh, I am sure she won't,' Georgie said. 'Not if you look after her.'

The girl stuck her thumb in her mouth and sucked it, considering for a moment or two before asking, 'What is your name?'

'Georgie.'

'My brother is called George,' the girl said. 'He is horrid. He never wants to play with me, only Shirley.'

'That is a shame,' Georgie said. 'But brothers are like that sometimes. I dare say he doesn't mean to be horrid to you.'

'Would you like to hold Rosie? She likes you.'

'Yes, why not,' Georgie said. She held out her hands for the doll, cradling it carefully as if it were a real baby. Rose got up and came to sit beside her on the straw. 'You're nice. I thought all boys were horrid like my brother, but you're not.'

Georgie laughed. 'I expect you will find that some boys are nice when you grow up,' she said.

Something made her turn her head at that moment to look up at the inn windows. Captain Hernshaw was standing looking down at her, an odd expression in his eyes. She smiled a little uncertainly and turned back to the child. He was suffering, she was certain of it, but he would not ask for help, though perhaps he would accept it from Henderson if he really needed it. She knew a longing to go to him and offer her help, but she was certain he would send her away; he did not need her, for he had his manservant, but it was becoming increasingly clear to her that she needed him.

Richard watched Georgie for a few minutes before she became aware of him. When she was laughing she looked too pretty to be a boy and he smiled wryly as he wondered just how long they could continue with this masquerade. He had decided it was too dangerous to let her travel alone, but travelling with her had its own dangers—for him. She was too damned attractive, and the outrageous clothes she was wearing were provocative, though of course she had no idea of it.

Damn it! Why was he even letting himself think how good she would feel in his arms? He had no room in his life for a woman—not one like her, anyway. He had no wish to marry, or to form a lasting attachment for anyone, and though he would enjoy seducing Georgie, he was too much of a gentleman to do it. For her it must be marriage or nothing. But it hurt too much to lose the people you loved. A curse escaped him. He was allowing Georgie to distract his mind from the purpose in hand.

He needed to concentrate on the task ahead. He knew that the little band of plotters he sought consisted of both French and English dissidents, men who were for one reason or another at odds with the establishment. Some he had no doubt worked for money and would have been loyal to the highest bidder only for as long as it pleased them. However, this plot was taken seriously enough by those in high places for Richard to have formed an idea of the man behind it, because there had to be someone masterminding the affair. He had an idea of who that person might be, but as yet had no proof.

Whoever this person was, he was clever and he knew people—people who mattered. Richard knew that there had already been two assassination attempts, presumed to be the work of this group. One was on Wellington, who had wrestled the man to the ground, taking him prisoner, and the other on the Regent—and that had been prevented by the intervention of a lady who happened to be there and saw what might have been the end of the prince had she not acted swiftly.

Two key figures in British politics, Richard mused with a frown. Had the assassins been luckier they might already have succeeded in causing the chaos they clearly desired. He did not truly think that Georgie was mixed up in the plot, at least not knowingly—but if this man, whose name he had heard whispered too often for comfort, was the same man to whom her uncle had been bent on marrying her, it could not hurt to see her safely to her family.

Richard was angry with himself for falling so neatly into his enemy's trap. He had been alert all the time he was carrying the papers, but, returning from his second journey of the night, he had allowed himself to relax his guard. The pain in his thigh was warning enough that he must never let his guard slip again, even for a moment.

'Curses!' he muttered as he sat on the side of the bed. Every movement was like having a hot knife thrust into his thigh. Henderson had warned him that it was too soon, begging him to wait another week before attempting the journey. His natural impatience had made him ignore his man's warning, but he was paying for it now. 'To hell with it!'

He lay back against the pillows. Rest was the only thing for it! He would not take the laudanum he knew would ease the pain, because it all too easily became addictive. Brandy would have eased him, but if he drank enough to dull the pain it would dull his wits, and his instincts were telling him that he needed to remain alert for the next few days.

Georgie had wondered if Captain Hernshaw would keep to his bed and send word that she should order a tray in her room, but he did not. He was downstairs in the private parlour at the appointed time, where Henderson, who had followed them to the inn at a discreet distance, joined them a little later.

Georgie watched the exchange between the two men. She could not hear what they were saying, but Captain Hernshaw nodded and looked pleased, so she supposed it was good news. The three of them took their places at table, and the host's wife served them with a dinner as good or better than they might have found at the more fashionable inn they had been headed for. Roast capon, cold ham, pigeon in wine sauce and a remove of parsnips in melted butter, carrots and mashed turnip, all served with delicious gravy. She returned a little later with a large treacle tart and custard, for the young lad. This was said with a smile and a nod, which made Georgie feel she must eat a piece of the gorgeous tart, even though she was already full.

'If you eat like that all the time, you will get fat,' Richard remarked, a flicker of amusement in his dark eyes.

'Well, I had to eat some of it since she made it especially for me,' she said, feeling miffed. 'Besides, I never get fat. I take after Papa in that and he was always thin.'

Richard nodded, his expression thoughtful as he looked at her. 'I fear I must leave you to amuse yourself this evening, Georgie. I need to rest if we are to continue our journey first thing in the morning.'

'I'll take a look at your wound before you retire,' Henderson said. 'It may have opened again.'

'I do not think so,' Richard replied. 'But take a look by all means.'

'You do not need to worry about me,' Georgie said. 'I shall go to my room. I would be happier with a book to read, but I dare say I shall fall asleep soon enough.'

'Poor Georgie,' Richard murmured. 'I am sorry I have nothing to offer you—unless you would care for the book of poetry you discovered at my London house?'

'Oh, yes,' she said. 'Thank you. I should enjoy reading that—I had hoped to subscribe to it myself.'

'Wait here and Henderson will bring it to you,' Richard told her. 'Had we stopped at the inn I intended to use, you would not have been safe, but this place is much quieter and I think you may stay here by the fire for a while should you wish.'

Georgie watched as he walked from the parlour, limping on his injured leg though obviously trying not to. Henderson gave her a nod and she settled down by the fire to wait for his return. They had not been gone more than a few minutes when Georgie heard the wheels of a carriage outside the inn. Something made her get up and go to the window. She glanced out at the curricle that had just arrived, giving a squeak of fear as she saw the gentleman throw his reins to a groom. She knew his face at once, for he was Monsieur Thierry—the man she had run away from her home to escape!

What was he doing here? It was a terrible mischance that he should come to this place! Georgie drew back hastily as he glanced towards the lighted window. Her mind worked feverishly. Would the host give him a room for the night? He would probably want supper, and, knowing that Captain Hernshaw had retired for the night, the host would think it acceptable if he allowed the newcomer to have the parlour.

She had to escape before he saw her! Georgie was not at all sure that her disguise was sufficient to fool a man she had met on several occasions at her uncle's home. He must not be given the chance to recognise her!

She left the parlour and hurried up the stairs, reaching the top seconds before she heard voices below in the hall. Thierry was asking for a room for the night, but the host was telling him that his rooms were full.

'You will at least allow me to take supper here?' The voice of the man she disliked followed Georgie as she fled up the stairs and along the landing to her own room. Once inside, she locked the door and leaned against it, her breast heaving in a sigh of relief. Had she not glanced out of the window, he might have walked into the parlour and found her there alone.

Trembling, Georgie sat down on the edge of the bed. She would certainly not be venturing downstairs to the parlour again that night, and she would be careful in the morning. Henderson would go to look for her in the parlour, but when he saw there was a new occupant he was sure to come here to bring her the book. Georgie decided that she would tell him Monsieur Thierry was here, because it might not be coincidence. It was just possible that he had followed them here for some reason.

She guiltily remembered the calling card she had discovered at Captain Hernshaw's house and not given him. In the morning she would have to tell him if he should mention the Frenchman by name.

Georgie spent a couple of hours reading the book Henderson brought her, but once again she found herself decoding the messages she found scribbled into the margins. She soon discovered that there was a fresh notation in one of the margins, but when she used the code to unravel it she was left with a riddle.

Where the stars and sword unite, the plotters lie in wait and plan their deadly deeds. The fox is in the hole and will not come unless you knock thrice and thrice again.

Now what on earth did that mean? Georgie stared at it for ages before closing the book. Perhaps she had made a mistake with the code? The first message had been simple to understand, for it said that there was a plot afoot to murder some important members of the government and hinted at the Head of State, who could only be the Regent. But this riddle did not make sense.

Her work had made her tired and she fell asleep with the book in her hand.

Henderson had told her that he would warn her if the Frenchman was still around in the morning, but as he did not do so she washed, dressed and went downstairs to the parlour. Both Captain Hernshaw and Henderson were there and she noted that the captain looked a little easier.

'Did you sleep well, sir?' she asked.

'Yes, thank you,' he replied. 'I hope you were not too bored, Georgie?'

She caught something in his tone and realised he was looking at her with interest, and then she knew that he had intended her to find the code and the riddle. 'Yes, I slept well enough, after I had finished puzzling over the book you sent me.'

Henderson stood up, saying that he would make sure the horses were ready for them in twenty minutes.

Richard's brows lifted as his man left the parlour. 'You found something to interest you?'

'A riddle I could not solve,' she said. 'Have you changed the code or did you discover a riddle too?'

He nodded, a smile on his mouth. 'Irritating isn't it? As if the code were not enough, there is yet a further puzzle.'

'You wanted to see if I got the same result as you?' Georgie said, because she understood why he had given her the book. 'Why didn't you just tell me?'

'Because I thought you would be curious enough to discover it for yourself.'

'I was,' she admitted and laughed. 'One of these days I shall read the poetry instead of working on your wretched messages.'

Richard's gaze narrowed thoughtfully. He had set her a little test and was satisfied with the result. 'You told Henderson that Thierry was here last night. It frightened you. Did you think he had discovered you were here?'

'I was afraid of it at first,' Georgie confessed. 'It seemed strange that he should come to the same inn— especially as it is not one of those most frequented by travelling gentlemen. We should not have stayed here had you not needed to rest.'

'That is true,' Richard agreed. 'He may have followed us, though I do not know why—do you?'

Georgie reached into her coat pocket and brought out the calling card. 'This was left for you in London. I saw him come to the house when I looked out of the landing window, and I hid it because I did not wish you to meet with him.'

Richard gave her a stern look. 'Jensen told me he thought a card had gone missing. It crossed my mind that you might have taken it, but I could not think why. When did you intend giving it to me?'

'When we reached my great-aunt's house,' Georgie said, feeling awkward under his interrogation. 'I know I had no right to take it. I am sorry.'

'You should not have done so,' he replied, but did not seem particularly incensed. 'It may be important that he approached me; it may mean nothing—but it is better that I know these things. Please do not hide anything from me in future.'

'You have every right to be angry,' Georgie said. 'Especially if he is mixed up in this…affair.'

'What makes you think he might be?' Richard's gaze became hard, intent. 'Do you know more than you are telling me? If so, confess it now, because it will not go well with you if I discover that you are in league with him later.'

'In league with that odious man!' Georgie was horrified. 'I hate him! I would rather die than have anything to do with him. I swear it on my honour...' She saw the look in his eyes and flushed. 'Very well, on my father's honour—and he was a good man.'

'Very well, I shall believe you,' Richard said. 'So, we have a little problem. Monsieur Thierry is possibly following us, but for the moment we do not know whether he is after you—or me.'

Georgie shuddered. 'Do you think he might have something to do with the attack on you?'

'If he is involved with the people I am after, he may well have done.' Richard frowned. 'I had not expected to be followed. I think I may have exposed you to danger, Georgie. Should I find a respectable woman to escort you to your aunt's house and let you continue alone?'

'No! I want to stay with you until we get there,' Georgie said, shivering as she turned cold. 'When I saw him last night I realised that I cannot be safe until we reach my aunt's home. If you abandoned me, I should be anxious every moment.'

'You are certain?' Richard accepted it as she nodded. 'I think perhaps you are right, though if I thought it was me he wanted...' He shook his head, his gaze narrowing. 'So you discovered the riddle last night—what do you think it meant?'

'I have no idea,' Georgie confessed. 'I thought perhaps the first part of it referred to the place where the plotters meet, but it was so strange that I could not make it out—and the bit about the fox in the hole...'

'Perhaps it refers to their leader?' Richard said. 'The

fox may be a name for the ringleader, and my informant is saying that he will not leave his lair until the right moment.'

'Why did he not just say so?' Georgie demanded, exasperated. 'It makes no sense to get a message to you and then not say straight out what you need to know.'

'I agree with you,' Richard said. 'Of course, had it fallen into the wrong hands it would have been safer. It may be that my informant is a member of the group who wishes to lay information without getting caught.'

'I hadn't thought of that,' Georgie said, giving him an appraising look. 'He must think that you are clever enough to work it out for yourself.'

'Yes, perhaps,' Richard said. 'Or it might have been sent to mislead…if my informant had been turned or…'

'Or murdered?' Georgie felt cold all over. 'Do you think that the first message was genuine and this one was false?'

'I think that may be the case,' Richard said. 'Whoever is behind this needs time to complete his plans. He is afraid that I may have more clues than I actually do and he sent this message to lead me on a false trail.'

'To force you to waste time trying to work out something that means nothing—is, in fact, nonsense?'

'Yes, it could be that,' Richard agreed, smiling oddly at her. 'You are an intelligent girl, Georgie. Talking to you has made me see that I could have wasted a lot of precious time. I wondered when I was told the location for the meeting that night. I believe the attack on me was meant to happen only after I had delivered the new message to colleagues—because I am not the only one involved in this affair.'

'So he wished to confuse you all,' Georgie said. 'Had you died in the attack, you would have been one less for him to deal with, but he knew you were not working alone.'

'I am not alone, but perhaps I have some information others do not,' Richard said. 'The trouble is, if I have it, I do not know what it is…unless it is a name.'

'Raoul Thierry,' Georgie said, looking at him intently as a suspicion came to her. 'You've heard his name before. You suspect him of being involved, do you not?'

'Perhaps,' Richard said. 'His name has been mentioned by several people as being suspect, but I have no proof. We should go. Henderson will have the horses ready and my groom will be waiting for us.'

'No, not yet,' Georgie said. She looked angry, two spots of red colour in her cheeks. 'You made me wait until you could travel because you thought I might be involved in this horrid affair, didn't you?'

'It crossed my mind,' Richard admitted. 'You did try to steal from me, Georgie. That package was important—or I thought it was at the time, though if it were a hoax he would not have sent you to steal it.'

'No one sent me to steal it,' she said indignantly. 'I would never do such a thing!' She blushed as she met his mocking stare. 'Well, only if I was terribly hungry, which I was—and I didn't know what it was!'

'No, I am certain you did not,' Richard said and laughed softly in his throat. She was magnificent when she was angry! Despite his determination to stay aloof, she was gradually worming her way under his defences. 'Do not look so outraged, Georgie. I have acquitted you of all malice. You only stole from me because you were hungry, so naturally that makes you blameless.'

'Oh…' She threw him a wrathful glare. 'Well, if you had ever been as hungry as I was, you might have done the same!'

'I have been and I did—when in Spain with the army,' he said. 'Forgive me. I could not resist teasing you. You are very pretty when you are angry, you know.'

'Please do not!' Georgie said. His smile was teasing but she knew he must think her a ridiculous scamp. 'I know I must look awful, not at all respectable.'

'Well, there is that,' he agreed, a sparkle in the depths of his teasing eyes. 'But I must say that I find your disguise rather attractive—though of course I deplore the behaviour that brought you to this masquerade.'

Georgie understood that he was teasing her. She had finished eating her bread and ham and got up, walking out into the yard with dignity. He deserved that she should ignore him for the rest of the journey!

Chapter Four

Georgie's spurt of temper lasted for the first mile or so, by which time she had realised that it merely made her seem childish, for he was determined to be a charming companion. He had allowed his young groom to drive and sat with her in a more comfortable seat.

'Well, I suppose it does no good to fall out with you,' she announced as they passed a pretty village. 'I have to thank you for making it possible for me to complete my journey. Had we not met, I might have suffered a worse fate than to be teased.'

'Very nicely said,' Richard observed with a faint smile. 'I was wondering when you would remember your society manners, for I dare say you were brought up to behave with decorum.'

'Certainly I was,' Georgie replied. 'Mama would have been shocked if she knew what I had done these past days—though I believe she would understand I had no choice. My father would have thrashed my uncle, but of course had either of them been still living it could not have happened.'

'Have you thought about your future?' Richard inquired for all the world as if he were an uncle and they out for an afternoon drive. 'You spoke of setting up your own establishment if your aunt did not wish for your company, but you are a little young for that, are you not?'

'Yes, perhaps,' she agreed. 'But I dare say I might hire a respectable companion to keep me company. If I had no relations, I must have done so anyway.'

Richard nodded. He was thoughtful as he watched her, wondering how he could ever for a moment have been deceived into thinking her a youth. She was extremely pretty even dressed as she was; indeed, there was something fascinating about a young woman in a boy's clothing, and he had to castigate himself severely for thinking that had she not been so well born he might have made her his mistress.

What was he thinking! It was a rogue thought and one he hastily dismissed, even though she was wholly enticing, especially when she got on her high horse. There had been moments when he had been tempted to kiss her simply to see her reaction, but each time he had crushed the unworthy impulse. No matter what she had done, she was a young lady of good birth and fortune and as such deserved his protection. He had no right to be imagining what she might look like without those ridiculous clothes—or what her hair would smell like as it lay spread on the pillow beside him!

'Do you think anyone would consent to be my companion?' she asked a little naïvely, looking uncertain. 'Perhaps my great-aunt will be pleased to have me and I shan't need one.'

'Yes, we must hope so,' he replied. 'I should imagine

any number of ladies would be happy to come and live at your expense, Georgie—but you must be careful that you choose the right one.'

'Yes…' She looked doubtful. 'Do you think—?'

Before she could continue a shot rang out. She ducked forward as she felt the air rush past her cheek and realised that it had almost hit her. The horses had taken fright and the young groom was having difficulty in holding them. She controlled her little squeal of fright as she saw Richard move swiftly to the driving box and grab the reins from the hands of his valiant groom.

It took only a few minutes before he had managed to slow their pace to something more manageable, though he did not immediately bring them to a halt. She realised that he was putting some distance between them and whoever had shot at them, and when she heard two more shots behind them she guessed that Henderson had arrived and was making sure that the assassin did not attempt to follow them.

It was perhaps fifteen minutes later that Richard slowed his horses to a walking pace, then gave the reins back to his groom and climbed back to sit beside her. He looked at her for a moment, his intent gaze registering that after her first fright she had taken the incident well.

'Good girl,' he said and picked up her cap, which had come off in their mad flight. 'It is a pity to hide that glorious hair, but I think you should. It won't do for you to be seen like this, you know.'

'No,' she agreed and blushed as he helped her to gather her long hair and tuck it back beneath the cap.

Richard smiled at her in a manner that suddenly took

Georgie's breath. Her heart was hammering so hard against her ribcage that she was relieved when Henderson rode up to them and he turned away. 'Did you see him?'

'He chose his spot well,' Henderson replied. 'He was sheltered by the trees, but his very vantage meant that he could get off only one shot, for the trees sheltered you too after you had passed. I shot at him twice as he fled and I think I may have winged him.'

'Not dead?' Richard asked, brows arched.

'More's the pity,' Henderson growled, looking at Georgie. 'He might have killed you, miss. A fraction either way and he would have shot you through the head.'

'Don't!' Georgie shuddered. 'Do you think he meant to hit me or Captain Hernshaw?'

'I think it was you, miss,' Henderson replied, his expression grim. 'From what I saw, he couldn't have been aiming for the captain.'

'But why would he want to kill me?' Georgie asked. She had imagined the shot was meant for her companion, and the idea that she had been the true target was frightening. 'Who could want me dead? Monsieur Thierry wants to marry me. I should be of no use to him dead.'

'No…' Richard was thoughtful. 'Who would inherit your fortune if you died unmarried? You have not made a will?'

'No.' Georgie screwed up her forehead. 'My aunt did suggest it once, but I told her I had no intention of dying for years. I suppose my uncle is my nearest relative, though my great-aunt might also have a claim. There is no else.' She held back a sob. 'Surely my uncle would not try to have me killed for money?' She had made just such a story up for Mrs Jensen, but the suggestion that it might be true was shocking.

'He was willing to sell you into a marriage you disliked.'

'Yes, but it was to clear a debt, and he was afraid of Raoul Thierry.' Georgie looked at him, feeling slightly sick. 'It might have been him—if Monsieur Thierry thinks that I can tell you something he doesn't wish you to know.'

'That would mean he knew who you were,' Richard said. 'You told me you saw him in the street in London. Could he have seen you—for long enough to know it was you?'

'I don't think so...though he might have seen me last night,' Georgie said. 'I saw him clearly in the inn yard, but the lights of the candles in the parlour were behind me. It is possible that he saw me. He might not have known it was me then, but he perhaps realised it later.'

Richard's eyes went over her. 'If I knew you before we met, I should not have been fooled for a moment,' he told her. 'To a stranger you might pass for a pretty youth, but to anyone who knows you...'

'Then he must think I am with you for a purpose,' Georgie said. 'He may think that I can help you to recognise him...or something of the sort...'

'Yes, perhaps,' Richard said and looked thoughtful. 'You are certain that no one else would benefit from your fortune other than your uncle?'

'My father was an only child,' Georgie said. 'I have only my uncle and my great-aunt.'

'Then we must assume it is either Thierry for reasons of his own or your uncle for money,' Richard said.

'When we reach the next posting inn I shall hire a closed carriage. If your life is in danger, I must protect you.'

'But we cannot be sure the shot was meant for me,' Georgie said, frowning. 'Perhaps the rogue who fired at us thought you would be travelling alone and fired without being sure who he would hit.'

'Yes, that is possible,' Richard agreed. 'But in future I do not intend to give anyone the chance to shoot at you again. We shall travel on by closed carriage.'

Georgie kept her silence. To drive with him in a closed carriage would do little for her reputation if it were discovered, but then she had already lost any claim to respectability and must hope it could be recovered when she reached her great-aunt's home.

However, he winced as he moved and, glancing at him, she saw the blood spotting on his otherwise immaculate breeches. 'Your wound,' she said. 'It must have opened when you moved so suddenly to grab the reins.'

'Yes.' He glanced down dispassionately. 'It may be as well, for there was a little festering, which is why it was causing me pain. Sometimes it is better to open a wound and let the blood flow to cleanse it.'

Georgie felt doubtful, guessing that he was in far more pain than he would ever say. She made no comment; she knew that he would not thank her if she offered sympathy. He settled back into his seat, telling his groom to drive on, though she noticed a little pulse beating in his throat and sensed that he was having difficulty in holding back his pain as the carriage rattled over a particularly bumpy road.

At the inn, a bustling, busy place at a crossroads, Richard secured both a private parlour and a bedchamber. He left Georgie to herself in the parlour while he and Henderson went upstairs. They were gone for half an hour, during which time she amused herself by staring out of the window at the inn yard. Several private vehicles drew up during that time, their owners calling for refreshment while their horses were being rested or exchanged for fresh. She saw no one that gave her the least need for anxiety, her thoughts centred on what was happening upstairs, and she turned with pleasure as she heard the door open.

Richard had changed into fresh breeches, and there was evidence of a bandage beneath the clinging material. As he seemed to walk a little more easily she assumed that he was feeling better for his man's attentions.

'We may as well stay and eat,' he told her. 'I am sorry that this journey is taking longer than it ought, Georgie. Had we not been forced to break our journey again, we might have reached your home by this evening. As it is, I am afraid we may have to stay at an inn for one more night.'

'It doesn't matter,' Georgie said. 'It wasn't your fault that we came so close to an accident. Besides, I shall be sorry when we part, sir.'

'Shall you?' Richard arched one eyebrow. 'I thought you could not wait to get away from me when we were in London?'

'Well, yes, I did think it would be better to leave, but…Jensen did not have a good opinion of me, you see. Mrs Jensen was kind, but she would not let me help her and I felt that I was in the way.'

'I am sorry if you were made to feel uncomfortable.'

'Oh, no, it wasn't their fault, and Mrs Jensen was

very kind, even though her husband obviously thought I was…no better than I should be.' She bit her lip. 'You must not blame him, for the circumstances were unusual to say the least.'

'Yes, I suppose it was inevitable that he should have thought the worst,' Richard said. 'It might have been better if I had let them think you were my niece or something.'

'They wouldn't have believed you. No one would.' Georgie pulled a rueful face. 'I told Mrs Jensen I was in desperate trouble. I think she half-believed me, but I am very certain her husband did not.'

'I have placed you in a difficult position,' Richard said, eyes narrowed, thoughtful. 'You stayed at my home without a chaperon and have had only my tiger and Henderson as our companions on this journey. I have, in fact, compromised you, Georgina.'

'I did that for myself,' she admitted, a blush in her cheeks. 'Besides, you were only trying to help me when you took me to your home—and no one needs to know.'

'Your great-aunt will know,' Richard observed. 'At least she will know that you have arrived at her house with a gentleman she does not know and no luggage.'

'You are a friend of the family,' Georgie said, 'and my luggage was lost on the way. We were attacked by ruffians who stole our baggage and that is how you were wounded.'

'You have a fine imagination,' Richard said and he wasn't smiling. 'How much can I believe of what you say, I wonder?'

'Everything!' She sparked with indignation. 'I did tell you a little white lie when we met, but I had to be wary, for you might have been anybody. Besides, it was not so far from the truth.'

'But you have made up a string of lies to tell your great-aunt.'

'Yes, well, I didn't know what else to say. You talked of having compromised me and…and you must not feel obliged or anything.' Her cheeks were deep rose with embarrassment. 'I would not want you to feel that you had to marry me.'

'Believe me, I don't!'

'Oh!' Georgie glared. 'Good, because I do not want to marry you. In fact you are the last man I would marry!'

'Perhaps you would prefer to marry Thierry?'

'No, of course I wouldn't! You know I would rather die. I told you so…' She understood that he was mocking her and threw him a fulminating stare. 'I never know when you are funning! Of course you don't want to marry me, and I shan't expect it—even if my aunt says I am beyond the pale.'

'Poor Georgie,' Richard said and smiled. 'You have got yourself into a pickle, haven't you?'

'Yes, I know it was a mad thing to do—but what else could I have done? My uncle meant to force me to marry that odious man and I did the first thing that came into my head. There was no one to help me.'

'Impulsive,' Richard murmured. 'But brave too. I am not sure what else you could have done, but perhaps a little more planning would have had better results. You could perhaps have gathered enough money to hire a post-chaise to your great-aunt's instead of taking the public stagecoach and getting robbed.'

'Yes, it would have been better,' she agreed. 'I was afraid my uncle would lock me in my room, and then I was careless…' She lifted her head, giving him a frank look. 'I think I should have starved or ended up in prison if you hadn't helped me. I am very grateful, you know—and sorry if I have caused you a deal of trouble.'

Richard looked into her eyes, which just now were soft brown, slightly moist and heart-wrenchingly appealing. He felt something stir inside him, an emotion he could not recall ever feeling before, something warm and tender, an urge to sweep her into his arms, carry her off and hold her for ever in his protection. In another instant he had quashed it. Love was foreign to his nature, an emotion he had long dismissed as being behind him, too dangerous to encourage. There had been women to share his bed, of course, but none of them serious and there had been no one at all for a long time. Perhaps that was why he had been experiencing these sudden swathes of hot desire as he looked at Georgie in her youth's clothing. Something he felt disturbing and not to be indulged.

He did not want to face the notion that he might truly have feelings for this girl who had come into his life unasked. His work was too dangerous for him to think of marriage; he could be killed by an enemy at any time, and that would leave her a widow before she was a wife.

Besides, they hardly knew one another. It was ridiculous to even consider marriage. Neither of them truly wished for it! If he ever married it would be for an heir, as his sister never tired of telling him he ought to do, but never for love. His experience of these things was that they led only to pain. His mother had died in childbed, leaving his father distraught, a broken man. He had seen his uncle decline after Justin's death, and the memory still haunted him. No, love was not something he wished to experience.

'I am glad to have been of help,' he murmured huskily and meant it. 'Do not worry, Georgie. If your aunt should turn you away I shall think of something.'

'I do not wish to be more of a burden than I have been already.'

'You are not a burden,' Richard said, his tone becoming harsh all of a sudden. 'Excuse me, I must speak to Henderson. I trust you have no objection to his joining us in the parlour for our nuncheon as usual? He serves me, but I have been used to treating him as a friend rather than a servant.'

'Of course not. Why should I?' Georgie said, though she knew it was something that would not happen when their lives were back to normal. But when that happened she would not see Richard again, except perhaps as a casual acquaintance in town, if she should be fortunate enough to visit.

Georgie felt a hot burning behind her eyes when she realised that she had only a few hours left in his company. In the morning Richard would deliver her to her great-aunt's home and go on his way, relieved to be rid of her no doubt.

When had she begun to think of him as Richard? And why did the thought of parting weigh heavily on her, making her breast feel as if it were being crushed? After all, he was merely someone who had come to her rescue when she needed him.

That was just it, of course. He had been there when she needed him, and insensibly she had come to think of him as her special friend, someone she could turn to in need. She must put that notion out of her mind. Richard had been considerate, kind and gentle towards her, but he must have found her a nuisance, especially at a time when he was wounded and in danger of his life.

She must not make him feel he owed her anything. He must be free to go on his way and forget her. Even as she made her silent vow, she knew that she would not forget him! Georgie sensed instinctively that this brief interlude would remain with her for a long time. Perhaps for the rest of her life. The thought made her want to weep.

What was she going to do with her life now? Georgie hardly knew what she wanted. Her great-aunt was elderly. It was not likely that she would entertain often, which meant that Georgie would be forced to spend long hours alone or with just her aunt for company. For a moment she sank beneath the weight of such a prospect, but then she put it behind her. If Great-Aunt Mary did not wish to take her to London or Bath she might know someone who would take it on for a consideration. There were bound to be widows of good family who did not have sufficient money for their needs.

And what then? Georgie wondered. It was usual for girls of good families to marry, settle down and provide an heir for their husbands. She did not know why the prospect of marrying an unknown gentleman did not appeal. When she was younger she had dreamed of falling in love, but as yet she had met no one who appealed to her…as much as Richard.

Oh, no! She was appalled at her thoughts. She must not even consider such a prospect. Richard had no desire to marry her, did not believe himself obliged to despite their circumstances these past few days. And she did not wish to be married simply to rescue her good name!

Georgie buried the renegade thoughts that told her she would not find it a hardship to marry Richard Hernshaw. She liked him despite his deplorable habit of mocking her—in fact, if she were truthful, she liked him a little too much for her own good.

Richard returned some twenty minutes later with his manservant, and the host followed almost immediately with their dinner. They were served cold beef, a dish of calves' liver in sweet sauce, chops and jugged hare with a remove of mashed potatoes and swede, carrots and baked onions. This was followed by a quince tart and an apple turnover with fresh cream.

She was pleased to notice that for the first time Richard did justice to his food, eating almost as much as Henderson and more than she could manage. He looked at her as she refused the apples and cream.

'I ordered that especially for you. Did you not like it?'

'I have eaten more than enough,' she replied. For some reason she had lost her appetite. 'I do not usually eat as much as I have recently. I think I was making up for having gone without for some days, but now I am back to normal.'

'It is not because I teased you about getting fat?'

'Oh, no, of course not,' she said and smiled a little wanly. 'I just do not feel hungry.'

'Well, it is only a few hours since we broke our fast,' Richard said. 'I should not have stopped so soon had it not been necessary. However, we shall go on again shortly. If you are worried about getting to your aunt's, we might see if we can get there. The carriage I have hired will make good time, I dare say.'

'Oh, no, I am in no hurry,' Georgie said. She frowned

and looked down at herself. 'I must try to find a dress before we get to my great-aunt's house.'

'I have thought of that,' Richard said. 'There are some things for you with my luggage and Henderson will bring them to you this evening before you retire. I shall order your breakfast in your room and we can leave immediately afterwards so that hardly anyone will see you.'

Georgie was silent. It would only need one person of quality to see her leaving the inn to ruin her reputation, but she would say nothing more on the subject. After all, it did not matter so very much since she had no real desire to marry. Perhaps she never would marry. If only she had some burning desire, something she truly wished to accomplish—like becoming an actress or a famous explorer, perhaps.

She wondered if she should do something of the sort once she had her inheritance. She could engage a companion and travel abroad. For a few minutes pleasant thoughts of all the countries she might visit filled her mind, but unfortunately she kept thinking that it would be much better to travel with a gentleman for company—and one particular gentleman would not stay out of her head.

It was most disobliging of him! She struggled to change her thoughts, becoming aware that his eyes were on her, mysterious and intent, the colour of wet slate.

'What? Have I done something wrong?'

'Nothing,' he said and shook his head. 'I shall pay the host and then we shall continue our journey—if you are ready?'

'Yes, of course,' Georgie replied, though her heart said something entirely different. 'I dare say you will be glad to deliver me to my great-aunt so that you may go about your business in peace.'

'It is true that I have business of my own in Yorkshire,' Richard replied, his expression serious. 'However, there is nothing urgent. I intend to make certain that you are settled and happy before I move on.' He frowned. 'It has occurred to me that I have no idea of our eventual destination. You have not told me the exact location of your aunt's home or even her name.'

'Did I not?' Georgie pulled a face. 'I am not certain of the location…I know it is near a village called Shrewsbury Morton and it is not far from York, for in her letters to me she talks of dining with friends at an inn in York. Her name…she is Mary, Countess of Shrewsbury and Morton. She is usually addressed as Countess Shrewsbury.'

'Good lord!' Richard stared at her, obviously shocked. 'I know the lady well. She was a great friend of my late mother and my sister resided with her for a few years before she married.'

'Oh…' Georgie's mouth made a little moue of surprise. 'How strange that you should know Aunt Mary…'

'Well, that makes things a little easier,' Richard told her. 'It is possible that she will accept the story of my being a family friend since she knows me and does not entirely disapprove of me.'

'Yes…' Georgie felt a sinking sensation inside. 'I did not know that your family came from these parts.'

'You know very little of me,' Richard said, frowning. 'I do not live in Yorkshire myself, but my sister does. She married a gentleman she met while living with the countess, and I visit her occasionally—though not as often as she would like. Jenny is a fond sister, though these days she has her hands full with her children.'

'What are they—boys or girls?' Georgie asked, because this was the first she had learned of his private life. 'And how old?'

'She has a boy and a girl, and hopes to have more,' Richard replied, a little smile on his lips. 'The girl is about the age of the girl you talked to at the inn we stayed at last night, and the boy is scarcely two.'

'How lucky she is to have one of each,' Georgie said. 'I always wished that I might have had a sister or a brother, but Mama lost one baby and Papa would not risk her health again. He loved her too much…' She sighed, her smile dimming. 'It was terrible to lose them both as I did, but I do not think that either of them could have supported life without the other.'

'But you were left alone,' Richard said. 'My parents also died when I was still young, but at least I still had my sister—and I have her family when I am in need of some of the comforts of home. You have no one who truly cares for you, I think?'

'Aunt Agatha was not unkind at first,' Georgie said. 'But her life was difficult. My uncle was for ever gambling and there were times when money was short. I am sure it was he who wanted to settle his debts by selling me to Monsieur Thierry. My aunt was shocked, but could do nothing but obey her husband.'

'Will the countess be prepared to stand against them for guardianship?' Richard asked. 'Have you considered that your uncle may have the right to force you to return to his house until you are older?'

'Papa's will states that I should be free to live as I please once I come into my fortune,' Georgie said.

'There are two lawyers applying the terms of the trust, and I think they might support me if I tell them what he tried to do.'

'Yes, perhaps,' Richard said. He hesitated, then, 'My sister can always reach me if she needs me. I shall furnish you with her address and you may apply to me if you are in trouble.'

'Oh…' Georgie looked down because her heart had begun to thump madly in her breast, feeling as if it would burst free of her ribcage. 'Surely you would not wish to have the trouble of such things?'

'I would help you if need be,' Richard said and his eyes held hers. 'Can you doubt it?'

At that moment Georgie would have believed anything he told her. She felt as if she were drawn to him, bound to him by invisible threads and her mind sought for something to say that would make him understand how she felt, but at that moment someone came in to announce that their carriage was waiting.

Georgie turned, preceding the others as they all went outside. She hoped that Richard had not noticed her confusion, because she did not want him to see that he had set hope flaring inside her. His promise that he would help her made her feel that perhaps she might see him again after the morrow.

Their journey that afternoon was uneventful, perhaps because Richard had hired grooms to accompany them. His young tiger had stayed behind with his master's horses and rig, and would wait at the posting inn until he was told what to do next. Richard sat opposite her. He made conversation for a while and then leaned back, his eyes closed. She thought that he was sleeping and felt pleased, because she knew he had had little sleep the previous night. If he could relax now, it must mean that his wound was feeling a little easier.

At the next inn they were shown to their rooms, and shortly after Georgie had washed and made herself comfortable she heard a knock at the door. She opened it to find Henderson standing there with a valise, which he handed to her with a smile.

'Can you manage, miss?' he asked. 'I could ask the innkeeper's wife to send a girl up to help you.'

'No, thank you. I am sure I can manage,' Georgie said. 'I shall not come down this evening. I think it best if no one sees me—and I am not hungry.'

'I'll ask for a light supper to be sent up, miss,' Henderson promised as he left.

Georgie smiled and closed the door, locking it once more. She carried the valise to the bed and opened it, taking out a gown of primrose muslin. It was the fashion of two seasons previously with a high waist, puffed sleeves and a white sash, which she could tie at the front or the side. It was a little creased, but she shook it out, laying it over the back of a chair as she examined the rest of the clothes. There was a shawl of white silk, some dainty white leather half-boots, which were a little too large for her, but wearable once she had laced them, silk stockings and garters, a fine silk petticoat— which, considering the cold weather of the past few days, she thought it advisable to wear—and a heavy pelisse of dark blue for travelling. She pulled everything out of the valise to make sure, but there were no pantaloons. Of course some fashionable ladies did not wear them under their clinging gowns, but Georgie had been accustomed to such items of underwear and felt that it would be very daring of her not to do so. However, as there were none, she would simply have to brave it.

No one would know, of course, but she felt it a little shocking. However, it might have been even more shocking if they had been there for her bag must have been packed by Henderson, who was more used to serving a gentleman.

She considered dressing in her finery just to see how she looked, suddenly keen to be a young lady again. However, the hour was late because Richard had wanted to make up for time lost earlier in the day, and she decided that it could wait for the morning. When she undressed she placed the youth's clothing into the bag, apart from the shirt that she had used as nightwear the previous night and would use again.

The Countess of Shewsbury and Morton would no doubt think it very odd when she arrived with no baggage, but they must hope that she was prepared to believe Georgie's story of having lost it on the road. She would have to send for her things, or wait until she had her money and could buy more, though that would be awkward.

Her life would be less than comfortable even when she reached the safety of her aunt's home, Georgie realised, and there was no guarantee that the countess would be willing to defy her uncle. As Richard had pointed out, her uncle was her legal guardian, of course, and could demand her return at least until she came into her inheritance.

Notwithstanding her troubled thoughts, Georgie slept soon after her head touched the pillow.

She woke as soon as the first rosy fingers of dawn began to creep through the partially drawn curtains, and was dressed and ready when the maid brought her a breakfast tray containing soft rolls, honey and a pot of dark chocolate.

Once she had eaten, Georgie gathered her things and went downstairs. She discovered that Richard and Henderson were already in the hall, and by the sound of it they had something important to discuss. However, they stopped speaking as one and turned to look at her as she reached the bottom stair, a picture of youthful beauty in her yellow gown and white shawl, the pelisse over her arm. She had no bonnet or even a ribbon to tie up her hair and so it fell on to her shoulders in a riotous tangle of shining curls and waves.

'You are ready, then,' Richard said, his eyes seeming to dwell rather too long on her slender form. 'I was about to send the maid to see if you were. I trust you slept well?'

'Very well,' Georgie replied. She thought that some of the shadows had gone from beneath his eyes and assumed that he too had rested. 'Is something wrong?'

'Henderson says he thinks we were followed here yesterday evening. The grooms told him someone was inquiring for a gentleman travelling with a youth, but since I had warned them to be on their guard they told him nothing.'

'Was he a Frenchman?'

'Yes, they seem to think so—at least they said he had a queer accent, so it seems likely it was Thierry or one of his cronies.'

A little shiver ran down Georgie's spine. She had hoped that Thierry would be left far behind, but if he had followed her here he might have ideas of snatching her from beneath her great-aunt's nose. She would have to be careful not to go out alone.

'Well, are you ready?' Richard looked at her, a crease forming on his brow. 'You need not be afraid of him, you know. I think it must be me he wants. He believes I know something about him—and perhaps I do, if I could but think what it is.'

'You have never met him?' Georgie asked. She tipped her head to one side, considering as he shook his head. 'Some might think him very handsome, but I do not. He is a fine figure of a man, but there is something…greasy about him. And he has a horrid way of looking at one.'

'Yes, I think I know what you mean,' Richard said. He had met characters he would describe as oily in the past and understood what she was trying to say. It was a slyness, a smoothness of manner that was too ingratiating to be believed, and an unpleasant feeling of being laughed at secretly. 'Well, are you prepared for what comes next?'

'Yes…at least I must be,' Georgie said. She moved towards him, laying her hand on his arm. 'You did mean it when you said I might call on you if I needed you?'

'I never say what I do not mean,' he told her with an encouraging smile. 'Come, be brave, Georgie. You faced a shot that might have killed you and bolting horses with courage—what can be so terrifying about one elderly lady?'

'Nothing, of course,' Georgie said and gave him her hand, allowing him to help her into the carriage. She was puzzled when he closed the door. 'You are coming with me?'

'Naturally. I shall ride. My wound has almost healed and it does not pain me now; I think the exercise will do it good. That rogue who fired at us did me a favour, for when the wound split open the poison seeped out, and since then I have felt much better.'

'I am glad,' Georgie said. She watched from the window as he mounted his horse and set off a little ahead of the carriage, Henderson following to ride at his side. 'So very glad.'

Her eyes felt moist as she sat back, clasping her hands in front of her. Her heart was beating very fast, but she raised her head, a gleam of pride in her eyes. She was determined not to be anxious. If her great-aunt refused to take her in she would simply…well, she did not quite know what she would do, but perhaps Richard would be able to suggest somewhere she might go.

Georgie relaxed as best she could for the next half an hour; then, seeing a village sign which proclaimed itself as Shrewsbury Morton, she sat forward and looked out at the view. They were passing through a pretty village with a fine church. It seemed something was going on at the church, for several carriages had arrived and people were getting out of them. Georgie saw that they were all wearing black and, hearing the mournful toll of a church bell, realised they must be attending a funeral. It was clear that whoever had died must be a person of importance, for the carriages belonged to good families, and the service was well attended.

Her driver had been obliged to halt the horses because of the traffic and she saw that Richard had also reined in and was talking to someone. She could see his face clearly and it was obvious that something was wrong. She shivered as he looked back at her, sensing bad news. He dismounted, gave the reins to Henderson and walked back to her, opening the door and climbing inside. His manner was thoughtful, sympathetic, as he reached forward to touch her hand.

'I am afraid I have some bad news for you, Georgie,' he said, a serious expression on his face. 'There is a funeral today and…they tell me it is for the Countess of Shrewsbury. Apparently, she died of an illness that has plagued her for some months. It was not unexpected, but sudden at the end.'

'Oh…' Georgie stared at him. Her eyes pricked with tears. 'How very sad. I had no idea she was ill. She wrote to me only occasionally, usually on my birthday or at Christmas, but she always sent a gift and her letters were kind.'

'I asked who was attending the funeral and it appears that she has no immediate relatives. Her great-niece has been informed, but has not replied…that is you, Georgie. The letter must have gone to your uncle's home after you left.'

Georgie looked at the church. 'Do you think I should attend? Would it look strange if I went in wearing these clothes?'

'Do you wish to?' he asked. 'You hardly knew her after all.'

'She was my great-aunt. I suppose I may explain my lack of proper dress if anyone asks.' She looked at him shyly. 'Will you accompany me?'

'Of course. She was my sister's friend for many years.' He frowned. 'I dare say that means Amelia may be here.' He nodded and gave her his hand. 'Wear your pelisse, for it will cover most of your gown—but your hair should be covered.'

'I'll wear my cap,' Georgie said and undid her valise. She set the brown cloth cap on the back of her head. 'It may look odd, but will be better than showing disrespect in church.'

'It looks…different,' Richard said, a gleam in his eyes, because there was something very appealing though slightly shocking in seeing that masculine cap set on her luxuriant dark hair when she was wearing feminine apparel.

They joined the last stragglers, taking up places right at the back of the church. One or two turned their heads to look, but as she was not known to anyone local few thought it odd—except for the rather strange attire she wore. However, since she was seated at the back only a few noticed.

Georgie sat staring straight ahead. She felt close to tears, though she was not certain whether her emotion was for the death of an elderly lady she had never met, at least since she was a very small child, or her own situation. The shock of realising that all her hopes had vanished in a puff of smoke was one of the reasons she had asked to attend the church service. It would give her a little time to consider what she ought to do now.

Clearly, she could not expect to live at the countess's home in the circumstances. It would probably be shut up with just a few staff to care for it until the new owner took it over. She had no idea who that person was, but suspected it might be a distant cousin of the late countess's husband. Since she knew nothing of him, whoever he might be, she could certainly not throw herself on his mercy.

It was very awkward, Georgie realised. She must either beg Richard to help her again or return to her uncle—and that she was determined not to do! Perhaps he knew of a respectable widow who might help her to set up an establishment of her own?

She could think of no alternative and thrust the worry from her mind as she listened to the vicar praising the goodness of her great-aunt. Tears trickled down her cheeks, because she felt very much alone. She had hoped that her great-aunt would be pleased to see her and the disappointment was hard to bear.

After the ceremony was over, the congregation followed the coffin out to the graveside. Richard and Georgie stood well back, feeling that neither of them was properly dressed for such an affair. Georgie was about to turn away when Richard took her arm and steered her towards a small party of mourners, one of whom was a very pretty young woman of perhaps seven and twenty. She turned her head as they approached, a look of astonishment in her eyes.

'Richard! How came you here?' Her bright eyes took in his dress, which was not at all suited to the occasion. 'I wrote, but was not sure you had my letter in time to make the journey.'

'I did not have your letter at all,' Richard said and went to kiss her cheek. 'You look very well, Jenny.' He smiled at the tall gentleman standing beside her. 'Maddison, good to see you. I had no idea the countess had died. It makes things rather awkward, for I had escorted her great-niece to stay with her…' He turned to Georgie, bringing her forward. 'Georgie, this is my sister, Lady Maddison, and her husband, Lord Edward. Miss Georgina Bridges.'

Jenny looked startled and then remembered her manners, offering her hand. 'My dear girl,' she said with a warm smile that gathered Georgie to her like an embrace. 'What a terrible shock for you—to arrive for a funeral when you had expected to be received by your aunt. It is strange that the countess did not tell me. She did speak of you once or twice, but I did not know that she had sent for you, though I had not seen her for a week or so.'

'Oh…' Georgie felt her cheeks flush. 'I dare say it was not important.'

'Well, what are you to do now?' Jenny said, her blue eyes curious as she looked at Georgie. 'I see you had no hat, though that cap rather suits you. You might set a fashion, at least if it were made in a different colour to match your toilette.'

'May we throw ourselves on your hospitality?' Richard asked. 'Georgie is in some difficulty, which I shall explain to you later.'

'Naturally you will stay with us,' Jenny said at once. 'How could it be otherwise? Shrewsbury House is closed up, though there are servants there to take care of it, but the lawyers have taken a room at the inn to entertain the countess's neighbours. We had no intention of attending, but if you wish to make yourself known…'

'Oh, no,' Georgie said, her cheeks flushed with embarrassment. 'I would rather not. I am hardly dressed for it.'

'No…' Jenny threw a very odd look at her brother. 'Shall you follow us to the house, Richard? I am not perfectly sure of your travelling arrangements.'

'Georgie is travelling in a closed carriage,' he told her, a gleam in his eyes. 'I am riding—but have been travelling with her for some of the time. I was injured, you see.'

'Good grief!' Jenny looked shocked. 'I begin to see why…but no matter. You shall tell me it all when we are home and comfortable.' She tucked her arm into Georgie's, giving her an encouraging look. 'You may accompany me, my dear girl, and tell me everything. Edward, ride with Richard if you will, my dear.'

'It may have escaped your memory, my dearest, but I came in the carriage with you. However, I shall ride on top with the coachman if you wish to be private with your new friend.'

There was a glimmer of mockery in his dark eyes, which Jenny seemed to accept without a flicker, her mouth curving in a smile of content, as if she were accustomed to having her way.

'Yes, Edward, whatever,' she said, dismissing his gallant offer as expected. 'Come along, Georgie. I sense a mystery here, and you are going to tell me everything.'

Georgie heard the note of determination in her voice, and guessed that beneath her sweet manners and pretty smiles was a lady who knew how to get what she wanted. She quailed inwardly, for she sensed it would do her no good to lie, and she could only hope that Richard's sister would not think her lost beyond all hope when she learned the truth.

'Well.' Jenny Maddison's deep blue eyes lit with admiration as she heard Georgie's tale through to the end. 'I think you were exceptionally brave and did exactly as you ought—though it was a pity you did not come straight to Mary. She was a lovely lady, Georgie. It is a shame you did not know her better. I always wondered why you did not accept her invitation to stay last Christmas.'

'Her invitation?' Georgie stared at her, bewildered. 'I did not receive an invitation last year—or ever to my knowledge.'

'How can that be? I know she wrote to your uncle asking if he would send you to her. I believe he said that you were unwell and could not manage it at that time.'

'I wasn't ill,' Georgie said, feeling a surge of indignation. 'Oh, how could he tell such lies? He must have done it to make certain that I did not leave his house. Had I known my aunt wished to see me, I should have come at once. She did say that I would always be welcome in her letter to me, but I did not know she had asked for me. When I spoke to my aunt about the possibility of a visit, she told me that the countess was elderly and did not wish for visitors. I was not sure if she would take me in.'

'I am sure she would have done so despite her health,' Jenny told her. 'Just a few days sooner and you might have seen her…' She sighed. 'Well, there is no point in crying over something that cannot be helped. The thing is, what are we to do about you now?'

'I shall never return to my uncle's house.'

'No, of course not,' Jenny said decisively. 'That would be to play into his hands and cannot be thought of.' Her cheek dimpled as she studied Georgie. 'You know, you are very pretty—even beautiful if you were dressed in something suitable.'

Georgie blushed, but made no mention of the compliment in her reply. 'I thought I might pay a respectable widow to bear me company once I have my inheritance.'

'Well, you might, of course,' Jenny said and gurgled with soft laughter. 'On the other hand, you could be my guest. I have been a little down these past months, you see. I do not care for the winter and it took me a little time to get over the birth of my son so I have stayed at home for an age. However, Edward has promised to take me to Bath if I will take the waters.' She pulled her soft mouth into a grimace of distaste. 'I do not enjoy the prospect, but I shall enjoy being in company again. We shall take a house big enough for nurse and her assistant, besides Jemmy's tutor and my maid, and Edward's man, of course—and you, Georgie, my love. Richard too if he should care for it, though I dare say he will be off on some horrid business of his own before we know it. I have been nagging him for an age, you know. It is time he gave up all this dangerous stuff and settled down. He should think of providing me with a sister-in-law and a nephew or two, but he is stubborn and will not listen.'

Georgie looked at her in dawning delight. 'Would you really let me live with you—visit Bath with you?'

'I should like it above all things,' Jenny told her in her engaging way. She clapped her hands, pleased with her solution, which, since it suited her, she imagined would please her family. 'If you would like to be my friend, of course?'

'Oh, it is exactly what I should like,' Georgie said impulsively. 'And so very kind. You do not know me. I might be a terrible person. Your brother thinks I am not always truthful since I lied to him at the start.'

'Oh, brothers,' Jenny said in a dismissive manner. 'They are for ever on at one, telling one how to behave, at least until one marries.' She looked thoughtful. 'And after if they can get away with it. My dearest Edward will not allow anyone to bully me.' A smile of content settled over her face. 'He always wishes to please me and I know he will say it is just the thing to lift my spirits. You will want lots of clothes, I am sure, for even if we sent for your own things they would not do for Bath, you know. I have some things that you may borrow. I see that Richard has given you an old gown of mine that I left somewhere once. He might have bought you something new! It was very stingy of him!'

'Oh, no,' Georgie said, instinctively protecting him. 'He has been very kind to me, Lady Maddison. You must not think otherwise. He fed me when I was hungry and then brought me all this way when I am sure he has other more important things to do.'

'What could be more important than showing gallantry to a lady in distress?' Jenny said. 'I dare say he thought that gown would do—and it does look well enough for travelling. However, I shall find you something much better when we are home, and in Bath we shall commission only the finest of everything.'

'I am not certain how much I am to inherit from my father,' Georgie said a little uncertainly.

'What can that signify?' Jenny said, taking her breath away with her next words. 'The countess was wealthy in her own right you know. The estate may go to a distant cousin of her husband, I dare say, for she said as much—but everything else is to come to you.' Her eyes went over Georgie in a satisfied way. 'You will be very rich, my dear—and, dressed as befits your consequence, you will take society by storm.' She tapped a finger against her velvet muff, which hung from a chain made of moonstones and gold. 'I am not sure whether it would not be better to open the house in London…that is where Richard found my gown, no doubt. He must have sent to the housekeeper, Mrs Maunders, for something.'

'You must not go to so much trouble for my sake,' Georgie said. 'Your husband wishes you to take the waters for your health—besides, I suppose I ought to be in mourning for my aunt.'

'Nonsense,' Jenny said, determined not to see her plans squashed by convention. 'You hardly knew her and she would not have wanted it. Mary would not have been pleased to see everyone wearing black today and never wore it herself, even when she was in mourning for her husband. I shall change into colours once we are home, and you must not think of going into black.' Her eyes went over Georgie again. 'You might wear a pearl grey for evening, and I think lilac would suit your colouring—also some blues. We can brush through it if we wish, and no one needs to know anything.'

'But if I am the countess's heir...' Georgie was doubtful. 'I should not wish to show disrespect.'

'And you shall not,' her determined hostess said. 'Yes, you may wear grey and lilac and white, I think. We shall not attend anything too large or noisy—but we shall contrive to enjoy ourselves just the same.'

'Oh, yes,' Georgie said, feeling relieved that she need not wear black again so soon after wearing it for her parents. 'Are we stopping?' She looked out of the window at what was a large, but not huge, country house with long windows, bricks that looked the colour of musk roses and an impressive front porch. 'What a lovely house.'

'It is not as big as Richard's,' Jenny said. 'But I like it better. Our home was always a little cold. If I were Richard, I should set the builders on to improve it, but he has been so busy that I dare say he has not had the time.'

Georgie had been so busy talking with her hostess that she had not noticed the gardens, but as the carriage door was opened she took the hand of an obliging groom, looking about her as he helped her down. The gardens were formal with smooth paths of bricks interspersed with neat beds of roses and flowers. As it was only late spring some of them were still in bud and had not yet bloomed, but she thought it would be a pretty place to walk in summer. To the side of the house she saw shrubbery and guessed that the gardens at the back would be less formal.

'Do you ride?' Jenny was asking as she took Georgie's arm once more. 'It is a must in the country, I think, for otherwise we should be confined to the house unless someone took us driving.'

'Yes, I can ride,' Georgie told her. 'My aunt did not encourage it, but my father taught me when I was a child. I can drive, too—a gig with one pony, though I should like to drive a proper rig.'

'I have never driven myself,' Jenny told her. 'My father thought I was too delicate and my husband thinks a puff of wind might break me—but he takes me driving as often as I want so I do not complain.'

'We must ride together,' Georgie said. She felt that she had known her companion for ever and was quite content to let her plan her future. She saw Richard giving her a quizzical look as she walked towards him. He and Lord Maddison stood by the front door, waiting for the ladies to come up with them. 'I shall enjoy living here with you, Jenny.'

'I dare say you will marry and leave me too soon,' her hostess told her with a naughty look. 'But we shall remain friends and you will visit me sometimes—will you not?'

'Yes, of course,' Georgie assured her and wondered at the satisfied gleam in her eyes. 'But I am not sure I shall marry very soon. I would not want to be married for any money I might inherit. I am determined it shall be for love and nothing else.'

'Well, I dare say you may fall in love,' Jenny said and her fond gaze travelled to her brother, dwelling on him for a moment. He might not be as handsome as her beloved Edward, but he was a fine strong man and kind. She thought he would do very well for her new friend, and determined then and there to bring about a match between them if it could be managed.

Chapter Five

It was amazing how quickly Lady Maddison's servants overcame their surprise at having two unexpected guests and almost before they had finished taking refreshments in Jenny's parlour, the housekeeper returned to announce that rooms were ready.

'I instructed that a pale lilac silk gown I had three summers ago be put out for you,' Jenny said. 'I was very much your size then, though my waist is a little larger now since I had my son. I think it will fit you and I shall look out some more things for you, Georgie. They will do until we can have you fitted for your new wardrobe in Bath.'

'I have no money of my own until my birthday, which is next week,' Georgie said, remembering suddenly. 'I must write to my lawyers and let them know where they can find me.'

'Well, we shall be in Bath by then,' Jenny said. 'They may set up an account for you there, and one of their people can visit you once we know where we shall be staying. Edward and Richard may arrange it all between them, you know. As for your clothes, you may have the bills sent to me. I shall make a present of them to you, to thank you for agreeing to be my friend and companion.'

'Oh, no, you must not,' Georgie said. 'I shall repay you once I have my funds, and I thank you for the kindness you have shown me. Some sisters might have thought the worst had they seen me with their brother and wearing a dress they knew to be their own.'

'Oh, no,' Jenny replied blithely. 'I know Richard. His flirts are always married ladies with obliging husbands, and they would not be seen dead in a cast-off gown. I dare say he has to make them a handsome present for their company, though of course I am not supposed to know these things. Most single gentlemen have their high flyers, of course, but I do not approve of it continuing after marriage. Edward would never look elsewhere and knows I should leave him if he did.'

This was plain speaking indeed, and Georgie might have been shocked had such a speech been made by anyone else, but Jenny said it so charmingly that she merely laughed and took it in the spirit it had been meant.

'I believe I should feel as you do,' she admitted. 'That is why I do not wish to marry simply for the sake of it.'

'Oh, no, you must not,' her hostess agreed. 'I am sure you will meet someone you like well enough to marry, and perhaps sooner than you imagine.'

'Yes, perhaps,' Georgie agreed. 'But supposing he did not feel the same about me?'

Jenny tipped her head to one side, her expression one of complete innocence. 'But I am sure that he does…I mean, will,' she corrected herself hastily. 'Once you are dressed as you ought to be, no man of good sense could resist falling in love with you—except for Edward, of course.'

'Because he loves you,' Georgie agreed. 'But might it not be the case for someone else…?' She faltered and flushed under Jenny's bright gaze.

'I believe you are speaking of Richard,' his devoted sister said, clapping her hands in delight. 'Do tell me you like him, Georgie! I am quite determined that you would do very well for my brother.'

'Yes, I do like him a lot,' Georgie admitted. 'How could I not when he has been so kind to me? I think he quite likes me—but perhaps not enough to marry me.'

'Then he must be quite without sense,' Jenny said and laughed. 'Besides, he will be no match for the two of us, Georgie. I know he has been reluctant to marry because of his work, but he has a fine estate and it is time he devoted himself to it and the getting of an heir. I shall remind him of his duty to the family, and you must smile and look a little aloof, as though you did not care a fig. He will understand then that he must court you if he wishes to win you.'

'Do you think that will work?' Georgie asked dubiously. 'I think he may know me too well to be taken in by any pretence of my being a fine lady he must court.'

'You mean because he found you in desperate straits?' Jenny frowned. 'But that was then, and you are a double heiress now and as such will be courted by all kinds of beaux when we get to Bath. I am sure it will bring him to his senses when he realises that he could lose you.' Jenny smiled serenely. 'We shall make him realise it if he does not.'

Georgie was not as certain that Richard would

respond to the tactics that his sister was suggesting. However, she supposed that it must be worth a try because whenever she thought of marriage, which she had a few times of late, it was always his face she saw.

She suspected that she had fallen for him while he was ill. The fear that he might die had wrenched at her heart, even though she hardly knew him. Since then she had been in his company more often and had grown to find him pleasing to be with, his touch making her heart race wildly. Once she had thought he might kiss her and it had caused her stomach to spasm, but he had turned away, and she felt he had made a conscious decision not to flirt with her.

After Jenny had delivered her into the care of her housekeeper, who took her up to her bedchamber, Georgie was left alone with her thoughts. Would Richard think she was beautiful once she was dressed properly? He had seen her in a dress for the first time that day, but since then they had not been alone, since he had chosen to ride. He had said it was because he wished to exercise his leg, but she thought it might have been to save her reputation, so that she should not be seen riding in a closed carriage with a gentleman by her aunt's neighbours.

Georgie's thoughts switched to her great-aunt. It was very sad that she should have died just a few days before she arrived. She would have liked to know the countess better than she had from the few letters she'd received from her, and wished she might have visited sooner. If Jenny was right and she had been invited to stay the previous Christmas, her Uncle Henry was much at fault for keeping the invitation from her. Or had it been her aunt? No, she thought Uncle Henry must have made the decision. Her aunt was not evil, but weak and easily led. Georgie's uncle must even then have had hopes of controlling her fortune.

Georgie frowned, because if Jenny was right about the countess leaving her some money, Sir Henry Mowbray might think it even more prudent to regain his hold over her.

She would never return to his house. Once her fortune was her own, she could appoint her lawyers as her guardians or perhaps Lord Edward would take on that position? She would say nothing for the moment, but if her uncle exerted pressure to try to get her to return, she would ask Jenny to speak to her husband. Surely with Lord Maddison's backing she would be in a position to defeat her uncle's schemes?

Her future settled in her own mind, Georgie looked at the pale lilac gown laid out on the bed for her. It was a pretty afternoon gown fashioned of quality silk and made in very simple lines, the waist high and bound by a fixed sash of violet. Sprigs of violets were embroidered on the hem and around the cuffs of the sleeves, which finished at the elbow with a slight flare. She slipped out of the yellow dress and pulled on the delicate undergarments she found with the gown, discovering that they all smelled faintly of lavender, as if they had been carefully packed away. She also found ribbons to match the sash, some pale grey leather slippers that almost fitted her, and a shawl of soft cashmere and silk in a toning shade of violet.

Once dressed, her long hair tied back with ribbons, Georgie was well pleased with the transformation. She looked much more elegant in this ensemble than the yellow, and guessed that it had been expensive when made, and scarcely worn. She thought that it needed something in the neck; discovering that one of the ribbons had some pearls sewn along the edges, she tied it around her throat and finished it in a bow at the back.

Satisfied that she had done all she could with her appearance, Georgie left the bedchamber and went along the landing and down the stairs. She had reached about halfway when a gentleman came to the foot and looked up at her. She paused, very aware of Richard, who had changed into a tight-fitting coat of blue superfine and some pale grey breeches with long boots. His linen was still casual, for she did not think he went in for the intricate cravats many gentlemen aspired to, but his style suited the man and she thought him very attractive, her heart catching as he smiled.

'Georgie,' he said, waiting for her to reach him. 'That colour looks well on you. I am glad you have not gone into black. It is not necessary in the circumstances.'

'I am glad you approve,' she said, trying to remain calm as her senses reeled at the touch of his hand. She did find him so very charming when he was like this! 'Your sister wants me to accompany her when she visits Bath, and she says that I may wear pale grey, lilac and perhaps blue—do you think she is right?'

'Perfectly right,' Richard said. 'Jenny may appear fragile and a little ingenuous, but believe me, she is up to the mark on all matters of propriety. She will look after you.' His eyes were so warm at that moment that Georgie felt she was wrapped in comforting arms. 'It was my intention to bring you here had your aunt refused you. However, Jenny has told me that that would not have happened. She believes the countess would have been delighted to see you.'

'It seems my Aunt and Uncle Mowbray refused to let me visit her last year,' Georgie said, frowning. 'I think it very wrong of them, for I should have come had I known.'

'Very wrong in the circumstances,' Richard agreed and seemed thoughtful. 'I wonder why they kept her request from you, Georgie? It might be that they thought you would choose to make your home with her, of course, and wished to keep control of you and your fortune.'

'I can think of no other reason,' Georgie said. 'It is hard to believe that my mother's brother could behave so badly to his only niece.'

'I agree,' Richard said. 'Unfortunately, money is at the root of many such instances. I am sure you are not the first young girl to suffer at the hands of greedy relatives.'

'They won't try to make me go back when they discover where I am—will they?'

'They may try,' Richard said, his mouth settling into a grim line. 'However, you have friends now, Georgie. My sister would never permit you to be made unhappy, and her husband—and I, of course—will prove formidable opposition should they try to force you.'

'My father's lawyers could be guardians, unless Lord Edward would give me his protection.'

'If it came to it, I am certain he would,' Richard assured her. 'However, when I leave Yorkshire I shall make a point of calling on Sir Henry and making him aware of your wishes in this matter.'

His tone and expression were so stern that Georgie almost felt sorry for her uncle. She suppressed a smile as she said, 'I hope you shall not leave Yorkshire too soon, sir?'

'Jenny has made me promise not to leave too soon,' Richard told her. 'I may as well avail myself of her hospitality while I make some inquiries. You know why I am here, Georgie. These are dangerous times, for Bonaparte escaped from his island prison some weeks ago, and is even now in France preparing an army. There may be war and I must do my duty. You would not expect me to neglect it?'

'No, of course not,' she said, though her heart was saying something very different. 'But you will take care?'

'I am always careful,' he replied. 'What happened in London was an isolated incident. I shall not be caught off guard again.'

'I am glad. I should not want the assassin's knife to find its true mark next time.'

'I believe you would mind if I were killed?' Richard's eyes were suddenly alert, intent on her face.

'Yes, of course I should,' Georgie said, and then, mindful of what his sister had told her, 'You have been so kind to me, helping me, bringing me to my aunt…naturally I should not want any harm to come to you.'

'Is that all it is? Gratitude?'

Georgie's heart took a flying leap. She wanted to throw herself into his arms and declare that her feelings were so much more, but at that moment Jenny came to the head of the stairs. She called out to them and Georgie turned her head to look at her. Wearing a pale apricot silk gown, Jenny was a vision of loveliness as she came down the stairs towards them. Her eyes went over Georgie approvingly.

'You do look pretty, doesn't she, Richard? That colour suits you much better than it ever did me, my dearest Georgie. I am so looking forward to helping you buy your new clothes. It will be so exciting. Georgie will be a sensation, do you not think so, Richard? She is a considerable heiress, you know, for the countess told me she intended to leave her all her personal fortune. Dressed as she deserves, I am sure she will receive a bevy of offers from the gentlemen in Bath.'

Richard's eyebrows knitted in a frown. 'Yes, I imagine all the fortune hunters will be flocking around her once it is known she inherits both her father's estate and the Countess of Shrewsbury's fortune.'

'Come now, Richard,' his sister said in a scolding tone. 'Georgie would attract suitors had she nothing at all. The fortune hunters will no doubt be after her, but I shall warn them off, you know. I am confident that there will be sufficient gentlemen of fortune and good birth to give Georgie a wide choice.'

'I dare say you are right,' Richard replied.

Watching him, Georgie saw the shutters come down. He looked like the man she had met that first night, a pulse flicking at his temple, his expression stern.

'I shall not marry any of them unless I truly love them,' Georgie announced. 'My father's estate would have been enough to give me independence, but if I also inherit from my great aunt…I dare say I may set up my own establishment if Lady Maddison grows tired of my company.'

'That I could never do,' Jenny said, linking arms with her. 'Let us go for a walk before tea, dearest Georgie. I want to get to know you better. You must tell me about your life before your dear parents died, and I shall tell you what I did as a girl.' She glanced at her brother. 'Richard, shall we see you at tea?'

'I have an errand I must do,' he replied. 'I shall return for dinner, Jenny. Do not let my sister take you over entirely, Georgie.' He smiled briefly and walked away.

'Brothers!' Jenny said. 'Why can he never relax and forget about his work?'

'I dare say it may be important,' Georgie replied. She doubted that Richard ever confided totally in his sister, much as he clearly loved her. He would not have told Georgie what was going on if she had not discovered it for herself in that book. And then of course there were the two attempts to murder him…unless the second attempt had been meant for her and not Richard? A tiny shudder went through her, causing her companion to look at her in concern.

'Are you cold, Georgie?'

'No, not at all,' she answered with a smile. 'I was merely thinking of my uncle. He may try to force me to return to him.'

'Well, he shall not,' Jenny said comfortably. 'I have discussed this with my dearest Edward, and he assures me that once we are settled in Bath he will arrange a meeting with your lawyers. He is one of the countess's trustees—did I tell you that?'

'No, you did not.' Georgie was surprised.

'Well, she trusted him with much of her business,' Jenny said. 'He told me that he will acquaint you with the terms of your inheritance after tea. I believe he will be in a position of trustee for a year or two, and of course that gives him as much right as your uncle to have a say in what you do.' Jenny smiled at her ingenuously. 'Not that he would dream of interfering with our plans, but it does mean that his word must be taken seriously, and if he and your father's lawyers reach agreement that you should live with me until you marry or wish to live elsewhere…'

'My uncle would find it difficult to disagree, especially if I placed a charge of misconduct against him.'

'You must not think of it except as a last resort,' Jenny said. 'It would cause a scandal and you do not want that, my dearest. No, no, you may leave it to Edward and Richard. Between them they will settle the affair. We need not trouble our heads over it. Gentlemen are so much better at matters of business, you know.'

'Yes, I suppose so,' Georgie said a little doubtfully. She did not see why a lady might not be in charge of her own affairs, though she knew that a woman's property became her husband's on marriage. A settlement was usually made, giving the lady a generous income and in many cases the bulk of her fortune was settled on her future heirs, unless otherwise agreed in the marriage contract. 'I think my father's will lays out certain conditions, but I am not perfectly certain what they are.'

'As I said, the gentlemen will take care of it,' Jenny said blithely. 'All you need to think about is what you need for our trip to Bath. That ribbon is very pretty for afternoon wear, but you must have some jewellery, Georgie. Did your mother leave you anything?'

'I had one or two small trinkets, but the rest was put away in a bank until I came into the remainder of my inheritance,' Georgie said. 'At least that is what my uncle told me, though I thought I saw a necklace of my mother's in my aunt's chamber once. She put it away immediately but it did look like Mama's diamonds. My uncle must have told her that she must keep them from me.'

Jenny looked thoughtful. 'If some of your jewels have been misappropriated, it might be a part of the reason why your uncle tried to marry you off, Georgie. If he has been entrusted with something he disposed of without your consent, that is theft. He would be ruined if it came out.'

'That is what he was saying to my aunt when I overheard them,' Georgie told her, frowning. 'He did not mention jewellery, but he said that Monsieur Thierry knew something that could ruin him.'

'It might be another reason why you were not allowed to visit the countess,' Jenny remarked. 'She would have been sure to ask why you did not have your mother's jewels, for it is more usual for a daughter to be given those at once, you know.'

'My aunt gave me the trinkets. I took them with me when I left home, a gold cross and chain, but they were lost when my things were stolen.'

'She did not give you pearls or bracelets?' Georgie shook her head. 'It might have been considered right to hold back diamonds or emeralds, something of that kind, but you should have had your mother's pearls before this—and I am sure she had some. Pearls are always the first things a young lady receives from her mother and father.'

'If my uncle sold them, it is too bad of him,' Georgie said. 'I do not care for the diamonds so very much, for I should not have wanted to wear them until I was older—but I remember Mama's pearls. They were beautiful and I believed they were waiting in the bank for me.'

'They may be, of course,' Jenny said and squeezed her arm comfortingly. 'The countess had some fine pearls and I believe they may be yours very soon. I know it is not quite the same, but you will have a few pretty things to wear in Bath, dearest.'

'Oh…' Georgie stared at her. 'Shall I really? I had not thought I would receive anything for ages.'

'Well, the money may be tied up for a while, but Edward has the jewels. Mary recently gave them to him for safekeeping. I think she may have feared that her husband's distant cousin might try to take them if she died.'

'I see…' Georgie could not quite suppress her feeling of anger and disappointment over her mother's jewellery, which, she was now fairly sure, had somehow been kept from her and misused. But the news that she would have the countess's jewels had done something to alleviate it. 'Then…if I had not run away, Lord Maddison would have come to bring me the jewels one day.'

'Oh, yes, you were bound to meet us one day,' Jenny said, a look of satisfaction in her eyes. 'I am sure everything will work out just as we might wish, my love.' She squeezed Georgie about the waist. 'We shall take one more turn about the rose garden and then it will be time for tea.'

Georgie looked at the casket Edward Maddison had just placed in front of her, hardly daring to lift the lid. It was an imposing box fashioned of mahogany with a large silver lock; she inserted the key carefully and turned, lifting the lid to peep inside. An array of velvet jewellery boxes met her eyes, and, opening the first, circular-shaped box, she discovered a set of creamy pearls with a diamond clasp. There were also some ear-bobs and a bracelet of gold set with pearls.

'Oh, they are magnificent,' she gasped, lifting them out. 'I never expected to own something like this! Thank you for giving them to me, sir.'

'You will discover much more valuable things,

though some are not suitable for a young girl. Countess Shrewsbury entrusted them to me for you, but you may wish to place some of them into a bank? Perhaps you should choose the ones you like best and put the others away for a time?'

'Are all these things mine?' Georgie asked, opening a ring box to look at a diamond five-stone ring. 'I have never seen stones as fine as these. Even my mother did not have such a good ring as this…as far as I can recall.'

'Well, I know the countess would have been pleased to hear you say that. She was proud of her jewellery, which is why she did not wish the contents of this box to fall into the wrong hands.'

'May I keep the box tonight and then give you back what I think should be put away tomorrow?'

'Yes, of course,' he said and looked pleased. 'You will want to take them up to your room and look through everything in private. You may safely leave them in the drawers of your tallboy, Miss Bridges. My servants are completely trustworthy, though I will take charge of them if you prefer?'

'Perhaps later,' she said. 'I would just like to look at everything, but I do not need very much. The pearls are perfect, and perhaps one of the rings, but most of the rest can be put away until I marry.'

'Very sensible,' he agreed. 'I dare say when you marry your husband will have several things reset for you in a more modern style. I believe much of it may be old-fashioned, but good quality. As you may know, the countess was a wealthy woman in her own right. Her late husband left her most of his money, though the house and land was entailed—but she was married twice and she kept her own fortune through the marriage contract. I was able to make some profitable investments for her—and you will have somewhere in the region of one hundred thousand pounds when the estate is settled.'

Georgie gasped. She imagined her father's estate could not amount to much more than five and thirty thousand pounds, but with the addition of the countess's fortune she would indeed be extremely wealthy.

'I had no idea, either that she was so wealthy—or that she intended to leave me so much,' Georgie said, feeling her eyes prick with tears. 'I am not sure that I deserve it, for I did not visit her.'

'I believe at one time she intended to leave only a third to you,' Lord Maddison told her. 'She had a young relative who died suddenly, and she blamed his death on her husband's cousin, who was also to have inherited a third. She changed her will at that time, leaving everything to you.'

'Did her husband's cousin come to the funeral?'

'He was expected, but he did not show,' Lord Maddison told her with a frown. 'I have never met the man, but I understand he came down from the female line and his mother married a Frenchman.'

'A Frenchman?' Georgie's flesh tingled. 'Do you know his name, sir?'

'Yes, of course. Monsieur Raoul Thierry…' He frowned as he saw the colour drain from her face. 'You know the name?'

'Yes. He…he was the man who wanted to marry me, which was the reason I ran away from my uncle's house.'

'Good grief! You are sure?' Lord Maddison was stunned. 'Richard told me a part of the story, but he didn't mention Thierry's name. Your uncle tried to force you into marriage with this man against your will?'

'Yes. I thought it was because of my father's estate,' Georgie said. 'And I think my uncle may have sold him some of my mother's jewels—but this bequest is a far more compelling reason for Monsieur Thierry to wish to marry me.'

'Yes, I imagine you are right,' Lord Maddison replied. 'It would explain something else…the reason you were shot at on your way here, Georgie. If you had died first, Thierry would have inherited everything. The countess had no one else, you see, and her fortune would have gone to him by default.'

Georgie shivered. She closed the lid of the large mahogany box, her pleasure in the contents dimmed as she realised that her life must have been in danger all this time without her realising it. How would Thierry feel once he knew that she had inherited the money?

'Do you think my uncle knew? Is that why he refused to let me visit the countess?'

'Who knows what the pair of them cooked up between them?' Lord Maddison said. 'I must speak to Richard about this matter, my dear. I had thought we merely needed to consult with lawyers, but I believe we must employ someone to make sure that you are safe from any attempt on your life during your stay in Bath.'

'You won't stop us going? Lady Maddison is so looking forward to it—and so am I.'

Edward smiled at her and shook his head. 'I am certain that Richard and I can come up with something to protect you and Jenny from these rogues. I had not thought it was this serious, but what you have told me with what I already know of Thierry tells me that he is a dangerous man, Georgie. However, we shall make sure that he does not harm you. I give you my word.'

Georgie thanked him, leaving him to take her box up to her room. She frowned over what she had learned, for it had puzzled her why someone should want her dead. She had thought that no one but her uncle could gain from her death, which, in the case of her father's estate, was correct—but the legacy from her great-aunt was an unknown factor in this mystery. Monsieur Thierry had tried to gain her by marriage, which would have brought him her fortune and her person. Knowing that she had run away rather than take him for her husband, was it possible that he had taken the chance to shoot at her? He had perhaps meant to shoot Richard, but, seeing her at the inn the previous night, had hesitated before firing and then chosen her. If so, he had missed his target by the narrowest of margins. How long would it be before he decided to try again?

Raoul Thierry frowned over his wineglass. Damn the wench and the interfering devil she had run off with! Her precipitate behaviour had ruined his plans in more ways than one, and he blamed that fool Henry Mowbray. Somehow the girl had learned what was afoot and taken off before anyone could prevent her. But how had she ended up with Hernshaw? Was it possible that he knew of the connection?

Thierry was furious at the way he seemed to be thwarted on all sides. He had lost the bride he had chosen, for her beauty as well as her fortune. He would have treated her kindly enough had she taken him, at least until she began to bore him, which she would in the end, he had no doubt. Women always bored him once he had broken them to his ways, and he did not think she would be any different, though she was certainly spirited— perhaps more so than he'd imagined. Had he suspected her capable of running off alone and with very little money, he would have made sure of her first. He should have snatched her from Mowbray's house and seduced her, ensuring that she could not leave him and retain her reputation.

He wondered what she was doing dressed in a youth's clothing. Was it a disguise to keep him off the scent? Had she guessed that he would look for her after that fool told him that she'd gone? She couldn't know that his distant cousin's wife had left her all the money. It was cursed chance that had led him to fleece the countess's late sister's grandson at the card tables, and stupidity that had led the young man to take his own life. Stupid young fool! Why hadn't Hastings gone to his great-aunt for money to pay his debts? He was her closest relative apart from Georgina Bridges, closer to her in truth since she had been fond of him for years and had offered him a home after his parents died of a fever. She would no doubt have rung a peal over him, but then given him the money he needed. Instead, he got drunk and then put a pistol to his head, leaving a letter that blamed Thierry for leading him into a game that put him in debt over and beyond what he could pay.

Thierry had tried to explain it away, but the countess had required him not to visit her again. She could not deny him the house and land, for, though distant, his relationship to her late husband was indisputable, but the estate was worth a fraction of her own fortune. He knew for a fact that it must be upwards of a hundred thousand pounds—and she had left it all to that girl! He had thought it would be an easy task to turn Georgina's head with flattery. Women had always been eager for his attentions, but not her—not that proud bitch! She had made her dislike of him clear, but he would still have had her. He had fleeced her uncle of his last penny, telling him he could stay on in his own house providing that he gave the girl to him. It was then that the fool confessed he had stolen most of her mother's jewellery, given to him for Georgina by the lawyers six months after her mother's death.

Mowbray had caved in once Thierry told him that he would go to prison for theft and debt. He had promised that he would force the girl if she would not take him willingly, but she had fooled them all by running away. Mowbray was still running round like a headless chicken looking for her, but he had found her first. Had she been alone, she would have been his wife by now, and her fortune his for the spending, but she was with him…Hernshaw.

Thierry glowered at the rich ruby wine in his glass. He wasn't sure how much Hernshaw knew about the other business. He had dealt with the traitor, and the man would tell no more tales, and he had tried to lead Hernshaw astray. Had his ruse worked? He had tried to confuse his enemies, and then to have Hernshaw killed, but the assassin had failed—and he had paid for it, his throat cut, his life blood draining from him as he lay in an isolated ditch. No one must be allowed to stand in the way of *his* plans!

The British had defeated Napoleon Bonaparte, making him a prisoner on Elba, but they were careless jailers. He had escaped and returned to France in glory—and Thierry had been one of those who had worked for the emperor's freedom. Now that he was free, the people of France would no doubt rise to greet their Emperor, marching with him to throw off the yoke of the new regime, restoring him to his rightful place on the throne. Indeed, it was already happening. Money would see that the uprising did not falter. And then, when Bonaparte had won the inevitable war, crushing his enemies, Thierry would have everything that had been promised him: the lands and chateaux his family had lost during the revolution, riches beyond anything he might have had here. But he needed the countess's money to finance his project. Uprisings all over the country in the Emperor's favour would happen only if strings were pulled in the background—and that cost money.

And there was the other little matter. At just the right moment two assassinations would take place: the Prince Regent and Wellington. The British could find another prince to rule them and another general would take Wellington's place, but his was the brilliant mind that might secure the defeat of the Emperor and with it all Thierry's inflated ideas of grandeur. Once Wellington and the prince who had staunchly supported him were dead, the country would be plunged into chaos, and at that moment Bonaparte would march to victory against his enemies. By the time England recovered from the chaos it would be too late!

Thierry's eyes glittered. Money and property were not enough for him. His family had been humiliated when they were forced to flee for their lives during the revolution, and he had found a home here in this God-forsaken country, but not the respect he craved. The damned English aristocrats had looked down their noses at him, acknowledging him but shutting him out of the most exclusive circles. As Bonaparte's saviour and friend, he would be heaped with glory and honour, and then he could go home. The peasants who had driven his mother from her home, murdered his father and his older brother…they would pay the price they had long deserved. He had waited for his moment, made his plans carefully. There were always disaffected rogues to take his money and do his bidding, and few of them knew he was the mastermind behind the plot, for he took care to behave as though he too was taking orders from someone higher up the chain.

But to make sure that the Emperor's return was successful, he needed more money. Money was always the key to everything in his opinion—money and careful planning.

'You are certain Thierry is in league with the Bonapartists?' Richard asked, his gaze narrowing as he looked at his informant. 'I had heard whispers, but I thought the French dissidents were a spent force.'

'They cling to hope of his return to the throne,' the man sitting opposite him said. 'We have known of Thierry's activities for some time, but we thought they were a bunch of idle dissidents, great talkers and drinkers, but men of little action. It is only recently that we have begun to suspect that he might be the leader of another, more deadly group.'

'You think they were behind the plot to free him? Now that they have succeeded, do you think the French people will rise in numbers to greet Bonaparte as a returning hero?'

'The present regime is not particularly popular with many of the people,' the other man said. 'With the right measures in place the rabble could be roused—and there are soldiers still loyal to Bonaparte, bound to be. We already have reports of men flocking to him.'

'But sufficient for a significant rising?' Richard frowned. 'He was beaten by the Allies before and will be again if he attempts it. Surely his commanders must know it is hopeless? They will persuade him to treat for terms?'

'Perhaps…' The other man toyed with his wine-glass. 'But supposing Prinny were dead and Wellington too?'

'That would make a difference,' Richard agreed. 'The Regent had always been a staunch supporter of Wellington and the war against the French. Others are not so strong. It is possible that the pacifists amongst the government could sway the motion towards making peace with Bonaparte. They might think he has learned a lesson and will not cause trouble in future.'

'Then they are fools,' the other man said. 'Bonaparte will never be satisfied until he has England under his thumb. We English have been a thorn in his side too long. If he could quash all resistance from us…'

'He would crush the rest of them under his heel and rampage across Europe again,' Richard agreed. 'We have to make sure that Thierry doesn't carry out this plan of his to have the Regent and Wellington murdered.'

'God knows where he gets all his money from. He came here with virtually nothing, but my agents report that he always seems to be flush in the pockets.'

'Gambling, I dare say,' Richard said. 'You know the score—lure a flat into a game that's too deep for him and take everything he has. Men like that do not hesitate to cheat their intended victims. I know of at least one case involving a man who was driven to desperate measures because of Thierry's threats.'

'He is a dangerous man, Richard. My superiors have spoken of having him disposed of, but they want to learn as much as they can of his activities first.'

'Murder?' Richard frowned. 'You are not expecting me to do your dirty work for you, I hope? I won't murder for you, Rawlings.'

'I didn't expect you would,' his companion replied. 'Fortunately, there are others not so nice in their scruples. When the time comes he will be dealt with—we just need the names of his friends.'

'And that is where I come in, I suppose?'

'Exactly,' Sir Michael Rawlings, secret agent and government adviser, said. 'I can give you a clue—there is a tavern they are known to frequent. We need you to follow Thierry the next time he goes there to a meeting. We want the names of the men he meets—where they live, what they do, if you can get it—but we must have the information soon.'

'Supposing he doesn't meet them for a while?'

'We believe it will be in two days' time,' Rawlings said. 'You won't let me down?'

'Have I ever?'

'No—but this girl you've got mixed up with, where does she come into it?'

'She doesn't come into it at all,' Richard said. 'Keep her out of it, Rawlings. I'm warning you. If you cause her to be harmed, you will be sorry.'

'No need to get yourself worked up,' his companion said. 'But if she is anything to do with this business you had better make sure she stays out of it or she might get caught in the crossfire.'

Richard glared at him, angry that he had dared to bring Georgie into this business—damned dirty business it was, too. Richard knew that it wouldn't be the first time his information had led to the death of an enemy of the State. The knowledge did not sit well with his conscience and he wondered if it was time that he thought of calling a halt. In war his spying work had seemed natural and right, for the enemy had needed to be tamed, but some of the things he had been called upon to do in the last couple of years had left a nasty taste in his mouth.

'I shall,' he said and stood up. 'I'll let you know what I discover, Rawlings.'

Nodding to the other man, he left the inn. He stood for a moment contemplating the situation, taking note of the other people in the street, alert to the danger that might be waiting in dark alleys. He had promised his sister he would be back in time for dinner but the hours had flown. She was used to his lateness and broken promises, understanding that his work came first, but she was his sister, not his wife. A wife would not understand what took him away from home so often.

Richard frowned and pushed the thoughts of personal happiness from his mind. He was hardly in a position to think of settling down—his life could be forfeit at any time; besides, his former life made him unfit to be the husband of a young and innocent girl.

He was a fool even to think of it!

Chapter Six

'Oh, that was so enjoyable,' Jenny said as they cantered into the stable yard together the next morning. 'Did you not think so, Georgie?'

'Yes, indeed,' Georgie agreed. 'I thought I might find it uncomfortable since I had not ridden for a while, but it was not so. We must ride together again tomorrow if you please.'

'Yes, we must,' Jenny agreed. She smiled as the young groom helped her to dismount. 'Thank you, Andrews. Oh, look, here is Richard…' She stood watching as Richard came striding towards them just as Georgie dismounted with the help of a groom. 'I must tell you that I am at cross-stitches with you, sir! You promised to dine with us last evening!'

'Yes, I did, and you are right to be cross with me, Jenny,' Richard told her, but his eyes were on her companion. Georgie was wearing a dark blue habit, which suited her very well and might have been made for her, though he knew it to be his sister's. She had a fetching hat set on her head at a rakish angle and looked stunningly lovely. 'Georgie—Miss Bridges, you look very well this morning. I think riding must agree with you?'

'Yes, it does,' Georgie said, frowning as she noticed the more formal use of her name. She sensed that he had placed a barrier between them, as if the intimacy of the past weeks had never been. Why? Surely they were friends? 'I see that you no longer limp, sir. Is your wound completely healed?'

She deliberately reminded him of all that had happened, but his expression remained polite, cool, almost detached. It struck her a blow to the heart, for she had thought they were beyond such manners. Indeed, she had begun to allow herself to hope that perhaps he liked her well enough to make her an offer, but now she saw that that was foolish. He had gone out of his way to help her, but now that she was safe with his sister he clearly felt that his obligation was at an end. She lifted her chin higher, deciding that she must follow Jenny's advice and be a little aloof.

'Yes, thank you,' he replied. 'I am quite recovered now. Jenny, I must pay a visit this morning, but I promise I shall be back for nuncheon—by tea at the very latest.'

His sister gave him a severe look. 'I shall not take it kindly if you break your word again, Richard. We do not see you as often as we should like as it is. While you are here, you might make some effort to give us your company.'

'Yes, I promise I shall,' he said. 'I need to set something in motion, but after that I shall try to be a proper guest.'

'Well, we shall excuse you for now, but if you do not join us later we shall both be very displeased with you.

Come along, Georgie. I am not sure my brother deserves our attention.'

'Yes, of course,' Georgie said. She avoided looking at him, knowing that her expression would reproach him as much as his sister's words. She felt that he had abandoned her, and it hurt more than she liked to admit. 'Please excuse us—and take care of yourself. We should not want you to have another accident.' Heat surged through her and she wondered why she added those last words.

Georgie was conscious of Richard's head turning to watch her as she caught up the train of her riding habit and walked towards the house. She must not allow herself to show concern for him since he had made it clear that he was not interested in her other than as a mere acquaintance.

Watching her walk away, Richard knew that his coolness had offended her. He regretted it in his heart and yet knew that it was the wisest thing in the circumstances. His business here was about to become even more dangerous and he did not wish her to be caught up in something that might end in harm to her.

Richard did not return in time for nuncheon, nor did he put in an appearance at tea. Georgie saw his sister's quick frown, and could not help feeling anxious. Was he merely caught up in some business or had something happened to him? She found herself listening for the sound of his voice or his footsteps in the hall, but he had not arrived by the time she went up to dress for dinner.

Jenny had provided her with two evening gowns, a pale blue and a delicate pearl grey. Georgie liked the style of the grey and chose that one, dressing her hair with some silver ribbons and pearl pins that had also been given to her by her generous hostess. She had kept her great-aunt's pearls, also some small items of gold for daytime wear, but returned most of the more costly jewels to Lord Maddison. He had promised to lock them away safely until such time as he could place them in the strong room at her aunt's bank. She decided to wear the pearl necklace for the first time that evening, though it still felt a little wrong to be in possession of such jewels.

They suited her well, and she felt pleased with her appearance as she left her bedchamber and went downstairs. Her heart leaped as she heard laughter in the drawing room, where the others had gathered for dinner, because she knew at once that Richard was with them. His eyes sought her out as soon as she entered and for a moment she saw a gleam that made her feel weak at the knees. When he looked at her that way she believed that he must feel something for her, even if he was not prepared to admit it.

He came to offer his arm as dinner was announced, his smile warm and relaxed, a remarkable change from earlier that day. 'You look lovely as always,' he said. 'Jenny tells me that you are to leave for Bath in three days' time. She was asking if I would visit you all there.'

'And shall you?' Georgie lifted her eyes to his, unaware of the silent appeal they held.

'Yes, perhaps, when my business is done here.'

'Is it nearly over?'

'I hope it may be very soon. Forgive me, but there is little more I can tell you at the moment. In my work one learns to be patient. It is often a case of waiting to see what develops.'

'You know that Raoul Thierry would have inherited the countess's fortune if I had died before she did?'

'Edward told me the terms of her will regarding you,' Richard said and frowned. 'I think it must mean that you are worth more to him alive than dead, Georgie. Unless he can persuade you to be his wife, he cannot now hope to inherit.'

'But my uncle could—and vastly more than he could have expected,' she replied. 'My life might still be in danger from him—do you not think so?'

'Perhaps, though I believe he may be more of a fool than a villain.'

'Yes, he must be, for he would not otherwise have wasted his own fortune…' Georgie found herself agreeing with him. 'So you think I am safe enough now?'

'Oh, yes—providing Thierry does not try to abduct you.'

She felt a stab of alarm. 'You do not think he would try?'

'It is his only hope of the fortune you inherited from the countess, and your father's estate,' Richard said. 'However, if you take reasonable care and stay close to Jenny, I do not think you in any immediate danger—and perhaps all danger may be eliminated soon.'

'What are you going to do?'

'I am afraid I cannot tell you. It is best you do not know. I should never have embroiled you in my affairs.'

'But you did and I do not like being shut out now.'

'Forgive me. Things have changed,' he replied. 'Tell me, are you looking forward to the visit to Bath, Miss Bridges? Have you been there before at all?'

His change of subject brought the barriers down

again. Georgie was angry with him. She shot him a look of reproach, for he was doing it again, shutting her out. It was as if they were mere acquaintances and that wasn't fair! She had discovered the code and helped him make up his mind that the message it contained was false—and now he was trying to make out that she was not concerned in his affairs, warning her to stand back.

Georgie was silent as he drew her chair for her. Had they been alone she would have told him what she thought of his behaviour, but he was passing on to take his own seat and the conversation became general.

Oh, how could he? Georgie felt the heat in her cheeks. It was too bad of him! He deserved that she should treat him in like manner. He would be well served if she gave him the cold shoulder! Only, she wanted to be his friend, wanted to share the confidences of their earlier time together, and it hurt to know that he thought her just a silly little girl who needed to be put in her place!

Georgie followed her hostess from the room after the meal ended, leaving the two gentlemen to their port. They settled down with the tea tray in the drawing room, though Georgie was alert for the sound of male voices. It was more than half an hour before they came.

'Ah, there you are at last,' Jenny said when they entered together. 'I had almost given you up!' She threw her husband a reproachful look.

'Forgive us, dearest,' Edward said and leaned over to kiss her cheek. 'Richard had something to tell me. It was important.'

'I hope you have not forgotten that we have guests for dinner tomorrow?' Jenny said. 'It will be our last night at home before we leave for Bath, for we are engaged to dine there next. You will join us, Richard?'

'I am not certain,' he said. 'It is possible that I may be called away. I shall be here earlier, Jenny—but I may leave at any time.'

'Richard had a message,' Lord Maddison said. 'It was the reason we were longer than we intended, dearest Jenny. You must not be cross with him if he cannot attend your dinner party.'

'Oh, your work again, I suppose?' Jenny frowned at her brother. 'I think it is time you settled down. Surely you feel the need of some personal life?'

Richard's eyes travelled to where Georgie sat, her eyes downcast. 'Yes, at times I confess I do, Jenny. However, there is something important I must finish.'

'Oh, well…' Jenny sighed deeply. 'If you must, you must, I suppose. I think I shall retire. Are you coming, Georgie?'

'Oh…yes,' Georgie said and stood up, preparing to follow her.

'Miss Bridges,' Richard said, 'would you wait a few moments? I should like to speak to you privately.'

'Yes, you should hear what Richard has to say,' Lord Maddison said and went to his wife. 'I'll come up with you, dearest. I have something I wish to say to you myself.'

Georgie went across to the window, staring out at the moon as she waited for Richard to speak. The French windows were open and she stepped out on to the veranda. She heard his footsteps and then sensed his presence at her shoulder, turning to gaze up at him with wide eyes as she saw his expression.

'You have heard me say that Bonaparte has escaped

from Elba,' he said, looking serious. 'We knew that it might happen—indeed, some of us expected it for he was given too much freedom, treated as a prince. Unfortunately, we were not taken seriously. When it happened there were those who were surprised; I was not one of them. He has been rousing support, gathering his army and the Bourbons have fled to Brussels. Bonaparte is probably even now marching towards Paris in triumph.'

'You think that Monsieur Thierry had a hand in this?'

'Yes, perhaps. He or his friends—the men he employs in this business—though it could have been someone else. I dare say there has been more than one plot to bring Bonaparte back to the throne of France.'

'What will happen now?'

'I believe attempts may be made to murder various important people here in England in order to cause chaos and aid Bonaparte's victory. Restored to the throne, he would be grateful to his supporters, I suppose.'

'It is what all this has been about, isn't it? Your work, the attack on you… Thierry is involved in their plots to murder the Regent, isn't he?'

'Yes, I believe so,' Richard told her. 'I have learned that an important meeting of the conspirators is to be held tomorrow night. It means I shall miss Jenny's dinner, because somehow I must discover the names of the men at that meeting. We have little time to waste. It also means I must go out tonight. I have to see someone, to make sure that all the arrangements are made. These men will be arrested. We have to stop them now, before it is too late. We cannot afford to let this affair drag on any longer.'

Georgie gazed up at him. 'Why are you telling me this now? Earlier you made it clear that you thought it did not concern me.'

'Thierry was seen loitering near this house by one of the servants this afternoon. He was challenged and ran off. The incident was reported to Edward after dinner. I had to warn you, Georgie. Be very much on your guard. If he would dare to come here, he has something in mind. If I am not here to protect you…'

'What do you mean? Are you going away?' She felt alarmed, her heart racing. His expression frightened her. 'No, do not look like that!'

'I have tried to be sensible for both our sakes,' Richard said. 'I may be killed…anything could happen…' He reached out for her, his hands taking her by the arms. For a moment he stared at her, his face working as he tried to suppress his feelings. He was in no position to form an attachment! He did not want to become attached to her, but this feeling would not be denied. He groaned, lowering his head to kiss her. As his mouth covered hers in a hungry, demanding kiss, Georgie shivered, resisting for one moment before melting against him. His arms surrounded her, holding her pressed tightly against him as he explored the sweetness of her mouth with his tongue, tasting her. She moaned softly, giving herself up to the pulsing desire that raged through her. He drew back, looking down at her. 'I am not made of ice, Georgie, though you may think it. Seeing you dressed like as a youth…being with you in that carriage…I have wanted to do this for so long. Wanted more! You must know that I am deeply attracted to you?'

'Richard…you seemed to shut me out…' Georgie's

head was spinning because everything had changed so suddenly.

'And I should. I must,' he said, releasing her, his face twisting with emotion. 'I had no right to kiss you like that, Georgie. I am not free. There are things I must do—things I have done that make this impossible. I want you, desire you as any normal man would, but I cannot ask you to be my wife. You must forget this moment, forget all that happened between us, my dearest girl. If I die tomorrow or in the future, I would not have you think that I did not care—but you must not hope for anything. I can make you no promises.'

'Richard…' She drew back, staring at him, her face white with shock. What did he mean? He shut her out before dinner, then brought her here to kiss her until her senses swam—and then told her not to think of him. 'You are so cruel…so very cruel…'

Georgie broke from him and ran into the house. She was close to tears, her senses battered and bruised from a maelstrom of emotions. Did he not understand what he had done by kissing her, awaking her sleeping heart to a painful awareness of all that might be hers, only to deny her? And it was all a riddle! What could he possibly have done that made a marriage between them impossible?

Richard stood on the veranda for a few moments after she had gone, his expression bleak. He had not intended to kiss her or to tell her that she was special to him, because he could not see a future for them. He knew that his life might be forfeit, either that night or in the battles to come, because now that Bonaparte was on the loose again there would be war.

The thought of it sickened him. Men dying, lying in

pain where they fell, too many of them to be cared for, friends lost, minds shattered by the horror of war. He felt a surge of anger that he and others like him had not been able to prevent it happening again. He had worked for months to try and break the movement, but it lived on in dark places, swirling beneath the surface of decent life like an insidious mist.

Somewhere out there Thierry and his cronies were gloating at the success of their plans to get Bonaparte away from his island prison. But they would not live long enough to see their emperor restored to glory. He would make sure that at least one nest of traitors came to the end of the road tomorrow night…

'It is all such a nuisance,' Jenny said the next morning as they were riding together in the park, accompanied by their grooms. 'Edward told me that awful man was seen here, and we must be careful when riding or walking—but even worse is the news that Bonaparte is believed to have entered Paris or to be on the point of doing so. If there is a war, and of course there must be, Edward has told me he must rejoin his regiment.'

'Oh, no!' Georgie was shocked. She glanced across at her friend as their horses walked sedately side by side. 'He wouldn't leave you, Jenny? How could he?'

'Edward was in the army before we married,' Jenny told her. 'I married a soldier and I followed wherever he went for the first year or two. When my first child was born I came here and Edward visited when he could. He promised to resign his commission when Bonaparte was defeated and he did—but I know he will fight if there is a war.' She gave a little wail of despair. 'I do hate wars! They are such a waste of life, do you not think so?'

'Yes, I do,' Georgie agreed. She looked at her friend with sympathy. 'I know Richard must feel as Edward does—but he is not married.' She looked thoughtful as it occurred to her that he might have been thinking of the coming war when he told her that he could not ask her to marry him the previous night. 'But surely Edward will not go—he must think about you and the children. If you begged him not to, he would listen. He always gives you what you want, Jenny.'

'I couldn't do that,' Jenny said, surprising her. 'Edward gives me everything I ask for, Georgie—but I never ask for anything he could not give easily. It is an unspoken agreement. I am spoiled and loved, but I love him too. If I begged him not to join his friends when they need him, it would break his heart. I would not do it.'

'Oh…' Georgie looked at her thoughtfully. 'Yes, I understand—but perhaps it will not happen, Jenny.'

'I pray that it will not,' Jenny replied. 'But I fear that it will. Bonaparte did not break free of his prison to live peacefully somewhere else. He will fight for his country and the power that was his.'

'Yes, I suppose so,' Georgie agreed and frowned. 'Does this change our plans for Bath?'

'Oh, no, of course not,' Jenny said. 'Everything must go on as usual for the moment, though—' She broke off and shook her head. 'We shall see what happens. After all, there may not be a war at all.'

Georgie was introduced to her hostess's friends that evening as, 'My dear friend, Miss Georgina Bridges. Her great-aunt was the late Countess of Shrewsbury, you know. She has come to live with me and we are to visit Bath together very soon, but after that she will make her home with me.'

Georgie smiled, curtsied and made polite conversation throughout the evening, but her mind was not truly on the affair. She could not help wondering what Richard was doing, and, glancing at Lord Maddison's face once or twice when he was not aware of her interest, she guessed that he too was concerned. She knew that he must be aware of what was happening, and wondered that he had the patience to be the charming, considerate host.

However, he disappeared at about ten o'clock and did not reappear for an hour, just as his neighbours were about to take their leave. After the last one had gone, he came up to Georgie, taking her aside for a moment.

'Richard wanted me to tell you that he was unscathed by the evening's events. It was a successful raid and most of the traitors were taken after a mere skirmish. However, there was no sign of Thierry. It seems that he did not turn up for some reason.'

'Do you think he was warned?'

Edward frowned and looked anxious. 'Richard thinks he must have known something was going to happen. However, he did nothing to prevent the others being caught, so it may mean that he could not.'

'Unless he had no further use for his friends,' Georgie said. 'He is ruthless and would not hesitate to put his own safety first. Where is Richard? Are you sure he isn't hurt?'

'He is perfectly well. I think he knew you would be anxious and he asked me to give you his message. He had to ride to London, but he assures me that he will visit us in Bath when he can.'

Georgie nodded, her expression serious. 'Is it over now, sir?'

'I wish that it were,' Edward said with a sigh. 'If Thierry had been taken with the others, it might have been as far as you are concerned, but he was not—and we have no idea where he is now. He could be anywhere.'

'Do you think he has gone to France?'

'I suppose it is a possibility,' he said. 'With the arrest of so many of the conspirators his plans to cause chaos here may have been overturned, but much of his plan will be in France. If Bonaparte is to take the people with him in his attempt to regain all that he lost, there will need to be work done over there. It may be that Thierry has decided to transfer his attentions there.'

'I admit I should feel safer if I believed he had gone,' Georgie said. 'But Richard warned me I must be careful and I shall not forget his advice.'

'You will be wise to follow it,' Edward said. His smile faded as he looked at her. 'I am glad you have come to be a friend to my wife, Georgie. She may need you in a while.'

'Yes, she has told me,' Georgie replied. 'I shall not desert her. I give you my word, sir.'

'Thank you,' he said. 'But we must not be too gloomy too soon. We have the visit to Bath to look forward to—and I am confident that Richard will come when he can.'

'Yes, thank you,' Georgie said. 'You must not worry about Jenny if you have to leave, sir. We shall do very well together.'

'I am certain of it. And now I shall bid you goodnight, Georgie.'

Georgie smiled, dipped a curtsy and left him. She was thoughtful as she walked upstairs, but also conscious of a warm feeling of relief. Richard was safe enough for the moment, and the English supporters of Bonaparte had been routed this time.

Outside in the darkness, a man stood and stared up at the windows of the house as one by one the lights were extinguished. It was lucky chance that had brought him here the previous evening to hear Hernshaw telling that little witch about the imminent arrest of his friends.

He could have warned them to stay away from the inn, but he had decided to let the fools be taken. Very few of them had ever done anything but talk and drink wine at his expense. He could afford to let them go; they were expendable, and he had other men in place—harder, more experienced men who knew their business. He imagined that Hernshaw must be pretty pleased with himself over this night's work. No doubt he thought it was over, finished, and that might cause him to let down his guard.

Thierry wanted revenge on the man who had come so close to destroying him and all his work, but he also wanted the girl. He needed her money. She would inherit her father's estate very soon, but the countess's money was already hers, though no doubt the lawyers were still sorting it out. He still had a little leeway, and he wanted to make sure that nothing went wrong this time.

She was still wary. He had been watching the house since she came here, and he knew she never went far without company. He might handle the other woman, but he couldn't manage two grooms as well. Unless he killed all three and took her prisoner, but she would never accept him as her husband if she saw him murder her friend before her eyes. If his aim had been truer that day he fired at her, the money might already have been his. Thierry touched his right arm, which still pained him. The manservant had spotted him before he had the chance to get off another shot, and he'd been winged as he fled into the trees. It wasn't a deep wound, but it had annoyed him, made him aware that he had to be careful. He couldn't be sure that Hernshaw wasn't having her watched all the time.

He knew that the ladies were repairing to Bath in the next day or so. Lord Maddison would accompany them on the road, and he would travel with too many servants to make an ambush viable even with the men he had at his disposal. But once they were in Bath, it would be impossible for the girl to be protected the whole time. She would mix in company and one of these times she would forget to be on her guard—and then he would grab her. Once she was his captive, he could take his time persuading her to see his point of view. She was lovely and he would enjoy her for a while before disposing of her.

Besides, he would need her signature on various papers to force the lawyers to release her fortune. He wouldn't put it past the countess to have tied some of it up, but if he had all the deeds he could raise a loan, as he had on the property that had come to him through her late husband. He cared little about anything he owned in this country. He would not need any of it once he was restored to his rightful place in France.

Yes, he would abduct the little witch, force her to wed him, and make sure of the money before he took ship for France. He already had men there waiting for his arrival, just as the assassins he had paid to kill both the Regent and the Iron Duke were waiting for their moment to strike. He would present their deaths as his personal gift to the Emperor and take his place at his side when he swept to victory.

'Well, the house is comfortable,' Jenny said, glancing around the handsome parlour into which they had been shown by a friendly housekeeper. 'I am glad the journey is over for I felt that I should be shaken to bits, and I dread to think how poor Nanny endured it with the children.'

'I should think it could not have been easy for her,' Georgie said with a smile. They had travelled in Lord Maddison's very comfortable carriage, the children and nurses following in another almost as well sprung, but the road had been badly rutted, particularly in country areas. 'But we are all here safe and sound and that must be the important thing.'

'Yes, of course,' Jenny agreed. 'No broken wheels and no highwaymen, and that is something to be thankful for!' She turned to her husband as he entered the room. 'I have sent for some tea, Edward. Shall you take a dish with us or would you prefer something stronger?'

'Nothing, thank you, my dearest,' he told her. 'I fear I must go out almost at once. You and Georgie will be all right, I trust?'

'Yes, of course,' his wife replied. 'But you have ridden all the way here, Edward. Must you really go out at once?'

'It is just a small matter of business,' he replied. 'Nothing for you to worry about. Richard wrote to me here from town. I believe it concerns Georgie's lawyers, but I shall tell you when I return.'

'Oh, well, if it is for Georgie you must go,' his wife said. 'I do not think I shall stray far today, but I may send for the seamstress so that she can begin working on some gowns for us.'

'Yes, dearest, you must have something decent before you can be seen about town,' her loving husband agreed, though he knew that she had brought three trunks filled with beautiful clothes to Bath. 'I shall see you before dinner.'

Jenny sighed as her husband left. 'We shall have some tea before we do another thing, Georgie. I declare I am fatigued near to death, but I shall recover bye and bye. I caught sight of a lady in a beautiful blue gown as we drove here and it has given me an idea for your clothes…'

Georgie was sitting in the back parlour looking through a pile of swatches of silks and muslin when Lord Maddison found her that evening. She glanced up as he entered and smiled.

'The seamstress brought so many samples that I am not sure which to pick, and Jenny seems to think I shall want a deal of new gowns.'

'I am certain she is right; she always is,' he replied. 'I am the bearer of good tidings, Georgie. Your lawyer is staying at an inn not far distant and he will call on you in the morning at ten. I believe you can look forward to some good news concerning both your father's estate and your inheritance from the countess.'

'Oh…' She was a little surprised. 'I had thought it must be some months before the countess's affairs were settled.'

'I dare say it would if you required the capital,' he

replied. 'But I imagine you will wish for an income and leave the bulk of your fortune invested?'

'Oh, yes, certainly,' Georgie said. 'At least, I shall be advised by my lawyers—and you, sir. I understand you advised my great-aunt for some years?'

'Yes, I did, and I shall be pleased to do the same for you, Georgie—should you wish it?'

'Well, I have no family—at least none I can trust,' she said. 'Unless and until I marry, I should be grateful for your advice.'

'Your lawyers will do as you ask them. If I were you, I should continue with the investments your great-aunt held, and draw only a generous income for your pleasure. Since you are to live with us you do not need to finance an establishment of your own, but you will want clothes and pin money, of course.'

'Thank you, it is all I need for the moment.'

'It would be safer for you. If the money is invested in a mixture of bonds and property, it cannot be liquidated too swiftly—if someone should try to defraud you.'

'Yes, that is a consideration,' Georgie said. 'One I have not had to consider before. I am glad to have your friendship, sir, for a woman alone in my situation might be vulnerable.'

'The countess was very aware of it, which is why she did not trust her husband's cousin, my dear. He cannot in law touch what is yours, but he may try something.'

'Yes, perhaps—though he must know it is too late now that my great-aunt is dead, mustn't he?'

'We shall pray that he has given up and gone back to France,' Edward said. 'Now I must go and find my wife—I have a little gift for her.'

Georgie smiled to herself as he left. Jenny was very

fortunate to have such a charming man as her husband. She did hope that the talk of war would come to nothing, because it would be so awful for her friend if anything were to happen. She frowned as she put the swatches aside. Lord Maddison had said nothing of Richard coming to visit. She did hope he would come before too long. Surely there could be nothing to keep him in London now that his work was done?

'It cannot be over until Thierry is found, you know that,' Rawlings said as he leaned forward to pour wine into Richard's glass. 'I appreciate that you have given us good service, Hernshaw, but I cannot release you yet. With Bonaparte on the rampage we know it cannot be long before there is war. We have to beat him soundly, make an example—make sure he is finished this time.'

'Soldiering is one thing, and I shall of course rejoin my regiment when the time comes—but I am tired of all this other business. I want a life of my own, Rawlings.'

'The girl, I suppose?' Rawlings arched his brows. 'It might interest you to know that her uncle shot himself when the bank foreclosed on his loans. His wife left in tears to live with a friend and the house was closed. I believe it belongs to the bank for the moment.'

'Mowbray killed himself?' Richard exclaimed. 'Good grief! Things must have been worse than I imagined.'

'He had been selling jewellery for months, and the land was mortgaged. I think everything must be sold to cover what he owes.'

'Some of the jewellery he sold did not belong to

him,' Richard said. 'The lawyers entrusted things that had belonged to Georgie's mother to him, but she will not see them again, unless they can be recovered.'

'I might be able to help you there. We have been keeping an eye on him, because of his dealings with Thierry—if you wish to recover them I could give you the name of the jeweller who bought them.'

'Thank you, I shall be grateful.'

'Grateful enough to end this business?' Rawlings raised his brows. 'Thierry isn't finished, Hernshaw. Find him and stop him before it is too late.'

'And then I am free?'

'You will have paid the debt,' Rawlings said. 'Whether you are free or not is a matter of your own conscience, my dear fellow. You were not to blame for what happened to your men that day. If you could accept that, you were free long ago. However, we need you to do this one last thing.'

Richard inclined his head. 'You are right. Thierry isn't finished. I doubt anything less than a ball in the heart will stop a man like that.'

Georgie's heart quickened as she entered the house after Jenny one morning later that week and heard the sound of male laughter. She knew at once that Richard had come, and despite his last words to her she was filled with a sense of hope. He cared for her, she knew he did, even if he did not feel able to ask her to marry him.

'Ah, here are the ladies,' Lord Maddison said as they entered the parlour, a handsome room with fine proportions and a particularly pleasing aspect over the garden at the back. 'I trust you enjoyed yourselves? Lady

Maddison, if you have overspent your allowance you may send the bills to me.'

'Naturally I should do so, Edward.' The adored wife offered her cheek for his kiss, a wicked smile in her eyes. 'However, we have been spending Georgie's money this morning. I may have ordered a few gowns for myself…' a mere dozen was not so very many after all '…but Georgie has been enjoying herself buying bonnets and trifles of no account. She has ordered some new gowns, of course, and one of them is to be delivered in time for this evening.'

'Jenny,' Richard said, 'you look wonderful as always. Miss Bridges, I believe Bath agrees with you.'

'If that is a compliment, it is a poor one,' his sister scoffed. 'You must have noticed how beautiful she looks in that bonnet, Richard. It is a new one and it suits her admirably, do you not think so?'

'Yes, I do,' Richard replied, amused by his sister's remarks. 'I think Georgie knows that I admire her in many ways.'

'Then you might say so,' Jenny replied, but looked pleased. Her brother was not often given to compliments, at least within her hearing. 'We have been here but three days, and already several young gentlemen have called to pay their respects. Is that not so, Edward?'

'Yes, my dearest. I do not even know some of the gentlemen who have been wishing to make themselves known to me, and I am sure it must have something to do with Georgie.' Edward grinned, joining in the teasing with alacrity. 'Despite their earnest desire to talk to me on matters of horseflesh, I am not deceived. I know I owe my popularity to the fact that I have the latest beauty as my guest.'

Georgie blushed as she saw the mockery in Richard's eyes. 'You may well look like that,' she said, pulling a face. 'I dare say word of my good fortune has got around and all the fortune hunters will queue up to know me.'

'Georgie! They are not all fortune hunters,' Jenny reproved her, eyes twinkling. 'Mr Davenport has a fortune that surpasses your own, even though you will have nearly two hundred thousand when it is all done. And the Duke of Marling's heir was very taken with you at the Assembly Rooms last night. He asked a great deal of questions of me, you know.'

'As much as two hundred thousand?' Richard arched his brow. 'I think you are right, Georgie. You will have a string of admirers. You must take care that you are not alone with any of them or you will find yourself compromised.'

Georgie gave him an odd stare. 'I should not consider that reason enough for marriage, sir—as I believe I told you once before.'

Richard laughed softly. 'Touché! I think the honours are yours there, Georgie. Since you have so many gentlemen asking for your favours, may I dare to hope you will allow me to take you driving one day?'

'You may take me this afternoon if you wish,' Georgie said and smiled at him. 'We have a free afternoon, though we are engaged for a private dance this evening.'

'Indeed? Then I shall call for you at two-thirty precisely,' Richard said. 'And now I must leave you since I have an appointment—but I promise not to be late.'

'You had better keep your promise,' Jenny warned. 'If you do not, we shall be very cross with you, shall we not, Georgie?'

'If Richard fails to keep his word, I dare say he will have good reason,' she replied, raising her eyes to meet his. 'I shall look forward to seeing you later, sir.'

'Thank you,' Richard replied. 'Before I leave I must give you some unhappy news. It may distress you, but you should know that your Uncle Mowbray killed himself after his bank foreclosed on his debts—and your aunt went to live with friends when the house was closed.'

'Oh…' Georgie was stunned for a moment. 'That is terrible news indeed. I know they treated me ill, but I believe it was the fault of Monsieur Thierry. My uncle was led into things he did not properly understand.'

'As to that, a man must always know when his play is too deep,' Richard said. 'However, Thierry does know how to draw men in and how to entrap them. I think you uncle was not his first victim. Still, your uncle did things that would have led to his being arrested for theft and worse. He took his life rather than face disgrace.'

'Well, I am sorry for him and my aunt—her mostly, I think,' Georgie said. 'I know that neither of them deserve my sympathy, but I shall ask my lawyers if something may be done to help her.'

'That is your decision,' Richard said. 'But be careful she does not take advantage.'

'Oh, no, she will not,' Georgie said. 'I have good advisers, you know. Besides, I am not foolish enough to do more than I wish, which is a small pension a year to keep her from poverty.'

Richard nodded. 'You are a generous young woman. Some fortunate gentleman will be lucky to secure you. I shall see you later.'

Georgie followed him with her eyes as he left the

room, feeling a little pricking behind them. However, she fought off any feelings of self-pity. She was young, not unattractive and wealthy beyond her dreams. It was ridiculous to feel as if her world were empty.

'Well, I think that was very satisfactory,' Jenny said as her husband followed Richard from the room. 'Richard is an odd creature, you know, dearest, but I am convinced he is in love with you.'

'What makes you think that?' Georgie's heart leaped insensibly, because she knew his intentions did not include marriage.

'Because I know Richard, and I have never seen him look at another woman the way he looks at you,' Jenny replied. 'He may not realise that he has met his match yet, dearest—but believe me, he will.'

'I do love him,' Georgie said, the words coming out in a rush. 'Promise me you won't tell him, because I do not think he means to ask me to marry him—but I cannot help myself.'

'Oh, I have known that from the beginning,' Jenny told her. 'I am perfectly sure of Richard's affections for you, my love—it is just that the foolish man does not know what is good for him! It may be because of our childhood, you know. After my mother died I went to live with your Aunt Mary, but poor Richard was often alone. He was very close with our cousin at one time, but Justin died—I am not sure of the details, but I believe it was tragic.'

'Justin? He was your cousin?'

'Yes, why do you ask? Has my brother mentioned him?'

'Oh, no,' Georgie said, because she would not betray Richard's secrets. 'Do you really think he likes me?'

'I am positive it is much more—but the ridiculous man may need to be told before he realises it is true!'

Georgie laughed, because it was impossible not to when faced with Jenny's optimism. 'Perhaps we shall have to teach him?' she suggested and saw that her companion was laughing too.

Her spirits lifted once more. Richard was here in Bath for the time being and he had promised to take her driving that afternoon. She would not flirt with him or throw herself at his head, for that was not her way—but perhaps if she showed herself amenable he might speak.

Chapter Seven

Richard was on time and waiting for her when Georgie came down promptly at two of the clock that afternoon. She was wearing a dark green silk carriage gown with a matching pelisse, her bonnet of chip straw trimmed with crimson cherries and green ribbons. Her half-boots were of soft kid, her gloves York tan, proclaiming to the world that she was a young lady of fashion.

Richard smiled inwardly as he saw her. She was beautiful, his sister was entirely right on that score, but he could not quite quash the memory of an urchin with dirt on her face. She had made an attractive picture once she was clean, and the sight of her neat, rounded buttocks in youth's breeches had had a powerful effect on him. At the moment her quality made him very aware that she was both beautiful and wealthy, much admired by a great many gentlemen. Georgie the urchin would have thrown propriety to the winds and followed him to the ends of the earth, but this young lady of fashion was an unknown quantity. Would she accept him if he proposed to her—and did he have the right?

He pushed the uneasy thoughts to the back of his mind. He did not wish to dwell on the darkness in his past for the moment. It was to be an afternoon of pleasure for them both. Time to think of more serious things when his work was finally finished.

'Green is your colour,' Richard said as he handed her up to his high-perch phaeton. His tiger released the reins to him and sprang up at the back. 'I am glad that you decided against going into blacks, Georgie. I am perfectly certain that your great-aunt would not have wished for it.'

'She made it a stipulation in her will,' Georgie told him. 'I am not allowed to wear mourning for her. She always hated the custom and said in her letter that she wanted me to enjoy my life and I was not to grieve for her since her only regret was that she had not done more for me sooner.'

'That was kind of her and shows thought on her part,' Richard said. His concentration was on his horses as he steered them through the press of traffic in the fashionable Crescent. 'It shows the quality of the lady and it is a great pity that you were prevented from knowing her better.'

'Yes, I cannot forgive my uncle for that,' Georgie said with a frown. 'It was far more unkind than selling my mother's jewels, though I wish he had not done that either.'

'In that small matter I have been of some service to you,' Richard told her with a smile. They had passed through the busier streets and were passing the Abbey, soon to be leaving the town for country roads. 'I could not locate some of the items, the diamonds having disappeared without trace—possibly broken up so that they could not be found—but I managed to retrieve some pearls, an opal-and-diamond brooch, a sapphire pendant, a set of rubies and pearls and a gold bangle set with rubies. I shall give them to you tomorrow when I dine with you at the house.'

'Oh, you are not leaving at once, then?' Georgie's cheeks flushed as she realised that she had focused on what was more important to her. 'I meant—thank you very much for your kindness in tracing my mother's things. You must give an account of any money you paid out for me and my lawyer will settle it.'

'I hope you will allow me to bear the small cost,' Richard told her. 'I have not forgotten that you assisted so ably when my life hung in the balance. I would count it kind in you to allow me this favour.'

'You know that it was Henderson who did it all,' Georgie told him, 'and I am already in your debt for bringing me to your sister—but if you truly wish it, I shall accept your generosity. You must tell me if I may do anything for you in return, sir.'

'You might call me Richard,' he told her, a little smile on his lips. 'I believe it would not go amiss—at least within the family.'

'Yes, of course—if you return the compliment. When you address me as Miss Bridges I know you are cross with me.'

'No, never,' he said, glancing at her. 'It is a mere politeness—besides, I was not sure if you were angry with me after the way that I behaved before I left Yorkshire.'

'Angry?' Georgie thought for a moment. 'I was a little hurt at first, but then I thought that you were not truly a cruel man. If you felt unable to offer me marriage, it must be for a good reason. Richard…' She turned her eyes on him, seeing a little pulse flick in his cheek. 'I would not wish you to think yourself obliged to offer because of what happened, but—' She broke off abruptly, because she had gone as far as she could without betraying herself.

Richard brought the horses to a standstill. They had reached one of the beauty spots that people came for miles to see, and he took her hand, helping her down from the curricle as his tiger sprang from the back and took the reins.

'Shall we walk to the top of the rise?' he asked. 'The countryside is accounted very fine in this area and the weather is mild for walking.'

'Yes, thank you,' she said. She took his arm. The grass was firm and dry beneath their feet as they walked to the brow of a small hill. They stood in silence for a moment, enjoying the vista of gentle slopes, water trickling over rocks into pools, sparkling in the sunshine. In the distance, the smudge of a wood dark on the horizon. 'It is very beautiful here, Richard. Thank you for bringing me.'

'You are beautiful,' he told her softly. 'If I do not ask you to be my wife, it is because I have my reasons, Georgie. I am not an evil man and would not have you think it, but there are things in my past—things that shame me. I had put all thought of personal happiness behind me.'

'I do not think you could have done anything that would make you unworthy,' Georgie said passionately, her eyes filled with fire as she gazed up at him.

'I have killed men,' he said. 'I do not say murder, but when necessary—and not just in battle. There have been times when I had to shoot to save the life of another or my own.'

Georgie shivered, because although at the back of her mind she had known his work must sometimes entail this kind of thing, to hear it spoken openly was still shocking.

'I dare say you had no choice…'

'None at all,' he replied. 'But that is not the worst of it, Georgie. Because of me, a blunder on my part…nine of my men were killed needlessly.'

'But that must have been in war?' She gazed up at him, reading the horror the memory occasioned in his eyes. 'Surely you cannot be held to blame for that?'

'I was not blamed,' he said. 'I was given orders and I followed them, but I was young, inexperienced and should have taken more heed instead of leading them blindly into a trap. I have tried to atone for that mistake, but it has lain heavily on my conscience all these years.'

'It could have happened to anyone, Richard.' She read the agony it had caused him over the years and knew that he was still haunted. 'Surely the officer in charge overall was more to blame?'

'Perhaps, but it was I who led the men that day, and though I managed to bring five of them back alive, nine died. I learned a hard lesson that day, Georgie. It changed me. I was but twenty, eager for the glory I imagined was to be found on the battlefield. I found death and pain and blood that day. I learned to be more cautious, to care for my men at all times and protect them, but the needless loss has haunted me.'

'Is that why you continued to work for the government even after Bonaparte was contained?'

'Yes. I was asked if I would undertake secret work and it is for that work that I have killed,' Richard said. 'And then I lost someone who meant a great deal to me. He had fallen in with evil men and I felt I had failed

him by not being there to save him from his own folly.
He died in pain in my arms. I buried myself in work,
and I was ruthless, careless of my own life. For a long
time I cared for nothing else, but that changed when an
urchin with dirt on her face tried to steal from me and
later helped to save my life. You made me realise that
there might be more to life, Georgie. There have been
times when I have come close to proposing to you.'

'Oh…' Her heart took a great leap. 'But if you care
for me, why…?' She stopped, casting down her eyes as
she waited for him to speak.

'Why do I not ask if you will marry me?' He reached
out, tipping her chin with his hand. 'Because it would
not be fair to you, my very dear Georgie. I must go after
Thierry and stop him. We know that he plans to move
against the Regent soon. He can't be allowed to. And
after that there will still be a war. I must rejoin my
regiment. We have a job to do, Georgie, and until Bonaparte is stopped for good I must play my part.'

'Edward has told Jenny that he means to fight too,'
Georgie said. 'She accepts that he must do his duty. I
would not try to stand between you and your duty. If
you care for me…'

'You must know that I do,' he told her and smiled.
'I think that if I felt able to marry it would be you I
would ask to be my wife, but for the moment I cannot
marry. It would be unfair, because I may be killed at any
time. You are young and beautiful and I do not wish you
to become a widow before you have been a wife.'

'Surely that should be my decision?' Georgie asked,
staring up at him. She knew that he must be able to see
her desperation. Surely now he would take her into his
arms and tell her that he loved her?

'I know you to be as brave as you are lovely,' Richard said. 'I care for you, but I cannot marry you, Georgie. I ask you to forgive me if I have raised hopes that I cannot fulfil.'

Georgie turned away. She had hoped when he suggested this drive that he intended to ask her to be his wife. Indeed, she had almost thrown herself at him and yet still he refused to speak. It must mean that he did not love her in the way she loved him.

'You have done nothing so very terrible,' Georgie said, turning back. 'I thought that you were attracted to me, but I see that I was wrong.' Tears trembled on her lashes.

'Forgive me,' he said, his voice harsh with the emotion he was fighting. 'You are very beautiful and I have been tempted. Seeing you in that youth's clothing…it was too provocative! Yes, I have wanted to make love to you—what man wouldn't? But I do not wish to marry.'

Georgie stared at him. 'I see…you make yourself plain, sir. I have been very stupid. When you said that you cared for me I thought…but I was mistaken. I apologise if I have embarrassed you. I think we should return to your sister now.'

Richard hesitated as she turned away again. He was tempted to go after her, take her into his arms and tell her that he was a heartless wretch for hurting her so. She had been so very brave and he knew that she would willingly risk being a widow just for the joy of being his wife, but he could not let down that last barrier. He was afraid of loving her too much. He knew that all his excuses counted for nothing in the face of Georgie's love, and he was saddened to hurt her so—but better now than in the years to come. Thinking of her alone, wearing black for a husband she hardly knew, was heartbreaking.

Richard knew only too well the pain of losing someone he loved and he did not wish to feel that pain again or to inflict it on Georgie. Better she should believe he was a heartless wretch and find someone new—and yet he did not wish to lose her entirely.

'Wait for me,' he said, as she set off down the hill, her back very straight, her head turned from him. 'Please do not hate me, Georgie. I should always wish to be your friend.'

'Of course you will always be my friend,' she said and turned to him. Her face was frozen, her eyes cold and distant. 'How could I not be after all you have done for me? It was foolish of me to imagine there was anything more than friendship between us.'

'Georgie…' Richard's heart wrenched because he did not know this new Georgie. She was so distant, so reserved, and he knew that it was his fault. 'Forgive me…'

'There is nothing to forgive,' she said. They had reached his curricle and he gave her his hand to help her up. She took it, but did not look at him.

Richard knew that she was both hurt and angry. He wanted to take back all that he had said, but to do that would be pointless. He could not ask her to marry him and therefore he must accept this new coolness. Perhaps in time she would forgive him and they could become friends again, but he was very much afraid that he had lost her trust. For the moment all he could do was take her to his sister and hope that time would heal the hurt he had inflicted.

* * *

Thierry watched as his enemy drove away from the house in the Crescent later that day. He had been following the little bitch's triumph from a distance since she arrived in Bath. People were gossiping about her, because she had a large fortune—money that should rightfully have been his! Her beauty might have brought her admirers had she been in possession only of a small competence, but with the wealth left her by the countess she had become an heiress of considerable importance.

He knew that his chances of winning her by fair means had virtually vanished into thin air. If she would not have him when she was nothing, there was little likelihood of her favouring him now. Besides, it was difficult to get close to her. Hernshaw had made certain that she was well protected. Damn the man! He should have made sure of him that first night, done the deed himself instead of leaving it to one of his underlings. Hernshaw had others watching his back these days, and was impossible to touch. The girl would not be easy to snatch, but he would manage it somehow.

His preparations were made. He had the house waiting to receive her. She would be at his mercy and, once she was his, he would find it easy enough to persuade her that she should marry him to save her reputation. After he had done with the little bitch, no decent man would have her!

Richard frowned as he looked at his informant. The man had come to him as he was preparing to go out, bringing unexpected news. Thierry had been seen in Bath and that was worrying. Richard had been intending to return to London in the morning, because he felt that his continuing presence in Bath could only be uncomfortable for Georgie. The knowledge that the Frenchman was here shocked him. What had brought him to Bath when his business must be in London?

'You are certain of this?' he said. 'You saw him yourself or you heard that he had been seen?'

'I saw him,' the man said. 'He was following two ladies—one of them was the lady you told me to watch for.'

'Damn him!' Richard frowned. Obviously, Thierry was still angry about the loss of the inheritance he had hoped to make his. 'Was he alone at all times?'

'He has met with some gentlemen, but there was nothing in it,' the agent replied. 'I saw him with some rogues one night at a seedy tavern on the outskirts of the city. I couldn't get near enough to hear what they said, but I saw money change hands.'

'Then he is planning something,' Richard said and frowned. 'It cannot be the other business, so it must concern Miss Bridges.' His fingers drummed on the table in front of him. He knew that he had hurt Georgie and it was likely that she now hated him, but that made no difference to his determination to ensure her safety. 'Make sure that she is followed wherever she goes, do you hear me? I am afraid that he may try to harm her in some way, though…' A muttered curse escaped him. 'Of course! Abduction is his only option now. He must know that he could never hope to persuade her to marry him in the normal way. Damn him!'

'The men are ready,' his agent said. 'We could take him tonight, sir.'

'But we still lack the evidence we need.' Richard stared at him uncertainly. 'Without that final piece he might walk free.' He struck his fist against his knee. 'We take him tonight. It cannot be left longer. Once we have him, I dare say Rawlings will make him talk.'

'Tonight it is,' the man said. 'I'll alert the others, sir.'

Richard nodded, watching as the man walked away. He had been waiting until the right moment so that Thierry was caught in the act of conspiracy against the throne, but he could not afford to wait any longer when it meant that Georgie's safety might be at risk.

He had planned to attend the ball that evening so that he could dance with her and then say goodbye. Somehow he had to mend fences with her, to show her that she was still his friend...that he cared for her even if he could not marry her. He prayed that she would understand he had held back for her sake rather than his own, though in his heart he knew that only a part of that was true. A part of him was not sure that he could love, at least not wholeheartedly in the way Georgie deserved. For the moment he must concentrate on her safety. He must put his mind to tracking down the dangerous man who was intent on harming Georgie.

Jenny looked at her young companion's face as she came downstairs that evening. Something must have happened to make her this way. She had been distant ever since she returned from her drive with Richard. Jenny had been expecting good news, but the expression in Georgie's eyes had told her that they must have quarrelled. Her friend had looked so strange, not a bit like herself.

'Is something the matter, my love?' she asked. 'You seem a little quiet.'

'Oh, I have had a wretched headache,' Georgie said,

'but it is getting better. You must not worry, Jenny. I shall do well enough in a little while.'

'Would you prefer to stay home this evening? It is only a small affair and I shall not mind at all if we do not go.'

'Oh, no,' Georgie said and smiled brightly. 'It is nothing. A mere irritation of the nerves! I shall be perfectly well once we get there.'

'You would tell me if there was something wrong, my love?'

'Yes, of course.' Georgie laughed. 'I told you not to worry, Jenny. I had a headache, but it has gone. I am quite ready to leave if you are.'

'Then we must go, for the carriage is waiting…' Jenny led the way outside. She guessed that her brother and Georgie must have had a quarrel. Drat Richard for being an insensitive fool! She would have something to say to him when they met that evening!

Georgie was wearing a gown of pale lilac silk that evening. It suited her well, its slender skirt flaring over her hips and ending in a little flounce. She had draped a spangled stole over her arms, because the night air was a little chilly, but inside the ballroom it was extremely hot because of all the candles in the chandeliers. She had danced every dance, determined not to let anyone see that her heart was breaking. Richard had said he would be here this evening, but he had not come, and she supposed she knew why. He was staying clear of her because she had embarrassed him.

Oh, why had she made such a fool of herself? She had practically thrown herself at him, almost begging him to ask her to marry him, and he had refused her. It was so humiliating, and she had only herself to blame. Richard had gone out of his way to help her from the beginning. He had been kind and considerate, and he was right—the clothes she had worn had been nothing short of shameless. If she had aroused his baser instincts, she was at fault. Just because he had kissed her, it did not mean that he wished to marry her. She had hoped it might be so, but she was mistaken, and now she had to pay the price. She was not sure how she would ever face Richard again! What a fool he must think her!

All evening, Georgie had laughed and flirted prettily with the young men who flocked about her. She had accepted their compliments and danced with them, but she could hardly remember their names or their faces. She was hurting so much that she felt she was being torn apart, but she had kept a smile in place. Now she needed a moment alone, and she turned instinctively towards the veranda.

She would go outside for a few moments to cool herself. Jenny was nowhere about, and Georgie imagined she had gone upstairs to tidy her gown because the rooms were crowded and one became rather too hot after a while. Lord Maddison was talking with some other gentlemen, and she knew the subject was war, for most of the men present that evening had at one time been officers. Many of them were thinking of rejoining their regiments at the first call to arms.

Not wanting to intrude on their conversation, she decided to go out alone. Her admirers had for the moment abandoned her and she was alone in a room that had been deserted by people in search of refreshment or respite. There were lights strung from the trees in the gardens and Georgie felt no fear as she went out to take the air. She would stay only a moment and then go in search of Jenny, but she really did need a little air to cool her.

One or two ladies were strolling on the veranda, though mostly in pairs. Georgie had met most of them, but formed no real friendships as yet, at least none that made her feel comfortable about joining the other ladies unasked.

She walked down the steps of the terrace for there were people about and she did not feel nervous or think herself in any danger. They had heard nothing of Monsieur Thierry and there was no reason to think him in Bath, and here at the house of an acquaintance she could surely not come to harm. She would stroll just as far as the shrubbery and back. Surely there was no danger in that, she told herself, holding her stole over her shoulders. Besides, she needed to take the air, to be alone, because her face was beginning to feel as if it might crack from smiling and she was close to tears. How could she continue to laugh and tease when she felt as if she were dying inside?

The moon was bright and with the lanterns in the trees she was able to see clearly. Georgie breathed deeply as she reached the shrubbery. She must learn to accept the pain inside for what it was. She had suffered a disappointment. In time she would get over it...she would learn to be happy again, and yet she felt as if a part of her had died.

There were some fine examples of camellias and she bent to look at a flower. What happened then was quite without warning. She heard a slight rustling sound and raised her head, turning to glance behind her just as someone threw something thick and dark over her head. She gave a shriek of dismay, struggling against her unknown attacker. However, she found herself being lifted, thrown over someone's shoulder, her head hanging down as she kicked and yelled. Even as she did so, she knew that her cries were muffled, the blanket getting into her mouth, choking her as she found it becoming difficult to breath.

After what seemed an age, but could only have been minutes, she was thrust into somewhere, falling hard and striking her head. The blow robbed her of her senses temporarily and it was a while before she came to herself sufficiently to realise that she was moving, being carried off in what felt more like a wagon than a carriage.

She tried to move and discovered that a rope had been bound around the blanket, trapping her in a cocoon of smelly wool that made her gag. The blanket smelled of horses and the stench was overpowering. She realised that she must breathe deeply despite the smell, and she must stop fighting what was happening, because otherwise she would not be able to breathe. If she did not wish to suffocate inside this blanket, she must lie quietly and wait to be released.

But would anyone come looking for her? Georgie knew that Richard had other things on his mind. Why should he bother about a girl who had caused him nothing but trouble? Had he loved her, wanted her as his wife, she would have known he would come for her, but now she felt very alone—and very frightened.

'Damn it!' Richard cursed furiously. 'What do you mean you lost him? You were told to follow wherever he went. How could he have slipped away without your seeing?'

'He must have gone across the roof at the back of his lodgings,' the Bow Street Runner said with a scowl. 'We had someone stationed there the whole time, sir, and at the back door into the alley behind. The only way he could have got away without being seen was across the roof.'

'He must have known we were watching him,' Richard said. 'I should have had him snatched off the street in broad daylight instead of waiting for darkness.'

He paced the floor of the private parlour, where he had arranged to meet his agent when the business was done. Thierry should have been in custody now or dead, shot in the attempt to escape. He had given permission for his men to shoot first, even though Rawlings had wanted the Frenchman taken alive. Thierry had outwitted them! He must have spotted his shadow and made his plans accordingly. It meant a setback to Richard's personal plans, because he would need to find Thierry again before he could return to London and his duties.

He went to the window, staring out at the night, feet apart, hands behind his back. He cursed and turned sharply as the door opened behind him, hoping that there was further news and the Frenchman had been caught trying to slip away from Bath.

'Edward?' He stared at his brother-in-law, ice sliding down his spine as he saw his expression. 'What has happened? Georgie…' He felt a shaft of fear. 'Is she hurt?'

'She has disappeared,' Edward said, tight-lipped. 'Someone told us she went into the garden to take the air at Lady Marten's house just before supper. She has not been seen since. I am so sorry. Jenny had gone upstairs and I did not notice. I feel I have let you both down.'

'Nonsense,' Richard said roughly. 'How could it be your fault, either of you? Georgie should have known—' He broke off with a groan as he realised what had happened. 'Thierry must have snatched her. He was seen in Bath. We had planned to take him tonight, but he escaped by climbing over the roof and my men were fooled into thinking he was still inside. When they went in after him he had gone.'

'My God!' Lord Maddison had turned white. 'Jenny is beside herself, weeping and blaming herself for not waiting for Georgie before going upstairs. Neither of us dreamed this could happen, Richard, at the house of a friend. What can we do? You know I will do anything to help you get her back.'

'Yes, I know,' Richard replied grimly. 'We shall have to find him again. I had thought he might return to London, but he will hardly try to take her that far. He must be somewhere not too far distant—a house where he can keep her until he can force her to become his bride.'

'You think that is his intention?'

'He needs money,' Richard said. 'His plan to have the Regent assassinated and help Bonaparte regain the throne of France will require a great deal of it. He must hope to get some of it from Georgie.'

'He will be unlucky,' Edward said, looking anxious. 'I advised Georgie to tie up her capital. She has a good income, but hardly enough to pay for such grand plans.'

'He will be angry when he discovers the truth,' Richard said, a pulse flicking at his temple. 'If she tells him that, he might…'

'Kill her?' Edward supplied. 'She would be of no use to him without the money he needs and her testimony could hang him.'

'Will hang him,' Richard ground out. 'His other deeds have been well disguised and we were not sure we could convict him of anything. We know that he has cheated his victims at the card tables, ruined young men by introducing them to evil drugs, and that he is involved in plots against the State—but proving it was always going to be hard. Rawlings wanted him dead at one time, but I refused to do it. He has changed his mind now, wants him taken alive and questioned. If I catch him now, I shall not be so nice!'

'Nor I,' Edward agreed. 'If he has harmed her…' He saw Richard's look and stopped. 'I am sure he will not, at least until he has done his best to force her to be his wife.'

'And what will that entail?' Richard asked, feeling sick. 'Rape or assault, both perhaps? I know Georgie. She will not give in easily, Edward. It might be better for her if she did, but she won't.'

'I know…but we'll find her, Richard. We shall find her in time.'

'Where do we look?' Richard demanded. 'It will be like looking for a needle in a haystack. He could have taken her anywhere.'

'Yes…' Edward frowned. 'I wonder…'

'What? Out with it, man!' His anxiety made him harsh, almost rude.

'He inherited the countess's property, at least that which came to him from her late husband—but she had a house some ten miles from here. It was hers of her own right, not her husband's, and should belong to Georgie, but it has been empty for some years. I know about it because the lawyers asked me what should be done with it. They thought it best to sell because it is in poor repair and needs a great deal of money spent on it. I told them to leave it for a while. I thought Georgie might like to see it before she decided.'

'Do you know exactly where to find the house?'

'It is called Mulberry Place and is near the village of Munkstowe,' Edward said. 'It is about ten miles from Bath, as I said.'

'Would Thierry know of it?'

'Yes, I believe he almost certainly would,' Edward replied. 'Is it worth a try?'

Richard hesitated for a moment. If it was a wrong guess, it would waste precious time. On the other hand, he had nothing better to offer.

'It is worth a try,' he said harshly. 'I'll send word to Rawlings and they can keep an eye out for him in town, but something tells me that you are right, my friend. I am certain he won't try to take her too far tonight. If we chance lucky, we may stop him before he can harm her.'

Richard prayed that he was right, prayed that it was not already too late. There were perhaps a dozen inns on the road between here and the house Edward had spoken of. Thierry could have taken her to any of them. Some landlords would take no notice if a woman screamed, only too glad of a handful of gold to keep them sweet.

He gritted his teeth. If Georgie was hurt…but he dare not let himself think that far ahead. The only thing clear in his mind was that if he found the man that night he would kill him!

Georgie had lost consciousness by the time the blanket was removed. She did not hear Thierry berate his underlings for their careless treatment of her, nor did she feel anything as she was carried upstairs and deposited carefully on a bed. Fortunately, she did not see the look of annoyance in his face as he stood looking down at her in the light of a candle.

'Damned idiots!' Raoul Thierry's handsome face twisted with anger as he looked at Georgie's pale face. 'I told them to take care of you, not kill you!'

If the girl died, he would be no better off than he had been before this rash kidnap! She would have been advised to make a will by her lawyers, and he would not be a beneficiary. Besides, she had an aunt and the money would have gone beyond him even if there were no will as yet.

His only hope of her money was to marry her. He had arranged for a vicar to marry them in the morning, judging that a night in his company would break her will. The Reverend Thorpe was not too nice in his principles that he would refuse a new roof for his church, and if he refused at the last, a pistol to his head should make him see the light.

He wondered how soon the money could be released. He needed it now if his plan were to work. His agents were at their deadly work even now and by tomorrow evening at the latest the Regent should be dead.

It annoyed him that so much depended on the girl lying so pale and still on the bed. Without her his plan would founder because he did not have sufficient funds, even with the money he had cheated her uncle and others of at the card table. He had been so sure the countess's money would be his until he learned she had planned to leave it all to a girl he had not known existed until it was too late. Georgie Bridges had refused to listen when he tried to flatter her—but she would not refuse him now. His mouth tightened. He must wait for a few hours longer, but when she woke he would show her no mercy. She would beg him to wed her once he had finished.

Cursing once more, he turned away, taking the candle with him. The girl could die for all he cared if only he could get her money somehow. Hernshaw might ransom her if he asked, but it would not be enough for his needs. It must be all or nothing. No, he must keep her alive somehow, at least until he had her signature to their marriage. After that, he did not care what became of her—though he could not allow her to have her freedom, of course. She would have to die sooner or later, but he might keep her for his amusement for a while.

He would fetch some water, see if he could revive her.

Georgie moaned, her eyes flicking open as she felt something cool touch her face. Her head hurt and she felt as if she had been beaten, her body tender. Someone put a cup to her lips and bid her swallow. She did so, though it hurt her throat as she gulped the water down. She opened her eyes, giving a moan of fear as she saw the face bending over her. She thrust her hand out, knocking the cup away and spilling the water over herself.

'Foolish girl,' Thierry muttered. 'I am only trying to help you. Those rogues almost killed you, tying you in that blanket. You were near suffocated when I released you. It is their fault you feel so ill, not mine.'

Georgie pushed herself up against the pillows. She was in a strange bedchamber, somewhere she had never seen. She struggled to recall what had happened before she lost consciousness, and moaned as she remembered that she had been abducted.

'You did this,' she whispered, her voice rasping. 'You told them to take me from the garden. It must have been you.'

'Yes, it was me,' he growled, glaring at her. 'You've given me a fine chase, girl. If you had married me, it would have saved all this bother. Why did you run off like that? Surely it was not such a bad bargain? I would not have harmed you had you consented like a sensible girl.'

'I would rather die than wed you,' Georgie spat the words at him. 'You are evil. You tried to have Richard killed. I hate you.' She tried to roll across the bed and get up, but found she could not stand as a wave of dizziness swept over her and she fell back to the bed. 'No, don't touch me! I am going to be sick.'

She lurched over to one side, retching on an empty stomach and bringing up the water he had given her mixed with a foul-smelling bile. Thierry turned away in disgust. All thought of seduction fled for the moment. He would leave her to come to her senses for a few hours.

'I would have asked you to wed me in all honour had you not run off,' he muttered. 'It is your own fault that I was forced to such measures. The countess had no right to leave her fortune away from me. It should have been mine. I need if for a purpose…'

'You want to help Napoleon Bonaparte regain the throne of France,' Georgie said, sitting up against the pillows and looking at him warily. 'Why should I let you take my money for such a purpose?'

'Once you are my wife, it will be my money.'

'But I shall not marry you. No matter what you say or do,' Georgie declared defiantly.

'You will do as I bid you when the time comes.' Thierry's eyes glittered. 'If you resist, you will be sorry. Besides, I shall return in a little while and when I've finished with you no decent man will want you.'

Georgie gasped and shrank back against the pillows, feeling a shaft of fear strike her. She knew that he meant every word and her mind reeled from the awful threat. She must find some way to prevent him from carrying out his intention. She shuddered with relief as he slammed the bedroom door shut behind him and she heard the key turning in the lock.

She was safe for the moment. Georgie guessed that it was the acrid smell of her vomit that had driven him away for the moment. It was pretty horrid and she could feel her stomach turning in protest. She got up from the bed and moved away, feeling glad that he had at least left her a candle. She went across to the window and glanced out, her heart sinking as she realised that she must be on the second floor of the house. It was a long way down, and if she tried to jump out of the window she might break her ankle. Had there been a tree close enough, she might have climbed into it, for she had often climbed trees as a young girl, but there were none.

Her head ached and she moved away, feeling that she needed to rinse the bitter taste from her mouth. Thierry had at least brought her water, and she discovered there was also a glass of wine and some cake. She thought the cake might help to settle the bile in her stomach and ate a piece of it, drinking a few sips of the wine. It was easier on her than the brackish water, which she had used to rinse her mouth, and she felt a little better in herself. Her mind was working furiously as she looked about the room, seeking some way she might escape from her captor.

'I won't let him force me,' she muttered to herself. 'I won't...' But how to stop him? She looked for a weapon, but the room contained only the basic furniture of a bed, chair and table. She thought it had probably seen better days, but was obviously neglected.

Where was she? She had no idea how far they had travelled from Bath, because she had been close to suffocating inside that awful blanket and must have fainted. It was probably the reason she felt so unwell now, she reasoned, because her stomach still felt uncomfortable and her head ached badly. Perhaps she was sickening for something?

She discovered a chest in the corner of the room. Lost in the shadows, she had hardly noticed it at first. Now she was drawn to it, hoping to find something inside the drawers that might help her keep Thierry at bay for a few hours longer. Jenny and Edward would know she was missing. They would tell Richard—but would he come looking for her? She had been nothing but a nuisance to him and he would be annoyed that she had been so careless as to let herself be kidnapped.

Jenny cared about her. She still had friends, and surely Richard would help in the search if he knew— but she was not sure he was still in Bath. She must find some way of escaping herself.

If she could just find something to help her... She came across the small porcelain pot in the drawer of the dressing chest and opened it, discovering the old rouge inside. It smelled awful and had a hard crust over the cream, but when she pushed her finger in deep she discovered that some of it was still soft. It stained the end of her finger red and she smiled as she began to hatch the beginnings of a plot.

It was almost dawn when the small party of men brought their horses to a standstill in the trees at the end of a short drive. The house could be seen clearly at the end of the drive, and a candle was burning in the window of an upstairs room, but there were no lights downstairs that could be seen.

'It looks as if you were right,' Richard said, feeling a thrill of triumph. 'The light means someone is here—and it surely must be him, as you guessed.'

'Do you think that is where she is?' Edward whispered. 'If we had a ladder, we might climb up and look in.'

'Too much risk of being discovered,' Richard said. 'We are four of us and armed. I do not know how many men he has, but I think we should go in and make a fight of it. Take them by surprise.'

Edward looked at him doubtfully. 'It would be better if we could somehow sneak her away…'

'Thierry has had her for a few hours,' Richard said. 'If he has harmed her, he is a dead man—if he attempts to harm her I shall shoot, but if he gives her up unharmed we'll take him alive.'

'And what then?'

'I shall hand him over to Rawlings and his cronies, though God help him, he might be better off dead.'

Edward nodded. 'Well, you've more idea of what to expect than I have. I just hope Georgie is somewhere safe and out of it. If she is locked in, we can break the door down once we've taken care of Thierry and his rogues.'

'We'll split up into two groups and go in at the front and the back. If he has men here, they will probably be at the back, and hopefully sleeping or drunk, because they won't be expecting us. He must think he has got away with it.'

Georgie was lying on the bed with her eyes closed when she heard the key in the lock. She had smeared the old rouge into her cheeks, forehead and over her neck and hands. There was no mirror so she could not see the result of her work, but the candle had burned low in its socket and as yet there wasn't much light coming from outside. With any luck it would look as if she had some kind of a fever.

She moaned as she heard the door open and then footsteps coming into the bedchamber. She threw her arm out as if in a fever and turned her head further into the pillows, whimpering and moaning. If she could just make him think she was ill, he might leave her alone for a bit longer.

'What is the matter with you?' Thierry muttered, his voice thick and slurred. He had been drinking for the past couple of hours and was not quite steady on his feet. 'Crying won't help—' He broke off as he saw her red face and neck. 'Good grief! Are you sickening for something?'

Georgie rolled over towards him, her eyes flicking half-open. 'Help me,' she whimpered. 'I think I have the scarlet fever…it was the gypsy child…'

Thierry jumped back as if he had been scalded. 'What child?' he muttered, suspicious and yet nervous of catching some foul disease. She might have the pox or some other dread sickness. 'Tell me, what child…?'

Georgie whimpered and retched as if she was about to be sick again, and he drew back. 'Water…please help me. I feel so ill…'

'If you are trying to trick me…' Thierry grumbled. His mind was not as clear as it ought to be and he hesitated, not sure of what was happening. He needed more light here, damn it! He carried his branch of candles to the table near the bed and set it down, peering at her as she lay tossing and turning in the covers. 'What exactly is wrong, girl?'

Georgie jerked up and snatched a glass of wine from the table beside the bed, throwing it into his face. He gave a snarl of rage and jerked back, temporarily blinded as it stung his eyes.

'Damn you!' he yelled as she was off the bed and running for the door, which he had neglected to lock. She wrenched it wider and was about to flee through it when she heard shouting from somewhere at the back of the house and the sound of gunfire. 'Come back here or you will be sorry!'

Thierry stumbled after her as she ran from the room, cursing and shouting as he started along the landing. She could hear more voices and another shot was fired and then she saw someone coming up the stairs. In the half-light she could not see his face, but instinct told her it must be Richard and she gave a cry of relief and welcome. He had come for her despite their quarrel. He might think she was a troublesome girl, but he had not let her down.

'Come back here, damn you, girl,' Thierry cried. 'I have a pistol. I am warning you, I shall fire.'

Georgie disregarded his warning, running towards the stairs as swiftly as she could. She heard the sound of a shot, felt the sharp sting as Thierry's ball found its mark. Her body jerked and she tumbled to the ground at the feet of the man who had just reached the top. She heard the crack of a pistol above her head and then a scream as the ball found its mark. Her senses were spinning as the blackness gathered around her and she sank into oblivion.

She was not aware of the man who knelt by her side, gently lifting her as the tears ran down his cheeks, or the sound of running feet.

'Is she alive?'

'Yes, just about,' Richard said, his voice harsh, guttural. 'I was not in time to stop him. I think he is dead, but you had better see. My aim may not have been true in the half-light.'

Edward walked further along the landing to where Thierry lay face downward where he had fallen. He turned him over on his back, noting the small round hole where Richard's ball had struck him between the eyes.

'Dead instantly, I should imagine,' he said and left the Frenchman, coming back to where Richard was gathering Georgie into his arms. 'Get her to a doctor, my friend. You can leave me to tidy up here.'

'Rawlings will not be best pleased. He was hoping for information. He says he believes an attack will be made on either the Regent or Wellington at any time now.'

'Well, Thierry will not be taking part in any more plots against the State,' Edward told him with grim satisfaction. 'You are a crack shot, my friend. Had it been me, I should probably have winged him. Your shot was deadly.'

Richard nodded, his expression grim as he cradled the unconscious girl to his chest. 'I could have wished him to live to answer for his crimes,' he said. 'A quick death for him is not enough if she dies.'

'You must get her to a doctor,' Edward urged. 'There is a chaise behind the house, probably waiting for Thierry when he was ready to leave. Take it and find the nearest physician. When he has done his work, take her back to Bath. She cannot travel to my home yet, even if she lives, but we shall go there as soon as she is able.'

Richard nodded grimly, but said nothing as he carried his precious burden down the stairs and out to the chaise. The men he had brought with him were quick to harness horses, saying nothing as they saw his face. His plan to use the element of surprise had worked well, for Thierry's men had been sleeping, waking to find themselves prisoners, and only a couple of them had gone for their weapons; they were nursing their wounds and wishing they had never met the Frenchman, who had not yet paid them for their work.

Richard nodded as his men wished him Godspeed. He would reward them when he had time, but for now all that mattered was to get the girl he loved so much to a surgeon. If she died, he would blame himself, for had he gone to the dance as he'd promised he would never have allowed her to wander outside alone.

Chapter Eight

'Thank God you were in Bath,' Richard said as Henderson finished tending Georgie's wound and straightened up. 'I would trust you to tend her as much as any doctor, and it avoids the scandal as much as possible, though I dare say Jenny will have the doctor to her in the morning.'

'I've done what I can with the wound,' Henderson said, a harsh note in his voice. 'But it is the first time I've taken a ball out of a woman, captain, and I can't vouch for her life. You are strong and made a good recovery, but she's a delicate lass…' He sighed. 'What were you about to let that devil take her in the first place?'

Richard flinched at the note of accusation in his servant's voice. He had endured reproachful looks from his sister when he first carried Georgie up to her bedchamber, but he needed neither of them to tell him that it was his fault Georgie had been taken. He had no doubt in his mind that she had gone outside because she was unhappy—and no one but Richard was to blame for that, because if he had been there with her it could not have happened.

'It was my fault. I do not deny it,' Richard said. 'I should have made sure of him before this—and if she dies...'

'We must hope she won't,' Henderson said and gave him a hard look before he went out.

Richard looked down at Georgie's pale face. Her hair was streaked with sweat and she looked almost lifeless as she lay there, her eyes closed, only a whimper of pain now and then to show that she was still living.

Richard sat on the edge of the bed. He reached for her hand, carrying it to his lips, stroking it against his cheek as the tears slid down them.

'Forgive me, my dearest one,' he said. 'I do care about you—more than you will ever know—but I was afraid to let myself love you. I am not worthy of you, Georgie. You should have a younger man, one who can be all that you need him to be.'

He leaned forward, brushing his lips over hers. Georgie whimpered, her eyelids flickering without opening. He smiled and stroked the hair from her forehead. He was needed in London, but he would not leave her until he was sure she was out of danger, and if she died... Richard's expression was harsh as he realised that the world would seem empty without this girl. She had caused him nothing but trouble, but for him life was hardly worth the living without her.

Georgie moaned as her eyes flickered open and she stared at the person bending over her without truly seeing who it was. She was aware of the pain in her shoulder, a burning, searing pain that hurt so much she could scarcely bear it. She did not know what was the matter with her for she had been ill for some days now, a fever raging in her mind and body. She was not as hot now as she had been, but the pain was still very bad.

'Where am I?' she asked, the mist clearing enough for her to see that it was a woman who tended her. 'What happened to me?'

'Oh, my dearest Georgie,' the woman said and placed a cool hand on her forehead. 'You are awake at last. I was so afraid that you would die and Richard has been beside himself with fear for you. You looked as if you had a terrible fever, but it was only rouge and I washed it off.'

'Who are you?' Georgie asked, frowning as she struggled to remember. She knew that something terrible had happened, but for the moment it escaped her. 'Who is Richard?' She gave a little cry as the pain stabbed at her shoulder.

'You ask who Richard is?' Jenny said, looking at her in dismay. 'He is my brother. Do you not remember him? He rescued you from the streets of London when you were near starving. Surely you must remember? You told me once that you loved him.'

'Did I?' Georgie tried to remember, but could only think of the pain throbbing in her shoulder. It hurt so much and she felt so ill, her mind confused. 'I am sorry. I cannot think…'

'You must not try for now,' Jenny said and smiled at her tenderly. 'You have been very ill, my love. It is more than a week now since Richard brought you back to us.'

'What happened to me?' Georgie stared at her. She sensed that she did know this kind lady, and she smiled a little tentatively. 'I feel so strange…my mind is full of mists…'

'You will remember soon,' Jenny soothed, smoothing back her damp hair. 'That wicked man Monsieur Thierry stole you from the garden of a friend's house. He planned to make you marry him, but Richard and Edward found you—and he will never harm you again. You need not fret, for he is dead. You are safe with me, Georgie, for I love you and will take good care of you.'

'What happened to him—the man who kidnapped me?'

'Richard killed him. He shot you, tried to kill you—so Richard killed him.'

'Richard…' Georgie sighed. A face came into her mind. It was a stern, harsh face and she remembered that it was Richard's face. He had been angry with her, but she did not know why. 'I wish he had not killed anyone for my sake. It is a sin to take the life of another…' Her eyelids fluttered and she fell back into a deep sleep.

Richard looked towards the bed from the doorway. He had visited her every day, spending hours at her side until the doctor told them that she would live. Since then he had left Georgie to the care of the women, but he still visited regularly to see how she progressed.

'Oh, Richard,' Jenny said, realising he was there. 'I did not know you had come in. Georgie was conscious for a little, though she did not truly remember anything that happened to her. I am sure it will come back to her a little at a time.'

'Yes, I am certain it will,' he agreed, but his expression did not lighten. His eyes held a distant expression, remote and cold. 'What she says is the truth. It is a sin to take life.'

'But you did what you had to do,' Jenny said. She

did not like to see that look in her brother's eyes, because she had hoped that he was learning to put the past behind him, to forget whatever it was that haunted him. 'You could not be certain that he would not shoot her again. Besides, he abducted her and then tried to kill her. He deserved to die.'

'Perhaps,' Richard said, a pulse flicking at his temple. 'However, it is not my right to take life. I should have done better to wound him and hand him over to Rawlings.'

'So that he could be tortured and hung?' Jenny said, because she knew that her brother had been stung by Georgie's words. 'I dare say he would have chosen the clean death you gave him if he could. You should not castigate yourself for doing what you did, Richard. Georgie will not once she is herself again, I promise you.'

'What Georgie thinks is only a part of it,' he said. 'In the course of my work I have done many things. It isn't the first time I have killed with one shot. You know nothing about the work I do…the things I have done.'

'In the line of duty,' Jenny reminded him. 'I know you, my dearest. You are a good man, a decent man. You would not stoop to murder.'

He smiled oddly. 'There is a fine line between these things, Jenny. When I shot Thierry I was angry. My aim was true. I meant to kill him because of what he had done to her. Does that make me a murderer? I am not sure.'

'Georgie will not think so once she understands.'

'I am sure you will explain it to her so that she believes me a hero,' Richard said, a grim smile in his eyes. 'I have been called to London, Jenny. An attempt to murder the Regent was thwarted yesterday. They have the man in custody and he has given names, places and dates. Rawlings wants me to make certain of a few more of the traitors, but it looks as if we have it all sewn up. With Thierry gone there will be no more grand designs for creating chaos here. We still have the problem of Bonaparte. Even without Thierry's support he is managing to raise a strong army; he has control of Paris and much of France…'

'So there will be a war?'

'Yes, I am certain of it.' Richard's gaze went to the bed once more. 'I would not leave if I were not certain she was better.'

'It may be for the best,' Jenny told him. 'If she is uncertain in her mind, she will need time to think about what happened. When will you return?'

'It depends how much work Rawlings has for me.'

'But surely you've done all they asked of you? That terrible man is dead. You've done your part, Richard. They have no right to demand more of you.' Jenny sensed that her brother was hurting inside. She went to him, reaching out to touch his hand. 'I believe Georgie loves you.'

'It would be better for her if she did not,' Richard said. 'She must forget me, Jenny. Thierry may be dead, but I still have dangerous work to do—work that may take my life.'

'Please, Richard, do not speak to me like this,' Jenny begged. 'You are my brother and you have done more than your duty. Why do you not give up this life and retire to your estates?'

'While that madman Bonaparte remains at large, free to rampage all over Europe again, I cannot refuse my services,' Richard said and frowned. 'It may be a few days, perhaps longer. Tell her I shall return when I can if she asks for me.'

'Yes, of course,' Jenny assured him. 'But she will wonder what was so important that you could not stay to make sure she was truly better.'

'You know I would come if she needed me. She has you and Edward. I shall return as soon as I am able.'

'You should think of yourself. Georgie deserves to be spoiled and loved, Richard. If you care for her, you should ask her to marry you.'

'I cannot,' Richard said. 'You should not encourage her to think of it. If I return from the war…perhaps then.' He shook his head. 'There are many others who could give her a better life, Jenny. I carry too much baggage with me. She should choose someone nearer her own age, and I am sure she will once I am gone. You should tell her to look for a more suitable husband.'

'Well, I certainly shall not tell her anything of the sort,' Jenny said, giving him an indignant look. 'I do not know what is wrong with you, Richard! I would swear you love her.'

'It is because I love her,' Richard said. 'I want Georgie to be happy, and I would not see her a widow before she has been a wife.'

'Well, I think you are a fool,' his sister told him frankly. 'Georgie loves you, I am sure of it. She would make you an excellent wife, and surely you must wish to marry one day? You cannot wish to live alone all your life?'

'I may have to,' Richard said harshly. 'I simply wish to give her time to think. Is that so very terrible?'

'No, but it is foolish,' Jenny said. 'We have had a dozen or more gentlemen calling to see how she does.

I dare say some of them are fortune hunters, but some seem genuine. If you do not make certain of her, you may lose her.'

'Better that than she should regret her choice later,' Richard said. 'She hardly knows me. She did not even recall my name until you told her. If she truly loved me, I do not think she could have forgot me that easily. I dare say she will meet someone and fall in love—and perhaps that would be for the best….'

Jenny watched as he went to the bed, looking down at Georgie for a moment or two before bending to place a gentle kiss on her forehead. She stirred in her sleep and smiled, but did not wake. Richard watched her for a moment longer before turning away.

Leaving his sister's house, Richard mounted his horse and rode away without a backward glance. Georgie had been hurt by his decision not to ask her to be his wife, but it seemed that her feelings for him were not as strong as he had feared. He had thought his refusal to marry her might break her heart, but she had forgotten him so easily that he was sure her infatuation had been merely the fancy of a young girl.

Georgie was many years younger than he, and it was another reason he had held back. As enticing and beautiful as she was, he knew her to be innocent. It would have been wrong of him to take advantage of that innocence. She would soon recover from any disappointment and fall in love again.

Whether he would recover so easily was another matter. However, his life was not his own for the foreseeable future. He had his duty to his King and country, and if he died in the coming war there would be few to mourn him. At least he would not leave a grieving widow behind him.

Georgie stirred and stretched, her eyelids flickering before she finally opened her eyes and looked about her. She was in her bedroom in Bath—the house that Jenny had taken for their visit. So where had that other room been? The one that was so bare and neglected? Had it all been a dream? The events of that night were a blur in her mind, but as she moved and realised that her shoulder was beginning to feel less sore, she understood that it had been real. She had not been able to remember it properly at first, but Jenny had told her little things and it had come back to her piece by piece.

She remembered smearing her face with that awful old rouge. Her ruse had worked, for Thierry had bent over her to see her more clearly and she'd smelled the wine on his breath, guessing that he had been drinking heavily and might be a little fuddled in his thinking. It had given her the courage to throw the wine in his face and make her bid for escape, but he had followed and he had fired after her, hitting her in the back of her shoulder. The doctor had since told her that she was lucky, because it had not been as deep a wound as it might have been. She had been ill because she had taken a fever, which had been severe and caused all her friends a lot of worry.

Seeing all the vases of flowers set about her room, Georgie smiled because Jenny was always telling her about various people who had sent her gifts of flowers and fruit, many of them calling to see how she went on. None of the flowers had come from Richard.

She remembered Jenny telling her that Richard had

killed the Frenchman. Somewhere at the back of her mind she recalled hearing one shot after she fell. Richard must have been afraid that Thierry would shoot again, and he had made sure of his own aim. She shuddered, because it was unpleasant to think that a man had died because of her—even though he was a wicked man and deserved his fate. However, Richard had shot him on the spur of the moment and she could not have expected him to do less.

But why wasn't he here with her? Everyone else seemed to care how she was, but Richard had gone away, leaving her to the care of his sister and her family. He had put his work first and she found that hard to bear. But, of course, she was only a troublesome girl to Richard. He had rescued her more than once and he had promised to be her friend, but he did not love her as she loved him. He did not wish to marry her. She meant so little to him that he had gone away while she was still desperately ill.

Her eyes stung, but she blinked hard, refusing to weep. She had always known that Richard's work was important to him, but surely she was important too?

If he truly cared for her, he would not have left her when she was so ill. But he only wished to be her friend. The humiliating memory of the day she had thrown herself at him came flooding back, bringing such a sharp stinging pain that was worse than all the physical agony she had endured. Richard did not love her. He had made that very plain.

She had to forget him, to move on with her life. Perhaps one day she would find someone else to love, but for the moment she felt as if her heart had been torn in two.

* * *

She had sat about in the house too long, Georgie thought, feeling restless. She was much better now, but she had not ventured further than the garden despite Jenny's encouragement. However, the glorious weather made her feel that she would like to go out somewhere. She was at the window musing whether or not she felt strong enough to walk to the lending library when Jenny entered behind her.

'Would you like to come with me to the Pump Room this morning, my love?' Jenny asked. 'It will be my last visit, because we are to go home tomorrow.'

'Your visit has been spoiled,' Georgie said, looking at her regretfully. 'You have done hardly anything you wanted to do, Jenny—and it is all my fault.'

'How could it be your fault?' Jenny demanded. 'You did not ask to be abducted by that wicked man, dearest. Caring for you was more important to me than visiting, though, as you know, friends have continued to call here and I have been to one or two small affairs. It is you that has missed out on all the treats I planned for you.'

'Well, I think I shall walk to the Pump Room with you this morning,' Georgie said, smiling at her. 'I shall wear the new gown we ordered before I was hurt. At least I have lots of new clothes to wear, Jenny—and I dare say you will entertain at home.'

'Yes, certainly, once we return—at least until Edward goes away.'

Georgie saw the anxious look in her eyes. 'He has not said when he will rejoin his regiment yet?'

'Not yet, but I am sure it cannot be long,' Jenny said. 'Everyone is talking of the war as inevitable and

I know Edward will rejoin once he thinks us settled at home again.'

'Then we must make the most of the little time left to us,' Georgie said. 'Perhaps we could postpone our return for a day or so?'

'Well, I suppose we might prolong it by two days,' Jenny said, looking pleased. 'If you are sure you wish to, my love?'

'Oh, yes,' Georgie said. 'I am feeling so much better now. I am not sure I should wish to dance, but I would not mind attending the theatre or going for a drive somewhere.'

'Edward will take us driving this afternoon,' Jenny said. 'We shall go to the theatre tomorrow evening and go home the following day. Yes, I should like that—and now, I'll ring for your pelisse and then we will walk to the baths.'

'This was a good idea,' Georgie told her companion after they had been walking for a few minutes. 'It is so refreshing to be out of the house again, and it is such a lovely day.'

'Yes, it is,' Jenny replied. 'Are you sure you feel well enough to continue, dearest?'

'Yes, I feel perfectly well,' Georgie said. Her shoulder was still a little sore, but she thought it nothing to complain of; the searing pain had gone and she felt a return of her strength in the sunshine. 'Besides, it is not so very far…' She did not notice the young lad following close behind her and was shocked when he suddenly seized her parasol and made off with it down the street. 'Oh! He stole my parasol…'

'How very annoying…' Jenny began, but even as she

did so a gentleman grabbed the fleeing urchin, holding him by the scruff of the neck by one hand and relieving him of the parasol with the other. He gave him a sharp tap with the parasol and then let the youth go. 'Did you see that, dearest? The gentleman has retrieved your parasol for you.'

The gentleman in question was coming towards them. He removed his hat, making Georgie an elegant leg. 'Your property, Miss Bridges. I let the rogue go for I dare say he was desperate to attempt such a thing in broad daylight and does not need more punishment.'

'Oh, no, it does not matter. I have my parasol back,' Georgie said and smiled. He was a tall gentleman, his hair fair and wavy, his eyes blue. She thought him handsome, but was not sure she knew him. 'You seem to know my name, sir, but I fear that I do not recall yours.'

'We have not been introduced,' he told her, his eyes bright with amusement. 'I saw you briefly one evening at a party. It was my intention to ask you for a dance later, but unfortunately you had left.'

'Not by my own wish,' Georgie said, her smile dimming. 'I do not know if you have heard the rumours?'

'I believe there was some tale of abduction and of your being hurt before your family rescued you?' His eyes were soft and concerned. 'If that is true, I must offer you my sympathy, Miss Bridges. I am Captain Philip Lowe, at your service... Lady Maddison, you will vouch for me, I believe?'

'Yes, of course, sir,' Jenny said, giving him a warm smile. 'Georgie, my dear, this gentleman is a friend of my husband's. They served together some years ago.'

'I had that honour,' Captain Lowe told her. 'I was hoping to call on Edward this afternoon to pay my respects. I would have come before, but I was called home for a few days. My grandmother was ill, but I am pleased to say she made a full recovery.'

'I am glad of that, sir,' Jenny said. 'We dine at home this evening—perhaps you would give us the pleasure of your company?'

'I should like that very well,' he replied. 'But I must not delay you. I dare say you are on your way to an appointment.'

'We merely visit the Pump Room,' Jenny told him. 'This is Georgie's first day out after her illness.'

'Then I shall hope it is a happy one. Lady Maddison, Miss Bridges. I shall see you this evening.'

He nodded and walked on past. Jenny watched him for a moment, her expression a mixture of thought and apprehension.

'You are thinking that he wishes to speak to Edward about rejoining the regiment?' Georgie asked.

'Yes, I am sure it will be spoken of this evening,' Jenny said and sighed. 'But it cannot be helped, Georgie. I know Edward means to go and I cannot say anything to stop him.'

'I suppose not,' Georgie said. 'It is a pity that more was not done to make sure that Bonaparte remained a prisoner on Elba!'

'Yes,' Jenny agreed and gave a rueful laugh. 'I think we ladies would run things much better if only we had the chance—do you not agree, dearest?'

'Certainly I do,' Georgie said. Her eye was caught by a bonnet in the window of a milliner nearby. 'That would suit you, Jenny. Why do you not buy it?'

'I have so many bonnets,' Jenny said. 'But you are right, that shade of cherry red is very becoming to me. Shall we go in and see if it looks as well on as off? And you might like to buy something, my love. You have not had nearly as much chance to purchase new trifles as you should.'

'I think I might like that blue one,' Georgie said, indicating a very fetching concoction of silk velvet trimmed with flowers under the brim. 'Yes, I think we should both buy something new.'

'Are you tired, my love?' Jenny asked as they paused at the head of the stairs as they retired that evening. 'You look a little pale. Does your shoulder hurt?'

'Only a very little,' Georgie said. She smiled, because she could not explain that she was missing Richard. 'I think the men will talk for ages. It seems that they are sure the war is certain.'

'Oh, yes, I think it must be,' Jenny said and a tiny nerve flicked in her cheek. 'I think it was hoped they might be able to stop it quickly, but Bonaparte's march brought him more supporters than expected. I dare say Richard will know more when he comes.'

'Do you think he will come soon?' Georgie held back a sigh.

'I think he has been gone too long already,' Jenny said, frowning. She looked at Georgie oddly. 'What did you think of Captain Lowe this evening?'

'He seems pleasant,' Georgie said. 'Full of stories about the Regent.'

'Yes, he is one of that set,' Jenny said. 'I believe he is a favourite with the prince, though younger than some of that set. He spoke to Edward of wishing to settle down soon, which I found surprising, for I had thought him a confirmed bachelor.'

'Perhaps he wishes for an heir. He seems a decent man, Jenny.'

'Yes, I am sure he is.' Jenny nodded as if Georgie's answer had settled something for her. 'We are engaged to visit the theatre tomorrow. After that, I dare say we shall be ready to return home in a day or so. Shall you be sorry to leave Bath, Georgie?'

'No, not at all. It has been pleasant, but I am looking forward to riding with you again, Jenny. We have not been out with the horses once here.'

'No, we have not,' Jenny agreed. 'We were busy at first and then you were ill—but it will be nice to be home again, dearest. I think I shall write to Richard and ask him when he intends to return.'

'Yes, I wish you would,' Georgie said with a little choke in her voice. 'I do miss him.'

'Do you truly?'

'Yes, of course. Why do you ask?'

'I thought you might like Captain Lowe?'

'I like him,' Georgie said. 'He is a pleasant companion—but he isn't Richard. I have met no one else I like as much as your brother.' She blinked away her tears. 'Unfortunately, Richard does not feel as I do. He is kind and generous to me, but he thinks of me as a friend.'

'Richard is sometimes thoughtless,' Jenny said. 'He is my brother and I love him dearly, but I love you too—and I want you to be happy.'

'I am happy,' Georgie said, forcing a smile. 'But I shall be happier when Richard comes back.'

'I am so glad,' Jenny said and kissed her cheek. 'The

foolish man does not know what he might lose if he continues to neglect you.'

Georgie shook her head. She blinked her eyes to stop the silly tears of self-pity from falling. Jenny continued to hope for a marriage between them, but Richard had made his feelings plain. He had helped Georgie and would help her again if need be, but she meant no more to him than any other friend.

Georgie had known that Captain Lowe was attracted to her and had she wished she might have aroused his interest, but for the moment her heart ached too much to even think of allowing another man to court her.

Richard stood in the prow of the ship, looking out through the sea mist that had fallen over them soon after they left the shores of France. He had not wanted to leave England, and would not had it been at Rawlings's bidding, but the request had come from higher up. He was to go over in secret and discover the lay of the land, test the mood of the people to discover how they truly felt about the Emperor's return.

His command of the language was such that he had found it easy enough to mingle with the people, but he felt it had been a waste of time for he could only say what he had seen and heard. People gathered in the streets to cheer whenever Napoleon Bonaparte rode past on his white horse and it was true that many of his old soldiers were flocking to join him. However, Richard had noticed that after the parade was over some of the faces were sullen and ordinary folk grumbled that there would be too high a price to pay for the Emperor's return.

War might bring glory to the few, but for the poor it brought only more hardship. The price of food would rise if there were battles and riots, and some would not even be able to find the price of a loaf. There were some who grumbled that even when the Sun King sat on the throne conditions had been no worse. Bonaparte had begun as a great champion of the people, but his ideas of grandeur had brought him to disaster. Many were afraid it would end in tears once more.

He had nothing conclusive to tell his superiors, Richard thought as he peered into the mist and longed for England's shores. His own feeling was that there might be relief if Bonaparte were beaten once more. People wanted peace and did not much care if they had a King or an Emperor, though some murmured that France would do better as a Republic. They did not need a dictator in any guise, merely a leader they could elect or dismiss at will.

The French were a volatile people in Richard's opinion. A revolution such as they had passed through some years earlier could never happen in England. Even had the plot to kill the Regent not been foiled, it would never have succeeded to the extent that Thierry had hoped.

His frown deepened as he thought of the man that he had killed to prevent him shooting Georgie for a second time. She should be well recovered from her injury when he returned, for he had been away some weeks—but would she have forgiven him?

He knew that she found the thought of his killing Thierry distasteful. Would it lead her to feel revulsion for him?

Georgie was returning to the house with a basket of spring flowers over her arm one morning when she saw

Richard standing outside the house. He seemed to be looking for someone and, when he saw her, began to walk in her direction. Georgie's heart jerked with sudden fright, because she did not know how to greet him. She was tempted to run away, but she knew that she must make this first meeting as easy for both of them as possible. Raising her head, she looked at him, but did not smile. It was impossible to smile, because her face felt frozen.

'You are back, Richard,' she said, finding a new dignity from somewhere deep within her. She would not show him that she was delighted to see him. 'Jenny has been anxious for your return.'

'Jenny has been scolding me for deserting you,' Richard said and frowned. 'Are you completely recovered? You look very well, Georgie.'

'Thank you, I feel much better,' she said. 'My shoulder aches a little sometimes, but I dare say that will go in time. You made a full recovery from your wound, I believe?'

'Yes, but I am a man and these things are easier for me to bear. Henderson has a good salve that may ease any stiffness in your shoulder, Georgie. I shall ask him to make some up for you.'

'That is very kind,' Georgie said. 'I believe I have him to thank for patching me up in the first place. You must thank him for me.'

'He needs no thanks, but will be glad to hear you have recovered.'

Georgie nodded. He seemed concerned and it was difficult to keep up this reserve with him, but she was determined that she would not throw herself at him again.

'How long will you stay with us this time, sir?' she asked.

'A few days only,' Richard told her. 'I wanted to visit my sister one last time before I leave for Brussels. It is as well to say one's farewells in case…' His eyes dwelled on her face for a moment. 'Will you forgive me for allowing that brute to harm you?'

'Yes, of course,' Georgie replied. 'How could it be your fault? I went outside to take the air alone. I ought to have remembered your warnings. If anyone is to blame it is I, not you.'

'I feel to blame—' Richard began, but was interrupted by the arrival of his sister. 'Jenny…'

'Edward is home,' Jenny said. 'You wanted me to let you know the moment he came in. He is in his study—he wanted a word with his bailiff—but he will be ready for you in a moment.'

'I shall go to him,' Richard said. 'I have important news that he will wish to know immediately. Excuse me, Georgie—Jenny…'

Georgie stared after him as he walked away. She felt tears stinging behind her eyes, but was determined not to let them fall. Richard was concerned for her as a friend, but he did not love her. She would do nothing while he was here to make him aware that her heart was breaking.

Richard knew that he deserved this new coolness from Georgie. She had changed since that day on the hill, seeming older and less confiding than she had been when he first met her. He could not blame her, because he had not behaved well, but it was a barrier between them. While he was away he had thought of nothing but this meeting, and in his thoughts he had taken her in his arms and kissed her, but he was no longer sure that she would welcome his attentions.

With war so imminent it was perhaps for the best that she should have thrown up this barrier. Nothing had changed since that day on the hill, except that he now knew his life would be empty without her—but he could still be killed at any time and it would not be fair to give in to his selfish urges to take what happiness he could. Far better if he did not attempt to break down Georgie's new reserve. If he returned from the war, it would be time enough to court her and hope that she might forgive him for the way he had hurt her.

Chapter Nine

Wearing one of her prettiest gowns, Georgie went downstairs to take nuncheon at twelve of the clock. She discovered that both Edward and Richard were already there together with Jenny. It seemed that they had been arguing, because Jenny looked heated, but no one said anything as she entered and she wondered if she had been the subject of their dispute.

'Here you are, my love,' Jenny said, an odd tearful expression on her face. It was strange to see for she was usually such a bright, happy person. 'Come and sit with us. I am a little cross with Edward and my brother, but we shall not talk about it anymore.'

Georgie was aware of some constraint between the husband and wife, but Richard smiled at her, as if trying to ease the tension.

'You look very elegant in that gown, Georgie. Is it a new one?'

'One of several,' she replied. 'I hardly got a chance to wear the things I ordered in Bath, but it does not matter—Jenny means to take me visiting with her and we are invited to several parties this summer.'

'Oh, yes, I know my sister entertains often. You will not be dull here—either of you.' This was said with a significant look at his sister, who made a face at him. 'Time soon passes when you have good friends and neighbours.'

Jenny uttered a sound of disgust, but made no comment. It was not until she and Georgie left the table to retire to the parlour they used for the afternoon that the truth came out.

'Edward will not allow me to accompany him to Brussels!' Jenny exclaimed. 'Richard came to tell him that it was time to rejoin his regiment. He will do so a few days after Richard leaves—and I begged him to allow us to follow him to Brussels so that we might be near each other until the last moment. It is what many other wives do—what I did when we were first married—but he says my duty is to the children and I must stay here.'

'Oh, Jenny,' Georgie said, seeing her distress. 'That is true and yet it is unfair. You have nurses and maids to care for them and you would wish to be near if Edward were wounded in battle.'

'You understand me perfectly,' Jenny said, giving her a grateful look. 'But Edward simply refuses to listen…and I cannot bear it.' Tears stood in her eyes. 'We have never been parted for more than a day or so since we were married.'

'Perhaps he will change his mind,' Georgie suggested.

'He got quite cross with me, and he never is as a rule, no matter how I plague him. He says that I might come to harm if things go wrong and then our children would be left without father or mother…' A tear slid from the corner of her eye but she swept it away with her hand. 'I refuse to cry! He is so unfair!'

Georgie did her best to cheer her friend, but

although Jenny smiled and nodded, she could not be comforted. When Richard came in a few minutes later, she turned away and pretended to be examining a fashion sheet, which had been sent with Edward's newssheets that morning.

Richard glanced at his sister with a frown and then at Georgie. 'Will you walk with me?' he asked.

'Yes, if you wish it,' Georgie replied and got up, following him through the open French windows into the gardens. 'Jenny is distressed because Edward will not allow her to follow him to Brussels.'

'I know,' he said. 'He thinks it might be dangerous if things should go wrong. He is afraid for her safety and the children's future.'

'I do understand that,' Georgie said. 'But if he were wounded he might be glad that she was there to care for him.'

'Perhaps, but he is adamant,' Richard said, and turned to her. 'I wanted to ask you if you would stay with her, Georgie. I know I have no right to ask such a favour. You are an heiress and the fashionable drawing rooms of London are open to you.'

'Oh, how dare you?' Georgie cried, a spot of angry colour in her cheeks. 'To imply that I would think of deserting Jenny for the sake of society. If that is what you think of me, I have nothing more to say to you!' She turned away, her throat tight with emotion. How could he think such things of her!

Richard caught her wrist, holding it firmly but without exerting pressure. She could not escape him and was forced to turn and look at him once more.

'I am sorry if I offended you,' he said. 'It was not my intention.'

'You cannot think much of me if you think that I would leave Jenny alone when she has been so kind to me.' Georgie blazed at him.

'Forgive me,' Richard said. 'You must know that I do not think badly of you, Georgie. I have always believed you brave and—'

'You thought me a liar when we first met because I did not tell you my story at once.' Georgie rounded on him, really angry now. 'I know you think me nothing but a nuisance, and it is true that I have caused you a deal of trouble, but I love Jenny and I would never hurt her.'

'You have caused me far more trouble than you will ever know,' Richard said. He reached out for her, pulling her hard against him. For a moment fire leaped in his eyes as he gazed down at her, and then he pulled her fiercely against him, his mouth crushing hers in a demanding, punishing kiss that drove the breath from her body. As he let her go, Georgie reacted instinctively, raising her hand and slapping him hard across the face.

'I hate you!' she cried. 'Go away and leave me alone!'

Richard stared at her for a minute. 'Yes, I should go,' he said and then turned and walked off without another word.

Georgie ran in the direction of the shrubbery. She was close to tears and did not know how she felt. How was she to understand Richard when one minute he refused to ask her to be his wife even though she threw herself at him and the next he kissed her as if his life depended on it! And to accuse her of being so heartless as to leave Jenny when she would be alone—it was too much! She was hurt and angry and she did not know if she could ever forgive him.

* * *

It was teatime when Georgie came downstairs. She had spent two hours walking alone in the garden, and since she had been crying she had needed to wash her face in cold water and change her clothes before she was respectable again. Jenny looked at her as she entered the parlour, and there was not much to choose between them, for both were in low spirits.

'You have quarrelled with Richard,' Jenny said as she saw her. 'He went off with a face like thunder and you have been crying.'

'Yes, we did quarrel,' Georgie said. 'I wish I hadn't slapped him now, but I was so angry.'

'Oh, Georgie, you didn't?' Jenny looked at her in horror. 'Whatever did he do to make you? Richard will not like that, dearest.'

'No, I do not suppose he will,' Georgie said in a small voice. 'I feel dreadful. I should apologise. Do you know when he will be back?'

'I do not think he intends to return. He said that he would be leaving for Brussels in two days and had work to do—but I am sure he had meant to stay longer.'

'It is my fault,' Georgie said. 'I am sorry, Jenny. He implied that I might leave you here alone when Edward is gone and then…he kissed me. Not in a nice way, but almost as if he wished to punish me and I hit him. I am sorry now, but there is nothing I can do—though if you write to him you can tell him I am sorry.'

'Richard has behaved very badly to you through all this,' Jenny said. 'If he kissed you like that, I am not surprised you hit him. Men have no sense at all sometimes.'

'In Bath I almost threw myself at him the day he took

me driving,' Georgie said. 'But he said that he could not ask me to wed him because it would not be fair…I might be a widow before I had been a wife.'

'Oh, how foolish of him! You would rather be his wife for a few hours than never know such happiness. Men are such ridiculous creatures. Edward will not let me go to Brussels with him—and Richard will not ask you to be his wife because he might be killed.'

'If Richard loved me, I would put on my boy's clothing and join the ranks as a drummer boy to be near him,' Georgie said dramatically. 'How can he think that I would prefer to be mixing in society rather than with you? You are my dearest friend and I shall not desert you—if you still want me after what I did to Richard?'

'Of course I do, my love. It may do my foolish brother good. I do not think any woman has ever slapped him before.' Jenny laughed. 'Oh, I can just see you dressed as a drummer boy, Georgie,' she said. 'Yes…' she looked thoughtful '…how clever of you to think of it.'

'What are you thinking now?' Georgie asked, because there was an odd expression in her friend's eyes.

'Oh, nothing very much,' Jenny said and looked away. 'Just a thought that occurred to me, but I am not sure. I must think about this carefully.'

Edward came into the room at that moment and Jenny's expression changed to a smile of welcome. Georgie withdrew to the window to allow them some privacy.

Richard had gone off in a temper because she had slapped him. Whatever must he think of her now?

Richard rode furiously for more than an hour. He had been outraged when Georgie hit him, but his anger had left him after some hard riding. He knew that he had deserved no less. She was perfectly right to be angry, because he should not have used her so ill. His need of her had broken through and he had done something he had vowed never to do, forcing a kiss on her. Instead of melting into his arms as she had in his dreams, Georgie had slapped him—and with some force.

If Georgie had once cared for him, he had killed her love. It hurt more than he had believed possible, and he cursed himself for a clumsy fool. Instead of acting as judge and jury, he should have confessed his love, begged Georgie for patience and asked her to marry him when the war was over.

It was too late now. She would never look at him in the way that made him ache with desire again. She would despise and hate him, and he could hardly blame her, because he had brought it on himself. His motives had been noble, but Georgie would scorn them because she was brave—much braver in truth than he…

Remembering the time they had spent travelling together when she was dressed in that ridiculous clothing, Richard found that he could smile. Perhaps if he survived the battles to come, Georgie might forgive him after all. At least she was not indifferent to him if the force of that blow was anything to the point…

For the next two days, Georgie lived in hope that Richard might return, but he did not, and she accepted that he must have decided to join his regiment, which was already being shipped to Brussels in anticipation of the war to come.

On the third morning Edward took his leave of them. Jenny waved him goodbye with a pale face, but when she returned to the parlour she was weeping. Georgie put her arms about her and they clung to one another, both crying as they tried to comfort each other.

'I cannot bear the thought that I may never see him again,' Jenny said and drew away from Georgie to wipe her eyes. 'If he should be wounded…'

'I know how you must feel,' Georgie said. 'If I were Richard's wife, I should follow him no matter what he said…' She faltered as she saw the look on Jenny's face. 'I do not mean that you should, dearest. You have your children to consider. Edward is right. You do need to be with them.'

'I am torn in two,' Jenny told her. 'My head tells me that Edward is right, but my heart says that I should be with him. If he needs me and I am not there… As you said, the children have their nurses. If I could just think of a way to be certain they would be properly protected if…' She shook her head. 'I love my children, Georgie—but Edward is my life.'

'Yes, I know,' Georgie said and her heart bled for her friend. 'I feel as if I am in chains. I know that Richard is in danger. He may be killed or wounded—and he does not know that I love him.' She gave a little sobbing cry. 'Why did I let him go thinking I hated him, Jenny? I love him so much. If he dies, I shall want to die too. If only he had cared enough to marry me.'

'Poor Georgie,' Jenny said and opened her arms. 'At least I know that Edward loves me. He has forbidden me to follow only for the children's sake.' She sighed deeply. 'I wish I knew what to do for the best—for all our sakes.'

'It is all such a coil,' Georgie said and hugged her

friend. If she knew for certain that Richard loved her, nothing would keep her here when he was in danger, but she must say no more for Jenny was already in turmoil. It was going to be a hard time for them both, waiting and worrying.

Jenny came into the bedchamber the next morning; she was carrying a tray set with soft rolls, honey, a pot of chocolate and two fine porcelain cups. Georgie had been just about ready to get up and face the day, but when she saw Jenny she sat up against her pillows, knowing that this honour was because her friend understood how she was feeling.

'I thought we would have breakfast, just the two of us,' she said, smiling as she sat on the edge of the bed. 'Afterwards, we might go visiting or we could ride out together if you prefer?'

'I should like to go riding, if you would?'

'Yes, I think I should enjoy it. Besides, we must not sit about moping. We must get on with our lives as best we can.'

Georgie looked at her. 'What are you up to? I know there is something, because I can see it in your eyes.'

'I can't tell you just yet, but I do have a plan.'

'What kind of a plan?'

'I shall not involve you just yet,' Jenny said with a mysterious look, 'but I believe you will be pleased with me. And now we must eat our breakfast before the chocolate goes cold.'

Georgie gave her a hard look, but Jenny merely smiled and shook her head. It was obvious that she had come to some kind of a decision, but for the moment she clearly wished to keep it to herself.

* * *

Some days later, Georgie woke from a dream as someone entered the room, swishing back the curtains. She sat up with a name on her lips, but it was not Richard, only her sister-in law.

'Is something the matter? It must still be early,' she said, her heart racing. It had been more than a week since Edward followed Richard to Dover where they had been due to embark for Brussels. 'It is not bad news?'

'No, excellent news. I have heard from my husband's cousin Martha and she is coming here later today. She has promised to stay while we are away and take care of the children. You must get up and summon your maid to pack a trunk, Georgie. As soon as Lady Randall is here we shall set out.'

'But where are we going?' Sensing Jenny's air of suppressed excitement, she threw back the covers and swung her legs over the edge of the bed. 'I knew you were up to some mischief!'

'We are going to Brussels,' Jenny told her, her eyes bright with the spirit of adventure. 'Edward refused to take us, because he said he could not have the worry of looking after us. Well, we are going to show him that we can fend for ourselves. We shall find a ship, take passage, and when we get there we shall rent a house for ourselves.'

'Jenny! Are you sure we ought to?' Georgie said, feeling stunned. 'Edward may be angry…' She could not imagine what Richard would say, but her heart had begun to race, for it meant that she might see him— might be able to tell him how sorry she was for hitting him and beg his pardon. 'Do we dare?'

'I do not care if Edward is angry,' Jenny responded, a militant sparkle in her eyes. 'I know he is afraid that some harm might come to me if he is not there to watch over me, but I do not see why it should. I am well able to take care of myself. Besides, I shall have you for company—shall I not?'

'Yes, of course.' Georgie smiled at her as the excitement stirred inside her. 'You know that I would never desert you, dearest. Besides, I understand how you feel. You need to be nearby in case Edward should be wounded and call for you. And I...should be there if Richard should need me.' She drew her breath in sharply. It was a bold plan, but full of dangers. 'Are you sure you want to do this, Jenny?'

'I knew you would understand,' Jenny said, laughing softly as she embraced her warmly. 'It was you that first gave me the idea. When you said that if Richard truly loved you, you would dress as a boy and follow the drum.'

'Oh, dear, was it that?' Georgie said, feeling guilty. 'I did not mean to give you ideas, Jenny. I know I said it, and indeed if I were sure Richard loved me—but you must be perfectly sure that this is what you want to do. Please do not be swayed by anything I said. Make your own decision.'

'I have and I am perfectly sure,' Jenny told her. 'It was not easy, but Aunt Martha will stand guardian to our children if need be. My place is with Edward at this time, whether he knows it or not. As for the journey, we shall both take a maid and two of the grooms will accompany us—but I am certain we shall manage for ourselves. They are merely there to provide security if we are set upon by thieves or highwaymen.'

'I do not think it likely,' Georgie said. 'We shall be

perfectly safe if we have our maids and two grooms—
who will be armed.' She frowned. 'I think I shall take
a pistol, too, for I am sure I could fire it if need be.'

'Do you think so?' Jenny looked sceptical. 'I am
sure I could not, but I shall feel safe enough with two
burly grooms. After all, I have travelled as far as York
without Edward—so it cannot be so very different to
travel a little further, can it?'

'Brussels is quite a lot further,' Georgie said. 'But as
long as we are careful and do not flash our money carelessly we should do well enough. I managed to travel
to London alone without harm. It was only after I got
there that I lost my money. With you, the maids and two
grooms, I am sure we shall be perfectly safe.'

'Well, I am glad you think so,' Jenny said. 'I am determined to go. I would have gone alone if need be, but
I shall feel more comfortable if you are with me.'

Georgie smiled and nodded. She would not dream of
letting her dear friend set off without her. Jenny was far
too pretty and trusting to set off on such an adventure
alone. Besides, it was she who had given Jenny the idea
and it was her duty as well as her pleasure to accompany her friend. It was quite an undertaking for two
ladies, but like Jenny she felt that it would be much
easier to endure the hardships of a long journey than to
sit tamely at home.

Despite some misgivings at the start, Georgie discovered that the journey to the coast was uneventful.
When they reached the port, they discovered that they
were not the only wives who had had the same idea. A
lady by the name of Mrs Feathers was staying with her
daughter Sally at the inn they chose. Sally was a pretty

blonde-haired girl of eighteen years, and engaged to a gentleman who was on Wellington's staff.

'How fortunate that we should all meet,' Mrs Feathers exclaimed when she learned that they were travelling to Brussels to be near their husbands. 'My husband is too old to be in the army, but he is engaged in the business of helping to oversee the logistics of supplies—and of course Sally is engaged to Captain Malvern and she simply could not wait at home. Do you think it would be a good idea if we were all to travel together? I know that there are still some places on the ship we have bought passage on. I could send word to the captain and book for two ladies, their maids and two menservants.'

'Oh, we shall not need the grooms now we have found friends,' Jenny said. 'They may as well return home with the carriage—for I dare say we may hire one over there.'

'That is what we plan to do,' Mrs Feathers told her with a smile. 'My husband will meet us at the port and we may all travel on to Brussels together—if that will suit you?'

Jenny agreed that it would. Georgie felt it would have been better to retain at least one of the grooms even if coachman and the other groom returned to Yorkshire. However, she made no objection for the matronly Mrs Feathers seemed very capable. She had been with her husband in the Spanish campaign a few years earlier, and had experience in acquiring both accommodation and means of travelling.

Mrs Feathers entertained them at dinner that evening by telling them how she had once travelled by donkey when the army had been routed, and how she had hidden in a cellar for days when the village they were staying in had been overrun by the French.

'It is often hard following one's husband on campaign,' she told them. 'Sometimes you have to be prepared to sleep under the stars, and food isn't always plentiful. A friend of mine who was caught up in a siege once had to eat rats and mouldy bread, but she survived to tell the tale and I dare say we shall too, my dears.'

Georgie saw the look on Jenny's face and wondered if she were having second thoughts, but when she asked her later she shook her head.

'I should not like to eat rats. Indeed, I think I might prefer to go hungry, but it has not made me change my mind. If I stayed at home in safety and Edward was left to die on some forgotten field, I should break my heart, Georgie. At least if we are there we shall be able to help if they are wounded.'

'I have been hungry enough to risk stealing,' Georgie told her. 'In fact, that is how I met Richard—but I think I would need to be starving before I ate a rat.' She shuddered. 'However, I do not think it will happen. Why should it? Wellington and the Allies will never allow the enemy to get near Brussels.'

Georgie stood in the prow of the ship looking towards the shore as its outline became visible through the early morning mist. She had not suffered from sea-sickness at all, though she knew that Jenny and both the maids had suffered varying degrees of it during the night when the waters had been choppy. She turned as Jenny came up to her, looking a little pale, though decidedly better than she had first thing.

'How are you feeling now, dearest?'

'Much better than I did,' Jenny said. 'I am not a good sailor at the best of times and it was rough last night.'

'Yes, it was,' Georgie agreed. 'We shall be docking in a short time. Do you wish to continue in company with Mrs Feathers or shall we find our own carriage?'

'I know she does talk a lot and rather loudly,' Jenny said. 'But she has been very friendly, and we may need help when we get to Brussels, Georgie. She said that her husband wrote to her a week before she set out from home, and said that it was almost impossible to find accommodation. He had secured something for her and Sally, but apparently it was not what he had hoped to find.'

'Well, we must hope that we can find something, even if it is only a room somewhere,' Georgie said. 'I suppose that may be one of the reasons why Edward thought it best if we stayed at home.'

'Yes, well, he may have done,' Jenny said, looking mutinous. 'But I am willing to put up with anything if I can be there if he needs me.'

'Yes, I know.' Georgie put an arm about her waist. 'Do not worry, dearest. I am sure we shall find something…'

Georgie looked out of the carriage window as they entered the town. It was teeming with people, many of them soldiers wearing British uniforms. She saw a group of ladies walking along the pavement, laughing and talking in the sunshine, their parasols shading them from the heat. She caught a few words of English as the carriage passed by, and realised that she and Jenny were not the only ladies to have followed their husbands and lovers. Ahead of them a wagon loaded with bales of hay was blocking the road, and just to the right a noisy fight had broken out as some men came tumbling out of an inn.

'They are drunk, I dare say,' Mrs Feathers remarked. 'If their commanding officers hear of it, they will be reprimanded, but it is always so in a garrison town. Most of them will be on the move before long, but the worst of times is always before the battles begin. The men become bored when they are idle.'

'It looks as if the city is full to bursting point,' Jenny said with a frown. 'It is good of you to offer us a bed for the night, ma'am, but we must begin the search for our own house tomorrow.'

'Perhaps your husband has suitable accommodation,' Mrs Feathers said. 'Does he expect you today?'

'Oh, he expects us at any time,' Jenny said airily. 'Either he or my brother will have something for us, I imagine.'

Georgie looked at her, but kept her silence. In truth, they had no idea where to find Edward and Richard, though they had already been shown what was known as Headquarters as they drove through the town and an inquiry there should give them some idea of either Edward's or Richard's direction.

The house that Mr Feathers had found for his family was small and in a back street away from the better area of the town. It did have three bedrooms, however, which meant that Jenny and Georgie were able to share a room for one night. Their maids were given makeshift beds in the kitchen, which caused some long faces, but was the best that could be achieved in the cramped house.

When they passed through the hall, which was dark

and smelled of boiled cabbage, Jenny wrinkled her nose in distaste. She was used to better and found it difficult to hide her dismay, though Mrs Feathers had declared herself well pleased.

'It is not home,' she remarked, 'but it is large enough and will do for the moment—will it not, Sally?'

'Yes, Mama, if you say so,' her daughter replied. 'I do not care, for Captain Malvern will call on us later and I dare say I shall spend much of my time out with him.'

Her mother shook her head. 'It will not be all balls and fun, Sally,' she told her. 'It is true that there is a ball being held quite soon in honour of Wellington and his officers, but you must remember that there is a war about to happen. The gentlemen may have to leave at any time.'

Sally pouted, but said nothing. Georgie smiled at her, because she liked the girl even though she did seem a little empty headed.

'Perhaps when Captain Malvern calls you could ask him if he knows the whereabouts of Captain Hernshaw or Lord Maddison?'

'Yes, of course I shall,' Sally said, because she was a sweet, friendly girl when her mother was not scolding her. 'I am sure Reggie will be only too pleased to help you. I dare say he knows everyone.'

Georgie was beginning to feel a little apprehensive. Jenny had every right to follow her husband if she wished, for she was Edward's wife. However, Richard might be furious that Georgie had encouraged her on this escapade. He might not have forgiven her for that slap and might refuse to speak to her.

She decided that she would not fly into a temper

whatever he said to her. She would be calm and reasonable, and she would beg his pardon. She loved him so very much, and she wanted to be with him for whatever time was left to them. Perhaps when Richard realised how short time was, he would understand that it was important to share their love and not deny it. After thinking about it, she had begun to believe that perhaps the reason that Richard had kissed her so fiercely was that he could not help himself.

If he did love her, but had denied it for her sake, she would make him admit it somehow. She had not come all this way to waste what was perhaps the last opportunity she would have to be with him.

Chapter Ten

Sally was not far wrong in her estimation, for her fiancé did indeed know most of the officers and had heard of both Richard and Edward. He was not sure if Captain Hernshaw was actually in Brussels at the moment, but he was almost certain that he had seen Lord Maddison at Headquarters the previous day. He did not know where he was quartered, but promised to make inquiries that evening and give them what news he could the next day.

However, he did not keep his appointment with Sally the next morning, and Georgie decided that they must go out to look for their own accommodation, because they could not presume on Mrs Feathers's good will for ever.

Since the town was so crowded with soldiers, Jenny thought it would be prudent to take their maids with them.

'It will give us more consequence when we are looking for somewhere to rent,' she told Georgie confidently. 'I know it may be difficult, but I am sure we shall find something soon.'

Georgie agreed, though she was not quite as hopeful as Jenny, but in that she was wrong for they found two rooms in a very pleasant house before they had been searching for more than an hour.

'I had a lovely lady before. She stay here with her daughter for two months,' the landlady explained in her broken English, which she appeared to understand better than Jenny's attempts to speak to her in French. 'They go only this morning. I was to put a notice in my window—but I shall be pleased to take you. I do not allow gentlemen; they can be *difficile*. You understand? Your maids can share a room in the attic, *n'est-ce pas*?'

'Yes, of course,' Jenny said, smiling at her sweetly. 'We do understand and this will be perfect for us, *madame*.'

They returned to Mrs Feathers's house in high spirits, pleased to have found such a good place. The lady was pleased for them and wished them luck. She told them that Captain Malvern had sent a note to say he had been sent on an errand, which he naturally could not explain, apologising for being unable to give them any news of Lord Maddison at present.

'Oh, well, it does not matter for the moment,' Jenny said to Georgie as they arranged for their luggage to be transported to their new lodgings. 'Once we are properly settled we can make inquiries ourselves.'

'Yes, I expect so,' Georgie agreed. 'It is perhaps a pity that we did not bring one of the grooms with us, because he might have done that for us.'

'I thought as we were travelling with Mrs Feathers we should not need them,' Jenny replied, 'but you are perfectly right. I ought to have thought a little harder before I sent them home. However, I dare say we shall mange very well on our own.'

'Yes, I am sure we shall,' Georgie said. 'We have got here without mishap and we found ourselves very comfortable lodgings. I see no reason to start worrying now.'

It took them most of the day to settle in and unpack their belongings. Georgie went up to look at the attic room that the maids were to share. It was large enough, but a little hot and stuffy.

'Will this do, Milly?' she asked Jenny's maid, who was the senior of the two and might take offence at the arrangement. 'I am sorry you have to share, but for the moment this is the best we can do. When we find Lord Maddison it may be better.'

'It will do for the moment, miss,' the maid replied with a sniff. 'It isn't what I'm used to but I dare say we might have done worse. At least this house smells of lavender and herbs rather than boiled cabbage.'

'Yes, it does,' Georgie agreed. 'But it would be better if we had a house of our own. In the morning we must go to Headquarters and discover where Lord Maddison is quartered.'

'You must not go unescorted,' Milly replied in a warning tone. 'Either Rose or I should go with you. It's a foreign city, miss, and there's a lot of strange people about—drunken soldiers and the like. I told Rose to be careful when she goes shopping. It's a pity Andrews didn't come with us.' She gave another sniff to show her disapproval.

'Yes, I think it was a mistake to send both the grooms home. We should have been more comfortable with a man to help us if need be, but it cannot be helped now—unless you think we should try to employ someone?'

'Employ a foreigner?' Milly looked horrified. 'No, miss, especially a man. We're better off without them! Besides, if anyone tries to accost you or her ladyship, I am more than a match for them—drunken soldier or not!'

Georgie thanked her for her assurances, deciding that when she went shopping she would buy a gift for Milly. Perhaps a new velvet bonnet or some pretty lace she could use to trim an undergarment.

Madame Bonner proved to be a good cook and they enjoyed their dinner that evening, spending the hours before retiring in Jenny's bedchamber, where they played cards to pass the time.

After a night spent in clean, sweet-smelling sheets, Georgie woke refreshed. She found Jenny a little pensive at breakfast and asked what was on her mind.

'Oh, nothing…' Jenny said. 'I am just wondering what Edward will say when he discovers we are here.'

'He may be angry at first, but I think he is sure to be pleased once he knows how well we have managed.'

'Yes, he must be proud of us, mustn't he?' Jenny brightened. 'We should go to Headquarters this morning, do you not think?'

'Milly says that she should go for us. She says if you give her your card with our address she will have it delivered to him.'

'Yes, perhaps that is best,' Jenny said. 'And then we could take Rose and go shopping. I am eager to explore a little of the fashionable part of the city. I am sure there must be a lot of people here that we know and it would be nice to meet acquaintances.'

Georgie agreed that it would. She secretly suspected

that Jenny was a little anxious about her first meeting with her husband, because he had refused to take her with him. However, she said nothing, because Jenny was obviously trying not to think about it. Georgie was more than a little apprehensive about meeting Richard. He was bound to be angry with her, both because she had accompanied Jenny to Brussels—and because of that slap. However, her resolution to remain calm was firm. She would not be provoked into a show of temper whatever he said!

Milly was dispatched with the card and the rest of them set out on a shopping trip. It was very warm and they needed their pretty parasols to shade them from the sun. Noticing that Rose seemed to be suffering a little from the heat, Georgie decided to buy her a plain blue parasol with lace edging for her own use. She bought an untrimmed straw bonnet for Milly, some lace, a length of green ribbon and a bunch of artificial cherries so that the maid could trim it for herself as she wished. For herself she bought a very smart hat, and Jenny bought gloves, lace and a length of green silk, which was to be delivered to their lodgings. However, they were all loaded with small parcels and they decided to stop and indulge in a bowl of the fragrant coffee being sold at a pavement café.

It was as they were leaving the café that Georgie saw the tall figure striding towards them. She knew that he had seen her at almost the same moment, and his expression was serious, even grave. Her heart raced wildly, and she braced herself for the scolding to come.

'Miss Bridges,' Richard said as he reached them. His expression was serious, but as far as Georgie could see not angry. She swallowed hard, waiting for what would come next. 'I couldn't believe it when I saw Milly at Headquarters and she told me she had come to deliver a message to Lord Maddison. How you managed to get here and why, after you both promised to stay at home, I do not know. However, it is fortunate that you did, because I have grave news.'

Jenny had come up to them, her face pale as she heard her brother's words. 'Edward!' she cried. 'Something has happened! Please tell me at once, Richard— is he dead?'

'Not dead, Jenny,' Richard told her in a gentle tone. 'Edward was sent on a scouting mission while I was away on a similar errand. Unfortunately, he ran into an enemy patrol. He realised almost at once and tried to outride them, but he was shot in the shoulder, and again in the leg. It happened two days ago, but I did not know until I returned. He was taken in by a village woman, who then sent word to Headquarters. I fetched him back last night, but he has a raging fever and knows no one. I was wondering how best to send word, for I did not wish to leave him unattended—and I must leave again soon. It is a blessing that you ignored his wishes and came, Jenny, for he will need you.'

'You must take me to him at once,' Jenny said. 'Is he in hospital?'

'A small hospital run by a religious order,' Richard said. 'I thought it best for I did not have the time to nurse him at my lodgings—and it is hardly suited for the purpose. Are you well situated where you are? I know it is hard to find good accommodation. Edward had been staying at an inn, which would not be suitable at all.'

'We have two rooms, though the landlady does not

take men as a rule,' Georgie told him. 'But Edward would be better in a private house as soon as it can be arranged. I dare say the nuns are good, kind people, but Jenny needs to be with him, and she will nurse him better than anyone else.'

'Yes…' Richard nodded. He glanced at her, a speculative look in his eyes, and then back at his sister. 'He could have my room, which is large enough to hold a truckle bed. If that would suit you, Jenny?'

Jenny hesitated for she did not wish to be parted from Georgie, but Edward's well being had to come first. 'Yes, of course,' she said. 'Will you be all right at Madame Bonner's without me, Georgie?'

'Yes, dearest. You must be with Edward. It is why we came,' Georgie said. 'I shall manage and I shall come every day to help you look after Edward, dearest.'

'It will be a day or so before he can be moved from the hospital,' Richard said. 'I shall take you both there now, and then I must go—but I shall return this evening, and in the meantime I shall see if better accommodation can be found for you. You need a house of your own if it can be found.'

Jenny thanked him, all her desire for independence fled now that she knew her husband was desperately ill. 'I shall be grateful for anything you can do.'

'You had best send poor Rose back to your present lodgings with those parcels,' Richard told them. 'I shall escort you to the hospital.' He looked at Georgie, seeming hesitant. 'There is something I must say to you, but it must be for another time. I am sorry I cannot stay with you for longer, but I have much to do.'

'Of course you have,' Georgie said. She did not smile, for the news that Edward had been injured was sobering and she could only feel grateful that the man she loved was alive and unharmed. 'Do not feel that you must worry about us, Richard. We managed to get here without help and we shall manage now. You have your duty. We both understand that.'

His eyes seemed to convey a message that had Georgie's heart racing. 'I shall see you this evening. Please wait at the hospital with Jenny. I may have good news for you when I come. At least I shall try.'

Jenny was given permission to sit with her husband in the small ward. There were three other beds, each with a male patient, only a curtain separating one from the other. Waiting in a little room just off the ward, Georgie found the smell of strong soap mixed with sickness a little nauseating, but she passed the time looking out at the nuns' pretty garden and reciting poetry to herself. It was almost two hours before Jenny came back to her.

'He is very ill,' she said, tears in her eyes. 'Oh, Georgie. If this fever does not break, I fear he will die. The nuns said that the woman who took him in was well meaning, but the cloths she used to bind him were not clean and his thigh wound may be infected.'

'He is not so lucky as Richard was when he was wounded in the thigh. Henderson tended him so well that he scarcely had a fever at all.'

'They say that they might try to cauterise the wound if it does not look better by morning.' Jenny made a little choking sound. 'If it turns bad, he could lose his leg...'

'Oh, no,' Georgie said. Her heart wrenched with pity for she loved Jenny as a sister and knew how much she was suffering. 'I wish that Henderson were here. I am sure he would not waste time, but do whatever was needed at once.'

'I wonder that Richard did not suggest it,' Jenny said. 'I know that he has helped my brother often in the past.'

'Perhaps Henderson is not here,' Georgie replied, frowning. 'Richard would surely have thought of it if he were.'

'I must go back to him,' Jenny said. 'You can do nothing here, dearest. When we have him home you may help me, but I do not like to think of you wasting your time here.'

'Richard told me to wait for him,' Georgie said. 'But you may tell him I have gone back to Madame Bonner's house when he comes. I shall ask her if she would be prepared to have Edward there if Richard's lodgings are not suitable. At least we have two rooms, and you and I could take turns to sleep in mine.'

'I think she will not like it,' Jenny said. 'Richard will do what he can for us, but I think it will be hard to find a house for they are all taken.'

'I shall go and talk to Madame Bonner,' Georgie promised. 'I shall go now, dearest.' She kissed Jenny's cheek. 'My prayers are with you.'

After leaving the hospital, Georgie set off confidently enough, believing that she could easily find her way to the house she was staying at. However, after half an hour of walking, she realised that she must be going in the wrong direction, for the streets had become progressively meaner and she was beginning to feel uncomfortable as she saw that there seemed to be an excessive number of inns and, as dusk gathered, the noise coming from inside sounded loud and rowdy.

It was as she was passing one of them that some men came tumbling out, fighting and brawling amongst themselves, and almost knocking into her.

'What have we here?' one of them cried, leering at her in a manner that made her start back in alarm. 'Don't be frightened, my pretty doxy. I won't hurt you. I only want to lift your skirts and pleasure you.'

Georgie gave a squeak of fear, turning and fleeing back the way she had come, the man giving chase with a cry of raucous laughter. She was in such a hurry as she turned the corner that she did not notice the man coming towards her until she bumped into him.

'I am so sorry…Henderson!' she cried with relief as she looked up and saw his face. 'Oh, thank goodness! I was trying to get back to my lodgings and I took a wrong turning and then a man…he seems to think I am a lightskirt or something of the sort.'

'You shouldn't be in this part of town alone, miss,' Henderson told her with a look of disapproval. 'You're not running away again, I hope?'

'No, of course I am not,' she said. 'Have you seen Captain Hernshaw recently?'

'No, for he sent me on an errand and I have just this minute returned to Brussels.'

'We are in terrible trouble,' Georgie said. 'Lord Maddison is badly hurt and Richard took him to the nuns, but they do not seem to know what to do for him. His wound is infected and we are afraid he might die— and we have nowhere to take him.'

'Can he not stay with you at your lodgings?'

'Madame Bonner says she does not take gentlemen.'

'Madame Bonner?' Henderson looked thoughtful. 'I think I might know the lady. Take me to her, Miss Georgie—and let me have a word.'

'Well, I would, except that I am lost, but I can give you her address.' She repeated it to him parrot fashion and he smiled.

'I do know the lady, and I believe we may be able to persuade her.'

'I should be so pleased if you could,' Georgie told him. 'Because it would mean that you could help us to tend Lord Maddison's wounds.'

'As to that, the captain might have work for me— but I'll do what I can,' Henderson promised. 'Come along, Miss Georgie. You took a wrong turn just back here.'

Watching Madame Bonner's face when she opened the door to them a little later, Georgie was amazed. For a moment she just stared, then she broke into a string of excitable French and seized hold of Henderson, kissing him on both cheeks and crying noisily. Her fingers stroked the terrible scars on his face lovingly, her eyes soft and gentle. He patted her on the back, smiled and spoke to her for a few minutes, but so quickly that Georgie could only make out a few words. Whatever he said did the trick because she was all smiles as she looked at Georgie.

'Bring the poor gentleman here,' she said. 'And you, Jacques—you must come too and look after him. You may have my parlour. You can be comfortable there, *n'est-ce pas?*'

Henderson took a step forward, kissing her on the lips, which made her smile even more. 'You are a good woman, Belle,' he said. He turned to Georgie. 'Stay here, Miss Georgie. I'll go back to the hospital and make all the arrangements. We'll do what we can for his lordship, I promise you.'

'Thank you,' Georgie said. 'And thank you for coming to my rescue earlier. You need not say anything of that to Captain Hernshaw?'

'Mum's the word, miss,' he said and winked at her. 'Don't want him worrying for nothing, now do we?'

Georgie smiled as he went off. She thanked Madame Bonner again, and went upstairs to change.

It was nearly three hours later when a carriage arrived outside the front door. Madame Bonner opened it to admit Richard and Henderson, who were carrying an unconscious Edward between them. Jenny followed behind, looking pale and tearful.

'It was terrible,' she said in a choked voice. 'The doctor wanted to take Edward's leg and Henderson wouldn't let him. There was a row and they were going to throw Henderson out when Richard arrived. He told them he was taking Edward away—and here we are. Henderson says that if Edward had stayed there much longer he might have died. He has promised to do all he can for us.'

'My dearest Jenny,' Georgie said, putting her arms about her. 'I saw Henderson at work when Richard was hurt. I am sure you could wish for no one better. He will save Edward's leg if anyone can.'

'Why did it have to happen?' Jenny cried. 'It wasn't even in a battle—just a scouting mission. I wish he had never come here.'

Georgie put her arms about her, holding Jenny as she

wept. After a few minutes she drew back, wiping her cheeks with a kerchief. 'Oh, it is selfish of me to give way to my feelings! I should be upstairs helping them to tend Edward.'

'I think perhaps it is best if you stay here,' Georgie said, remembering the harrowing scenes she had witnessed when Richard had been so badly injured in London. 'Richard will help Henderson. He will come and tell us when it is all done.'

'I should wash my face and change. I smell of the hospital.'

'Come to my room,' Georgie said. 'You can borrow one of my gowns, for we must share for the next few days at least—unless Richard found us a house?'

'No, he could not,' Jenny said, looking at her. 'How did you persuade Madame Bonner to let us bring Edward here?'

'It was not me,' Georgie said. 'It seems that Henderson knows her...quite well, I should say.' She laughed as Jenny raised her brows. 'No, I must not say for she has been truly kind, and I will not gossip about her— but if you observe them together you may draw your own conclusions...'

'Henderson is one of the most resourceful men I know,' Richard said when he came downstairs an hour or so later and found Georgie alone in the parlour. 'It was good fortune that you happened to meet him, for I understand he persuaded the landlady to let you have Edward here?'

'Yes, he did,' Georgie said. 'I believe they know each other quite well?'

'They met while her husband was still living,'

Richard said. 'I believe the attraction was mutual, but she could not bring herself to leave Monsieur Bonner, even though he was a bit of a brute.'

'Ah, I see,' Georgie said and smiled. 'That explains it of course.'

'It does not explain why you left the hospital when I asked you to wait until I came.' Richard looked at her, his gaze narrowed but not angry.

'Jenny told me to leave. There was nothing I could do and she thought I might do better here.'

'A garrison town is a dangerous place for a woman alone. I would prefer that you took one of the maids with you when you go out—preferably Milly.'

'Yes, Richard. I shall do so in future, I promise you.' Georgie hesitated, then took a deep breath. 'I must apologise to you for our last meeting. I should not have slapped you. It was very wrong of me and I have wished that I might say how sorry I was ever since.'

'You have less need to apologise than I, Georgie,' Richard said, looking oddly uncertain. 'What I did that day was unforgivable. I have had time to think since we parted and I have realised that my behaviour towards you has not been all that it ought. I hope you may find it in your heart to forgive me?'

'I forgive you for the kiss,' Georgie replied. Her pulses were racing, but she knew that this might be her last chance to speak of what was in her heart. 'However, I cannot forgive you for not loving me as I love you, Richard. I know that I have been a great deal of trouble to you and—'

Richard pressed his fingers to her lips. 'If you will have the truth of me, Georgie, you have been a constant delight and torment almost from the first. Dressed in

your youth's clothing I found you unbearably provocative and it took all my strength of will not to carry you
off somewhere and make love to you.'

'Richard!' Georgie stared at him, not certain she had
heard him right. 'Are you saying that you do care for me?
I do not mean as a friend—but as a woman you love?'

'Can you doubt it?' he asked, a glimmer of mockery
in his eyes. 'Even from the beginning when you came
into my bedchamber looking so delectable in your
breeches and that thin shirt…it was sheer torment travelling with you and knowing that you were beyond me.
Had you been the lady's maid you pretended to be, I
have no doubt that you would already be my mistress.'

Georgie gave him a straight look. 'Not your wife?
Is that all I mean to you—someone to share the delights
of your bed until you are tired of me?'

'No, damn it!' Richard moved closer, gazing down
into her lovely eyes. 'You must know that I adore you,
Georgie. I would never have deserted you, even had you
become my mistress—but…' He shook his head. 'I am
a fool. All I do is hurt you when I want to love you, to
kiss you until your eyes darken with desire and you melt
with love.'

'Then why will you not marry me?' she cried in a
tone of exasperation. 'You are the most vexing man,
Richard. You say that you adore me…want me…and
yet you do not ask me to marry you. Pray tell me why?'

'I am older than you and have seen too much of the
darker side of life. I killed Thierry because he hurt you
and I have killed others when it was necessary.'

'You killed him because he might have shot me
again. It was in defence of my life and your own, and
I dare say it has been the case at other times. This is ri-

diculous! You are a good, caring man and I will hear no more of this nonsense.'

Richard's gaze did not waver. 'I did not wish you to suffer the pain of losing a husband before you have tasted the pleasures of marriage. You know that I may be killed in battle very soon. You would be in mourning and might never recover from your grief.'

'An hour of happiness as your wife would suffice a lifetime,' Georgie said, her eyes challenging him. 'It will not do, Richard. If you love me as you claim, you would marry me.'

'If you will have me, I shall marry you—as soon as this damned war is over,' Richard told her, a smile lighting his eyes. 'I have been such a fool, Georgie, and the truth may be that I was afraid of loving you too much—but it was already too late from the first and I should have known it. When I thought you might die, I knew that my life would be empty without you, but you had forgotten me and I believed it might be for the best.'

'You foolish man!' Georgie said and there was a militant sparkle in her eye. 'You have wasted so much precious time—time that we might have spent together.'

'Forgive me,' he said, his eyes dwelling on her face so intently that she shivered. 'Will you marry me when the war is over?'

'Yes, I shall,' Georgie said. 'When must you leave?'

'I have tonight, but then I must leave. I have told Henderson he is to remain with you and Jenny, no matter what happens,' Richard said, his mouth thinning to a grim line. 'The Duchess of Richmond holds a ball for Wellington and his officers tomorrow evening. However, I shall not be here to take you.' He hesitated, then, 'I believe that the conflict is very near now, Georgie. The French have been spotted moving this way. We thought Bonaparte would not dare to attack us, but it looks as if he might try to cut us off from our allies. Wellington is waiting for news, and when he has it we shall make our move.'

'I do not care for a ball in times such as these,' Georgie said. 'Even if you could take me, I should not attend while Edward is so ill. I would not dream of leaving Jenny alone.' She raised her head, looking into his eyes. 'Let me spend this night with you, Richard.'

For a moment his eyes took fire, but then he shook his head. 'I cannot take advantage of your sweet innocence, my love. Think of the consequences if I should die and you were to fall for a child.'

'Do you think I care for reputation when I might know the happiness of being truly yours?' she demanded, eyes flashing with pride. 'I might lose all the world, but I should have your child and Jenny would still love me. I am brave enough to face it, but are you, Richard? Are you brave enough to give me your heart and then leave me to face the enemy on the field of battle?'

'Can you truly face the thought that I must leave you in the morning?'

'I can bear anything except that you take your love from me.'

'Then come with me to my lodgings,' Richard said huskily. 'God forgive me, I am not strong enough to resist you when you look at me that way.'

Richard closed the door of his chamber behind them. For a moment he stared at her, a hungry yearning in his eyes that made her sway towards him, her lips opening on a sigh as she waited for him to come to her.

'You are quite certain?' he whispered huskily.

'Quite, quite certain,' she replied, and turned round. 'You must unhook me, Richard, for I cannot do it myself.'

He came to her, and she felt the touch of his hand at the nape of her neck, and then his lips as he kissed her, making her tingle. His fingers moved slowly down the line of tiny hooks, opening each in turn carefully and kissing the silken flesh as it was revealed to him. And then the gown fell away and she stepped out of it. She untied the laces of her bodice, and then Richard eased it over her shoulders. And then she was naked, standing before him as his eyes feasted on the glories of her slender form.

'Georgie, my love,' he murmured huskily. 'I want you so much. You know that I adore you…will always honour and treasure you above all others.'

'As I shall you,' she whispered. She trembled as he reached out for her, pulling her to him, clasping her to his body as if he hungered for the feel and scent of her. She felt the tiny shudder as he bent his head to kiss her. He caught her up in his arms, kissing her tenderly but with such need that she trembled in his arms as desire surged up in her.

'So beautiful…' he murmured. He stroked her cheek, his hand trailing down her throat, caressing the sweet swell of her breasts. He ripped open his shirt, shrugging it off, and tugging off his boots so that in seconds he was naked as she, and making her catch her breath as she saw the finely honed strength of his body and the evidence of his arousal. 'Let me love you, my darling. I shall be gentle and you must forgive me if I hurt you this first time.'

'You will do nothing I cannot bear,' she said. 'I welcome the pain if pain there must be to be yours in all ways.'

Richard made a throaty moaning sound, sweeping her up and carrying her to the bed where he placed her tenderly amongst the fine linen sheets and then lay down beside her. He turned on his side towards her, gathering her to him so that she felt the heat of his flesh and the slight tickle of body hair where it arrowed over his taut stomach. She smiled into his eyes trustingly, her arms sliding up around his neck, tangling in his hair as his lips touched her throat and he kissed her…tiny feathering kisses that made her arch and moan with need.

She could feel the heat deep down inside, and the moisture running from her intimate places as his lips moved lower. He caressed her with his mouth, tongue and hands, lavishing sweet tenderness on every part of her willing body. She moaned softly in her throat, making little mewing noises as he drew her along the path to a place she had never been.

She had known his kisses could arouse need in her, but this was more than she had ever dreamed, making her arch and whimper with longing as his hand parted her legs. She could feel the burn of his flesh, and the hard bulge of his manhood as it throbbed with desire, probing at her moist warmth. His entrance was careful and slow, so sensuous that she opened to him easily, her moisture making it easier so that when he finally broke through her maidenhead it hardly hurt at all. His mouth covered hers, smothering the small cry, and then she was arching up to meet him, welcoming him as he thrust deeper and deeper into her silken warmth.

'Richard…oh, my love…' she cried out as a spasm of sheer pleasure shook her and she felt his release, understood that he too had felt the exquisite sensation she had known at the moment of climax. 'Oh, Richard…'

Afterwards they lay still, Georgie still gathered in his arms as he stroked the arch of her back and she relaxed into sweet contentment.

'I never knew there could be such pleasure.'

'Nor I,' he murmured close to her ear. 'No one— nothing—has ever given me so much as you have, my darling. I think that we must have been made for each other.'

Georgie felt the wetness of tears on her cheeks, but knew that they were tears of happiness. She laid her head against his chest, breathing in the smell of his sweat, loving it, loving him and this wonderful feeling between them. She wished that they might stay together like this for ever. The knowledge that they had only this one night was close then, despite all her efforts to shut it out.

She could hardly prevent herself crying out in protest. She loved him so. How could she bear it when the time came for him to leave? And yet she would bear it, for she must.

Georgie yawned and stretched, feeling her body tingle as it remembered the sweet loving she had known the previous night. She opened her eyes to see Richard dressing. He was wearing his riding things and his sword lay near to hand. She knew that he was about to set out on one of his scouting missions for Wellington, but this time he would not leave her without saying goodbye.

She threw back the covers and went to him naked as she was, throwing her arms about him, looking up at him, her love shining from her eyes.

'Take good care, my love,' she said. 'Come back to me when you can.'

'You know that I shall,' he said. 'Know that I regard you as my wife, Georgie. You and you alone hold that place in my heart. We shall marry as soon as I can arrange it once I have leave to come to you—and if…' His eyes dwelled on her. 'At least you know that I love you. Whatever happens keep that thought with you, Georgie.'

'I shall,' she promised. 'But you will come back to me, Richard. I love you so much that my love will bring you back.'

He nodded, his eyes hungry, devouring her as she lifted her face to receive one last kiss. 'I must do my duty, but I pray that I shall return to you, my love. I fear that I must go now—can you make your own way home?'

'Yes, of course. Do not worry about us, Richard. We have Henderson now and he will take good care of us.'

'Yes, I know. He did not wish to be left behind, but I told him it was his duty to me, and he agreed. You will do well enough with him here—just in case. If things go ill and he advises leaving town you must listen to him, Georgie. I believe we shall hold the French, we may beat them—but nothing is certain. If they were to overrun the city…'

'Yes, I understand,' Georgie said. 'Go now, Richard. Do what you must and do not worry for my sake.'

'You are so brave,' he said, touching her cheek. 'Keep that brave heart, my love—no matter what.'

Georgie held back her tears. She had spent one wonderful night in his arms, and she would let him go to war without showing her pain. She would keep her tears for the nights she spent alone.

Chapter Eleven

As soon as she arrived back at their lodgings, Georgie went up to the bedroom to inquire how Edward did. Jenny was with him, because she had persuaded Henderson to take a rest.

'He was with Edward all through the night,' she said. 'I sat up for some of the time, but Henderson made me rest—and now I have sent him to his bed. The fever seems a little better, and I am assured the medicine Henderson has made up for him will help.'

'And his leg?'

'Henderson opened the wound and cauterised it,' Jenny said, her face pale. 'It brought Edward to his senses for a while, because he screamed with the pain, but Henderson said it was necessary.'

'You can rely on him to do all that is possible.'

'Yes, I know,' Jenny said. 'Mrs Feathers sent a note round this morning. We are invited to the Duchess of Richmond's ball this evening—but I sent her a letter back explaining we could not go. You did not wish to attend?'

'You know that I would not while you are so distressed and Edward is ill. Besides, Richard has gone again. He left this morning…'

Jenny looked at her. 'You spent the night at his lodgings, didn't you?'

'Yes.' Georgie met her eyes bravely. 'Please do not condemn me, Jenny. It maybe the only chance for me to know what it is to be loved by him. You may think me wanton…'

'No, Georgie, I do not think it. Richard should have married you weeks ago. If I were in your situation, I would have done the same.'

'Thank you.' Georgie gave a little sob of relief. 'I should not wish you to think ill of me—but I love him so much. I would have done anything to have that one night in his arms. Even if it is all I ever have.'

Jenny reached out and touched her hand. 'Do not be anxious for him, dear one. He is more skilled in these things than Edward. Richard has never given up his work, while Edward became used to living at home with me in peace.'

'Yes, I know you are right,' Georgie said. 'He made Henderson stay with us, you know, just in case things go wrong. He says that if Henderson advises us to leave Brussels, we must go.'

'I shall not go unless Edward is well enough to travel,' Jenny said with a frown. 'But if it seems the French will overrun us, you must go.'

'And leave you?' Georgie shook her head. 'No, if you stay, I stay—but it may never happen. I am sure that the Iron Duke knows exactly what he is doing.'

'Yes, I am certain of it,' Jenny said and glanced back at the bed. 'I believe he is a little easier now, Georgie. Do you not think so?'

Georgie went to the bed and looked at their patient. She placed a gentle hand on his brow. 'His fever has not gone yet, but perhaps it is on the wane.'

They heard the morning after the ball that the British army was on the march. News had come during the ball that the French had made a surprise move and Wellington's officers had slipped away one by one, hoping not to distress the ladies. Wellington himself had left Brussels, though no one seemed to know much about his plans; he was playing it very much close to his chest and rumour was flying. Some said that the French had stolen the high ground, while others declared that Wellington would outfox Bonaparte and come through in the end.

Mrs Feathers came to call. She seemed complacent, assuring the ladies that there was no need to panic.

'Wellington will have it all under control,' she said. 'My husband has gone off somewhere. He told me to stay put and not panic whatever I hear. He is confident that the Allies will win the day.'

However, as the next couple of days passed, rumour of battles lost and defeat started to circulate. One day there was even talk of the French overrunning Brussels. When the first wagonloads of wounded came in, a mood of panic began to spread. If there were so many killed and wounded, the Allies must have been defeated.

Mrs Feathers sent a note telling them not to worry, reminding them that Wellington was a brilliant commander, and warning them to hold their nerve.

In the town opinion was divided. Some of the townspeople were fleeing, packing up their belongings, stunned by the news that the French had got this close. The streets were jammed with carriages and wagons as some tried to flee from what they thought was a disaster.

Georgie asked Henderson if Lord Maddison was fit to travel.

'No, Miss Georgie, he is not,' he told her with a grim shake of his head. 'His fever is a little better, as you know—but it might start again if we tried to move him. I know the captain would say you should stop here for the time being. As yet I haven't heard anything that tells me the defeat is certain. I think it may have been just a setback.'

'All those wounded men,' Georgie said. 'They are coming back by the wagonload, as well as those that can walk. They say the lists of the dead are circulating. Do you think…?' She swallowed hard. 'How can we find out if Richard is on them?'

'I'll do that for you,' Henderson said. 'Stay in the house with her ladyship, miss. I'll see what I can find out.'

Georgie waited patiently for his return.

Henderson had been gone for three hours. When he returned the news for her was not good.

'The captain was last seen taking a message for Wellington, Miss Georgie,' Henderson said. 'No one saw him come back—but the news of the war is better. Wellington did retreat, but only to a position of advantage at Mont-Saint-Jean. Far from being beaten, it is the French who were broken. It is over for Bonaparte. They say he is in retreat towards Paris and some of our men will follow and finish it.'

'I am glad that the Allies were successful,' Georgie

said. 'But it is Richard I am anxious for. Where is he and is he alive or dead?'

'I do not know.' Henderson frowned. 'He would have me stay here—but Lord Maddison is recovering at last. I am no longer needed. I shall go to look for him.'

'And I shall come with you,' Georgie said. 'No, do not look like that, Henderson. I shall wear my youth's clothing and ride astride so I shall not hamper you. I brought it in case it was needed, and I am glad I did.'

'The captain will not like it, miss.'

'If he is hurt, I must find him,' Georgie said. 'I cannot wait here when he may be lying injured by the side of the road. If you do not take me with you, I shall go alone.'

'The devil you will!' Henderson shook his head at her. 'You would too, miss. You had best go and change because I shall be ready to leave in ten minutes.'

'I'll be with you in less,' Georgie promised, and she was.

They had been riding for nearly three hours. Georgie's heart was breaking as she saw the stragglers making their way back to Brussels. Some had bandages around their heads, some were limping, others had their arms in a sling. They were the ones with slight wounds, men who could make their own way back. Others lay moaning in hastily set-up tents where they were treated by hard-pressed doctors and local women who had come out to help.

Once they saw a line of bodies lying on the ground. Set out neatly, there were men of several nationalities side by side, Allies and enemies united in death. Henderson refused to let Georgie look, but came back to her

with a shake of the head after he had made an in-
spection.

'He isn't there, miss.'

'Thank you,' she said, her face pale. 'What will
happen to those poor men?'

'If no one comes to claim the bodies, they will be
buried together. It can't be helped, miss. It is the way
things work in war.'

'Richard isn't going to be buried in a grave with no
name,' Georgie said fiercely. 'We have to find him,
however long it takes.'

'We'll try, miss, but he could be anywhere. You
mustn't get your hopes up…' His voice drained away
as he discovered that he was talking to thin air.
Georgie had scrambled down from her horse and was
flying across a stretch of land to where several
wounded men were grouped, sitting or lying on the
ground. 'Wait for me, miss! You never know what
they'll do for a horse.'

Georgie didn't look back. She had seen a man sitting
with his back to a tree. He had a bandage round his head
and there were bloodstains on his breeches, but instinct
told her that she had found the man she sought.

'Richard,' she cried. 'Richard, my darling…'

He glanced up, staring at her for a moment as if
dazed, but then as she flung herself to the ground beside
him, her arms going about him, he made a little
grunting sound low in his throat.

'You shouldn't be here…dressed like that,' he said,
but even as he spoke his tears trickled down his face until
he brushed them away. 'Troublesome girl! Damn it! I
must be mazed in the head. I thought I might never see
you again. We saw some of the citizens fleeing and I

thought you must have left the city when the news was bad.'

'Edward could not be moved when everyone was fleeing,' she said, wiping his tears away with her fingertips. She kissed his brow, her hands running lightly over his beloved features. 'But the news is not bad, my love. I do not know when you were wounded, but Wellington won the day. The French are fleeing back to Paris with their tails between their legs and some of our men are following. They will finish it for good this time.'

'God be praised,' Richard said and tried to push himself up, but his head spun and he fell back. 'Damn it! We made an attack and I was wounded. I was unconscious for a while and someone found me, brought me this far and then left me. I couldn't raise enough energy to move on.'

'Well, you do not need to now,' Georgie told him with a smile. 'Henderson is with me. Do not blame him for bringing me with him, dearest, because I told him I should come alone if he did not.'

'I can imagine,' Richard said, giving her a stern look. 'I'll deal with you when I have my strength back, but I must admit I am glad you came to look for me. I might have sat here for days. They are taking the seriously wounded first.'

Henderson came up to them then. He stood looking at Richard for a moment. 'You can't ride in your condition, captain. I've agreed to swap our horses for a wagon and a carthorse.'

'The devil you have! Have you any idea what they cost me?'

'They were purchased for war,' Henderson replied.

'You'll not need them again. What you need now is something to get you back to Brussels.'

'Yes, you're right,' Richard agreed and looked at the other exhausted men lying on the ground nearby. 'Have we room to take them too?'

'Aye, I dare say,' Henderson said. 'You'll have to sit on the box with me, Miss Georgie, but I dare say you won't mind that?'

'You know I won't,' she said, smiling at him. 'I don't care about anything now that we have found Richard— and these poor men need help too. We must get as many of them back as we can.'

'Aye, well, I dare say we can manage these and maybe come back for more once the captain is settled.'

'It's no more than a scratch,' Richard told him. 'It is just that I can't stand up by myself at the moment. I dare say it is the shock.'

'Mebbe,' his manservant said with a stern eye. 'But you'll go back to Belle's and you'll stay in bed until I tell you you can get up.'

'Yes, you will,' Georgie agreed. 'And I shall make sure you do!'

'Well, there's one way you can do that,' he replied, giving her a look that made her blush. 'I think I have told you before that you have a very fetching rear in those breeches.'

'Richard!' Georgie said. 'Behave yourself or I shall think that the wound to your head has turned your mind.'

Richard grinned as he was assisted to his feet and helped into a wagon that a farmer was bringing to them. He muttered something about an old nag in exchange for prime cattle, but was ignored both by Georgie and his servant. They exchanged glances, but remained silent as he was helped into the back of the wagon, which had a mattress of straw already stained with the blood of the wounded.

Once Richard was settled, Henderson went to help the other men climb up. Some of them were in better case than Richard, but exhausted by all they had endured, all pathetically grateful for the transport back to Brussels and somewhere they could receive rest and treatment.

The wagon was soon filled, and they were forced to leave others they passed on the journey back to Brussels, but they saw other wagons and carriages coming out from the city and knew that people were daring to venture out in search of the wounded. Now that the news of the Allies' victory had reached them, the people were no longer afraid of being ransacked by the French army.

It was a journey she would never forget, Georgie thought as she looked about her. She was happy that she had found Richard, but tears came to her eyes as she thought of all those men that would not return to their wives and families.

'I think I shall get up this morning,' Richard said two days later as she entered his room carrying a tray of soup and fresh bread. 'You should leave this to one of the maids, Georgie. You do not have to wait on me.'

'But I want to,' she said and smiled at him. 'When we go home I can be the wealthy Mrs Hernshaw, and play the society lady, but for this time I just want to be the woman who loves you, Richard—as indeed I am.'

'You know that you will be Lady Hernshaw one day,' he said. 'The Regent has decided that I am to be made a Baron for services above and beyond the call of duty.' He gave a moan of frustration. 'The sooner I can get out of this bed and make an honest woman of you the better!'

Georgie made a little curtsy and laughed. 'Yes, Sir Richard. Mrs Feathers called earlier this morning and told me that everyone was talking about you. Apparently, you have been quite a hero, my love. Wellington mentioned you in dispatches, and you have been summoned to London to report to the Regent himself.'

'Damn it!' Richard said. 'Henderson brought me the letter a moment ago. How does that woman know?'

'Mrs Feathers knows everything,' Georgie said, her eyes bright with mischief. 'To hear her talk, you would think she was an aide to the Iron Duke himself. I think she has been everywhere with her husband and seen all there is to see. It was she who told us to stand firm when most were panicking.'

'At least in that she was right,' Richard said. 'But I would have preferred to tell you my news myself.'

'Well, you did, but she told me first,' Georgie said and her laugh was husky and delightful. 'Do not look so cross, my love. She likes to talk and there is no harm in her. She has been of great help to us one way or another.'

'Then I shall forgive her,' he said. 'Providing that you take that pap away and tell Rose to bring me bread, cold beef and pickles—and a glass of good red wine.'

'Are you sure you should, Richard?'

'I am perfectly sure I should,' he retorted. 'And it is the last meal I shall eat in bed. When I have eaten it I shall get up and come downstairs. If I am summoned back to England, the sooner I am on my feet again the better. I have enough of this damned business! I want to marry you and take you home, Georgie—to my home.'

'And so you shall, my darling, just as soon as you have done your duty.'

'Damn my duty,' he growled. 'I want to be with you. And I want to be home, my love.'

'I want that too,' she replied and then gave him a teasing smile. 'But I think I have a fancy to be Lady Hernshaw.' She threw him a mocking glance as she went out and down to the kitchen where she found Henderson and informed him of his master's wish to have cold roast beef.

'The wonder is he hasn't demanded it before,' Henderson told her. 'If you had not been so insistent, he would have been up before this. He would not stay in bed this long at my behest.' He grinned at her. 'I think the captain is in for some shocks once you are Lady Hernshaw. You will run rings round him, my lady.'

'I'm not a lady or even a wife yet, Henderson,' Georgie said and laughed. 'Though Richard is impatient to make an honest woman of me.'

'I know that, but it's my chance to use the title,' Henderson said. 'I haven't told the captain yet, but I shall not be coming back to England with you, my lady. Belle has asked me to stay here and help her run a boarding house. She's got a taste for it, and with my help she can buy something bigger.'

'Henderson…' Georgie was half-dismayed, half-amused. 'We shall both miss you but…are you going to marry her?'

'Yes, that is part of the bargain,' Henderson said and frowned. 'I never thought to see the day when I was petticoat-led, my lady—and I never expected to leave the captain. I wouldn't have done if I hadn't known he was in good hands. You'll keep him right now.'

'I hope he means to give up his work and settle down now,' Georgie said with a little frown. 'I believe he does, but—' She broke off on a sigh.

'You tell him it's what you want and he'll do it,' Henderson said. 'He loves you—and I never thought I'd ever say those words either. He was always a loner and I couldn't see him changing, but he has—and that's your doing. I've likely shown you more familiarity than I should, but you are a lady and the captain is lucky to have you.'

'That is very kind of you, Henderson,' Georgie said. 'And you have always shown me respect. More than that, you've given me friendship. Captain Hernshaw will miss you too.'

'He will and he won't,' Henderson said. 'We've been together through thick and thin, but we've both had a bit of good fortune and that's why we'll go our separate ways.'

The wedding took place two days later, as soon as Richard was able to stand straight long enough to walk down the aisle of the church. It was a brief service with just Henderson and Jenny, who had left her husband's bedside long enough to be a witness.

'This is not the way I intended to marry you,' Richard told Georgie afterwards. 'But when we are home we can have a blessing in an English church and invite all our friends to witness it and share a feast with us.'

'I shall be happy to invite our friends to a grand affair to celebrate our wedding,' Georgie told him with a teasing look. 'But I do not care what kind of a wedding we have—as long as it is legal?'

'Oh yes, it is legal,' Richard said and his arms tightened about her. 'You are mine now, Georgie—and I have no intention of letting you leave me ever.'

'Then it is fortunate that I have no wish to leave you,' Georgie said. Her eyes were bright with mischief as she tipped her head to one side to look at him. 'It took me long enough to get you, Richard—but now I have you—and I can be quite as stubborn as you, my love.'

'You have no need to tell me that,' Richard replied, giving her a rueful look. 'I have met my match in you, my darling. From the start I knew that you would be a troublesome girl and it seems that I was right.' He laughed and ducked the blow his new wife aimed at his ear. 'But it was worth it just for the pleasure of seeing you in those wretched breeches.'

'Well, that is over, my lady,' Richard said as they looked at one another in the comfort of their well-sprung carriage. 'We've seen the Regent, received his thanks and I've resigned my work for the government. We're going home at last, and the next time we come to London it will simply be for pleasure.'

'Oh, Richard,' Georgie said. 'We are so lucky, my dearest. When I think of all the women who lost their husbands…Jenny has her darling Edward back and I have you. We could easily have lost you both.'

'I bear a charmed life,' Richard said, glossing over the slight matter of a dozen lives saved because of his own bravery in leading a charge to get them when they were cut off from their own side. 'Edward should never have been out there. I tried to dissuade him, but he would not listen. I believe he knows how fortunate he was to get away with it this time and in future he will not stray far from Jenny's side.'

'I do hope so,' Georgie said. 'She was quite determined to follow him, you know. At first we intended to take two of the grooms with us to Brussels, but when we met Mrs Feathers Jenny sent them home. I think she thought we could manage for ourselves—but we are not all as intrepid as that lady. She told us about hiding in cellars and riding on donkeys when they had to flee from the enemy in Spain.'

'An intrepid campaigner indeed,' Richard said and reached for her hand in the carriage. 'But even she might have balked at dressing in a youth's clothing and setting out to look for her husband alone.'

'I had Henderson,' Georgie demurred, but her eyes sparkled. 'Poor Henderson—I wonder how he will like living with Madame Bonner and running a boarding house.'

'I dare say he will be in his element,' Richard said, his mouth quirking. 'I told him that he always has a place with me, but I doubt he will use it. I dare say that when we go to visit in a year or two he will have become the perfect innkeeper, very French—or Belgian, perhaps.'

'Yes, perhaps.' Georgie giggled at the picture his words brought to mind. 'Can you see Henderson in a white apron?'

'I'm not sure,' Richard replied. 'Minx! Yes, he will do very well, I think.'

'Perhaps…' Georgie sighed as she glanced out of the window. 'How long before we are home?'

'Three hours, I imagine,' he replied, his eyes narrowing. 'You look tired—are you?'

'Just a little.'

'Then rest your head on my shoulder and sleep for a while.' He put his arm about her protectively. 'Sleep and we shall soon be there, my love.'

He frowned as she closed her eyes. It was not like Georgie to want to sleep in the middle of the day, but perhaps all the troubles of the past few weeks had caught up with her at last.

Georgie woke as the carriage came to a halt. She yawned and looked at Richard apologetically, because she must have slept for such a long time.

'Your poor shoulder must hurt,' she said. 'You should have woken me, Richard.'

'You were tired,' he said. 'I did not want to disturb you and my shoulder is fine. I would not have woken you now, but everyone is waiting to greet their new mistress, my love.'

Georgie looked out of the window and saw the house that was now to be her home. It was larger than Lord Maddison's but newer, no more than fifty years old, and very attractively built in the Palladian style with a portico of white pillars and long windows that glistened in the sun.

'Oh, it is beautiful,' she said. 'I love it, Richard!'

'I am glad,' he said. 'My grandfather had it built for his bride, but she did not live long enough to enjoy it, and died giving birth to my father. My mother survived my birth and Jenny's, but died giving birth to another son, who died with her.' He gave a little shudder, his eyes intent on her face. 'I hope we shall not have a child too soon, my dearest. I do not want you to suffer as she did.'

GEORGIE

~~Jenny~~ gave him her hand as he helped her down from the carriage. She kept her face turned from his in case he should see her expression. She had held back from telling him her news, for fear that it was premature, but she was almost certain now that she was having his child. It needed only a doctor's confirmation, but now she felt unsure about telling him. He did not want their baby…

Georgie looked round the beautiful suite of rooms she had been shown to after being introduced to all the servants lined up waiting for her arrival. It seemed that Richard had been accustomed to living in some style, though he had not chosen to spend much time here in the past—perhaps because of some secret sorrow he had not yet shared with her?

She knew that the loss of his mother in childbed had affected him, but was there something else he had not told her? Perhaps a lost love?

She was standing at the window, staring out at the view over the park when the door opened behind her and Richard entered, coming to stand at her back, his arms going around her.

'You seem pensive, my love?'

'I was wondering why you spent so little time here, Richard. It is such a lovely house, and the grounds are beautiful. Is there something you have not told me?'

He gazed down at her. 'My father grieved so long for my mother,' he said. 'He spent most of his time in London or Newmarket. Jenny and I were thrown into our own company, and then she went to live with the countess. After that I was alone, even before my father died. Justin was my best friend and I told you how he died. I decided to join up when I was quite young, and I got drawn into the life. I saw no point in coming here other than to make sure my agents were caring for it as they should.'

'But you do want to live here now?'

'Now that I have you,' he agreed. 'I have given up soldiering and the old life, Georgie. We shall spend all our days together—and our nights, my love. When I go to London, you will come with me.'

'And supposing I could not come for some reason…?'

He frowned as he gazed at her. 'I do not understand, Georgie. Why should you not accompany me? You are not ill?' He was suddenly anxious. 'You were so tired in the carriage…'

'Jenny said she was very tired when she was having her children.'

'Having…' He stared at her, his expression so mixed that she felt a shaft of disappointment. 'Are you having our child, Georgie?'

'I am not sure,' she said. 'I wasn't sure at first, but I have not seen my monthly flow since we left Brussels…'

'My love,' he said. 'You should have told me. Last night we danced and then I made love to you…I may have hurt you.'

'Do not be foolish, Richard,' Georgie said. 'I talked to Jenny before we parted. She told me it does not harm the child in the early months. It is only later that you must take care—and I have not even been certain, but I have not seen my courses for a while and I feel different.' She saw his frown. 'You are not pleased. I am sorry. I wish it might have been different for your sake.'

'Of course I am pleased—if you are?' She nodded. 'But we have had so little time together and…I do not want to lose you.' She heard the underlying pain in his voice. 'I cannot lose you now, my dearest love.'

'You will not lose me,' she said, pressing herself closer, lifting her face for his kiss. 'I am strong and the thought of childbearing does not frighten me, Richard. Your mother died in childbed, but it is not so for all women. I shall carry our child well, and I shall survive the birth. I promise you.'

'Yes, you will,' he said, and bent his head to touch his lips to hers. 'You are my brave, troublesome girl and I shall not let the past cloud my mind. What happened to my mother and grandmother will not happen to you. I shall not let it!'

'We shall not let it,' she said and laughed as she saw the laughter in his eyes. 'Remember, this is me, Richard—not a fragile flower that wilts in the sun.'

Afterword

〜〜〜〜〜

'You may go in now, Sir Richard,' the doctor said as he came out of Lady Hernshaw's chamber and found her husband pacing the floor restlessly. 'Her ladyship has been delivered of a fine son, and is wishful to see you.'

'Thank you,' Richard said, relief in his eyes. 'How is she?'

'Perfectly well, just as I told you she would be,' the doctor said and smiled. 'Your wife is a very brave lady. She made little of it, though it was not easy for her. But you should go in now, because she says she will not rest until you do.'

'That sounds like Lady Georgie,' Richard said and laughed. 'I thank you again for coming here to stay for the birth, Dr Forrest. Georgie said it was not necessary to bring you all the way from London, but I insisted.'

'You were concerned for her,' the doctor replied, a faint smile in his eyes. 'But she is very strong, you know. I do not think you will need me again for a while, but I shall not leave for London until later this afternoon.'

Richard thanked him again, and then went in to see his wife. She was sitting up against the pillows, her lovely hair spread out around her, looking as beautiful and fresh as ever. She showed no sign of having suffered anything untoward, though he knew from the doctor that the birth had not been easy—but she was alive and that was all that truly mattered.

'My dearest love,' he said as she beckoned him forward, offering him the child she held in her arms. 'You have a son.'

'*We* have a beautiful son, Richard,' she told him. 'Look at him and tell me if he was not worth all the trouble.'

Richard took his son, looked and saw the beautifully formed features, his wife's eyes and hair—and fell in love.

'He is wonderful,' he said. 'What shall we call him?'

'Richard?' she suggested. 'We can shorten it to Dickon while he is a child, if you wish.'

'I think we should call him George,' Richard said. 'He looks very much like you, my darling.'

'Very well, he shall be George, Richard,' she said and smiled up at him. 'You had better give him to the nurse now, my dearest, and then sit with me, here on the bed, because I am really rather sleepy and I want you to hold my hand.'

Richard bent to kiss her on the lips. 'Go to sleep, my love. I shall sit with you while you rest.'

He held her hand, watching her as she slipped into a peaceful sleep. His little urchin, the troublesome girl he had fallen in love with while she dressed as a boy and tortured his dreams, now the most beautiful woman he knew. How much she had brought him, his darling Georgie. He felt the fear leaving him, slipping away, the loneliness of years vanishing into the air he breathed. She had given him his beautiful son and he did not doubt that she would give him more children as the years passed, but she would not die and leave him as his mother had left his father. They would live in peace and content until they were both old…until they had grandchildren to fill the house with love and laughter.

* * * * *